Her damp hair stirr..., ...ht about the time she re... ...es, she saw the purple ... ...he remembered she wa... ...le-stained underwear.

Oh . . .

Shit . . .

Heat splashed through her, and she knew her face had just gone the color of a bad sunburn. Her eyes darted to the waves, but her yellow robes were long gone. Every swear word she had ever known—in any language—cycled through her mind, but she refused, she absolutely refused, to cover herself up or make excuses or do anything at all to let this man know she felt humiliated.

Somehow, she stood there. Just sort of hung out like it was no big deal, being almost naked on a beach with the biggest jerk on earth.

Jack folded his sunglasses and slipped them into his suit pocket. His throat moved, but his mouth stayed closed and not a sound slipped out. Andy saw his eyes dip, then snap back to meet hers again.

He wants to look at mē, but he's trying not to. Good for him. He might live to get off the damned beach.

"I—ah—hello. You—" He gave up again. Rubbed his hand across the back of his neck. "Saul and I tried to call ahead, but your phone's not working."

Andy held his gaze, amused and surprised by his reaction to her. "A Motherhouse full of Sibyls does that to technology. There's not a stable digital signal or a functioning computer within five miles of this beach. You could have had yourself transported directly here instead of going to Motherhouse Greece and making Saul ferry you over to the island."

Jack rubbed his neck again. "Didn't think that would be . . . polite."

Nervous, Andy's cop brain informed her, and her Sibyl instincts agreed. Well, that was an emotion she was familiar with, but what was getting to him? Was it her—or her underwear?

Books published by The Random House Publishing Group
are available at quantity discounts on bulk purchases for
premium, educational, fund-raising, and special sales use.
For details, please call 1-800-733-3000.

CAPTIVE HEART

A NOVEL OF THE DARK CRESCENT SISTERHOOD

ANNA WINDSOR

BALLANTINE BOOKS • NEW YORK

A Ballantine Books Mass Market Original

Copyright © 2011 by Anna Windsor

Published in the United States by Ballantine Books, an imprint of The Random House Publishing Group, a division of Random House, Inc., New York.

BALLANTINE and colophon are trademarks of Random House, Inc.

ISBN 978-0-345-51391-5

Printed in the United States of America

www.ballantinebooks.com

9 8 7 6 5 4 3 2 1

For all of Andy's fans who write me so frequently—
she's finally getting her due

You can't bargain with the truth.
—Yusuf Islam

(1)

Sibyls.

Jack Blackmore stood on a rickety Greek dock staring across the sunlit waves of the Ionian Sea. He had come to paradise. He should be enjoying himself, but instead he was thinking about Sibyls.

Saul Brent, one of the few men who called Jack a friend, yanked at a rusty pull chain on the boat they were supposed to take to the island of Kérkira, but the battered skiff's engine wouldn't catch. "Son of a bitch," Saul muttered, giving the chain another jerk.

Shirtless, tattooed, and with his brown hair barely crammed into a ponytail, Saul looked more like a biker on spring break than a decorated soldier and career police officer. His years undercover for vice and narcotics seemed to be etched into his essence. Saul's swearing did nothing to ease Jack's mind, and neither did the warm air or the scents of wet sand and salt.

Sibyls were still a puzzle to him.

He didn't like puzzles.

Every time he dealt with Sibyls, he seemed to do something wrong. He didn't like wrong.

Jack frowned at paradise.

He'd fought demons easier to get along with than the Sibyl warriors of the Dark Crescent Sisterhood—especially the one he had come to Greece to see. What the hell was he doing, trying to make nice with the most unreasonable woman he'd ever met? A woman with elemental powers so vast they defied his understanding.

She'd already tried to kill him twice. Maybe the third time, she'd get the job done.

The engine caught, but Jack didn't make a move to get into the boat.

"Second thoughts?" Saul asked as he struggled with the last rope lashing their skiff to the dock.

Jack wondered if his features mirrored his career like Saul's did, if his years in the Army and gray ops, both internationally and stateside, showed like subtle scars on his face.

"No second thoughts," he said in answer to Saul's question before considering whether he was telling the truth. Jack considered himself an honest man, but he never said much about what was really on his mind. Training—and reflex.

Saul snickered as he worked the rope's last knot. "The thought of seeing her, it's got you nervous, doesn't it?"

Jack didn't answer, but he got into the skiff. He wasn't nervous. He didn't do nervous. The reason his gut was tight—well. Just a lot riding on this little visit to Motherhouse Kérkira.

"She might finally drown you this time," Saul said over the roar of the engine as he steered them into the deep blue waters of the channel.

The skiff lurched, and Jack had to catch himself on the splintery rail. Sea spray coated his face, cooling him enough to say, "She'll hear me out. She thinks more like us than like the Dark Crescent Sisterhood."

"Andy Myles stopped being a police officer the minute she snapped her pretty fingers and summoned her first tidal wave." Saul gestured behind them, in the general direction of Mount Olympus and Motherhouse Greece, home base of the air Sibyls, where they had started this little late-afternoon odyssey. "She hasn't been in training since birth like the rest of them, but she's a Sibyl now, and you haven't made many friends among the chicks in leather."

Jack thought about the elementally protected body-suits the Sibyls wore into battle, and about how the tight black leather hugged every enticing inch of Andy's body. His fingers tightened on the skiff's railing until his knuckles hurt.

Let it go.

Yeah. Because he was good at letting things go. No distractions. Not on a mission.

Saul stayed quiet for a minute or two, then came back with, "You still haven't told me what you want with her."

"I want her back in New York City." Jack made himself ease up on the boat's railing before he broke the damned thing. "I want her mind on operations and planning. I've read her notes and reports—she's one of the best analysts in the Occult Crimes Unit."

"She's a Sibyl now." Saul cut to the left and pointed them toward the island they sought. "One of the few water Sibyls on the planet. Did it ever occur to you that Andy has other shit to do? That she might not be willing to come running just because the great Jack Blackmore gives her a summons?"

Jack considered various answers, but he kept coming back to one obvious fact and the thing he couldn't stop believing about Andy Myles. "Once a cop, always a cop. If I ask her, she'll come."

Saul's brown eyes narrowed. "When you took your little sabbatical at the Sibyl Motherhouses and came back all Zen, I thought you'd changed—but you're still the same cold bastard. Everyone and everything exists just to get you what you want."

"Not what I want." Jack went back to strangling the boat's railing. "What we need."

"Who is *we* this week, Jack? The Army? The FBI? You and the little voices in your head?"

"The NYPD. The OCU." Jack didn't expect Saul to understand or even to believe him, which was a good thing, because Saul laughed his ass off as he whipped the skiff through the crystalline waters leading to the tip of Kérkira.

"You're full of shit," Saul called over the roar of the engine and the slap of the boat through the waves.

Meaning, *When you're finished with whatever has your interest, you'll leave New York City and the OCU in your rearview mirror just like you've left everywhere else.*

Probably true.

Thanks to some pretty bad shit in his childhood, Jack had no real ties, not to any person or any place. Once upon a time, the Army had saved his life. He'd become a soldier, a commander who knew who he was, where he was supposed to be, and what he was supposed to be doing. Then he watched a bunch of tiger-demons crawl out of the Valley of the Gods in Afghanistan, the blood of his unit dripping from their claws and fangs, and he lost track of life's basics even though he always warned his men never to do that.

The tiger-demons, the Rakshasa, had been his reason for existing—or at least his reason for being a single-minded, single-purposed bastard—since the Gulf War, but they were dead now. The darkness he had tracked for years had been scrubbed from the planet.

But he could always find more darkness.

New York City was as good a place as any. For now.

As if he had heard Jack's thoughts, Saul made a vicious cut with the rudder and the skiff scooted sideways. If Jack hadn't had a good grip on the rail, he'd have busted his face on the rough floorboards.

"When Andy decides to kick your ass all over the island,

don't ask me for any help," Saul said. "I'm gonna hoot un-til I piss myself. And I'm staying on the boat. You're on your own with this one."

Jack studied the sands of the fast-approaching island as he tried to clear his mind and get ready to engage the—what? Enemy? Friendly? Hydra monster in a gor-geous redhead suit?

Damn, but the skiff's railing felt flimsy in his choke hold.

Even if Jack wasn't too sure about his own character, he had no doubt that Saul was an honest man. If Andy decided to wash Jack back to New York City, he was on his own—and Saul might very well get his chance to keep laughing.

One day you're a good cop with a decent career in New York City.

The next day you're the world's only water Sibyl, a warrior of the Dark Crescent Sisterhood sworn to protect the weak from the supernaturally strong.

And not too long after that, you're standing at the bottom of the Ionian Sea in your underwear, nose to beak with a big-ass octopus.

"Normal people don't have to deal with this shit." Andy Myles didn't dare take her eyes off the octopus to glare at her companion, a woman so ancient she looked more crusty than the debris in the shell midden under the octopus. Bubbles rose with each word, and Andy breathed in warm, salty breaths of her element, still amazed that she didn't need gills to treat water like air.

Aquahabitus. That's the fancy term for me being able to live underwater like a happy clam. See? I'm remembering more of this crap every day.

The octopus blew a load of black ink in Andy's face and scooted off across the seafloor, leaving tiny bursts of sand and rock in its wake.

Andy waved the stinky black cloud out of her face, but melanin coated her floating red curls. The effect was interesting. She had never given much thought to trying purple highlights. "Add this to the list of shit normal people don't have to deal with—what color will a wart with legs stain my hair today?"

"You frightened the octopus," Elana told Andy as her silver robes absorbed some of the coloring. "To approach water's many creatures, you must keep a broad view, a strong sense of purpose, and peace in your own heart and mind."

"Wonderful." Andy glanced down at her purple-stained underwear. "Let's not schedule any chats with sharks this week."

Elana stared at Andy, her eerie white eyes conveying nothing but acceptance. Andy wondered how much Elana saw, even though theoretically she saw nothing at all. How the hell did she stay so calm about *everything*?

"Let's finish for the day," Elana suggested. "You had quite a bit of success with the fish earlier."

"Sure. Three fin wounds and one tail in the face. I did great." Andy raised her fingers to the iron crescent moon charm she wore around her neck and watched currents rinse her curls, but shades of purple remained. Camille, the fire Sibyl in her quad, had made the charm for Andy. The metal's special properties increased Andy's aquasentience—her ability to move water through her essence and sense or track whatever the water might have touched—but of course, it couldn't do much to wash away octopus dye.

"The sea senses your unrest and it answers with its own."

"The sea senses I have no idea why I'm playing with fish instead of working with adepts or sailing back to New York City to fight with my quad." Andy let go of the necklace.

Elana sent bubbles of laughter swirling around her silver hair. "Water's creatures can teach you acceptance, my dear. They can teach you about vast freedom within vast limitations. We'll keep trying."

She offered Andy her small, wrinkled hand, and together they drifted up the slope of the seafloor, closer and closer to the sparkling blue surface above. The day had been bright and warm when they walked into the depths, and heat kissed Andy's freckled cheeks as waves gently helped the two women forward.

Her ears worked as well as her lungs when she was immersed in her element, but the world of water sounded so different from the world of air—richer, more nuanced, and unbelievably detailed. The slightest whistle carried for miles, like the swish of a tail or the crack of a tooth on a shell, and all the while, the ebb and flow of tides all over the world made a whispering *beat, beat, beat* she had come to know like her own thoughts. She had become fair at estimating how far sounds had traveled, and at judging their source and trajectory.

A slice-and-push noise caught her attention, and she glanced toward the Greek mainland. "Boat," she told Elana, but of course Elana already knew that.

"Five minutes until it arrives," Elana said.

Andy's head broke the surface. Ahead of her lay the steeply sloped beaches of Kérkira, where her Motherhouse had been hastily constructed. Andy could see its single turret peeking over the rise of the nearest hill. Elana's head didn't break through to air for a few more strides.

As they got a little closer to the beach, the small Motherhouse, tucked into a small, heavily treed valley near the ruins of old Turkish fortifications, came into clear view.

The place . . . lacked a little something. Like, maybe, sanity?

Air Sibyls, earth Sibyls, and fire Sibyls had built it all together and in one huge hurry when Andy first manifested her talent for working with water. Water Sibyls had been extinct for a thousand years, and their training facility, Motherhouse Antilla, had been destroyed in the tidal wave that wiped them out. Once Andy had started working with water, younger water Sibyls began appearing and seeking training, and these girls couldn't very well hang out in hotels, shelters, or anywhere else that couldn't tolerate a hefty dose of moisture. So Motherhouse Kérkira had been born, near Motherhouse Greece because air Sibyls had the most to offer in training a clueless water Sibyl. Air, like water, could be vast and fast-moving, difficult to control and unpredictable. Air, more than any other element, could control water, blowing it this way and that—or setting up an impenetrable moving barrier of wind to hold back an accidental tidal surge.

The common areas of the north section had gone up first, with old-style Russian architecture and heavy wooden walls and floors. The barracks in the western section had been laid together with Motherhouse Ireland's smooth Connemara marble and austere room design, while the kitchen and library in the eastern reaches had the open, airy look of carved crystal that marked Motherhouse Greece. In the middle, good old American brick and mortar formed an entry hall and a formal meeting chamber. Stone, crystal, wood, and brick—Motherhouse Kérkira had come out looking like a twisted fairy-tale castle, or something Picasso might have barfed after a particularly bad bender.

As Andy and Elana crested like tired waves on the beach, Elana moved her hands over her robes, absorbing all the moisture and dispersing its elemental components back to the universe.

"Aquaterminus." Andy named the ability before Elana could ask her to say it. "Halting the motion of water or absorbing small amounts. This demands significant energy and can be fatal if done on too large a scale."

"Excellent." Elana's small feet moved effortlessly over rocks and sand and branches as if she could see every hazard and shift in the terrain. "But I sense more unrest. Your tension increased the moment we walked out of the sea, my dear. What is it that troubles you so deeply—and so constantly?"

Andy grabbed her yellow Mother's robes off the rock

where she had draped them. "For starters, I hate yellow. I think it's a stupid color for water Sibyls." She pitched the robes back into the waves, feeling satisfaction as the annoying sun-colored cloth whipped under the surface and darkened as it moved out to sea. The nervousness inside her wound tighter even though she was gazing across an endless vista of water and ornate islands. Most people thought the Ionian Islands were perfection itself, but right now they just bugged the hell out of her.

"I don't know who's on the boat," Andy added, fishing for any explanation that might turn out to be the truth about why she was so jumpy when Elana's only purpose in life seemed to be helping her learn to relax.

Elana cocked her head like she was listening to something. "Yes. There's disruption onboard the approaching skiff. I won't deny that."

Andy squinted toward the mainland and sighed. "I hadn't picked that up. Thanks. Do you sense more tension now?"

Elana ignored her sarcasm, as she usually did. "What bothered you when we left the waves?"

The cranks in Andy's depths turned again, ratcheting her muscles. She sensed rushing and overflowing in her own essence, but at the same time, her emotions choked inside. She felt like a river battling beaver dams at every bend and juncture. She needed to kick out some logjams before her brain flooded.

"I don't know. I don't . . . well, the building. The Motherhouse bothers me. You can't see it, but I've told you it's freaky." Andy smeared water out of her eyes with both hands, then remembered she could absorb it and dried off her face. "It's crowded here, and too public, and I'm worried more adepts are on the way. What if one of them makes a mistake and we flood half of Europe?"

Elana's lips curved at the edges like she might be trying to smile. "Keep going. Let it flow, Andy."

"Flow. Right. That's supposed to be my job." Andy glanced at the tattoo that had marked her right forearm since her Sibyl talents manifested. Earth, fire, air—mortar, pestle, broom—in a triangle around a dark crescent moon. Sibyls worked in fighting groups, with earth Sibyls as mortars, responsible for protecting and leading the group. Fire Sibyls worked as pestles, handling communications, and air Sibyls served as brooms, cleaning up messes, archiving events, and researching information on just about everything. When Andy joined their ranks, Sibyl tattoos all over the world had changed. The lines connecting the symbols went from straight to wavy, symbolizing the role of water Sibyls in a fighting group.

Flow.

She was supposed to attend to the emotional flow and growth of her group.

Whatever the hell *that* meant.

"I'm a cop and a warrior, Elana." She lowered her arm, lifted her chin, and blinked at the sudden glare of sunlight off the too-blue sea. "I shoot things. I don't flow."

"The longer you live in water, the more water will live in you. Release, Andy." Elana put her paper-soft hands on Andy's bare belly. Her dark, damp skin seemed to glitter in all the sunlight. "Tell me all of what's bothering you. Don't think. Don't censor. Just let yourself flow."

Andy closed her eyes. The beat of the tides swelled in her mind, the gentle pressure of Elana's hand focused her, and she was able to come up with the next pain on her list. "I miss my quad."

"Bela, Camille, and Dio are brilliant fighting partners." Elana's voice seemed as hypnotic and rhythmic as the waves. "I'm sure they miss you these summer months when you have to be away. What else?"

Andy listened to the water around her, tried to let it wash through her and break free everything crammed in her chest and throat. The air smelled like evergreen and fish and brine. "The beach bothers me. Stupid as this might sound, it feels wrong."

Elana said nothing. Andy kept her eyes closed, listening to the waves dance with the beach. "The trees bother me. They don't . . . they don't speak to the water like I want them to."

Andy wondered if Elana was thinking she was screwy, but the old woman just asked, "And?"

And . . .

Great. She was starting to relax a little more, but only because she didn't have the energy to fight with more than one emotion at the same time. Gently, she moved Elana's fingers away from her and opened her eyes. "It's everything, okay? It's the whole place. I sort of hate it. No, I actually do hate it. I'll never get peaceful here without regular shipments of Valium, coffee, and all the chocolate I can eat."

Elana's hands came together like a young child clapping. "Good. I agree."

Andy wasn't sure she heard that right. "What?"

"This is not the right location for our Motherhouse." Elana's white eyes brightened with emotion. "The Motherhouse we water Sibyls build for ourselves—it won't be here."

Andy stared at Elana. It had felt like a miracle, finding a single surviving water Sibyl from time before time, fully trained and able to *really* teach her what it meant to live with water in her soul. Now she was worrying that Elana's ancient mind might be running dry after all.

Warm breezes teased Andy's stained hair and underwear, and the afternoon sun baked her freckles. "Build a Motherhouse," she said. "You and me?"

Elana gestured toward Motherhouse Disastro. "We have the adepts. They'll help."

Now Andy's mouth came open. "We have five teenagers, twenty-two kids, and three infants. Think the babies can hammer a nail?"

"And we have Ona," Elana said like she hadn't heard a word Andy spoke. Her robes and hair were completely dry, and she seemed enraptured by whatever she could see in her mind.

Desperate to make Elana talk sense, Andy said, "Ona's a renegade fire Sibyl who barely talks to anyone but you. And she sort of destroyed the last Motherhouse. And fire Sibyls burn shit up and want everything made of rock. And, and—she's as old as you are!"

Elana held up two fingers. "Two years older."

Andy smacked the side of her own head, sending a spray of water over the sand and rocks. "Does that matter when you're a thousand, for God's sake?"

Elana paused. "It's still surprising to hear you call on God instead of the Goddess."

"I'm from the American South and I didn't grow up a Sibyl. The whole Goddess thing—I'm ambivalent." Andy dried off her hands and legs in sheer frustration, soaking the water into her essence and firing it back at the ocean in a fast, arcing plume. "Assuming I go for the insanity of believing we can build our own Motherhouse, where would we put it?"

Elana faced her, her scarred face serious but kind, with that ever-present relaxation she seemed to have when they visited any beach. "Where our hearts take us."

"That really helps." Andy drew in more water and shot it out over the sea, using her palm to target the stream. Aquakinesis. She needed a lot more practice with that ability, but she felt a small release every time she did it. Nothing like a little violence to get a girl's pulse back to normal.

"When the time is right, the place will call to us," Elana said. "We'll both know."

Just the thought of moving her Sibyl training facility to some new and unknown location, never mind building a Motherhouse—Andy wasn't sure how she was supposed to ever find any peace now.

"Don't die," she told Elana. "There's no way I can fight alongside my quad in New York, figure out all this crap, and build a Motherhouse by myself."

Elana's shrug made Andy want to bury herself head-first in the sand. "I'll live forever if nothing kills me."

Andy grimaced because Elana was referring to the fact that not only was she one of the oldest Sibyls in the world, she was also the only half-demon Sibyl . . . ever. Tiger-demons known as Rakshasa had attacked her and infected her a long time ago, but she had survived and lived to help drive the bastards off the face of the planet—twice. Andy felt like she had to protect Elana at all costs, but that would be damned hard if Elana didn't quit putting herself on the front lines of demon battles.

"Our disruption has arrived." Elana pointed in the direction of the docks, and Andy saw a man striding toward them.

Weird.

Usually the locals who knew about Motherhouse Salvador Dalí's Worst Nightmare wouldn't let anybody approach this end of the island unescorted, much less march right up their private beach to bang on the front door. Which, for the record, was as ugly as the rest of the place, though Motherhouse Russia was quite proud of the carved wolf's-head door handle.

How had some guy managed to—

Andy looked closer.

The man had coal-colored hair and stoic, handsome features almost too perfectly aligned to be real instead of some Renaissance painter's fantasy. Those features were familiar, but what she really recognized was his scowl.

And who could miss the totally out of place *Men in Black* suit and the dark sunglasses?

Him.

Here.

Of all places.

Oh, yeah, *this* was really going to help her relax and focus on learning healing and flow and all that other water Sibyl crap.

"Fuck me." Andy put her hand on Elana's shoulder. "It's Jack Blackmore. Think anybody would care if I drowned him?"

(3)

The temporary director of New York City's under-the-radar Occult Crimes Unit walked straight toward Andy like he owned the whole damned island. The man had existed outside of mainstream society for so long he had no idea how to deal with real people. After his stint in the Army, he'd gone federal, and most recently he had been working for the FBI on special assignment to New York City to fight the Rakshasa. Since the first Gulf War, Jack Blackmore had been helping military and civilian law enforcement establish and run units like the OCU, and he was used to being in charge and giving orders.

Andy was used to plotting Jack's death every time he spoke.

Just the sight of him made her blood come to full boil. How could she hate somebody just for the way he walked? No. No. It was the suit and sunglasses. Or the tight way he held his athletic body, like he was always ready to fight with something.

Maybe it was the way he breathed.

Or the fact he breathed.

Truth be told, in the year or so she had been forced to be around him, she'd never had a real conversation with the bastard because they always started screaming at each other after a few sentences. Her palm itched like it was getting ready to slap him.

"Your sister Sibyls told me Mr. Blackmore spent time at all the Sibyl Motherhouses last year to improve his manners with the Sisterhood," Elana said. "I take it from your surge of stress that you don't believe his tutoring was sufficient?"

Jack was thirty feet from them and still coming. Andy glanced at the water on her right. Okay, okay, drowning him might be extreme—but what about washing him out to sea for a few hours? "Believe me, Elana, this jerk is beyond teaching. He doesn't want to learn."

Elana responded by moving off a little ways and seating herself on a rock. She turned her face to the sea, and Andy had to make herself stand still as Jack Blackmore steered himself to a stop directly in front of her.

She looked up to see his face. Otherwise, she would have been staring straight at his muscle-bound chest. So he was an arrogant shithead in a Flaming Bunch of Idiots suit—but she had to admit the stupid getup fit him like nobody's business. Did the guy hit the gym twice a day or something?

Blackmore's typical all-business expression remained in place for about three seconds. Then it faltered. For a long moment, he stood motionless, his mirrored lenses reflecting sunlight. His face softened and he pulled off those ridiculous glasses, but he still didn't say a word. He just looked at her like he'd traveled a few thousand miles to have a chat this afternoon, then completely forgot what he intended to say.

His dark brown eyes seemed almost black in the sunlight, and Andy could have sworn the man brought a host of fresh, warm breezes with him. He smelled like cedar with a hint of something earthy, which she had never noticed before, probably because every time she had ever gotten near him she had been in the process of doing him serious bodily harm.

Her damp hair stirred, blowing across her cheeks. Right about the time she reached up to brush it out of her eyes, she saw the purple streaks on the damp tips.

Then she remembered she was wearing nothing but lacy, purple-stained underwear.

Oh . . .

Shit . . .

Heat splashed through her, and she knew her face had just gone the color of a bad sunburn. Her eyes darted to the waves, but her yellow robes were long gone. Every swear word she had ever known—in any language—cycled through her mind, but she refused, she absolutely refused, to cover herself up or make excuses or do anything at all to let this man know she felt humiliated.

Somehow, she stood there. Just sort of hung out like it was no big deal, being almost naked on a beach with the biggest jerk on earth.

Jack folded his sunglasses and slipped them into his suit pocket. His throat moved, but his mouth stayed closed and not a sound slipped out. Andy saw his eyes dip, then snap back to meet hers again.

He wants to look at me, but he's trying not to. Good for him. He might live to get off the damned beach.

"I—ah—hello. You—" He gave up again. Rubbed his hand across the back of his neck. "Saul and I tried to call ahead, but your phone's not working."

Andy held his gaze, amused and surprised by his reaction to her. "A Motherhouse full of Sibyls does that to technology. There's not a stable digital signal or a functioning computer within five miles of this beach. You could have had yourself transported directly here instead of going to Motherhouse Greece and making Saul ferry you over to the island."

Jack rubbed his neck again. "Didn't think that would be . . . polite."

Nervous, Andy's cop brain informed her, and her Sibyl instincts agreed. Well, that was an emotion she was familiar with, but what was getting to him? Was it her—or her underwear?

He managed to get himself under control enough to say, "Besides, I thought since you could use a phone, maybe water Sibyls were different about the whole killing-electronics thing."

Whatever was bugging the guy, Andy didn't feel inclined to help him get more comfortable. Maybe if he hyperventilated, he'd leave faster. She stayed casual, like she was in no rush for him to get to the point. "I think I can still use electronic stuff because I didn't become a Sibyl until after I was an adult. Just different, I guess."

"Yes, you are." Jack looked at the sky like he was cursing himself, then quickly added, "In a good way. What I mean is—just . . . look." He met her eyes again, though he didn't seem to be having an easy time with that. "I came here to make peace and to ask you for a favor."

Okay, this was rich. Jack Blackmore coming to her for a favor? Andy really didn't care anymore about being almost naked. She folded her arms and watched, enjoying the warm beach breezes as he squirmed in his no doubt hot-as-hell suit. "Make peace? Are we at war?"

Jack's face slid through a few near-expressions, from irritation to surprise to something like determination. "We've been fighting since I came to New York City because—"

"Because you're a pushy, arrogant dickhead who gives orders instead of listening to people who know more than you do." Andy made sure her smile was sweet even though she wished she could grow fangs like some of her demon friends.

Jack kept his determined look, but he seemed at a loss for a response.

Andy waited.

He cleared his throat. "Pushy. Arrogant. I'll accept that—but I'm trying to learn more about working with Sibyls as equals. I spent time at every Motherhouse except yours, and I was hoping to remedy that."

"You want to stay . . . here?" This struck Andy about as crazy as Elana's announcement that they needed to build a new Motherhouse. She would have laughed, but she couldn't believe he meant what he was saying. "I'm sorry. We don't have any regular Assholes Anonymous meetings. You might fall off the wagon."

Jack looked away. Looked back. Was he actually smiling at her? Oh, she had no idea what to do with that or the ice water shock of seeing what that smile did to his obnoxiously handsome face.

Chills broke along her very exposed skin, cold at first, then warm, then hot. Her body ignored her common sense and vibrated under the force of his gaze.

"Yeah. Definite possibility." He was still smiling and she wanted him to stop, but she really didn't want him to stop, either. Ever. "Maybe some other time, then."

When pigs marry donkeys and fire Sibyls stop letting off smoke. That's what Andy wanted to say, but she couldn't really say anything because she was too busy being freaked out by a weird disappointment that he'd given up so easily.

"About that favor," he said, the smile slipping away until Andy actually felt the loss.

This wasn't quite as fun as she'd thought it was going to be. "Okay. Let's have it."

Jack raised one eyebrow. "You probably won't like it."

"Big surprise." Andy made sure to tamp down her elemental energy. If she blasted him with a wave here on the beach, she really might wash him out to sea. His boyish nervousness and that damned smile had earned him a few minutes without the risk of homicide. Maybe.

After a few moments of hesitation, Jack said, "Come home to New York City, either right now with me or as soon as you can work it out, Sibyl-fashion."

Surprise made Andy's eyes widen. "I'm not due back

until September—I have duties here since I'm the senior water Sibyl Mother." Her gaze drifted to Elana. Was that really true anymore? She and Elana had never formally discussed Elana taking her position as a water Sibyl Mother, but they should. Elana should rank as the eldest at the Motherhouse. "I can't come back with you, but why would you want me to?"

Jack pulled some folded papers out of his jacket pocket and handed them to her. She glanced down at them and realized they were copies of crime scene photos. The snapshot showed a pile of bodies with legs in jeans sticking out in every direction. Bloodied arms flopped out of the stack like they were trying to point at whoever had shot them so full of holes.

Her mind automatically took in every detail, from the glimpses of warehouse backdrop to the way no blood had pooled around the pile. So somebody had slaughtered these guys, then stacked them up like trash bags to be shoved to the curb. She couldn't see any of the faces, but she thought they were all male.

She looked up at Jack. "Who are they?"

His face was emotionless, but his dark eyes gleamed with an intensity that gave her a new round of shivers. "Desemov's men."

"Desemov? The Russian crime boss? You're shitting me." Andy looked back at the photo. Her nostrils flared and she took a deep breath, like she could smell the whole mess all the way across the ocean. "Who would have the balls to go after his operation like this?"

Jack took back the crime scene photos and slid them into his pocket. "Wish I knew. We've seen some bizarre crap happening in the Balkan crime families, too." He handed her another crime scene photo. This one showed a dead man with his head, both arms, and both legs detached. Andy stared hard at the picture. The bloody clothing plastered to the man's torso was intact. No cut marks—and the limb and head amputations had ragged, chaotic edges. It was like they had been—

"Pulled off his body?" A new kind of tension formed in Andy's belly. This one had nothing to do with her Motherhouse worries or her long list of issues with Jack Blackmore, and it made her shut out almost everything but the rocks surrounding her on the beach and the man trying to talk to her. "Something just . . . popped him apart like a doll?"

"We found most of Ioannis Foucci's crew in similar shape," Blackmore said. "Ripped to pieces, no tool or chain-saw marks, no hint of a machine involved, no bite or chew marks. Elemental energy traces suggest Samuel Griffen and his Coven were involved, but they can hide themselves from detection. So far, we've got nothing."

Andy knew whatever had been strong enough and evil enough to kill a person by yanking him to pieces, it wasn't human. The Coven had a history of making allies out of creatures most people would kill on sight—like the Rakshasa they invited to New York City. They also had a history of creating minor, simple elementally based demons like Asmodai—but this? Andy couldn't think of a man-made demon who could tear people apart at the joints. "What do you think it was?"

"I don't know." The intensity in Jack's eyes got down-right uncomfortable as he took the photo back from her. "What I do know is that your quad took down the Rakshasa, and I think you're the best fighters and best investigators we've got on the Sibyl side. You—you're the best of both worlds, and you've logged more time on the streets than any OCU officer I've got."

Andy looked away, flustered and hot all over again. For a lot of reasons, it dug at her to hear him give her compliments like a commander. To notice him using *we* and *I've got*. Possessive. In control, not of her, but of the police unit she helped start and had intended to lead.

Blackmore was a fixture at OCU now, no matter how temporary she had hoped he would be. Was he planning to stay in New York City instead of moving on to whichever crisis in the world needed an extra asshole on the case?

Was that why he'd showed up here offering to make peace?

OCU officers often accused Sibyls of reading minds, but Jack Blackmore was the one to dig straight into Andy's thoughts. "I'm sorry about how I rode into New York City unannounced and heavy-handed. And I'm sorry for the loss you suffered before I came. It must have felt like shit to see me take Sal Freeman's job. If you hadn't become a Sibyl, that position would have been yours."

Andy was past hot now and getting more pissed by the second. "Don't go there, okay? Just—don't."

Don't say Sal's name. Don't go where you're not welcome. She turned her face to the waves and made herself breathe. From the corner of her eye, she saw Elana in the distance, stiff on her rock like she was watching the whole conflict even though she couldn't see. She was probably picking up Andy's emotion and sensing the rise in the water level all around them.

Andy didn't like making Elana nervous, but she couldn't help it. She didn't want this bastard talking about her old life, her cop's life, back when she'd thought she was a normal human and would live a normal life, rising through the police ranks and kicking some ass along the way. She'd had a future that made sense to her. She'd had Sal Freeman, too, the previous captain of the OCU—and, Andy thought, her match in every sense of the word. But Sal had gotten himself killed, which created the departmental opening Jack Blackmore had . . . what? Muscled into? Stolen?

Jack went there like she'd asked him not to, but only

a little further. "From what I've heard, my predecessor was a hell of a guy. I should have paid more attention to how it would affect all of you for me to assume his duties."

Andy was about ready to agree to his damned favor just to shut him up and get him off the island before she killed him outright.

"I need you on this case, Andy." Jack sounded so earnest she wanted to double her fist and knock out five of his teeth. "I've got a bad feeling about it, and I'm not the only one."

A bad feeling . . .

The phrase made Andy's gut churn because it was law enforcement code for *Beware, one giant clusterfuck upcoming.* It was the closest most cops ever came to screaming for help, and it was probably the only thing in the world that could have made her look at him again.

"I'll think about it," she said, feeling the relief of doing the right thing mingle with the rage of losing a battle she hadn't realized she had been fighting. "You go back. I'll talk to my people here and check in with my quad, and I'll let you know."

Jack nodded. Then his voice dropped, quiet and low. "I'm sorry. I meant to do this better."

Andy stared at him.

The man actually seemed disappointed in himself and concerned about her. Did he really care what she thought about him?

He's probably worried I'll wash him into the Hudson the first time I get pissed.

But the longer she gazed into those brown eyes, the more she was sure something else was driving him. What, she couldn't say, and she didn't really want to give a shit.

She glanced down the beach in the direction he'd come, toward the distant figure of Saul and the boat they had taken from the mainland, then back at Jack. Her meaning was clear.

Jack didn't look happy, but he took the hint.

With a polite nod he walked away from her, and soon enough he was out of sight and back on his boat, leaving Kérkira before sunset like he hadn't just come here and tossed a grenade on her emotions and perceptions.

"Was that unusual?" Elana asked as she approached, picking her way more carefully than usual over the uneven layers of beach.

Andy reached out and caught her arm to steady her. "That was wrong on so many levels I can't even begin to explain it."

Yet it was right, too, in ways she had no words to describe.

Elana's disapproval showed in her frown and the way she hesitated before she spoke. "He made you even more tense."

"Jack Blackmore is a tension-creating machine. Come on. Let's get back to the Motherhouse. I have to check out some things."

"His boat is still idling if you'd like to speak with him again, Andy."

"Not happening." Andy shifted her grip to Elana's hand and led her up the beach toward the bizarre collection of building materials they called home. "Believe me, the last thing I ever want to do is spend an evening getting friendly with Jack Blackmore."

The words had no sooner left Andy's mouth than she had another thought, one that made her stumble on the rocks and almost bust her nearly naked, purple-streaked ass.

Now, why didn't that feel like the truth?

(4)

"So what happened?" Saul's voice rose over the steady thrum of the boat's motor as he piloted Jack to the Greek mainland.

Jack tried to ram his thoughts into work gear, but his brain groaned like a stripped clutch. "She—" he started, intending to give his opinion on whether or not Andy would come back to New York. Something turned loose in his mind and he blurted, "She was wearing lace underwear."

Saul gave him a look like he was waiting for the punch line, but Jack's body vibrated from more than the boat's engine. He'd never had the cutting wit that made his soldiers so popular. He was a commander. A natural straight man in any comedy routine.

And now—now he'd been knocked stupid by the sight of an old-school classy redhead in lacy underthings.

Wet lacey underthings.

With some kind of . . . ink or dye all over the cream-colored fabric. And her hair, too. And she'd just stood there in front of him, refusing to cover up like she wanted him to know he didn't intimidate her one damned bit.

God, she was beautiful.

And that Southern accent—damn.

Saul slowed the motor so he could face Jack more completely. "Did she bash you upside the head or something? 'Cause just then, you didn't make any sense."

Jack tried again to say something professional, but what came out was, "Underwear. Nothing else except her crescent moon necklace—the iron one she wears to enhance her abilities. Just that necklace and silk and lace, all stained like somebody splattered her with a purple paintball."

Saul laughed so loud it sounded like a hound barking. "She hit you with her underwear? Damn. I'd say you did a little better with her this time."

Jack rubbed his knuckles across both eyes. "Fuck you, Brent."

"I'm just sayin'." Saul shrugged and went back to steering their craft. "If there was underwear involved, Andy wasn't trying to kill you—so it's progress."

When Jack thought he could speak without being ignorant, he started over with, "The important thing is, she'll come back to New York."

Saul kept his shoulders forward, his attention on the water, but Jack heard more humor in his tone when he asked, "You psychic or just arrogant?"

"Arrogance is all I've got." Jack left it at that, because he, Saul, and Saul's brother Cal were unique among the hierarchy of the OCU. They had no magic powers, no demon blood, no secret weapons to deploy to clear the battlefields of New York City. For the three of them, their work to keep the streets safe from supernatural bastards who misused their abilities came down to the time-honored cliché of blood, sweat, and tears.

Heavy on the blood part.

Jack studied the brackish water churning away from the boat. Hot, salty air tightened his skin, and sunlight almost as strong as desert rays drilled at his cheeks and forehead. This beautiful, exotic place was about as far away from wartime deserts as Jack could get—but the battles had never really ended. Not until six months ago, when Andy and her Sibyl fighting group had finally put down the Rakshasa cats once and for all.

I might have lost track of most of the basics, but I guess I still know what I want.

That surprised him.

He didn't know what to do with surprises he couldn't shoot, cuff, or interrogate.

He let himself turn enough to study the island fading behind him, especially the area that seemed to shimmer and vanish from awareness.

Andy Myles might have a lot more surprises in store for him.

It wasn't just lace underwear or the cute freckles, the red curls or the Southern accent. Her eyes, dark brown and green depths, the color so blended he couldn't say which dominated—those eyes were gorgeous, but they weren't what intrigued him, either. She could handle a SIG like a third limb, fire an underwater dart pistol with a SEAL's accuracy, and cut a grown man to bloody shreds with a few sharp words and a look more brutal than a barbed-wire noose. He admired all of that, but still, there was something else about Andy. Something . . . more. He couldn't put it into words yet, even for himself, but he was determined to get a grip on how she affected him.

Jack forced his attention away from Kérkira and stared at the Greek mainland instead. Under normal circumstances, the Sibyls in New York City would have transported him and Saul directly to their destination at Motherhouse Kérkira—but Jack had figured his odds of getting close enough to Andy to actually speak to her were better if he used the element of surprise. She had never really liked him.

Okay, that was an understatement.

In their few previous interactions, Andy had made one thing very clear: she hated his guts and she'd love to find an excuse to drown him. She'd tried a few times and damn near succeeded—not that he hadn't deserved it— but all in all, he and Saul had opted for the safer option of moving through the earth's ancient energy channels to nearby Motherhouse Greece.

Underwear. Sweet God. How was I supposed to anticipate lace and ink stains?

Was it even possible to plan for scenarios involving that woman?

Jack massaged the back of his neck and tried to erase the image of Andy on the beach, but he already knew that hot little picture had been seared into his memory forever. It would be a long trek back up the slopes of Mount Olympus to the crystalline palace the air Sibyls called home, but at least he would be making it with no broken bones or punctured lungs.

Maybe Saul was right.

With Andy's temper in the equation, that was definitely progress.

From the communications platform in Motherhouse Greece, Jack and Saul moved through the earth's ancient energy channels directly back to OCU headquarters in a townhouse on the Upper East Side, above the Reservoir. Just like that, the late Greek afternoon became a fresh New York City morning, thanks to the time difference.

Built in the 1800s, the cavernous five-story brick townhouse had been donated by a couple of officers, who were also half demon, to give Sibyls, the NYPD, and all of their demon allies a safe place to stay, meet, and organize away from public scrutiny. Jack had a room in the townhouse, though he was considering getting his own place.

He took a sharp breath full of smoke and pine-scented cleanser as he thanked the fire Sibyl who managed their transport, then climbed down from the townhouse communications platform on the third floor. Saul coughed when he stepped through the big piece of projective glass that linked the townhouse with Motherhouse Greece. Several other projective mirrors hung around the round wooden table, misty and inactive but waiting to be opened if needed. Jack had almost gotten used to the weird portals, but he always gave them a quick check to make sure nothing was about to burst from far away to up close and eat off his head at the neck.

Saul stepped off the platform and made flirty eyes at the fire Sibyl as she danced around them to close the channel. The second she finished her whirling step, the young adept with strawberry curls and a lot of freckles hit Saul with a quick burst of fire, scorching the tip of his ponytail.

That only got Saul going.

Jack ignored their banter as he headed into the hallway. He barely glanced at the polished hardwood or heavy antiques as he blew down the stairs, gripping the carved banister despite the splinters left over from his boat trip.

"We headed to the brownstone?" Saul asked as he caught up, referring to one of the Sibyl houses near Sixty-fourth and Central Park.

"Yeah. I want to let Andy's quad know how the visit went and go over this morning's patrol reports." Jack hit the main floor and gave a quick nod to the plainclothes OCU officers, leather-clad Sibyl fighters, and demons and half-demons of several varieties who often paired with the patrols. They were grouped near the conference room where they received shift briefings, and nobody looked happy.

Cal Brent, Saul's older brother, strode out of the conference room and flagged them down with what looked like a new case file.

"Shit." Jack stopped at the front door as Cal jogged toward them, his sleeves shoved up, his brown shirt wrinkled, and his serious face tight with frustration. "We've got more dead people."

Saul watched Cal approach. The two resembled each other, but with his slacks, close-cut thick brown hair, and recent shave, Cal looked like the Ivy League brother.

"At least until now, it's been dead criminals," Saul said, wiping his hands on his faded jeans.

Jack's eyes fixed on Cal's folder. "That luck won't hold."

Cal reached them and thrust the jacket toward Jack. "This time it's Kristo, Ioannis Foucci's last surviving son. We found him an hour ago at one of Foucci's warehouses in the Garment District, along with a few of his friends."

Saul's whistle cut through the unusual silence in the townhouse. "If he's dead, the Foucci clan is finished. That leaves one hell of a power vacuum."

Jack looked at the photo. Body parts. Just a pile of bones and flesh. "I wish I knew why the hell this was happening. There's a bigger picture I'm not seeing yet."

Cal's frown made him look furious and close to exploding. "I'd settle for knowing what can yank arms and legs off human bodies like it's nothing."

"And who made it, or summoned it, or turned it loose." Jack closed the folder. "We better find out before our patrols run into it in some alley."

"The scene's secured." Cal kept his hands on his hips, a gesture Jack recognized from his service days, before Jack had talked him into starting an occult crimes unit in New Orleans, then transferring up to New York City when Jack needed extra manpower and a friendly face or two. It meant Cal had no answers and felt like he was running out of options. "I've got our patrols on max alert all over the city. Everybody's going slow and careful, checking even faint traces of paranormal energy and keeping backup close."

"We'll pick up Bela, Camille, and Dio," Jack said as Saul opened the townhouse's front door. "Duncan Sharp and John Cole should be at the brownstone. We'll meet you."

❨ 5 ❩

They were coming.

Samuel Griffen's impressive bloodline gave him some prescience, and he knew without dispatching a single watcher that the unusual Sibyl fighting group that had destroyed the Rakshasa Eldest had reunited. They'd be on his trail soon.

Around his neck hung a Rakshasa tiger-tooth necklace, enhanced by his own elemental workings. The charm blocked probes of his energy, and it would keep the Sibyls from finding him or anyone he gifted with a similar treasure. The serpent tattoo on his left forearm glittered with life, its elemental paints reacting to the power in the warehouse, and the blessed blood of his father surged in his body. The fingers of his left hand curled around the railing of the third-story walkway he was using to watch the training of his newest fighters below. The trail he was leaving for the Sibyls was, of course, a diversion. Griffen felt certain the Sibyls wouldn't have a clue about his real intentions until he wanted them to know. Griffen knew how to keep himself and his group hidden from detection even when the Sibyls were on the hunt.

He could feel the energy of the Dark Crescent Sisterhood pulsing through the city like a steady, dangerous heartbeat. He could feel *her* energy. Andy Myles. If Griffen accomplished nothing else in his life, he'd bring her to her knees and shoot her in the head, just like she'd done to his father. He glanced to his right, at his implacable half sister. Rebecca's pale blond hair curled in ringlets around her otherworldly face, and her bright blue eyes stared down at the warehouse floor. She seemed oblivious to what Griffen sensed, but the activities below had more than captured her.

She liked blood overly much, or perhaps it was suffering she enjoyed. In so many ways, physically and emotionally, she mirrored him.

Griffen followed Rebecca's gaze. His new soldiers, arranged in three groups of four by his Coven, had been dressed in all black. They stood quietly in front of the holding cells lining the warehouse walls—cells that had become their homes. The cells had been built small to fit in the space, but they looked more like mini luxury apartments equipped with all amenities, including fully stocked refrigerators and cable with porn channels. The rooms also had bars in the walls and across the windows and doors. The metal in the bars had been treated with layers of elemental energy, linked together until it formed barriers known as elemental locks. Inside the cells, under the influence of those locks, the soldiers became just men again, slow-moving and dull from the controls exerted by the locks and the Coven.

Outside the cells, they had to be controlled by the Coven, Griffen and twelve other men with strong elemental talents. He had chosen and trained the men, and they were loyal beyond all reasonable meanings of the word. Nine stood behind the soldiers, adjusting elemental energies to hold them in check until the trial commenced.

The warehouse's side door opened, and the other three members of the Coven ushered in a fresh set of captives. Fifteen gang-bangers, midrange punks, had been snatched off the streets just like he ordered, to be put to better use than using each other for target practice. The young men shouted and threatened, but Griffen knew they were just posturing. Disarmed, with hands bound behind their backs, they were no match for the firepower Griffen's men carried.

Rebecca's breathing picked up and her eyes got impossibly wider. Excitement. Griffen felt it, too.

A few seconds later, the gang-bangers had been lined up in front of the soldiers. Their captors stepped away and made a show of readying their weapons. The meaning was clear enough. Anybody who turned and ran for the door would get cut to pieces.

"Fight or die," Griffen muttered, and Rebecca's squeal of delight made him happy.

When the gang-bangers seemed to fully grasp what was happening, they turned back to the soldiers, who at least had no weapons. Griffen couldn't hold back a laugh. This warehouse in the Garment District, not far from the crime scene the Sibyls would come to investigate, would be the last place the bangers ever saw.

Donovan Craig, Griffen's second in command, ordered the other eight Coven members handling the soldiers into position behind them, far enough back to keep the warlocks out of harm's way. Craig was a big guy, all muscle and beard like a rugby player. Irish by birth, he had a loud determination Griffen appreciated and used as often as possible.

"This bunch looks completely human," Rebecca said, sounding almost disappointed when she got a good look at the black-clad men Craig and the Coven were about to set loose. "Are you sure anything changed when you gave them the serum?"

Griffen smiled at his sister. "Watch."

He raised both fists and opened his fingers.

The three armed Coven members sent out a burst of elemental energy that released the magnetic cuffs restraining the gang-bangers. At the same time, Craig's men released their elemental holds on the soldiers.

The soldiers charged forward, silent against the battle

shouts and swearing of the captives. Before the street fighters could take a good stance to throw a punch, the soldiers started killing people. Crushing blows to the face, rib-shattering kicks, organ-crushing grabs—and a few threw down their prey and stomped them to death in seconds. *Seconds.*

Rebecca's breath left her in a rush. Griffen thought she would have laughed or run down to join the mayhem if she hadn't been so shocked. He gave Craig another hand gesture, and Craig's men restored elemental control over the soldiers.

Like a disciplined military unit, the black-clad men stepped back from the carnage. Soon the Coven would adjust the elemental energies until the soldiers returned to the mental and emotional stasis that kept them manageable between battles. Except for the moans of the dying, the warehouse went silent.

"They're taller than they were before they took the serum," Griffen explained to Rebecca, "but just a few inches. Not enough to destroy their natural reflexes or make them clumsy. They're bulkier in the arms, shoulders, and thighs, too. They look completely human, but you just watched how easily they kill with nothing but kicks and punches."

Her piercing eyes studied each man as the soldiers stood silently below, never glancing in their direction. "How do they handle weapons?"

"Like they were born to shoot and stab. We'll give them a trial run soon, a real-life situation, and see how it goes." Griffen gripped the rail again and resisted the urge to jump up on the pipes and tightrope around the walkway in celebration. "The Coven controllers have more range with these, too—fifty feet, and we've pushed it to one hundred without losing a handle on their energy. I believe full remote management might be possible if we keep refining the formula."

"Why don't we just make them like him? He's more effective." Rebecca pointed below to the only real cell in the room, a double-barred space built into the farthest corner next to the other off-limits room, a small laboratory where Griffen did his most important work. This cell had no television or refrigerator because those could too easily be used as weapons. In the cell, Griffen's earliest effort at transforming a human with the serum he created prowled back and forth, snarling softly to itself.

"It takes all thirteen of us to control him," Griffen said. "Too much of his human mind and will asserts itself. He's good for strategic attacks, but he's impractical for warfare."

Rebecca's bright blue eyes still glinted in the low light of the walkway. "You mean he's not your slave."

Griffen caught where this little discussion was headed. "It's necessary for now, for everybody's safety."

"Was it worth it, old man?" she shouted down at the cage. "What do you think of immortality now?"

The creature hurled itself at the bars, making some of the Coven stop the cleanup process and work elemental energies to calm the thing. Griffen reached out and took hold of the chain affixed to his sister's wrist cuffs. If she tried to incite the creature again, he'd haul her downstairs and out of the warehouse. He told her as much with a stern look, and she went back to gazing down at the leftover blood and devastation.

What is she? Griffen had asked himself that question too many times to count. They shared a father, the most powerful of all demons, a Leviathan, and the last of his kind. He had taken the human name of Bartholomew August and lived for centuries before the Sibyls slaughtered him on a mountaintop in Greece. Griffen's mother had been elementally strong herself, a skilled Pagan practitioner who had passed along her talents to her son. With

August as his father, he could be nothing short of exceptional.

As for Rebecca's mother, some secrets Bartholomew August had taken to his grave. Griffen studied his sister's narrow shape and the unusual features that made her seem much younger than her actual years. Griffen wasn't certain, but he thought Rebecca's mother might not have been fully human herself. In his quest to restore his own kind to the world, August had mated with many different types of females. Griffen, August had explained, was exceptional among the offspring, and so was Rebecca. The two of them were closer to perfection, and so August had entrusted them with his legacy and his fortune. *Worthy*—that was how his father had described Rebecca when entrusting her to Griffen's care.

Worthy.

Good word.

But that didn't mean she was human in anything other than visible physical form.

August had also warned Griffen that Rebecca might manifest an impetuous and treacherous nature, especially as she aged. Never, under any circumstances, was Griffen to search for Rebecca's other relatives. If anyone or anything appeared in New York City claiming to be her kin, August had advised Griffen to kill first and sort for disposal later.

Some people might think the treated elemental cuffs Griffen kept on Rebecca's wrists constituted paranoia or excessive caution, never mind the chain that linked the cuffs and fastened them to his belt. Those people had never met her, and they certainly hadn't tried to survive her fits of temper.

When she bored with enjoying the blood-smeared floors below, she held up the cuffs. "Will I get time off for good behavior today?"

"When we get back to the apartment." Griffen made his smile match Rebecca's, a mix of genuine affection and murderous cunning.

She shifted her pretty features into a pout. "The elemental locks in that place stifle my senses."

"That's the point, my dear. When I know where you are and what you're doing, you can't get me killed."

"I would never harm you." Wide eyes at this statement. She let them drift halfway closed and frowned like a child desperately failing to earn craved approval.

"Not on purpose, I'm sure," Griffen said, but he wasn't sure. Not at all. Hence the precautions. Soon he'd find a worthy mate for her. Perhaps the right warlock or demon, or some other creature Griffen had yet to encounter, could continue the gentling of Rebecca and focus her on her true destiny—to produce worthy offspring and carry on the bloodline their father had given his life to establish and advance.

"Let's go down to the lab and check on our patient," he suggested.

Rebecca pouted anew. "Why? He won't be awake. You never let me wake him on purpose."

Griffen eased up on her chain lead so she could walk at her own pace when they started for their destination. "Maybe today you should have some fun."

This time her smile made Griffen shiver.

"That's my girl," he murmured, and led Rebecca toward the stairs to the warehouse floor.

(6)

The first part of the walk through the park to the brownstone went fast because Jack couldn't make himself slow down. The July heat stuck to him, and the smells of freshly mowed grass, mud, and his own sweat threatened to clog up his senses. Nothing like New York City in the summer. The place could get as hot as any beach—only without all the tropical perks.

"Normally, crime bosses and their foot soldiers slaughtering each other doesn't raise my blood pressure," Saul said as they neared the Central Park exit that would take them to the brownstone, "but this is fucked. Sooner or later we'll be facing some kind of freaky paranormal supermob with God only knows what leading it. I preferred it when supernatural shitheads didn't join forces with human dirtbags."

Jack thought about the OCU townhouse, nicknamed Headcase Quarters because of the Sibyls, demons, half-demons, and other creatures lurking through the hallways. "We have our alliances. Guess they had to do something to keep up."

They needed Andy's quad at the crime scene faster than right now. Bela, Camille, Dio, and Andy had special skills, an ability to use their elemental abilities to investigate crime scenes and track creatures and objects through the energy they left behind or contacted—but remnant energy faded fast.

"That's weird." Saul caught his arm for a second, then pointed at a clump of trees near the exit.

Jack saw some dark lumps on the ground and realized

they were squirrels. Looked like dead squirrels, and the grass around the furry little corpses had gone brown and dry. Jack's gaze moved left, then right, then up into the trees where he presumed the squirrels had been. Patches of dead leaves rustled against full, green healthy leaves.

"What the hell?" Jack muttered.

Saul narrowed his eyes at the dead animals. "Might be some kind of blight or disease, but usually that gets trees or critters, not both at the same time, right? Maybe it's a new thing."

"Or it's something weird, like you said." Unease made Jack's neck feel a little stiff, but his instincts didn't give him a full-on blast of warning. Weird, definitely. Important, probably. Directly related to their current case, maybe not. Time for an executive decision. "Call it in and ask the Sibyls on patrol tonight to give it a look."

"Done." Saul made himself a note on a pad he pulled out of his pocket, then retrieved his phone and called in the location and situation.

Jack tried to refocus as Saul hung up his phone, then the two of them angled out of the park, walked past an OCU panel van, and climbed the five steps to the brownstone's front door. With its rough stone exterior and lacy white curtains, the place seemed normal enough to the casual observer. On the inside, the décor was tasteful and modern, with sand-colored walls and neatly stained trim, but Jack knew he was passing through enough elemental protections to drive a hostile paranormal to its knees on the sidewalk below—maybe even bash its ass all the way into the fast-moving summer traffic on the street beyond.

Saul raised his hand to knock, but the front door opened.

The man standing in front of them looked almost Italian with his dark hair and eyes and his tanned skin. The sight of him still shocked Jack for the first few seconds, even though he'd had a few months to get used to the body John Cole had stolen from a Rakshasa demon. A longtime operative in Jack's secret special forces, John had traded his military career for the NYPD and marriage to Camille Fitzgerald, the unique fire Sibyl in Andy's fighting group.

"Knew it was you, Jack," John Cole said, his nose wrinkled like he'd caught a whiff of five-day-old garbage with his powerful demon senses. "You need a shower."

Saul grinned. "Maybe it's your litter box. You should check."

Before the two of them could throw another verbal punch, Jack said, "We've got another victim in the Garment District. I need to talk to Bela and the group—and I saw Andy this afternoon in Greece. Well, it was morning here, but you know what I mean."

"Yeah, we heard." John stepped aside to let them into the foyer. Above Jack's head, wind chimes tinkled softly in the summer breeze, a different sound from the coordinated jangle they gave off when carrying Sibyl messages.

Jack glanced at John to be sure he was serious. "That didn't take long."

"It never does. Bother one member of a fighting group and they're all after your blood." John's smile was sympathetic. "You should try to remember that, Jack." He gestured across the waterproof tile of the living room floor to the leather furniture in the room's alcove near the kitchen. On the brown leather couch behind the massive wooden communications platform that doubled as a worktable, Bela Argos Sharp sat next to her husband, Duncan, a longtime NYPD officer who'd survived a Rakshasa attack and learned to control the demon energy the attack set loose inside him. Bela's dark hair and exotic eyes contrasted with Duncan's all-American brown hair and cool blue eyes, but they moved like dance partners as they examined pictures from the earlier crime scenes.

Dio, the air Sibyl with wispy blond hair and a long, tall attitude, occupied the chair across the table from the couch. Arms folded, she studied the pictures at more distance with Camille. Camille's riot of auburn hair was pulled back into a ponytail, and her pretty face had an intensity Jack associated with her endless attention to detail.

As he got closer, another person came into view on the far end of the couch.

He stopped walking, and Saul literally bumped into him from behind.

Saul started grumbling, but Jack didn't hear anything he said because Andy was sitting right there, legs drawn up beneath her, studying him with her brown and green eyes. She had on jeans and a green tunic that made her shoulder-length red curls look dark and soft and rich, and Jack could have sworn he smelled her. Vanilla and the ocean, blended in a summer breeze.

Every curve of Andy's body spoke to Jack, and for one hot and bothered second, he couldn't do anything but imagine her in her underwear again, wet and vulnerable and beautiful on that island beach.

Had that been just a few hours ago?

Felt like a month.

"Jack?" Saul's questioning voice poked at his brain from somewhere far away, and Jack realized he was just standing there mute and stupid, holding the new crime folder in front of him like a shield.

"Jack," Jack echoed, trying to get his shit together and force his thoughts back to business and the present. This little-boy woo-woo crap just didn't happen to him. It couldn't.

He dragged his gaze away from Andy only to find her reflection in the host of projective mirrors hanging on the walls around the communications platform. He could see other reflections, too—Saul, John, Duncan, and all the other women, just staring at him, and then the group looked at Andy.

Dio tensed and Bela stood, even as Camille got to her feet and backed off a step. He figured they were getting ready for the flash wave that would finally crack Jack's skull, but all Andy said was, "Took you long enough."

Her slight drawl made each word longer. Sweeter.

Bela, Camille, and Dio let out a collective breath, though none of them seemed to relax. When Jack couldn't form any proper words, Andy pointed to the folder. "New case?"

"New case," Jack managed, handing the folder to Bela.

As she opened the jacket and frowned at the photos, he got himself in gear enough to say, "Another murder. We need to get to the scene while the energy might be traceable."

Once he finally got that out of his mouth, almost everybody moved at once, gathering papers and weapons and tossing away soda cans and chip bags. Saul moved past him to go over the location and victim with Duncan and John, and the Sibyls started talking about which other fighting groups to notify, and in what order.

Andy stayed on the couch, eyes locked on Jack. Her hair had gone damp in a matter of seconds, and the sleeves of her tunic dripped steadily on the floor. Aquakinesis. She was drawing water to her, moving it from nearby pipes or sprinklers. Jack had studied all the Sibyl abilities during his time at the Motherhouses. Water Sibyls had better control of their element than most fire Sibyls—but not by much. Water energy could be powerful. All-consuming.

Jack was beginning to understand that in ways he'd never expected. He wanted to peel off her wet clothing and see everything underneath, and there was nothing he could do to stop the wanting.

It's just physical. Ignore it and it'll pass.

His better sense talking again. Funny how quiet that rational voice seemed.

On the beach, Andy had seemed amused by him. Now she seemed distant, almost angry—or maybe this was how Andy did unsettled and afraid.

Did he unsettle her?

Jack thought he did, and he didn't believe he was just being nice to himself because she rattled him so completely. God, he'd been out of this game too long. One-nighters and quick meaningless encounters met his physical needs, and given his past, his life now, that was the best he could hope to achieve. This kind of thrust and parry, this kind of unspoken emotional sparking that could end up being meaningful, he remembered it from way too long ago, and suddenly realized he had missed it.

The lines of Andy's beautiful face tightened. "Don't think me saying yes to your little favor means anything."

Her firm assertion hit him like a slap. That should have restored his sanity, but his next words were, "It means something."

He heard himself talking, heard the loaded, suggestive tone and the way his rough voice cut under the chatter and activity. He'd made a statement of fact, born from instinct and a steaming, building certainty deep in his gut.

Her lips parted and her mouth came open. Her expression was supposed to be incredulous and mocking, but he saw it as sexy anyway. She knew that. Must have seen it on his face. He could tell by how fast she frowned at him.

"Think what you want, you egotistical jackass." She pointed at him, and the sprinkler over his head rattled like it was about to turn loose and douse him. The green highlights in her eyes came alive. Passion? Fury? He couldn't tell. Not much difference between the two sometimes. "I came back here to help my quad and the OCU. You—I don't give a fuck about you, so don't push me."

Jack couldn't move his eyes away from hers, and he couldn't stop himself from smiling at her. "I won't push you."

And again, he could tell they both understood his meaning.

I won't push you because I won't have to.

She stood so fast he readied himself for the blast of water that would break his ribs and crush his lungs.

He probably deserved it, but it never came.

She walked straight to him even though she could have gone around him on either side, put her hands on his chest, shoved him out of her way, and kept walking toward the stairs. She didn't look back as she climbed the steps, loosening the laces on her tunic.

"She's changing into her battle leathers," somebody said from behind him. Bela, Jack thought. Good timing, because he had almost followed Andy with zero memory of why he was here, what he was supposed to be doing, and how many other people were counting on him to keep a level head.

Instead of irritation over his lack of focus on the mission at hand, he felt impatience with the situation. Something was getting in the way of him going to have another word with that fascinating, infuriating woman, maybe daring her to tell him she felt no interest in him at all.

Jack figured Andy might do anything on a dare. She seemed the type. She seemed *his* type, and he wanted to know a lot more about her. He wanted to know everything about her, especially how she'd feel stretched out beneath him, giving him hell as he teased her with his mouth, his hands, his whispers in her ear, until she dug her nails into his back and demanded exactly what she wanted.

Bad, his rational mind told him.

But the rest of his mind had another thought.

Soon.

(7)

Bela drove her black SUV toward the warehouse, cutting around cabs and buses with a fluid grace developed over years of New York City driving. Camille rode shotgun with Dio and Andy in the backseat, and Duncan, John, Saul, and Jack followed behind them in one of the OCU's panel vans.

Andy never got nervous with Bela driving, but she often got nervous when Dio stared at her. At the moment, Dio was staring so hard Andy wanted to crawl out her tinted window. Her leathers would probably protect her if she jumped, right?

"What the hell was that little drama between you and Jack Blackmore?" Dio's tone didn't quite reach accusatory, but it got close.

"Nothing." Andy almost shouted the word because she was still so pissed over that—over the—over *him*. Just him. Unbelievable that she hadn't tried to drown the bastard all over again. Her own self-control amazed her.

Dio kept her chin high and turned her eyes forward, but Andy felt wave after wave of something coming off her despite the elementally treated leather suit that should have contained at least a portion of Dio's power. Some sort of energy that reminded her vaguely of the movements of water and the sea. Andy had no idea what it was or why she was sensing it, but the urge to say something about it grew like an itch until she had to scratch it.

"What's your problem, Dio?"

"*My* problem?" A sharp burst of air blew through the

backseat, stirring Dio's wispy blond hair all across her delicate face. She squeezed the door handle with one hand, and with the other she toyed with the vicious three-clawed African throwing knives forming her belt and hanging in long strips down both legs. "That whole scene back at the brownstone—too weird."

The energy surging from Dio increased. *Anger,* Andy's instincts told her. She felt like she was gazing into a pool, seeing layers of water flowing with different shades and temperatures. *Mistrust. Suspicion. Worry. But at base, deep in the well, the source is . . . confusion.*

"You felt surprised and confused by the undercurrents you picked up between Jack and me." Andy took a breath, trying not to let her thoughts speed up to match Dio's air energy. "Well, welcome to the club."

Dio let off another hair-raising burst of wind. "Surpr—confused? No way." She glared at Andy all over again, and this time suspicion crept into her storm-gray eyes. "Dear Goddess. Did Elana finally manage to teach you how to read emotions?"

Andy couldn't look away from Dio even though she knew it was probably a good idea. Her first instinct was to lie, but as usual, she reverted to honesty. "She's been trying to make me learn, but I didn't think I was getting it. I'm not sure—but yeah, I think I'm picking up feelings from you."

Dio's eyes darkened. From off in the distance came the ominous rumble of thunder out of a clear sky. "Stay out of my head."

Andy could almost smell the acrid lightning threatening to explode thanks to Dio's unusual and definitely unsanctioned weather-making talent. Dio had almost been denied the chance to join a fighting group because the talent had proved so dangerous in the past that the Mothers feared it, and she was absolutely forbidden to use it in battle. That wouldn't stop her from bursting

Andy's eardrums with thunder or planting a crackle of lightning across Andy's forehead. There, in the back of the SUV with Dio quivering from anger and discomfort, Andy understood why the Mothers wanted nothing to do with weather making.

"Emotion reading is one of her jobs, Dio." Camille, the most level-headed fire Sibyl on the planet, weighed in from the front seat, trying to calm things down. "Flow. As in the emotional flow of the fighting group. She's supposed to sense our emotions and help us work through them—not that your feelings are so hard to sense anyway."

More thunder turned loose, this time right above the SUV. "Bullshit!" Dio's hands stayed in her lap. Her fingers twitched. "Nobody gets to poke around inside me like I'm some sort of child who needs soothing."

Nobody said a word in response, because that was exactly how Dio often behaved. They all knew it—even Dio. Andy tried to make herself watch Manhattan's scenery flow by outside her window, but the buildings, sidewalks, and people all seemed like a sun-drenched blur.

"Something did go down between you and Jack Blackmore back at the brownstone, Andy." Bela's words carried the subtle power and force of her earth element, and her dark eyes seemed both kind and understanding as she glanced at Andy in the rearview. "I was afraid the air between you might catch on fire."

Andy felt her jeans and shirt get damp, both from sweat and from a surge of her water energy. "He made me madder than hell. You got that part right."

Bela and Camille and Dio waited, saying nothing, and Andy thought about Elana. Had the old woman been giving Andy's quad lessons on being silent until Andy spilled her guts?

Andy had no idea what to say because she wasn't

ready to think too hard about Jack—not that he or anybody else was giving her that choice—but she knew she had to come up with something. "Okay, okay. Jack seemed more intense than usual. I don't know why." She took another breath when she finished talking, and this time she caught hints of earth, fire, and hot summer winds as the elemental energy mingled with her own to help her calm herself.

"Looked like interest to me," Camille said. "Something too raw and powerful for Jack to cover up, so he just went with it."

Andy absorbed the water soaking into her jeans, but she had nowhere to send it. She slipped her hand to her side and let it flow onto the SUV's floor, intending to deal with it after they parked. "When he saw me on the island this morning, he acted a little goofy, but I thought it was because I was in my underwear."

"Oh, shit." Bela banged her hand on the steering wheel. "You didn't say anything about him catching you half dressed. I'm so sorry. If we'd had any idea he was planning to show up on the beach today to confront you, we would have warned you."

"Look, whether or not he's interested in me, I really don't care. It's not mutual." There. Andy felt triumphant, getting that out of her mouth. Nice and firm and definitive. A boundary. A limit. She tried to ignore the sudden silence and the furtive glances from three separate pairs of eyes that threatened to take away her victory, but that was hard.

Sometimes, living with three intuitive women who noticed everything sucked as much as the chaotic construction of Motherhouse Kérkira.

"Elana wants us to build a new Motherhouse," Andy said to change the subject, hoping like hell everyone would let her. "Just the water Sibyls."

"You've got to be kidding me." Dio whipped toward Andy, mouth open. "Where?"

Andy shrugged. "No idea."

"How?" Bela and Camille asked the question at the same time, almost in harmony. They looked as stunned as Dio, but not nearly as angry.

Relief began to trickle through Andy. She could hardly believe this was easier to talk about than Jack, but it definitely didn't make her feel like she was losing her mind. "Elana acts like Motherhouse Wherever will just rise from the sea fully formed. Maybe she's finally going around the bend. She's too old to even think about the actual number of years she's lived."

Bela gripped the SUV's steering wheel so tight her fingers seemed to pale. "Sibyls don't go senile. At least I don't think they do. Elana and Ona are the oldest ones I know."

"Ona's a nutcase, so that's comforting." Andy went back to staring out the window. "And, for the record, I'm not attracted to Jack Blackmore."

"Yes, you are," Camille said.

"He's so handsome he's almost pretty," Bela added.

Andy's jaw clenched, and she had to make herself relax before she could answer. "Pretty on the outside doesn't make up for asshole on the inside."

"I don't think he's a complete waste of skin," Camille said. "John considers him a close friend, and so does Duncan. And the Brent brothers stay close to him. He's got to have some redeeming qualities."

"He keeps them well hidden," Dio muttered, and when she made eye contact with Andy, Andy felt their tentative bond reestablishing itself. Andy nodded, agreeing with her, and Dio's air energy settled into little breezes.

Because of the air Sibyl–water Sibyl teaching connection, Andy shared living space with Dio upstairs in the brownstone. They had always managed to get along even though Dio was anything but the laid-back, supportive team member most air Sibyls strove to be. Like all of her fighting group, Dio was important to Andy, and Andy didn't relish the thought of ongoing conflict with her sister Sibyl.

What was it Andy had told Elana on the beach—that Jack Blackmore was a tension-creating machine?

Yeah.

That was accurate, wasn't it?

When they reached the curb in front of the warehouse, Andy finally got to bail out of the SUV. Thank God for the space, the warm summer air, the chaos of traffic and pedestrians. The normalcy of the New York City day, at least on the surface, did more to settle her nerves than anything in a long time, but her thoughts still spun like a big whirlpool, sloshing in her mind until she couldn't focus on the walkway, the surrounding pavement, or even the warehouse door to see if there were subtle traces of debris or energy that might be important.

I'm not attracted to Jack Blackmore. But if I am, it's only physical and I will never take it past looking and admiring.

She didn't even admire him that much.

Okay, he was handsome, but good looks didn't wash away months of him shouting orders and ignoring the fact that nobody else thought he was God's gift to anything.

"You okay, honey?" A hand gripped Andy's shoulder, and she jumped a foot before she realized it was Bela— and that she'd been standing, spaced out, her hand on the warehouse door handle.

"Fine, fine. Sorry." Andy let herself close her eyes for a second and imagine Bela, Dio, and Camille standing quietly behind her, waiting for her and counting on her to be at her best. The whole conversation from the SUV—it needed to be tabled now, especially in Andy's own mind. If she didn't settle down, she might wash the whole scene clean by accident, and she definitely wouldn't be doing her best job as a Sibyl.

She checked the Heckler and Koch P-11 underwater pistol she carried when she was suited up for Sibyl work. The weapon felt cool and solid in its holster. It wasn't a SIG, but it handled moisture a lot better. She tried to breathe, tried to think about the ocean, the beach, or any of Elana's dozens of wise statements and mantras.

Not so easy.

It took a few seconds, but she found the rhythm, and a few seconds later she settled into the focus she needed to be safe and walk into the crime scene fully aware. After a slow count to three, she pushed open the warehouse door.

The OCU officer on guard stepped aside to let her and her fighting group pass, and as the door closed behind them, Andy heard another vehicle pulling up outside.

Jack and the guys. Not waiting. They can catch up. Then, a few steps into the building, she had another irritating thought. *I should have listened better when Elana tried to teach me to shut out distractions in the ocean.*

As she walked farther into the crime scene, older and more comfortable instincts took over. Reality edged across her worries and confusion like a bloody shadow, and the details of the warehouse got a lot more salient—especially the fact that the place was empty except for the pile of body parts in the center of the concrete floor.

"I've seen gross before," Andy muttered, "but that's definitely a contender for Most Disgusting Ever."

Bela stopped short of the corpse pieces and glanced around the warehouse again. "This place could have housed an automotive showroom. It's huge."

Andy estimated four stories and noted the reinforced

ceiling—more floors on top. OCU would be determining ownership and working on access to those floors.

"Offices to the left," Camille said. "One door's open and taped off."

"No unusual scents. Just blood and decay and old moldy warehouse." Dio gave her report from a distance, and Andy knew she was keeping a broad perspective and paying close attention to everything. While the rest of them worked, Dio would make sure nothing snuck up on them. Even with the OCU presence, Dio would never trust the safety of her fighting group to outsiders. She was the broom, and she'd be the one sweeping up—or planting a throwing knife between the eyes of—any threat.

Bela put her palm over the copper crescent moon charm Camille had forged especially to enhance her awareness of earth energy, and Andy sensed Bela's power flowing into the sand and rock making up the concrete floor. Her eyebrows immediately came together. "Something came into the building and made contact with the ground there." She pointed to a spot under a smashed window around the three-story level.

Andy stared at the window, then at the floor. "Whatever it was scaled the building or climbed down its façade from the roof, broke through, and what—rappelled to the floor? Jumped?"

"I think it jumped," Bela said. "The trace is much stronger where it hit the ground."

"Great. Just what we need." Andy touched her dart pistol again for comfort and checked the ceiling one more time. "A homicidal Spider-Man."

"I can't get a read on the energy, but it moves from there to the taped-off office." Bela closed her eyes. "Then back out, but only once."

"To move the body into view and do the damage?" Camille asked, and Andy realized she was addressing the question to her.

She turned her gaze back to the body parts and the area around them. "Kristo Foucci was already dead when the thing tore him apart. No blood spatter, just a lot of pooling. His heart wasn't beating."

Camille knelt over the body's torso and closed her left hand over her gold crescent moon pendant. Tiny beams of blue fire left the fingers of her outstretched right hand, probing the pieces of the body from its detached head to its discarded feet.

Andy heard the outer door open and close. Footsteps came toward them, but Andy didn't turn around because she didn't want to see Jack Blackmore. Knowing he was in the warehouse threw her insides into a jumble of irritation and curiosity.

She fidgeted with her iron crescent moon charm, hoping the metal would help her focus her own awareness, but even after long hours of intense training from Elana, she felt leery of using her aquasentience to explore the crime scene. Projective elemental energy could be extremely powerful and dangerous, and that's what the charm most enhanced—and what she most needed in order to examine the body. When Andy tapped her projective abilities, she became a conduit for the power of water, letting it flow through her essence instead of summoning and controlling its course. She could gain so much valuable information by searching through what the water could tell her, but one mistake, one slip in concentration, and she could flood the building or, worse, most of Manhattan.

Her pulse picked up as she sensed Jack getting closer to her, and damn it, her body started responding again. He was staying quiet, staying out of her way, but his presence felt like hot geysers firing through her from her toes to her cheeks. The bastard was making her sweat.

Worse than that, she was sensing something from him. Something like concern. Or maybe . . . protectiveness?

Oh, that pissed her off.

She didn't need his protection. She didn't need anything from that man—and why the hell was she picking up his emotions, anyway? She barely had a handle on her own, or her quad's, and she was *supposed* to be reading theirs.

This was stupid. She had work to do.

She strode forward and knelt beside Camille, studying the mangled corpse with a detachment she had cultivated during nearly a decade of working homicides. She gripped her charm and made herself breathe, slowly, slowly, until—

Yes.

That was better. She could hear water now, hear it all around her, from the ocean and the bay and the river, from sewer pipes and water pipes and even the whisper of moisture hanging in the warm summer air.

More flickers of energy flowed into Andy's awareness. Camille. Camille's emotions swept across Andy like a sunlit river. Total focus. Total absorption in her purpose. Relaxed. Confident but with definite moments of self-doubt. And there was Bela, more like a cool mountain stream running deep in a rock-lined cavern, strong and determined and aware, perplexed by the data she couldn't interpret. Dio—Andy held herself steady, but the force of Dio's feelings nearly knocked her sideways. She couldn't sort a single emotion from the whirlwind. The woman seemed to be made of wind and weather instead of flesh and flowing blood with its obligatory portion of water.

Andy used her free hand to brace herself against the concrete floor and barely avoided swaying into Camille.

I should . . . do something.

She tried to ignore that thought, wanted to put it aside but couldn't. She should act on what she was sensing. She *needed* to act on it, but she had no idea what to do.

Strengthen Camille's confidence?

Relax Bela's tension?

And Dio—well. The best she would be able to do for Dio was make her own energy a buffer between Dio's inner tempest and everyone else.

The idea of intruding on anyone's private emotions came close to disgusting Andy. Everything she had been raised to believe, everything she had learned in life, and everything she had always believed to be true argued against doing anything like what she was considering.

Yeah, and until a few years ago, I didn't believe in demons, either.

She had to keep reminding herself that this was her new life. Andy version 2.0, complete with sister Sibyls and elemental energy and duties to her fighting group.

She allowed her water energy to flow out in small measure. A split second later, a hot shock rippled up her spine as she made contact with Camille's angst.

Great.

She had no idea what to do next, but a voice in her head almost like Elana's whispered, *Just let it flow.*

Andy let her water power touch Camille's fear and doubt, imagined the water soothing and cooling those emotions until they were nothing more than smoldering bits of debris. Camille's shiver of surprise and the resultant burst of fiery gratitude felt like a reward. Bela's earth energy joined the mix, and even a measure of Dio's wind. Almost at the same time, the four of them relaxed and their energies blended seamlessly, like they had always been part of the same source. A strange kind of harmony settled through Andy, and the corpse she wanted to examine came into crystalline focus.

Her eyes scoured each inch of the mutilated flesh, and bit by bit she pulled more water through her essence, reaching out with the moisture in the air and letting it rest on the body. New images and sensations came to her, from the stink of stale sweat and fear to the copper tang of blood. She saw each ragged edge of each wound anew, and if she'd had a pencil and pad, she might have been able to sketch out which limb got pulled off first and second and so on—she never knew what might end up mattering. All information was relevant.

"Broke his neck first," she said aloud so they'd all record it in memory. "That feels like the first point of damage. Quick and efficient and strong as hell."

Her thoughts shivered like ripples across a pond, and her attention focused on the bloodied sleeve pasted against the body's torso.

Something was there. She couldn't see it, but her water energy told her foreign matter clung to that sleeve.

"I need tweezers and an evidence bag," she said, holding her awareness as still and tight as she could. Couldn't lose this. Whatever it was, it was important.

Camille scooted away from Andy, and someone bent down to hand her a bag and tweezers. She knew who it was. Her teeth ground together as she made herself keep her attention on the evidence.

Jack withdrew quickly, giving her the space she needed to lean forward and follow her senses to . . . yes. Right there.

She plucked a thin strand of something out of the blood and smeared it into the bag.

"Hair?" Camille asked from behind her.

"No idea." Andy harvested the other strand she had detected, and this time she brought it closer, looked at it, and let her water touch it more completely.

The world around her shivered.

Then it blurred.

A picture expanded in her mind like a watercolor filling itself in, center to edges.

What the hell—?

What am I seeing?

The image tried to take over her awareness, and her lips moved almost outside her control.

"Arms . . . too big. Legs . . . not human. The rage. Ah, God, the rage!"

So betrayed. The energy seethed off the hair, hatred pure and cold. And determination to destroy every living thing in its path.

Andy rocked backward, lost her balance, and would have splattered all over the warehouse floor if someone hadn't caught her by the waist.

The hands steadying her felt strong as iron, yet gentle and caring, and new rivers of emotion flowed into her. Completely selfless concern. Gut-level apprehension. Genuine warmth and respect. It was enough to make her legs wobble. Her breath caught so deep she coughed, and she pulled away from Jack Blackmore so fast she almost fell a second time.

Camille got her by the arm and steadied her, then pulled her away from Jack and the body they had been examining.

Andy held herself like she'd been broken open, like her insides might burst through to the outside world.

I'm a cracked dam.

Her awareness spun. Images from the past, from this morning, from now washed through her mind, and she saw other pictures, too, of herself, of her quad, of Jack, of people she knew, the same but changed in ways she couldn't understand. They were nothing but fast snapshots rising out of water, then turning and vanishing below the surface again.

She could hear herself breathing, feel herself swaying as Camille's grip on her arm tightened.

"You okay?" Camille asked as Bela and Dio hurried over.

"I'm not sure." Andy's mouth felt numb as she spoke.

"I saw something, but I don't know what it was. I didn't expect it."

She didn't say the rest, but it screamed through her mind.

And I didn't expect him.

The plugged-in connection to Jack Blackmore and his emotions at the moment he touched her. The oh-so-undeniable confirmation from her own Sibyl abilities that maybe, just maybe, Jack wasn't ugly on the inside. Once more she was way too aware of him standing close to her, but relieved and a little surprised that he didn't shove his way past her quad to act on the worry steaming out of him like locomotive exhaust.

She heard male voices murmuring, but Jack said, "Let them do what they do. No medical examiner will find more, and the ME will miss all the paranormal traces. They'll tell us if they need our help."

"What is it?" Bela reached Andy, appraising her with the dark, steady eyes of a mortar and filling Andy with soothing earth energy. "What did the hair show you?"

"A—an—I don't know. It looked and felt human or human-like, but it wasn't. The composition was wrong."

Dio jogged to a stop beside Andy, obviously hearing her explanation because she said, "What the hell does that mean? What about its composition?"

"It wasn't natural." Andy glanced around the warehouse, glad it was coming into full focus again. "Whatever left those hairs behind, it's not human, but not natural paranormal, either. I can't say it any better than that."

"Unnatural paranormal?" Dio's confusion showed on her face, and Bela and Camille looked just as perplexed. "What does that look like?"

Andy thought about Elana again and all of her lessons in the Ionian Sea. "Vast freedom within vast limitations."

Not enough.

Damn it, get it together, Myles.

She fished for the right words, failed, sighed, and tried again to organize what she wanted to say. "I don't completely understand it myself, but in the natural world, certain laws have to be followed and certain realities can't be changed. Even in the paranormal world there are basic sets of energies and biological compositions, just like in oceans and seas and other ecosystems. Huge numbers of possibilities, but finite ways they can combine naturally." She raised the evidence bag with the hairs. "The water in these, the water that's moved through them—the flow was broken. This biology isn't natural."

Bela, Camille, and Dio stood in silence, looking from the bag to Andy. She could tell they were trying, but nobody was getting it. Andy had no idea how to explain it better, and she felt as clueless as the first moment she had seen someone—actually, her OCU partner and best friend at the time—shift into a demon. She had no words to describe what her senses perceived.

"The creature who shed these hairs is possible in nature," she tried again, "but it never would have come about or arisen on its own. It's like a hybrid, something human and paranormal, but not blended like half-demons or other paranormals we've encountered."

Okay, maybe that was a little better.

Lights seemed to be coming on, at least in Camille's face.

"Like a turcock?" Camille asked.

Then again, maybe not . . .

Dio stared at Camille like Camille's mind might have melted during one of her more intense play sessions with fire. "What the living hell is a turcock?"

Bela put her hand on Camille's arm. "What she means is, can you translate for those of us who don't live in books and laboratories?"

Camille, possibly the only fire Sibyl in history more

bookish than an air Sibyl and more science-oriented than an earth Sibyl, warmed to the task with lots of expansive gestures. "Turkeys and peacocks both belong to the pheasant family, so theoretically and biologically they can produce offspring. Only they can't mate and produce offspring in the wild. They can only make babies in laboratories with scientific help. So turcocks are possible, but they'd never happen in nature on their own."

As she finished, Camille smiled like a happy kid.

"And you know this because . . . ?" Dio's tone suggested she was trying to keep her impatience in check.

Camille shrugged. "Birds are interesting. I read about them in my spare time."

Andy felt grateful, because she never would have come up with an allegory that made any sense. This one might have been weird, but it worked.

"So somebody, somewhere, somehow, made a turcock or whatever," Bela said.

Dio lifted one finger. "A man-eating turcock."

"Man-ripping," Andy corrected. "It doesn't eat its kill, which also doesn't feel natural, since the act itself is so brutal it's like a wild animal."

"It should feed, but it doesn't." Jack joined the conversation without jarring Andy in the least, as if he had been watching, guessing, making deductions about the case—and learning on the spot how to better interact with her. "So either it can't feed or it was engineered not to."

"Engineered," Bela said, sounding far away as she stared at the body parts on the warehouse floor. "As in genetically. Or biologically, at least."

Bela's husband, Duncan, came forward and took her hand, while John Cole and Saul Brent kept their distance. Andy let herself look at Jack. He had his jacket and tie off, and his sleeves were rolled up to his elbows.

Casual suited him better than she would have imagined. He gave her a polite glance, nothing overstepping. This was work. He was at work.

So am I. God, I'm hopeless.

"Biologically engineered is more accurate," Andy said, instantly annoyed by the slight tremor in her voice. "If the creature had been built from genes up, I think it would be using water more naturally, more evenly."

"So we've got ourselves a New Age Dr. Frankenstein," Jack said. "Or maybe a bunch of them."

Andy gestured at the body parts. "And their monster, the mobster ripper."

"Ripper? Gross." Dio's delicate features twisted in disgust and a faint breeze stirred the cloying smells of old blood and older warehouse. "Don't you dare start calling it the Ripper."

"I'll settle for Frank." Andy held up the evidence bag. "Will you and Camille take this back to the brownstone so Camille can start figuring out how Frank's built? Bela and I can handle seeing what we can track from the leftover projective energy."

Dio grabbed the bag, still looking disgusted. "Have it your way. But I'm not sure I want anybody to find Frankenstein the Ripper."

"Better we sneak up on it than it sneak up on us," Bela said as Jack put in a call for additional OCU and Sibyl backup.

Dio and Camille took their leave with Saul Brent and John Cole escorting them. Andy watched them go, then closed her eyes. She let her awareness sink into dozens of nearby water sources—puddles, condensation, water pipes, mains, wherever water stood or flowed around the warehouse. She gripped her crescent moon pendant, and as she had practiced so many times with Elana, she drew the water toward her.

Not much. Just a little.

Too much and the ocean will flow across Manhattan to say hello.

She made herself breathe. Imagined being deep under the calming sea. The water's energy touched her, caressed her, and—

"There." She pointed. The word she had spoken sounded like something out of a faraway dream, and she had to bring herself back to the real world enough to look at Bela and add, "The last water Frank touched in this building. We should go out that door."

Jack and Duncan Sharp moved out behind Andy and Bela, leaving the warehouse behind as the two women took turns sampling water and earth with their elemental powers. To casual passersby, they no doubt looked like two women in leather getups, model-style, walking slowly down the sidewalk in the summer sun. Both of them had their smaller weapons concealed, and Bela's sword looked like a movie prop. Nobody gave them a second glance even though it was hot outside and most everyone who passed them had on short sleeves or no sleeves at all.

Andy hesitated at a corner, then gestured toward Canal Street. Bela stood still for a moment, then agreed. Something—some sort of power—made Jack's neck prickle.

"Feel that?"Duncan Sharp murmured, keeping a close eye on the earth Sibyl he had married. "They've really got the scent now."

Jack nodded and kept walking. This thing Andy and her group did with their elemental energy—projection—impressed him. It also disturbed him. The Mothers had made it clear that projective energy could be very difficult to control, and a Sibyl losing her grip on such power could cause natural disasters of global proportions.

"Have they got this?" he asked Duncan, knowing he'd understand Jack's concern. Duncan had been around for a lot of the bruises Jack had taken from elemental energy and pissed-off Sibyls. "They're in total control of that kind of power?"

Duncan's grin still made him look like a fresh-faced Army recruit. "They're fine. And if they're not, we probably won't live to give a damn."

Jack glanced in the general direction of the Hudson, wondering exactly how much water Andy could bring to bear if she really channeled that power of hers. A few seconds later, he saw an OCU van pull up, and a small squad of plainclothes officers got out, followed by the Sibyls in the East Ranger group—Sheila Gray, Maggie Cregan, and Karin Maros. He recognized Sheila easily enough from the no-hair-out-of-place ponytail and the creepy sort of calmness she seemed to radiate. Maggie's short red hair was distinctive, too, like Karin's stocky build—unusual for an air Sibyl.

Almost immediately, Jack's eyes moved to the sword belted at Maggie Cregan's waist, only partly hidden under the folds of a black cloak she wore to conceal it. Sheila had on a cloak, too, while Karin didn't need one since her throwing stars—*shuriken*—looked like belt decorations. But that sword of Maggie's kept nudging out from under the cloak.

Of course it was just the wind stirring through the hot summer day. The sword wasn't moving by itself, but still, something always felt off about that damned thing. Jack didn't much like being on the same block with it, and he really didn't like it being only a few hundred yards away from Andy.

Duncan saw where Jack was looking, and he acknowledged Maggie with a nod. "You've heard the rumors about her weapon?"

"That she's carrying a sword handed down to her by executioners in her family tree?" Jack made a quick visual check on Andy and Bela, who started walking again. "Yeah, I got that part from some of the OCU officers who work with her."

Duncan edged ahead of Jack on the sidewalk as Bela

took a lead over Andy in the tracking. "Bela told me that one of the women who used to carry that sword also hung people outside her own window, for the local jailhouse. After the victim died, she'd sketch the swinging body on her bedroom wall. Somehow one of those sketches ended up etched into that sword's blade."

Jack checked Andy. Checked the sword. He'd like more distance between her and that . . . thing, but the East Ranger Sibyls had responded to his call for backup. He couldn't very well order them off again and ask for a different group. "John Cole said the sword hates him. Think there's anything to that?"

"It tasted his blood. Now it can find him anywhere. I've seen the damned thing try to pull out of Maggie's hand to cut him when he got too close."

Jack closed distance with the Sibyls so he could watch Andy and the strange blade at the same time. "Why does she carry it?"

Duncan gave a quick snort of amusement. "I guess because it kills the bad guys."

Jack forced himself to stop monitoring the sword and how close Maggie was getting to Andy. He'd really rather that sword not be a part of this, though he couldn't say why. And he damned sure couldn't tell a Sibyl what weapon to carry, not if he liked staying alive with all his body parts still attached.

Jack figured that from above, this tracking operation looked like a leather-headed snake, with Andy and Bela up front and Sheila and Maggie close on their heels. Karin Maros had backed off and disappeared into the crowd like air Sibyls tended to do, keeping a broader view of the whole situation. Jack and Duncan walked a few steps behind the Sibyls, and four OCU officers kept pace right after them.

Bela and Andy followed a strange path, up and down different streets, first one way and then the other. Canal to Broadway. Broadway to Nassau. Back to Broadway. Over to Church. Finally they ended up on Greenwich, and the Sibyls made a sharp right behind what looked like an abandoned storefront.

On instinct, Jack's hand moved toward his Glock. His nostrils flared, picking up the doughy scent of pizza and, from somewhere close, something sweeter, like pastries. "Anything?" he asked Duncan, who could use his enhanced Bengal senses to pick up threats Jack wouldn't notice.

"Not yet. I mean, the monster thing smelled like stink and blood when it left the warehouse, so I've gotten a few whiffs of that, but the trail's old and degrading with every minute we're out here." His nose wrinkled as they got closer to the storefront. "Like now. I can smell the bastard, but not strong enough that I think he's here or anything."

As they moved down the small alley beside the storefront, Andy and the other Sibyls turned a quick left and Jack lost sight of her.

"Shit." He drew his weapon and broke into a jog. So did Duncan. The OCU officers tailing them stopped at intervals, covering the alley and making sure nobody followed them. A blur of movement on a nearby rooftop almost made Jack take aim, but he realized it was Karin, keeping her vantage point clear.

Jack rounded the corner and spotted Andy immediately, standing in the center of a small paved area with Bela. Looked like a private patio, enclosed—maybe one that used to be attached to a restaurant or bistro. Open crates and broken chairs and tables littered the ground, and the space smelled like musty concrete and motor oil.

As soon as he was close enough to Andy to grab her if anything went nuts, Jack stopped. He didn't holster his weapon, and neither did Duncan, who stopped beside him.

The Sibyls seemed to be studying something on the ground, and when Jack got closer, he could tell it was a gold coin. The design looked old, but the way the thing caught the light and glittered, somebody had polished it before dropping it—or placing it on the ground for the Sibyls to find.

Andy seemed particularly bothered by it, or maybe startled. Jack wasn't sure, but he thought he saw her twitch like she might be hearing something nobody else could perceive.

Bela cocked her head for a different perspective on the coin. "Looks Far Eastern or maybe Persian—kind of like a dinar, but a lot smaller."

"Are you getting anything from it?" Sheila asked Bela, her voice as serene as that of some yogi on a mountaintop. Andy's red curls and Bela's dark hair moved in the light breeze, but Sheila's ponytail stayed neat and still. Jack wondered if it was possible for an earth Sibyl to anchor herself so completely to her element that she turned frozen or something.

"Nothing." Bela stooped toward the coin for a better look. "It's like the energy's muffled, or the coin's never been touched by anything anywhere—even the ground beneath it. And that monster's energy ends right here, too. It doesn't trickle or dwindle. It's just gone."

"Same for me." Andy didn't seem inclined to get close to the gold piece. In fact, she took a step back, shook her head once, then rubbed her right ear. "If I weren't looking straight at that coin, I'd swear there was no metal on the concrete in front of me—and no traces of the altered creature. It's like somebody took out a big hose and washed away all the natural energy and traces we should be sensing." She rubbed her ear again, then lowered her hand. "Does anybody hear anything?"

"Not a thing but Karin's wind," Bela said. "You getting something auditory?"

"I thought I heard my name," Andy said. "Like somebody called me."

Bela gave her a quick glance. "Right now? Ongoing?"

"No," Andy said. "Only when we first got into the alley, and again when we got close to the coin."

"There's another one." Maggie Cregan broke away from the other three Sibyls, her short red hair so bright it gleamed like the coins. Jack caught a glimpse of her strange-colored eyes and fought off a ripple of discomfort as she went close to the boarded back door of the abandoned storefront. She knelt beside a second gold coin on the ground, but she didn't touch it.

"Sampling metal's more Camille's thing than ours," Andy said to Bela. "Should we have Jack call somebody to get her and bring her back here?"

"I can use my sword," Maggie offered. "It can assay metal as well as it does blood, only without some of the unpleasant effects."

Sheila nodded, and Maggie slowly drew the blade Jack wished she'd keep in its scabbard. The weapon had an oddly short hilt, but the flat blade was massive. Even at a distance, the details of its form seemed glaring and disturbing, and Maggie seemed to struggle to grip it for a few seconds. As she tightened her hands on the hilt, tiny flames caught along the blade, illuminating rune-like etchings.

Easy enough to see what those freaky little pictures showed. A hanging man. A beheaded man. A guy in pieces. A guy with a blade sticking out of his back. There were lots of them, and Jack decided to stop cataloguing them. The more the sword flamed, the brighter those pictures burned.

"Shit," Duncan whispered. "Are those pictures moving?"

Jack didn't answer because he'd stopped looking at the sword. At the moment he was more worried about

Duncan, because Duncan's voice sounded too forceful and deep.

Duncan held out his hands so Jack could see the swaths of orange and black tiger fur breaking across Duncan's knuckles and wrists. "The energy coming off that thing's enough to make me puke. Definitely projective, but contained in the blade somehow."

"Will it make you change?" Jack knew a full blast of projective energy usually brought out the paranormal aspects of half-breeds and other demon mixes. "Are you safe?"

"No, I don't think it'll make me change. And even if I change, I can handle myself." Duncan's gaze moved back to Maggie and the sword. "But I want that sword out of here pretty damned soon."

Maggie lowered the tip of her blade toward the coin and touched it, and Duncan, Bela, and Andy jerked like they'd been hooked to jumper cables. Duncan let out a loud howl. His skin rippled, then pulled as he changed completely and fully to his Bengal form. He collapsed on the ground, head covered and still howling, as Andy and Bela slumped to the concrete. Andy landed near the other coin and rolled away from it, shrieking like the damned thing had gutted her.

No fucking way. Jack bolted toward Andy with zero idea what to do.

Sheila ran toward Maggie, who seemed to be locked to her sword and the coin, rattling so hard her teeth clattered together. Jack jammed his Glock in his holster and dropped to his knees beside Andy. Her eyes had gone wide and her mouth hung open. She was breathing. Jack reached to touch her neck, to check her pulse, but he couldn't get his hand close to her. Something repelled him. Same with Bela. He fought like hell to push through the fuzzy-feeling nothingness surrounding them, but he couldn't.

"Damn it!" Jack turned to yell at Sheila, but wind blasted across the concrete and Karin Maros hit the ground beside him in a crouch.

"Wait," she barked in a tone so unexpected Jack did wait.

Sheila launched herself in the air, straight toward Maggie, arms out like an NFL tackle. Karin sent a rush of wind to speed her flight.

When Sheila slammed into Maggie, the two of them fell away from the sword—which stayed upright on its tip and flaming, attached to the coin.

Andy moaned. Jack reached for her again, but he got an even harder pushback from whatever energy held her hostage. Christ, she was going pale. Bela twitched beside her, ghost white, and he couldn't do anything. Nothing. Fuck!

Karin yanked a throwing star off her belt and hurled it hard and low. The howling wind she sent with it shoved Jack on his ass.

The star blasted into the coin. Sparks flew in every direction. The sword spun and gave off a wail like some writhing creature in hell—and the coin underneath it exploded like a flashbang.

Light ripped across Jack's vision and the noise punched at his eardrums. He fell like a discarded puppet, vaguely aware of pain as his head bounced off concrete.

For a few seconds, he saw nothing but white-blue flashes. He couldn't hear anything except his own pulse in his ears.

Shake it off. Now. Up, soldier!

His own voice from a million years ago. From the smoldering desert to the smoldering concrete where he lay now.

Up. Ass, then knees, then feet. Get up.

He struggled to sit. Blurred negative images of a burning sword seemed to dance on the ground in front of him. Then he saw what looked like a shadowy movie of three women staggering to each other and holding on—Karin, Maggie, and Sheila. The air smelled like fire and burned wood.

Jack forced himself to his knees, then crawled straight back to Andy. Big blobs of light swam across his visual field as he tried to focus on her. She wasn't moving. Eyes and mouth closed now. He reached for her—and this time his hand touched her shoulder.

Warm. Relaxed. Alive.

She opened her eyes and spoke.

Jack couldn't hear a word, but the relief of seeing her awake and moving nearly sent him back to the ground. She looked like somebody had wrung all the blood and energy out of her body, but she had fought off whatever energy had grabbed her.

Bela rolled to her side, vomited, then got to a sitting position. Jack turned his head to check on Duncan and saw him crawling toward Bela on hands and knees. The tiger fur on his hands and face slowly shifted back to skin as he worked his way in their direction.

The world tilted a little, and Jack had to catch himself with one palm on the still-smoking concrete. The muffled hearing, the blazing afterimages still popping across his eyeballs—way too similar to battlefield conditions. He repeated the date and time and his location to himself to keep himself grounded, but he knew from too much experience that he couldn't make his stunned senses recover any faster than nature would allow.

Andy put her hand on his wrist, and warmth flowed into him, hotter than the bright summer day. The sensation sped up his arm, then spread across his chest and face. Seconds later, he could see her more clearly. His ears popped open to sound again, and the world around him stopped swimming. Surprise made Jack look down at himself, then rub his ears to be sure they really had started working again. Amazing. He could hear traffic out on the road. He'd brought home so much hearing damage from the war it had been years since he could make out distant noises, much less sort them out and identify them.

Andy's hand fell away from his arm and her eyes closed again.

Almost as one, the three East Ranger Sibyls shuffled Jack to the side, crowded around Andy, and put their hands on her shoulders and arms. Jack didn't fight with them because he sensed they were helping Andy, doing whatever Sibyls did. Sharing energy. That's what the Mothers had taught him. That Sibyls could share energy with each other, and with children, and with adults who had paranormal sensitivity. Even though water Sibyls had the reputation of being best with healing, any Sibyl could help a sister Sibyl out with a little infusion of energy.

Sheila, Maggie, and Karin finished with Andy, then moved on to Bela. Bela seemed to do better with her dose of Sibyl healing, because she sat right up and crawled into Duncan's waiting embrace.

Jack listened to the sounds of everyone moving around and wondered how he could hear them so well. Had Andy done something to heal him? But that wasn't possible. He had no paranormal sensitivity. The Mothers had as much as confirmed that, yet Andy had touched him and given him back his eyes and ears a hell of a lot faster than they would have come back on their own.

Andy woke again, more slowly this time, and the East Ranger group got out of the way so that Jack, Bela, and Duncan could talk to her again—but Duncan and Bela were still busy holding each other. When Andy started to sit up, Jack supported her with one arm behind her back and his hand on her waist.

She hesitated for a moment and gazed into his eyes.

Jack felt more warmth, new warmth, generated from the closeness. He wanted to say something. No, what he really wanted to do was pull her to him and hold her there for a long time, just to be positive she was still breathing.

As if reading his thoughts, Andy slipped her arms around his neck and gave him a quick hug, so slight and so fast he barely had a chance to feel her softness or the powerful tension in her muscles. She turned him loose and hugged Bela and Duncan next, and then the four of them helped each other stand.

Jack kept his arm around Andy to be sure she didn't sag or stumble, and she didn't seem to mind. "What the living hell just happened?"

"The coins must have been a projective trap." Bela wiped her eyes with the backs of her hands. "It got triggered when the projective energy from Maggie's sword made direct contact with the metal."

Projective trap. Jack had heard that phrase before, but he couldn't place it or add up how two gold coins could flatten a bunch of elemental warriors. "Fill me in here."

"It's a Rakshasa trick." Andy leaned into him just enough to make him feel useful. "Or at least we ran into a projective trap for the first time just after they came to New York City. When we went after the demons in their lair and started using our elemental energy, we got hooked into what felt like an endless feedback loop. We couldn't stop sending out our energy, and we couldn't pull it back. All of our power got drained away from us."

"And the building blew up," Bela added, wiping her eyes one more time. Jack realized she had tears on her cheeks, probably leftover worry that the sword-and-coin trap had hurt Andy. "That part particularly sucked for me because I thought Duncan and my group and everybody else died in the blast. I didn't understand the projective trap had wounded my elemental senses, so I just couldn't pick up any signs of life."

Duncan stayed close to Bela, his expression grim, and Jack remembered now. He'd read those reports in detail. He hadn't gone on that raid because he was already at Motherhouse Russia, recovering from the last set of broken bones he'd gotten from one of Andy's waves. Seemed like a lifetime ago. "That explosion was a bad scene. Lots of dead and wounded—and Duncan, if you hadn't realized you needed to knock Bela down to separate her from the energy drain, she and most of the Sibyls in New York City would have been killed."

Duncan's expression got more fierce. "A projective trap was what held the Rakshasa in that temple in the Valley of the Gods for so many centuries, until John Cole and his patrol accidentally released them. The tiger-demons learned from their misery and got to be masters at building their own energy snares."

Jack wanted to wrap his arms around Andy and put himself between her and the still-glittering gold coin that lay only a few feet away. Scorch marks spread out from it like demented artwork, and he had no idea if the thing was still dangerous. He pointed it out, then looked at Andy. "That kind of trap affects you and your group even more because you have such strong projective talents, right?"

Andy confirmed this with a nod. "We need to gather that coin to study it, but nobody make direct contact with it. Wooden tongs, elementally locked gloves—all precautions, just like it's a paranormal bomb. Get it back to the townhouse and have the Russian Mothers come get it. They can do a component analysis faster than anybody else."

Jack got out his cell and called in a description of the situation and gear needed to the OCU's pyrotechnics and explosives squad as the East Ranger group finished dusting themselves off and rejoined the party.

"My sword fought the trap," Maggie said as Jack hung up and dropped his phone back in his jeans pocket. "It turned the coin's power back on itself—that's one of the things it does, drain energy from people and objects. It's kind of like a smaller, more stable version of a projective trap."

Jack thought about the brutal deaths etched along that strange blade. He wasn't sure *stable* was the word he'd choose to describe the weapon under any circumstances, but if it helped save Andy, he'd at least not insult it by putting those thoughts into words.

Okay, you're losing it. It's a sword. It can't be insulted.

Except he couldn't shake the feeling that the sword did have some idea about people's feelings, positive or negative. That the sword had ideas, period, or some type of consciousness.

Maybe he had been hanging around Sibyls and demons too long.

Andy slowly pulled herself away from Jack, leaving him worried about her safety and generally unsettled from the loss of her nearness. Damn it. He wasn't used to getting knocked off balance by a woman every five seconds. He automatically scanned the pavement, the walls, and everything else near them to be sure nothing posed an immediate threat.

After a second or two, Andy made eye contact with him, then Bela, then Maggie. "I think if a person with projective abilities had tried to pick up one of those coins, that person would have died instantly."

"No question." Maggie's voice dropped low, and Sheila and Karin both reached out to squeeze her hands. "I've never seen any energy powerful enough to best my sword, but that coin battled it to a draw."

Bela's sigh sounded like one part relief and two parts frustration. "We won't be able to use projective energy to track the monster from the warehouse."

"We probably shouldn't risk hunting for the Coven with it, either," Duncan added, "since they're twisted up in all this."

"So now we've got nothing, a little more than nothing, and less than nothing," Andy grumbled.

"We've got the coin and the trace from the warehouse," Bela said. "That's the best we can do for now."

Andy's irritated, impatient expression made her look a lot more like a pissed-off detective than a Sibyl, and that worried Jack. Pissed-off detectives tended to take too much into their own hands—and they took way, way too many chances.

Better head that off, at least for now. "Duncan, let me drive you and Bela and Andy home. The OCU can pick up our van." To the East Ranger group, he said, "Ladies, do you need a ride?"

"Walking will help clear our heads, thanks." Sheila didn't smile when she answered, but Jack had the feeling she didn't show emotion as a matter of course. He sensed friendly, peaceful acceptance from her, and that was probably the most he could hope to receive from the majority of Sibyls, especially given his unfortunate initial contacts with them. They made their departure as OCU crime scene techs and the bomb squad came screeching to a stop at angles outside the alley that led to the enclosed patio.

"We'll take you up on the offer," Bela told Jack. "I feel like I've been stomped on by some elephant-sized demons, and I bet I'm not alone."

Duncan and Andy didn't dispute the description, and Jack led them all away from the coin and the chaos, through the crowd of descending officers, to Bela's SUV.

(9)

Andy . . .

Andy tried to open her eyes, but she couldn't.

Aaandy . . .

Fog swirled around her, and not the cheesy B-movie kind. This stuff was thick and frigid and icy—and it stank when she breathed in the watery mist. The ground beneath her feet felt rocky and unforgiving, and even with her eyes closed, the darkness all around her seemed huge and endless and suffocating.

I'm high in the air, far from groundwater. On a mountain. And then she knew where she was. Káto Ólimbos in Greece, the home of the Keres—the lair of the death spirits.

If I open my eyes, I'll see him.

The Leviathan. The murdering demon who'd killed Sal and so many others would have one eye open, bloodied and awful, and he'd be ready for a fight.

No problem.

Andy tried to make fists even though her body seemed to be ignoring her commands. She had spat on the demon the first time she got close enough to kill him. She'd spit on him this time, too.

Open your eyes, Andy.

But she didn't want to. The Keres had a treaty with the Sibyls and didn't kill them on sight, but it was still damned freaky to watch shadows ooze out of the darkness and fog and solidify into tall, skeletal forms in gore-stained robes. The Keres had black, matted hair and pale faces. Their wings, always torn and ragged, shed black feathers when they moved. Their haunting screams could drive any human insane, Sibyl or no.

Last warning.

That voice. Andy knew it. She'd heard it before, and it came from the Leviathan—only this time the bastard wasn't half dead and waiting for her to kill it. Her breath stuck tight in her throat as her pulse jacked to two thousand miles per hour. She grabbed for her dart pistol, then for her backup weapon, and—

"Take it easy." Jack's voice brought her fully awake. She was sitting in her own bed, on the top floor of the brownstone, down the hall from Dio's room and archives. "You're all right. Everything's safe here."

His tone sounded surprisingly gentle.

Andy glanced around her small but functional space. Her shades had been closed, but a little sunlight crept through and left yellow lines on the olive walls and sandy trim around the door and near the ceiling. A few of her framed photos—her with her fighting group and other Sibyl friends—glowed in the partial lighting. She had other pictures, too, her with some of her friends from her detective days, and her with her parents on the Georgia farm where she'd grown up happy and healthy and having no idea she'd one day live in New York City and fight demons. Her pillow-top mattress felt soft underneath her, and her thick green comforter had been spread across her like somebody had tucked her in and made sure no wrinkles would bother her in her sleep. She still had on her battle leathers, but somebody had wiped off the grit and dirt from the explosion and the enclosed patio.

Her attention shifted to Jack.

He still had on the pants from his Flaming Bunch of Idiots suit, but he had no jacket and his shirt collar stood open. That and his relaxed posture in the chair beside her bed made her wonder if he'd been right there since— Christ. What time was it? How had she gotten here?

How had *he* gotten here?

Andy frowned at him. "How long have you been sitting watch?"

"Since I carried you up the stairs." Jack's voice stayed so unusually gentle that Andy didn't know what to make of it, or of him. "About three hours."

She stretched before she had a chance to get too uncomfortable with that thought, feeling tingly because he was so close to her. "I don't even remember falling asleep."

"Took you about three seconds once you strapped in for the ride home." Jack's smile didn't come across as mocking. More concerned and . . . friendly? Shit. Maybe she'd hit her head when she fell on the patio.

"Bela's out, too," he said. "I'm surprised Duncan got her inside before he fell out snoring. That elemental trap really took it out of all of you."

Andy's heart fluttered at the memory of the crushing pain of having her elemental energy jerked out of her body. Her breath. Her life. A few seconds one way or the other, and she might not have walked away from that attack. Her eyes jumped to her door, halfway open on the quiet hall outside. "The remaining coin? Where is it now?"

"Off to Motherhouse Russia like you suggested." Jack shifted his position in the chair and leaned forward. For a split second, Andy thought he might be getting ready to leave, and she didn't know if she felt glad about that or a little anxious.

Heat rose to her face, then flooded her. She had a flash of him leaning forward, lifting those big hands to grip her shoulders, pressing those sexy lips against hers . . .

Get a grip.

A fluttery sensation made her breath come short, and

her throat went dry from the force of his nearness. Some-how she managed to say, "You didn't have to stay."

"Duncan and Bela are down for the count, and John's with Camille and Dio at the townhouse, working on search grids moving out from the warehouse and where we found the coins." He kept looking straight at her with those brown eyes, and she couldn't do anything but stare right back at him. "Seemed like the right thing to do."

"Thanks." Andy didn't want to admit it, but she'd probably slept a hell of a lot better sensing his presence. Asshole or not, he radiated protection and safety, and everybody could use solid, dependable backup.

"Did you have a bad dream?" he asked.

A quick shudder moved through her before she could stop it, and she let out a breath to help herself relax. "More like a memory. No big deal, but no fun. It comes and goes in different ways, but in the end, I always wake up and nothing's as bad—or at least as fresh—as it seems in dreamland."

Jack's expression conveyed understanding mixed with a flash of dark anger she could tell had nothing to do with her. "I have a few dreams like that myself."

More strange things happened in Andy's belly. Was that a twinge of sympathy? Of kinship with Jack Black-more, of all people? Christ. Physical attraction was one thing, but actual understanding of some of what might make him tick?

She needed her head examined. Too bad she was the one who was supposed to handle emotions in her quad.

"Do you have dreams from the war?" she asked, sur-prised at the softness in her own tone.

He nodded. "The war and some of the work I've done since."

Damn it, she *did* feel like she had stuff in common with him. Maybe more than she'd like to contemplate. "Sometimes we see things we shouldn't."

"Sometimes we see things that shouldn't exist, period." He managed a sort-of smile despite the sudden sadness in his eyes. "Your dream—was it anything we should know about? For the case, I mean."

"No." As soon as she said it, Andy wondered if she might be brushing off connections a little too easily. When they'd been on the move down that alley toward the patio, she'd really thought there had been a voice, that the coins—or rather, the elemental trap itself—had spoken to her. And, yes, in a voice she almost recognized.

It wasn't like my dream, she told herself. *It wasn't the Leviathan.* Bartholomew August was dead forever, and she was sure of that because she'd killed the ancient demon bastard herself.

She realized Jack was still watching her, quiet and still, just waiting like he'd do her bidding if she sent him off for an aspirin or a glass of water. Which she should want to do, to get rid of him. Right?

Why don't I just tell him to go? I should say that I'm fine and I don't need him anymore. That would do the trick.

But . . .

She pulled the comforter and sheet aside, got her legs on top of the covers, then smoothed them again, beneath her this time. "Am I keeping you from anything important?"

Jack's gaze stayed as steady as his deep, engaging voice. "You're what's important right now."

More than Andy's face heated up as he spoke. The man could say the damnedest things, suggestive without being too pushy.

Yet.

In the end, Jack wouldn't have it in him to show restraint, so she knew she needed to stop this little interest or flirtation or whatever it was before it even got started.

Nothing about it was sane or even possible. Her stomach tightened, but she plunged ahead before he could distract her from what she needed to say. "If I've done anything to give you the idea that there's a chance we could—that we might—I shouldn't have, okay? I'm sorry."

That was easy. Her stomach stayed tight. *But harder than it should have been.* The fact that the intensity in his expression didn't lessen one bit made her wonder if he realized what she meant.

"You don't have to be sorry, because we could." That voice. It seemed to fill the room. Definitely her awareness. "And if the moment's right, we might—but only if that's what you want. Otherwise, I'm a fellow officer, and maybe in time a friend. You've got nothing to lose by letting me stand watch while you're too tired to defend yourself."

Andy knew she had to be turning red all over again. He'd seen her blush more times than most men would live through. She'd expected a lot of things from Jack, even with all his supposed reforms and insights from his time at the Motherhouses. But this side of him, the way he had taken care of her, and how he was handling her now, with no teasing or trying to get the advantage, just that matter-of-fact statement of his own interest and the fact that he realized she did feel some attraction . . . damn him.

She didn't even *want* to argue, which felt too weird for words. She hadn't imagined he could be so settling and relaxing. In addition to being arrogant and irritating. And handsome. And interesting.

Her body started a fresh, hot tingling, low-level, under the surface, like her skin knew secrets about how it might be to let herself get a little closer to Jack after all.

Shit, I've got to stop.

He sat back, easing up on the almost tangible connection she'd been feeling. "We rearranged the patrol schedule so your group is off tonight, but you'll be on tomorrow. We'll need all hands for an old-fashioned search, since it's not safe to use that projective tracking thing you do."

"Yeah. That's gonna be fun." Thank God for work. Safe territory. A place she could always go. *And hide.* Andy pinched the bridge of her nose to ward off a headache. "And boring as hell. With the Coven, we could look until hell's an ice-skating rink. All we'll get for our troubles is a big fat nothing, or maybe punched in the eye by some big ugly Asmodai demon. I always manage to end up face-to-face with fire Asmodai. I never get the earth ones or air ones."

Jack shrugged. "I hear they smell like graves, anyway."

She smiled at him even though she hadn't meant to.

His smile came back, too, slower this time, and full, and even sexier than she remembered. Andy realized she might be headed for a little trouble with this man.

"If you're okay," he said, "I'll go downstairs and check on Bela and Duncan, then let you get your rest."

"I'm okay," Andy said automatically.

Why did you do that? the confused part of her brain—the part she was trying without a lot of success to control—yelled at her, while the rational side congratulated her.

She *was* okay, really. But now he'd leave. And he should go. Only she really didn't want him to go. That headache was probably on its way no matter how hard she tried to relax.

Jack got up from his chair and moved it carefully back against her wall, right where he must have found it after he'd put her to bed. When he reached her door, he stopped, turned, and gave her another look that set off more blushing and shallow breathing. "If you need anything, say the word. I'll be right here."

That statement felt like a promise, and Andy sensed a

depth she didn't fully understand. Before she could sort out her thoughts and ask him what he meant, he was gone—and the sound of his footsteps on the stairs actually made her sad.

She listened for a long time, until she heard the soft opening and closing of the brownstone's front door. His energy. It had been tangible to her, like a steadying force, and now its absence made her even more sad. She dropped back against her stack of pillows, wondering what the hell to do with herself. Staying totally away from Jack Blackmore—that seemed like the sanest course. Definitely the safest.

"Who needs safe?" she muttered out loud, hearing the nervous edge in her own voice even as her tingles started all over again at the thought of him. "Safe is for sissies."

(10)

Three days after the scene in the warehouse and at the patio, Jack still couldn't forget what it had felt like to touch Andy. Just a few seconds, his hands on her sides to keep her from falling on the floor, and later, helping her sit up, then carrying her up the stairs. All of that had felt like holding everything warm and vital in the world.

He wanted to hold her closer.

It was the last thing he needed to do.

He set down the last of the boxes he had been carrying and rubbed the back of his neck, glancing around the office he was setting up for himself on the main floor of the townhouse. For the moment, it was organized. The single big window was clean, and the curtains were brown and professional-looking instead of lacy. Books sat straight and dust-free on the wall of built-in shelves, his three file cabinets were filled and not piled up with junk, and his nonprivate pictures, mostly shots of his Afghanistan unit, hung straight on the walls. His computer stood on the right-hand side of his desk, and for the moment, a few mementos took up the rest of the space along the desk's front edge. He'd kept a football from his service team, a drinking mug from a bar near NYU, a small commendation from the senator who'd overseen the formation of OCU units all over the United States, and some rocks he'd brought back from the Afghan desert—little stuff.

How long before the whole space became an explosion of files and stacks of paper he'd never be able to shrink, no matter how many hours he worked? Staying anywhere long-term, anchoring himself in any way, even with something as benign as designated and personalized office space, had downsides other than making him more vulnerable to old enemies.

As for the upside . . .

"No upside," he said out loud.

But Andy flickered through his mind anyway. Not the underwear- or leather-clad version, but the Andy who wore bright, obnoxious tunics and jeans. The Andy who smiled and teased and seemed to see right into his soul. The Andy who looked so soft when she slept that it had taken every bit of his self-control not to lean down and kiss her.

That Andy felt totally new to him, and even more exciting.

Jack opened the last box. Right on top was a framed photo of the only two people he had ever loved with no strings and no regrets. His mom and sister stared out at him with their big brown eyes, and their matching chestnut curls made them look more like siblings than parent and child.

The sudden ache in his chest didn't surprise him. It never got any easier, losing Mom and Ginger. Even after all these years, he'd give anything to see them again, just for five minutes—but that wasn't possible. They were dead to him.

They had to be.

Jack unlocked a drawer in his desk, put the photo inside, then closed the drawer and locked it again. It was the best he could do and the most he could let himself have, and seeing the family he'd lost reminded him of yet another reason why he didn't need to hang around New York City. Too damned close to bad memories.

Cal Brent stopped in the office doorway, smoothing

his brown suit. "The Sibyls still don't have anything on the hairs they recovered from the warehouse body?"

Jack wiped his hands on his jeans and turned to face Cal. "Even with supernaturally advanced science, genetic analysis takes time. I expect they'll let us know when they're ready, and I'm not pushing the issue. If you want to bug 'em, have at it."

Cal's grin filled up his whole face. "Nah. I'm impatient, but I'm not crazy. And you—jeans at work? Is there something I need to know?"

Jack gestured to the office. "Moving day. I dressed for the job."

"Uh-huh. I'm not crazy, like I said, but something's definitely up with you."

Crazy.

Now there was a word that resonated for Jack. It had been more than seventy-two hours since he'd let himself get near Andy, and she was still filling his thoughts more than the cases at hand. More than that, he hadn't expected to lose his mind when he saw her at the brownstone after she came back. Until he got a grip on the attraction he felt to her, he needed to keep his distance. Stay clear.

Saul joined his brother in the office doorway and pushed his way inside, glancing around. "Not bad. You really are an old maid at heart."

"Fuck you." Jack glared at Saul. He had on jeans full of holes and a battered Giants T-shirt, and he'd left his long hair loose for the day, making him look so different from Cal that only their similar build and hair color gave away any relationship.

"By the way, nobody can stand your mood anymore, Jack." Saul acted like he was studying Jack's library, but Jack saw the conspiratorial look Saul gave Cal. "Please go see your honey soon so we can live with you."

Jack tensed all over, heat rising to his face. Saul hadn't really disrespected Andy, but . . . almost, and Jack didn't like it. "She's not my honey. Christ, we're not in boot camp anymore, Saul."

This time Saul didn't hide the look he gave Cal or the smirk he turned on Jack. "I'm not the one acting like a teenager with a crush."

"He's got a point," Cal said, his tone pitch-perfect with Saul's.

Jack didn't bother to go at either one of them because he knew when he was outnumbered. Instead, he went with, "What do you think about a sketch artist?"

Saul's teasing expression faltered as he tried to add the question to the conversation and failed. "Excuse me?"

"We've had our heads crammed into the world of weird so long, it's easy to forget about regular law enforcement tools." Jack reached into the last box on the floor and pulled out some books. He walked past Saul and situated them on one of the bookshelves as Cal leaned against the doorframe. "Andy saw something in her mind at the warehouse. She couldn't describe it with words, but maybe she could lead a sketch artist through creating a reasonable image."

Silence ruled as Jack went back to the box, but then Cal said, "It's got potential."

Saul said, "Great. Now you've got a *good* excuse to call her."

"Call who?" Jack got the last of the books and slid them into place.

Saul laughed at him outright. "A certain hot water Sibyl."

"Yeah, about that, Jack. Seriously." Cal's voice changed from ribbing to more professional. "Some of the guys around here really are worried about what you're planning with Andy. The Lowell brothers, for example—"

"Can speak for ourselves, thanks." Nick Lowell's deep voice cut across Cal, chopping off any further discussion.

With a *sorry-pal* grimace in Jack's direction, Cal got out of the doorway, leaving room for Nick and Creed Lowell, a matched set of half-demon muscle and lots of combined years in law enforcement. On top of that, they had both married powerful Sibyls. They had black hair, black eyes, and similar dark expressions. Behind them stood Jake Lowell, the younger brother, nothing like the rest of his family with his blond hair and fair features, though he, too, had married a Sibyl.

At the moment, Jake seemed benign enough, especially since he had Creed's son, Ethan, propped on one hip and Nick's daughter, Neala, resting on the other. The children, both three years old, stared at him with too-wise and mischievous expressions. As for Mr. Uncle Demon, the look on Jake's face stayed neutral, but Jack read that as more menacing than the other two brothers put together. Jake had been turned into a full-blooded Astaroth demon by his psychotic parents, but he'd found his way back to his brothers, to sanity, to a pretty good life with his air Sibyl wife—and of course to the Lowell family profession of police work.

Saul didn't have the decency to leave like Cal did. He took a seat in one of the two leather armchairs on the visitor side of Jack's desk, and his amused expression carried an unmistakable message. *You're on your own with this one, too, and I get to laugh if you get your face busted.*

Creed Lowell came into the room first, followed by Nick.

Jake stayed in the doorway like he was standing guard, moving only to amuse the children and keep them calm. Good thing, because Jack was pretty sure the little girl could burn down the townhouse if she got riled.

Jack didn't flex or tense or get ready for battle, but his pulse was definitely up a few beats.

Creed fixed him with a hard stare, and one of his hands clenched into a fist. "Andy was my partner before she—you know—had the change. It's sort of my fault that it happened to her. She got attacked—"

"I know." Jack nodded. "By a low-level Legion cult bastard with water talent that activated hers. While she was out in the field with you. I studied everything I could in my time at the Motherhouses."

This seemed to ease Creed a fraction, the fact that Jack had taken the time to learn about Andy's past when he had the opportunity, but he still had a point to make. "I let her down then, but I won't let her down now."

"I've got her back, too." Nick Lowell always managed to sound like an angry prick, but Jack knew he was a good man and a first-rate officer. "Andy's special and I won't see her mistreated."

"What they're trying to say is, leave the lady alone." Jake Lowell, as usual, said the least, but his words carried more impact because he let his demon fangs and claws show when he spoke. Both children giggled and tugged at him, obviously amused by his demon essence coming forward.

Jack wasn't so amused. Even though Jake was standing behind his brothers, Jack caught the clear outline of Jake's full demon presence—white hair, shining golden eyes, translucent pearl skin, a double set of huge leathery wings, and yeah, those claws and fangs. Nick and Creed, if they shifted to their Curson demon forms, would be huge, hulking golden monsters, barely able to tell friend from foe. Jake, on the other hand, retained every bit of his sense of self, his purpose, and his cunning.

The thought of getting shredded by demons didn't bother Jack, but the possibility that the Lowell brothers hadn't come here of their own accord made his gut churn. When he glanced at Saul, he could tell Saul was wondering the same thing, because all the goading had drained out of Saul's expression. The man seemed concerned now, for Jack and maybe for Andy, too.

Jack looked the Lowell brothers in the face, one at a time, as he asked what he needed to know. "Did Andy send you here?"

Nick, Creed, and Jake gave away nothing in their stone-cold gazes for a few seconds, then Creed looked away and Nick glanced at the ceiling. Jake kept his gaze leveled on Jack, and he was the one who spoke. "No. Andy hasn't said anything to us about you."

"Andy!" Neala's gleeful shout echoed through the hall. "Andy soon?"

"Andy soon," Jake answered her, smooth as ever.

Jack's insides uncoiled so fast he wanted to shout from the relief. Instead, he settled for bargaining with the Lowells. "I don't plan to harass Andy or do her any harm. Is that enough for you three?"

"I'm not sure." Creed kept one fist tightly clenched. "What *are* you planning, Jack?"

The other two didn't speak, and Jack couldn't help seeing them as a posse of big brothers. Once upon a time, before his childhood went to shit and he lost his mother and sister to federal marshals and the witness protection program, he'd been a big brother. It didn't take much to dust off the memory, but it took a lot to handle the sudden chasm of loss that reopened when he thought about his father's death and the only two surviving members of his family.

"If she ever, and I mean ever, for any reason, lets on that I've done anything she didn't want, you know where to find me." Jack looked at them again in the order in which they stood, Creed, Nick, and Jake. He understood what they needed now, and he could give it to them, one big brother to another. "All three of you. And I won't bring any backup to the fight."

For a few seconds, nobody said anything. Then Creed's fist loosened, and Nick's body posture relaxed. Even Jake seemed to reel himself back enough to be fully human.

"That'll work," Nick said. "For now."

"What are you idiots talking about?" Andy's voice rang out in the hall behind Jake, loud and laced with curiosity.

"Andy!" Neala strained to get down from Jake's arms, and Ethan tried to climb over Jake's shoulder, shouting her name along with his cousin.

Andy called back to the children, and Jack caught a glimpse of her as she gave hugs and kisses.

Jake stood fast despite the wriggling of his niece and nephew. He and his brothers had gone instantly mute when Andy spoke, so it was Saul who had to save the day. "Ah, just . . . the weather." He got to his feet, smiling but looking ready to exit in a hurry.

"Yeah." Nick cleared his throat. "Hot as a bi—" He looked at the children, cleared his throat again. "Hot outside, isn't it? Well, we'll take the kids up and feed them. See you when you're done."

And with that, the Lowell brothers made themselves scarce so fast Jack could have sworn all three were Astaroth demons with the ability to go invisible and fly away. Saul didn't stick around, either, and Jack followed him as he hightailed it into the hallway.

Saul gave Andy a mock salute as he passed by her, then took off toward the conference room, probably pretending he had some kind of patrol report to give or receive. She stared at him, then turned her gaze to Jack, asking questions with her gorgeous two-tone eyes.

Jeans. She's wearing jeans, and this time, the tunic's rainbow-colored with great big sleeves. A pair of huge sunglasses had been propped in her unruly red hair, and she was eating the last of some freaky-smelling sandwich—artichokes and goat cheese on rye, if his nose wasn't lying to him. She looked like a glorious, happy mess.

It struck Jack that he could fall in love with her.

He made himself stop an arm's length from her even though he wanted to go closer. What he really wanted to do was smooth her hair and help her lose the sunglasses. Then he'd kiss her and drink in that feminine scent of vanilla and ocean wind mixed with the tang of that weird sandwich—but she was probably packing her SIG and a backup weapon. Even if she didn't drown him, bullets could do some damage.

A second or so ticked by before Jack realized Andy had finished eating. She licked her fingers and appraised him, too.

"Well, well." Her eyes moved from his face to his feet, and he felt every inch of that stare. "Look at you. Jeans and a sleeveless T-shirt. I'd have bet money you didn't even own clothes like that, Jack."

Jack really liked listening to that soft Southern accent, especially when she wasn't swearing at him. "You don't like my suits. Flaming Bunch of Idiots gear, right?"

The corners of her mouth turned upward, and her smile came slowly. Surprised. Maybe curious. "I didn't figure you for the kind of guy to change anything about yourself because of somebody else's opinion."

"No changes." He pulled up the neck of his black T-shirt. "This is as much me as the FBI costume. I just don't let my casual side come out to play too often."

"You play?"

"Yeah." Jack heard his voice drop. Damn, but she teased as well as she tortured. "I can play."

"The surprises just don't stop." The most beautiful blush fanned across her freckled cheeks. She looked away from him and a few drops of water spilled off the hem of her jeans.

Jack's blood surged like he'd just won something, but he didn't think he'd better try to claim any prizes.

"I'm due to babysit Neala and Ethan so Nick and Creed get a breather, but I thought I'd drop off what we've got on the hairs so far, and what the Mothers told us about the coins." She managed to look him in the face again and held out an envelope.

He took it, exercising every bit of his willpower not to brush her fingers with his own and push his luck.

"It's not much," she continued, the color slowly fading from her cheeks. "So far, all we know is whatever shed the hairs is definitely part human—or it used to be. The human cells have been altered. Strengthened somehow. Even our technology can't get a fix on them. As for the coins, they're definitely Coven work, but more advanced than we've seen in the past."

"The Coven. Part human." Jack glanced over the lab reports, picking out what he understood after years of studying analyses of paranormal creatures. "And the part that's not human?"

"The closest we can come is Rakshasa, or some kind of new Rakshasa mix, first generation, but with the Eldest all dead, that's not possible. Besides, this combination looks nothing like the demon infection we analyzed when the Rakshasa attacked Duncan. The Coven's up to something else, developing some other method for transforming fighters, but God only knows what it is."

Jack nodded, still studying the reports.

When the Rakshasa Eldest had been alive, they had created half-breeds that almost always went mad. A few managed to control themselves and preserve their human essence, and they called themselves Bengals. Duncan Sharp was a Bengal, and in some ways, so was John

Cole. Bengals could make other Bengals by biting or scratching humans, but second-generation infections were weaker, and third- and fourth-generation hybrids would be weaker still—more human than tiger-demon, and maybe not even able to access their demon essence. Whatever the Coven was doing, it had to be different from the usual methods the Rakshasa had always used—but what kind of infection were they working with? How could it even come close to Rakshasa essence?

Jack looked up to find Andy glancing from her watch to the townhouse stairs.

"How long will you be here?" he asked.

"A few hours, then I've got to hit the channels and head to Greece, then get back in time for patrol to-night." Andy's expression turned wry. "No rest for the wicked."

Jack didn't find the humor in her spreading herself so thin. "No time off?"

"Not this week. We're pretty certain the Coven's a part of all this, and we'll have to hunt hard every night to have a prayer of finding them."

He didn't like the sound of that at all, and his mind started churning out ways to divide patrol duties so that Andy's group didn't carry too much of the burden. "You need to rest."

Wry turned to sarcastic as Andy said, "Thanks, Dad. I'll manage."

Jack tucked the lab reports back in the envelope, more worried about her than about the case. "I know I'm the one who asked you to come back here, but I assumed you'd ease up on the Kérkira responsibilities. How are you going to manage both sets of duties?"

She gave a little shrug. "I'll be going back and forth."

"That sounds like a lot of work."

"I'm up for it." Her smile made him want to grab her

and kiss her—or shake her. He'd never seen a woman who could pull off half-vixen, half-stuff-it-up-your-ass so easily.

"I meant—I hate to see you exhaust yourself. If it gets to be too much, just say something." Jack folded the envelope and tucked it in his pocket. "Maybe Saul and I can do some of the commuting instead of running you ragged."

"Thanks." Her smile slipped away, replaced by an expression Jack couldn't read. Professional, maybe. Certainly a lot more distant—meaning he didn't trust the casual note of her tone when she asked, "So, you're definitely planning to stay in New York City now that the Rakshasa are dead?"

Was she hopeful? Pissed off? He wished he had a clue. He kept his own voice level as he said, "Seems like most of the action is here. Since we're asking questions, I've got one for you."

She moved away from him, not much, but enough to underscore the limit she set. "As long as it's not too personal."

"Fair enough. I don't think it is." He took a breath and cued up the first of the hundreds of things he wanted her to tell him about herself, about Sibyls, about anything she'd talk about. "If water Sibyls have so much control over water, how did they get wiped out by a tidal wave?"

This surprised her and, he saw with a measure of relief, relaxed her a bit, too. "Even the strongest Sibyl, or group of Sibyls, can get overwhelmed by an unstoppable force." Her tone and expression shifted farther toward professional, toward work and safety and not running away from him. "It's not common, but it happens. The wave that took out Motherhouse Antilla was created by projective energy, and it was so large and forceful even an army of water Sibyls couldn't stand against it. The weight and speed and force of the water crushed them, or they died from being battered by heavy debris."

Jack tried to imagine the magnitude of that wave, but he couldn't quite wrap his mind around it—though it did help him to understand a little better about the potential dangers of projective elemental energy. "I'm sorry they all got killed."

"It was hundreds and hundreds of years ago." She seemed comfortable now, even warming to the conversation despite her waiting obligations upstairs.

"But it left you alone."

"Not anymore, thank God." A smile. A real one, no smirk involved. "I've got Elana now, and she's like a miracle to me. She's teaching me so much."

She had started talking faster as she went, but she seemed to catch herself and put the brakes on before she went farther.

Progress. Jack would take it. He'd take whatever she chose to give him. "One more question," he said before she could take off upstairs. "What do you think about sketch artists?"

For a moment she seemed confused, then understanding flared in her eyes. "You mean, for me to try to describe what I saw when I made contact with the hair at the crime scene? Why didn't I think of that?"

"Want me to line one up?"

Andy looked at her watch again. "I'll try to get back from Greece an hour before patrol tonight. Will that work?"

It's a date. The words almost came out, but Jack caught himself in time. "We'll make it work. Thanks for your help. I'm glad you're here."

She started to say something, and he could have sworn it was, *I'm glad I'm here, too,* but that was probably wishful thinking.

Jack decided to quit while he was ahead. "Okay, then. Catch you tonight."

He turned and headed to do more unpacking, but Andy stopped him. "Hey, that's not your office."

"It is now." He faced her again. "I swapped out with the Brent brothers."

Her eyebrows lifted, then pulled together. "Why?"

"Seemed like the right thing to do. I need to carve my own niche here, and I didn't want it to bother you that I was in Sal's old space." Jack's throat went a little dry as he said all that, hoping it was explanation enough—and not too much.

For a few seconds Andy didn't say a word.

Right about the time Jack was about to decide he'd made yet another in a long line of bad mistakes with this woman, she said, "I don't know whether to be touched or pissed off. What are you trying to do, Jack?"

"Clean up a lot of messes I've made." He hoped she could hear the truth in his voice. "I want this to be a start."

Her voice broke to a whisper. "A start for what?"

"Whatever you want." He wanted to touch her so badly he could already feel her soft skin under his palms.

The blush came back, flowing across her freckles, and she actually leaned toward him, moved like she might take a step in his direction. He was more than ready to let her come even if she intended to slap him cross-eyed, but she seemed to think better of it.

"I'm . . . going upstairs now." She pointed toward the steps.

"Okay." That was the best he could do, and she did go, walking slowly away, and he couldn't stop looking until he lost sight of her heading off the first-floor landing.

Before he could stop himself, Jack let himself imagine Andy playing with the cute fire Sibyl kid, Nick's daughter

Neala. If they had daughters together, and if those little girls looked like Andy—now those would be some gorgeous children.

Jack stopped himself and walked into his office, but the image wouldn't leave his mind.

What the hell—was he trying to drive himself batshit?

He liked kids. He was good with kids himself, but he'd long ago abandoned the idea that he could have kids of his own.

Christ, this thing in my head about her—it's getting out of hand.

11

Mistake.

Griffen could have chosen to see the projective trap in that light, but he preferred to consider it experience.

He sucked in a breath of antiseptic air and crushed the can of soda he had been carrying in his hand. The liquid blew toward the ceiling, but he used his elemental ability to capture and curtail it so it wouldn't stain the white squares above his head. As an exercise in focus and self-control, he banked the can off the lab's refrigerator and watched it drop into the deep stainless-steel sink positioned along the right-hand wall. As soon as all motion stopped, Griffen made himself direct the trapped soda into the ruined can. Not an easy trick in the low lighting. *Sickroom theater,* Rebecca called it.

True enough.

The rhythmic click and hiss of medical machinery helped him stay calm, helped him regain his center and complete his task. Not a drop of soda spattered on the glass doors of the refrigerator, the white cabinets, or the countertops. Not a drop hit the sink itself, until it oozed from the ruined can and ran directly down the drain.

"Better," he said aloud, keeping all traces of emotion from his voice. Then he reminded himself that he was standing in his small but efficient laboratory, in the corner of his completely protected warehouse full of Coven members and their genetically enhanced fighters. All of this—all of it—testaments to his many successes. He'd had plenty of good moments, from his early alliance with the Rakshasa to his taming of Rebecca to the Coven's robust and powerful ranks. He still had an active under-Coven as well, thirteen ready and willing men who could replace anyone in his current group, should they fall in battle, and a training group beneath that. Everyone had backup. Everyone was dispensable.

Everyone but him, of course. And Rebecca.

Everything . . . is . . . under . . . control.

A soft knock on the lab door made him turn. "Open," he said, happy with the placid sound of his voice.

The lab door swung until he could see Rebecca standing there with one of his Coven, who was holding the chain lead to her elemental cuffs. Griffen smiled at his sister and gestured for the man to let her come inside.

She brought her chain lead past two lab tables lined with empty syringes. With a glance toward the full syringes visible through the refrigerator's glass doors, she handed the chain over without guile or protest. "What happened? Did the trap fail?"

"It worked beautifully." Griffen said this with pride, because that much was true. He and his Coven had never attempted such a complex elemental working without the Rakshasa assisting them—and they had done a fine job. "One of the Sibyls had a strange sword with properties and strengths no blade should have. She used it to smash one of the coins and break the trap. If she hadn't, Andy Myles would be dead now, along with Bela Argos Sharp and the other three Sibyls who were helping them."

Rebecca's lip curled at the mention of Bela Sharp. Bela had cost Rebecca a love interest in the past, and she apparently hadn't forgiven the earth Sibyl for her meddling. For his part, Griffen had been grateful. That boy had been useless and elementally barren. Absolutely not worthy of his sister.

"Perhaps the next time you attack, you can let me fight Bela," Rebecca said. Her eyes moved back to the full syringes, and Griffen didn't much like the thought of what might happen if his sister got hold of the various batches of experimental enhancement formula. Whom would she choose to inject—and what would be the outcome?

He tightened his grip on her chain. "I wouldn't risk you in combat. You're far too valuable for that."

She gave him a quick pout but let it go fast and walked forward, past the tables and Griffen, to the hospital bed where they kept their only patient. Heavy elemental shackles bound the creature's great clawed paws to four metal poles set into the floor, just outside the bed. A fifth metal pole, also elementally treated, riveted him to the bed, directly through his heart. A respirator forced oxygen into the Rakshasa's lungs. A set of IV poles held bags that carried food and fluid to his veins, while a second set stood ready to receive his blood the next time Griffen chose to access the permanent catheter he had placed in the demon's chest.

Tarek's eyes were closed and his fanged mouth hung open even though the machine did all his breathing through a trache in his throat. His golden fur had grown tattered and matted during his time in captivity, and some of his skin was bare and scarred due to poorly healed burn wounds from the molten ore attack that killed the rest of his kind. Griffen couldn't risk taking the elementally treated metal out of his heart long enough for him to heal himself. No guarantees Tarek wouldn't wake with enough strength and fury to deflect attempts to stab him again. As it was, Tarek was alive—or more to the point, he couldn't die.

"Sometimes he wakes up," Rebecca said, obviously hoping now would be one of those times.

Griffen studied the Rakshasa Eldest, who didn't show any signs of agitation and movement, as was usually the case just before the demon roused for a few seconds—

long enough to try to swear at him but fail due to the invasive placement of the respirator tubing.

"Now and then he opens his eyes," Griffen agreed, "but the elemental metal in his heart sends him right back to dreamland and keeps him immobile. I'm not sure he's really awake."

Rebecca leaned down until her ethereal face seemed dangerously close to the Rakshasa's big fangs. "If I behead him, he'll die."

"But he can come back if you don't burn his head and body and scatter the ashes." Griffen didn't let himself rise to the bait or the subtle threat, and used the opportunity for reminders instead. "If you do have to kill him, don't forget that part."

"Will you ever be able to make the enhancement formula without him?" She touched the tip of Tarek's fang with one delicate fingertip.

Griffen reached down and moved her hands away from the Rakshasa. "Once we have an ideal mixture, it's possible we can synthesize the blood. For now, he's not bothering anybody—and he doesn't eat much."

Rebecca didn't laugh at the joke because she was already focused on the laboratory refrigerator again. "What do you think the formula would do to me?"

"The effects on people with elemental talents aren't predictable." Dread crawled up Griffen's neck. "It wouldn't be a good idea."

"I'd end up like the Coven members you tried it on— crazy and dead." She smiled, and her slender features made her seem so young and innocent.

"Probably." Griffen relaxed a little. This was curiosity, not plotting. Rebecca's curiosity tended to be a good thing, and it often led to breakthroughs, like figuring out how to leave traces of sound in the elementally treated coins he used to make the trap, just to add a little extra touch of terror for his victim. To play with her mind. "My Coven members who volunteered and died, they were brave men. They gave their lives for our cause."

Rebecca's blue eyes twinkled. "If Andy Myles is your cause, she's still alive."

Okay, so it would be this way today. Tease and poke. Griffen didn't flinch. He could handle this mood from Rebecca, and he shrugged off his initial irritation with a teaser of his own. "For now. As for later—we'll see." He made sure to smile, to keep Rebecca's interest and attention. "I'm thinking she'll make a good test run for the fighters."

12

Andy sat in a dark leather chair in the dark wood and stone section of Motherhouse Kérkira, where the handiwork of earth Sibyls and fire Sibyls joined to create the largest—and maybe the worst—section of frankenhouse. The big stone room with its hardwood floors had a few redeeming features, like the giant window overlooking the ocean—and a few weird ones, like wooden etchings of wolves built into the walls and stone carvings of winged creatures fighting what looked like dragons sitting on lots of the shelves.

"Boxing gloves?" Elana didn't exactly sound disapproving. More like confused.

"They're twelve." Andy chewed the last few bites of her roast beef and pineapple sandwich, wondering if sourdough had been the right choice for the bread, as she watched the two brown-headed adepts through the big window. "I didn't want them to hurt themselves."

The girls walked with a lithe grace, like the waves beyond them, and they seemed to be talking instead of fighting. Blue-purple bruises still marked both of their cheeks, but Andy knew they'd heal quickly.

They're Sibyls, she thought with a bittersweet wistfulness she didn't fully understand. *They don't have any choice.*

Elana shrugged. "Having them punch each other silly with leather-padded fists under the water—I suppose it could have been worse."

"We used to do that all the time when I still walked a beat for the NYPD. Young kids would be going at it, have some beef, and we'd set them up in a ring with gloves and show them how to work it out with a little honor." Andy battled a surge of sadness, remembering all of that, because it seemed so logical and simple. "Lots of them went on to take up boxing as a sport," she added, her voice cracking on the last word.

Elana let out a sigh of sympathy. "You miss your old life."

"I don't know what I miss anymore, Elana. I just know I'm a Sibyl now, so that's what I have to be."

For a time the old woman didn't say anything, her fierce, concerned expression reminding Andy of one of the shelf dragons.

We have so got to get another place to live. And soon. Someplace right. Someplace more peaceful than this.

"You have a heart as vast as any sea," Elana said. "You can't deny one aspect of yourself in favor of another. The sea can't reject its mountains or its coral reefs, or turn its back on storms or whales or how moonlight ripples on night waves. It is what it is. *All* of what it is."

Andy scuffed her heel against the hardwood. "I don't have time to be everything I am. Or everything I want to be."

"That's because you're trying to make everything separate." Elana waved her hands in the air, then brought them together. "You have to flow, to make it all work as one stream."

That made Andy bang her head against the chair's leather headrest. "But everything *is* separate. I'm a Mother. I fight in a group. The two things don't seem compatible all the time."

Elana went quiet again, and Andy tensed, getting ready for another onslaught of tough observations.

"You used to work in law enforcement and still feel very loyal to that old fighting group also." Elana's observations sounded distant, almost scientific. "You're a friend to some, companion to others, trusted confidante to many more. And, if I'm not much mistaken, you're a woman, too. A woman with flesh and bones and emotions and . . . interests."

Waves crashed onto the beach below Motherhouse Kérkira, scattering the few young adepts who had gathered to play in the sand. Andy realized she'd brought the water flying toward her. Her jeans and yellow tunic dripped steadily on the stone floor, soaking her socks and sneakers and making her want to go home.

She just wasn't sure where home was anymore. Certainly not here, in this chaotic place. And the brownstone—it was okay, but she and Dio often felt like the odd women out with their married sister Sibyls keeping house all around them. She hated the townhouse where OCU was headquartered, since that's where she'd had to face Sal's death and see him so torn apart and cold. She didn't get to go to any other NYPD precincts too often. The park stressed her out because half the paranormal battles she'd been in happened in its fields and clearings. And New York City itself had turned alien to her as she developed the ability to sense supernatural energy around every other corner.

Tears melded with the water droplets on her cheeks, and she dug her fingers into the leather arms of the chair. Outside, adepts laughed and danced in and out of the crashing waves, and Andy wished she could be one of them—all girl, all kid, all Sibyl, with her future path clear in her mind again.

"Okay, we're stopping now," she told Elana before Elana tried any more therapy or teaching with her.

"You have much to reconcile."

"You say that like time's running out or something. I'm going to live hundreds of years. I'll get it figured out." Andy touched her tears with her fingertips and dried them. It felt like cheating.

"Andy, you must grow comfortable with reading and challenging the emotions of your group. Of all the pieces of your scattered life, of all the fragments of duty and purpose and self you're trying to pull together, that is the most important. The most sacred."

Oh, for God's sake. Andy didn't even bother to say anything to that. Elana might be ancient and wise, but *she* didn't have live with Dio—or Bela or Camille.

Elana leaned toward Andy and reached out, holding her fingers in the air until Andy touched them. "If I had taken my emotional duties to my group more seriously, I might have prevented the disaster that left us so damaged and alone in this world, and living here instead of where our hearts belong."

Andy gripped Elana's hand. "Come on. How could you have stopped the destruction of the water Sibyls?"

"I might have realized we were all being drained by tapping into such great but terrible power." Elana pulled away from her and sat back. "I might have understood action and reaction, decision and consequence. It's the flow, don't you see? How everything moves, how everything connects to the next thing? Patterns. They'll become familiar to you. You'll be able to follow them, sense them, perhaps even predict them."

Andy thought about Sal's death and how her former life had ended in a split-second paranormal attack that woke her water abilities. She thought about dead officers and dead Sibyls and how she and her entire group had lost everything at various times in their lives. Was Elana trying to say that if she understood flow, if she allowed herself to plunge into the stream of feelings and connect more fully with her sister Sibyls and the water of the world, she might sense such tragedies coming? That she might be able to stop them?

Is that wonderful—or horrible?

"Do you understand what I'm trying to say to you,

Andy?" Elana sounded strange, and Andy wondered if the old woman was scared about something. She didn't even want to ask.

"No, I don't fully understand it, but like I said, I'm going to live practically forever, so I'll have time to learn."

Elana turned her face away, like she could see everything happening on the beach outside the Motherhouse's big window. "Forever," she said, "can be shorter than it seems."

Andy got back to the brownstone in time to change clothes and get out the door to headquarters to work with the sketch artist. She more or less stumbled off the communications platform in the brownstone's living room and gave a quick wave to the projective mirror attuned to Motherhouse Kérkira.

Ona, the zillion-year-old fire Sibyl who had opened the channels for her, nodded. The mirror winked into darkness, and silence and stillness settled like a silky blanket around Andy's mind. She so wanted to collapse on the leather sofa, maybe after a gourmet sandwich and five or ten servings of corn chips—but that wasn't going to happen. Not now. Maybe later, or lots later, after patrol tonight.

Andy sensed the elemental energy of her sister Sibyls, familiar to her and welcome. Camille's fire rose from downstairs, while Bela's earth energy drifted languidly from the main-floor bedroom near the staircase closet. Dio's wind moved softly through the space, moving with a soft lack of pressure that only happened when Dio was sleeping. Andy assumed they were all napping, storing up energy for tonight's patrol. She'd love to do the same, but oh well.

She headed up the polished wooden stairs to the floor she shared with Dio and turned left, keeping her footsteps as quiet as possible. Her little bedroom seemed to welcome her, and did that bed ever beckon . . . damn it. No time, no time.

"Stretch, shower, and dress," she told herself as she gazed at the pictures on her walls. Neatly arranged. Fairly sedate—a big change from her previous life. In her old apartment, she'd had dozens of posters, covers from *Gourmet* magazine, concert prints and ticket stubs from bands she liked, and teetering stacks of romance novels. And crime novels. And a bunch of fantasy novels, too. Now, who had time to read? And concerts? Poster browsing? None of that was happening anymore.

"Maybe I should just get dressed. I'm not that filthy." She scratched at a layer of salt residue she'd probably picked up refereeing the underwater boxing match. "Well, maybe a little filthy."

The bathroom was centered in the hallway, between Andy's room and Dio's room-library combo, and it was pretty small, too. The tile, however, was top-notch and decorative, with little water-burst patterns Bela had grouted in just to make Andy feel welcome. Bela never mentioned it, but Andy sensed her care and attention each time she came into the bright little space, as if Bela had layered her soothing, accepting earth energy into each crack and seal.

Andy turned on the shower.

When she first met Bela, she had hated her. Bela had seemed arrogant and bossy and brash, but she had turned out to be the most solid, loving, and loyal person Andy knew.

She stepped into the shower thinking about Jack Blackmore.

Maybe there were similarities.

Bela had started off trying to kill Andy—or, more to the point, her then-partner Creed Lowell, who was half demon. Warm water struck Andy's face, rivulets and steam flowing across her body as she closed her eyes and soaked in the absolute peace and restoration of standing in the midst of her element.

Yeah, Bela had acted like a total ball-busting ass, but the minute she'd learned the truth of Creed's strong, good nature, she did a 180 and defended him to the death. And when Andy had needed somebody, really needed another human being for the first time in her adult life, Bela had been right there. It had been Bela standing resolutely and lovingly at Andy's side when Andy had to see Sal's mutilated body and tell her lover goodbye.

"Just goes to show, no asshole is totally beyond rehabilitation."

Except maybe Jack.

Andy put both hands on the heated tile in the shower, breathing in water and the mingled scents of Dio's coconut soap and her own rain-scented shampoo. She snitched Dio's soap and lathered herself up, then worked the shampoo into her salty curls.

What the hell was happening between her and Jack, anyway?

Andy opened her eyes as she stepped back into the water for a rinse. He agitated her. He knocked her off balance. But he also had her interest. What did she want it to be? Because he'd made sure she understood the call was hers to make . . .

Six months ago, this whole line of thinking would have been ludicrous. She'd hated the man worse than she'd ever hated Bela. She might still hate him—but no, that wasn't true. Not anymore.

So what did she feel?

Attracted?

In lust?

Terrified?

All of the above?

She rinsed more shampoo out of her hair and let it slide down her skin, relaxing her. A fantasy kindled in the multicolored hue of the bubbles. Jack, in the shower with her, working the soap into her skin with his big hands. She could imagine his dark brown eyes studying her naked skin, choosing where to touch her, exactly how to make her moan and whimper and beg him never to stop.

The screaming started a few seconds later.

Andy's heart skipped and she jerked her palms away from the shower's slick tile. It was all she could do to keep from pitching out of the tub.

Dio.

Dio was screaming.

She sounded terrified. Dio was never terrified.

Breathing hard, Andy threw back the shower curtain, jumped out of the tub, and pelted down the hallway, wishing like hell her dart pistol wasn't downstairs in the weapons closet.

"Dio? Hey!" Her own voice sounded harsh and desperate, almost as jagged as the screams. "Dio!"

Andy burst into Dio's bedroom looking left, looking right, natural and elemental senses running so hot she probably could have sighted a spider at twenty paces and blown it to smithereens.

Identify the threat. Left and right again. Nothing. The light blue walls seemed normal and free of blood spatter or smudges. The bookshelves covering every inch of Dio's walls looked neat as ever. Her half-dozen tan file cabinets stood undisturbed. Her desk was immaculate. All of that would have been a sign of psychosis in most air Sibyls, but Dio had been maniacally neat since Andy met her.

Andy's brain blasted along at a thousand miles per hour, her eyes searching each fraction of an inch. Dio herself sat on the edge of her bed gripping her covers, red-faced and wide-eyed. She looked like she was choking.

"Honey?" Andy made it to her in seconds, reaching

for her with wet hands but stopping just shy of grabbing her shoulders. "What is it?"

"I—I—" Dio's startling gray eyes stayed wide, like she could see things invisible to Andy's senses. A haziness in the depths let Andy know Dio had been sleeping, might still be clinging to some dream or horrible nightmare. In that instant, she seemed so childlike Andy wanted to wrap her in her arms and rock her.

Instead, she tugged a throw from the foot of Dio's bed and wrapped it around her own soap-covered body.

"Talk to me," Andy said. "Tell me what you saw."

Dio blinked, seemed to be trying to shake off her fear. But her teeth started to chatter and she shook so hard the bed trembled with her.

"Not good," Andy muttered, pulling the covers around Dio's bare shoulders. Dio had nothing but a silk shortie covering her to her knees, and the blue fabric seemed filmy and insubstantial even though it was summer.

"Dio?" Bela's voice. She was coming hard up the stairs with Camille right behind her. When they charged into the bedroom, Bela had her scary serrated blade drawn, which didn't jive with her WORLD PEACE T-shirt. Camille had on one of John's button-downs, red with a Crimson Tide football logo on the pocket. It hung below her knees, but her ivory-handled scimitar, an Indian weapon made for beheading with one vicious stroke, took away from the cute factor.

"I think she was dreaming," Andy said, aware of the fact that Camille didn't give off smoke and sparks like most fire Sibyls did. That didn't mean she wasn't deadly. For all her gentle looks, Camille could be more lethal than a volcano at full blow when she used her projective abilities.

"Dreaming." Bela didn't lower her weapon. "And she's still tranced out? Shit. It wasn't a dream. It was a vision."

Camille eased her grip on the scimitar and lowered it

to her side. "Dio doesn't have visions. She's never talked about seeing the future."

"Any air Sibyl can have prescient dreams," Andy said, studying Dio more closely and easing some cooling water energy in Dio's direction in case she wanted to accept it. Andy had learned about air Sibyls and their dreams from Elana. "So can any water Sibyl, or fire or earth Sibyl, too. It's just that air Sibyls are more likely to see the future because of their shared genetic heritage with the Keres—the death spirits near Mount Olympus. In ancient times, some people called the Keres the Fates, because they seemed to know what was coming, at least in general terms."

"Just a dream," Dio muttered, coming back to herself a little more each second. The bed slowly stopped shaking from the force of her tremors.

Bela sheathed her sword but kept her distance, which was always prudent when dealing with Dio. "What did you see?"

For a moment Dio seemed about to argue, to insist she had just repeated some childhood nightmare and maybe they should all just get out and leave her the hell alone. Indecision flickered across her features, followed by guilt, then resignation.

"Rakshasa," she said, more to Andy than anyone. "I saw the tiger-demon Eldest, or one of them. Tarek." She pointed to one of the dozens of drawings tacked to her walls, and Andy found herself staring at the sketch she liked the least. The picture showed three Rakshasa demons in full battle gear, fanged mouths opened in threatening snarls. One had white fur, one had black fur, and Tarek had golden fur with dark stripes down his legs and arms.

Just looking at the damned picture gave Andy the creeps because Dio could draw with a skill and power that brought the essence of her subject right into the room. Rakshasa essence was nothing but evil. Heavily muscled chests and arms, big swords, armor like chain mail suffused with tiny metal spikes—and the eyes. Blazing and soulless, yet sharply intelligent. Tarek's eyes seemed to be the brightest and most awful of all.

"He was here in the brownstone," Dio said. "He came after us and this time he got us. Me. He got me. He tore me apart."

She shivered and shook the bed again.

"How could that dream be prescient?" Andy asked Bela, confusion and concern mingling like cool streams in her chest. "The Rakshasa leader is dead. All the Eldest are toast. We saw what happened this winter down in the Croton Aqueduct offshoot. Camille called up molten ore from the earth's core, and it coated the Eldest. We took them out. All of them."

It had been a stroke of amazing fortune. To kill a Rakshasa Eldest, the heart had to be pierced with elemental metal, which immobilized the demon. Then it had to be beheaded, burned, and the ashes of head and body scattered in different directions. Otherwise, the Eldest could re-form and heal—literally pull themselves back together again. When Camille had summoned the ore from the earth's core, elemental metal hadn't just pierced the hearts of the Eldest. The metal had suffused through their hearts, then coated them externally as well, hardening them into statues so the Sibyls could work at leisure to dispose of them.

"We even destroyed the metal casings that held the Eldest," Camille added, staring at Dio. "There's nothing left."

Bela didn't ask any questions or make any challenges. Andy felt the flow of her earth power, wrapping them all like a soft, shielding cloak.

"In my dream Tarek came back from the dead," Dio said. Andy had never heard her sound so tentative. "He seemed stronger and more powerful, like one of the demons from time before time. Like the—" Dio's furtive glance at Andy told Andy she didn't want to say the name of the most ancient demon the Sibyls had ever battled, the one who formed the Legion cult—the one who killed Sal and almost killed them all.

"The Leviathan," Andy said so Dio wouldn't have to. Her heart chilled and tried to crust with ice at the thought of that fucking murderer straight from hell, her own worst-ever monster that she still had nightmares about, but she kept herself focused on Dio and what Dio needed. "Are you saying that the body and some aspects were Tarek, but the essence, the power, were like the Leviathan?"

Dio nodded and looked everywhere but at Andy. If it had been anyone else, Andy would have touched her arm or knee to soothe her, to let her know she was up for hearing the name. Touching Dio uninvited could get a person's skull split by lightning.

"Tarek becoming Bartholomew August." Bela used the Leviathan's human name, and Andy's teeth clamped together on reflex. "Has to be some kind of symbolism since Tarek and August are both dead."

"Tarek had help." Dio seemed to pick up strength as she got everything out of her mind, out in the open for them all to see and evaluate. "A group of chanting people, all men except one, like the Coven. Samuel Griffen and his sister, Rebecca—I never saw them clearly, but I think it might have been them. They brought him back with—"

Again, Dio couldn't keep going, and again she wouldn't look at Andy.

"I can take it," Andy murmured, making sure her voice sounded low and calm. She kept her gaze direct and tried to invite the answer. When Dio did catch her eye, Andy didn't falter. "I mean it. You're not hurting me. Just spit it out."

"They used a blood sacrifice. A child. And you." The words spilled out like a scream. "Tarek rose off this table thing, like an altar. He ate you and the little girl, then he came after the rest of us. He killed Bela and Camille, and when he started tearing me apart, I woke up."

"The little girl." Bela drew closer to Dio, letting her earth energy serve as a buffer to the air starting to move around Dio's shoulders. "Do you know who she was?"

Dio closed her eyes and grimaced like she was forcing herself to look back, or maybe step back, into the bloody nightmare. "I couldn't see the kid, either, but she had red hair like Neala."

New chills of dread prickled across Andy's neck. Since Sal's death, her fighting group and her godchildren had been what sustained her. Even the hint that something might take them away, that something wanted to hurt one of them, made her so angry water started to leak from her knees and elbows even as the rest of her went completely dry.

"We'll need to write it all down," Bela was saying. "We've known the Coven is involved in all of this, but the Rakshasa connection's been eluding us. Maybe this is some kind of hint. Make a record of it and let the Mothers evaluate it. They'll have a better idea of what to make of symbols like that."

Dio pushed herself off the bed and shed the blanket from her shoulders. "Maybe it wasn't a vision. I haven't had them before, not really, not like that."

Bela responded with a look that made Dio say, "Okay, it probably *was* a vision, but fuck, it was weird. It can't be literal. We know that."

"Write it down," Bela said again. "Every detail, every color and nuance. Anything might be important. We'll all keep it in mind until the meaning gets clearer. If you have any more dreams that even might be visions, we need to know, Dio, okay?"

"Write it down," Andy muttered, thinking about notebooks—then about sketches. Her heart stuttered as she remembered where she was supposed to be. "Shit. Sorry. I've gotta go."

"The proportions are good, but the face—the face doesn't feel right." Andy handed the sketch back to the artist she'd been working with for the last hour. "The too-big legs and arms, the disproportionately long midsection, all of that's dead on. Don't change any of that."

Saul Brent sat in one of the townhouse's interrogation rooms with Andy and the artist. He squinted at the picture, the tribal tattoos on his neck seeming to pulse with the effort of his concentration. "Bastard's muscled up enough to be a 'roid freak."

"His name is Frank, not bastard," Andy shot back. It helped her to give the thing a name, especially one like Frankenstein, so it seemed cartoonish and less real.

"Let's go over this part one feature at a time." The artist rendered the face blank again. "Start with any identifying marks, scars, moles, lines—anything."

"Christ, I only saw the image for a few seconds." Andy put her face in her hands and tried to breathe through her sudden irritability before she accidentally tore off sprinkler heads by sucking water toward her. Her mind kept flipping back to Dio, scared and shaking on her bed, and what Dio had said about a little girl, maybe Neala, getting killed. "I'm sorry. I'm not sure I'm up for any more this evening."

When she looked up, both Saul and the artist gave her smiles that communicated patience and understanding. Saul even looked worried about her, enough that she felt a flash of guilt. To the artist she said, "It looks . . . older in the face, somehow. Definitely male like you've got, and human-like—but not that close to human. More square. More ridged along the cheeks. Like some ancient movie star that had way too much plastic surgery. Or maybe Botox, you know? Where the features don't move?"

Saul listened, then watched as the artist roughed in some basics. "Maybe it's some sort of new human-demon hybrid? Maybe it used to be human?"

"No idea." Andy thought about Neala again. Was she upstairs with Nick and his wife, Cynda? Cynda and her triad sisters Riana and Merilee had introduced Andy to the world of the Sibyls. She still considered them her friends, though her bonds of the heart had formed more closely with Bela and Camille and Dio.

"Listen, I just need a minute, okay?" Andy pushed back from the table and got to her feet. Before Saul or the sketch artist could say anything to her, she left the room. With each step she took toward the townhouse stairs, her heart beat faster. She strained her senses, listening for Neala's giggle, searching for that hint of fire and smoke with Neala's subtle flavor.

By the time she got to the floor where Neala lived with Cynda and Nick, Andy was running. Her sneakered feet brushed along expensive oriental rugs covering even more expensive hardwood floors. The house was so well built that the bookcases, chairs, tables, and reading lamps in the long hallway didn't even jiggle as she shot past. Her breath caught in her throat, and her chest hurt and burned and ached until she turned the last corner and—

There she was.

Andy stopped running and forced herself to walk, slower, slower, until her pace seemed more normal.

Cynda Flynn Lowell stood outside her bedroom talking to her fighting group, Neala gripped firmly in her arms. The two looked like younger and older versions of the same person, with their green eyes, redder-than-red hair, and almost aristocratic features, and both of them seemed to be unharmed and in no immediate danger. Andy's detail-oriented brain registered that the fighting group had on jeans and casual shirts—street clothes instead of battle leathers. Another hint that all was well, no matter what Dio had dreamed.

Riana Dumain Lowell had Ethan with her, but the boy seemed to be asleep against her shoulders. Riana's black hair shielded his face like a curtain. Merilee Alexander Lowell smiled when she saw Andy coming, her pixie face brightening.

"Andy!" Neala squealed, wriggling to get away from Cynda and letting off a big puff of white smoke. "Let's play battle. Please? Please, Andy!"

"Can I just take her for a few?" Andy made eye contact with Cynda, hoping she didn't freak anybody out with her massive case of nerves. "I'll bring her right back." *As soon as I check every hair and freckle. As soon as I count her fingers and toes.*

Andy took a deep breath, taking in the familiar scents of pine cleanser, musty books, and old house, with the very welcome tang of fire Sibyl energy. It burned her nose and made her eyes tear, and she'd never been so glad.

"Sure." Cynda didn't even seem concerned. She grinned at Andy as she handed off Neala, who whooped with delight and grabbed Andy around the neck. "She only gives you second-degree burns. I think she likes you better."

"Blisters heal," Andy murmured as she carried the little girl past Cynda and her group, straight to Neala's room. The space reminded Andy of a cotton candy explosion, with its pastel pinks and blues and purples. The furniture had to be made out of metal, and of course, all the stuffed animals were fire-retardant.

"Have you been good today?" Andy set Neala on the purple rug beside her bed and knelt to be at eye level with the little girl.

"I'm a good girl. Watch me!" Neala raised both hands over her head, clapped, and sent a fountain of sparks raining down on Andy.

Andy caught a whiff of burning hair. Her own. She countered the small bits of fire with her water energy and shook a finger in Neala's cute little face. "I bet you're not supposed to do that anywhere but the gym and when you visit Motherhouse Ireland."

"Ireland's got bunches of rocks." Neala's frown charmed Andy as much as her smiles. "Motherhouse Ireland won't burn. Boring."

Andy ruffled Neala's curls. "But cheaper and safer."

A spectacular pout. "Boring."

"Okay, I'll take your word for it."

Andy had to admit she was beginning to feel a little stupid. Why was she worrying so much about Neala? Any monster who tried to snatch her would have to get through a house full of cops and Sibyls, not to mention come through her Curson demon father and uncle, plus Cynda, one of the most powerful fire Sibyls alive. If somehow the monster succeeded on that little suicide mission, the thing would have to contend with the full wrath and resources of Motherhouse Ireland. And Merilee and Riana—also way powerful in their own elements—wouldn't be far behind. They'd bury, burn, blow, and shred anything that tried to hurt Neala or little Ethan, Riana and Creed's son.

"Watch me, watch me!" Neala shouted, and Andy covered her face.

"No sparks!"

"No, silly. Hands."

Neala hopped on her bed, bounced twice, then got off and executed a decent handstand for about three seconds. Andy jumped up to grab her before she fell, but Neala's elbows gave way. She thumped her head on the floor and toppled to the hardwood.

In two seconds flat, she tuned up to whine, but Andy scooped her into her arms before she could make a sound. "Ouch, huh?"

"I whopped my head." Neala moaned like she'd snapped her leg in half. "It huuuurts."

Andy kissed the spot, right between her eyes. "I've done that lots of times. It sucks."

Neala's new moan broke off before it reached its peak. She blinked at Andy. "Not supposed to say *sucks*."

"Probably not. Except when you whop your head."

Neala glanced at her bedroom door, then back at Andy. "Sucks," she whispered.

Andy hugged her tight and kissed the top of her head this time.

"Battle now?" Neala smiled at her. "Demons are bad guys. I'll help you fight."

"Later." Andy hugged Neala again. Sometimes when she held the little girl close, she felt an emptiness inside, an emptiness that might have been filled with her own babies if Sal hadn't died. Before Sal, she'd never thought about having kids, and since his murder, she hadn't felt much interest in men or marriage or the idea of her own children. It was like she'd gone numb in a few places when she lost Sal. Maybe a lot of places. Just nothing. A dead zone. Until she met Jack Blackmore.

She straightened herself. *Gotta stay away from that kind of sob-and-Kleenex thinking.* She kissed Neala one more time for good measure, then let herself admit that Jack made all her dead spots buzz and tingle. So far, since he'd reintroduced himself to her, he'd made her feel like healing might be possible, like life might be possible, and—

And he was standing in Neala's door watching her.

Andy's heart did a big tumble in her chest.

Jack was watching both of them, actually, with the strangest look on his handsome face. She picked up his interest, his amusement. And deeper, way deeper, something like . . . longing.

She felt like she'd swallowed a warm wave.

When he realized she was staring at him, he didn't look away. "I—ah—came to see about you."

His expression didn't change, except to get more intense. Andy's heart kept beating, and she kept breathing, and she didn't look away, either. She could get used to him staring at her like that, never mind his low, sexy voice.

"Saul said you seemed wiped out." Jack made an effort to smile at her, but she saw the worry rise into his brown eyes.

Damn, but he was a sight in those jeans, wasn't he?

"Saul's a nag and a mother hen." Andy tried to sound serious despite the fact she was on her knees in a cotton-candy room in close proximity to a dozen stuffed animals—and some of her hair was probably still on fire.

"No argument, but he's usually right." This time Jack succeeded with his smile, which did nothing for Andy's composure.

Neala pointed her finger at Jack and sent a shower of sparks and smoke all across his shoulders and hair, then laughed as Andy quickly followed her blast with some cool water to put out the flames. Once more, the smell of singed hair drifted through the air. Jack never changed positions or expressions, but droplets ran off his hair and all over his face.

"Sorry." Andy balanced Neala on one hip, pulled back her water energy and dried his face as best she could, then turned and let the excess flow off her fingers into one of Neala's water glasses. "Life with Sibyls can be hazardous to your health."

"To my hair, for sure. She's gotten me a few times in the past." Jack didn't even sound annoyed. "Ever played battle with her down in the gym? She can explode exercise balls like nobody's business."

Andy wouldn't have figured Jack as a guy to play battle with the kids. The image amused her. Actually made her smile.

From the hallway, Cynda called, "Neala, that was a no-no. Come here right now."

Neala let off smoke as Andy put her down. For a split second, she looked like she might try to argue or cook some other part of Jack's body. Instead, she hurried out the door to her mother, stopping only to wave at Andy before she disappeared from view.

Jack's gaze followed the little girl, surprise obvious in the lines of his face. "That went a little too easily, don't you think? I mean, she's pint-sized, but she's a fire Sibyl, right?"

"Baby fire Sibyls don't argue with bigger fire Sibyls." Andy got to her feet, helpless to slow her own pulse in Jack's presence. "Just everybody else."

Jack turned his attention back to her, fixing her with a stare that made her insides tremble. "And what about baby water Sibyls?"

"So far, I've found that baby water Sibyls are even-tempered and peaceful as long as bigger water Sibyls are around." Amazing how dry her throat could get when the rest of her was slowly soaking from the water she couldn't help pulling toward herself. "If the bigger water Sibyls take a powder—well. Things can get messy."

Another smile from Jack, this one more devastating than the last. "People get hit with rogue waves?"

His tone sounded teasing, and Andy figured he could see the heat coloring her cheeks. "Yeah. That. Listen, about all the times I tried to kill you—I'd say I was sorry, but I'm not sure I am. Not yet."

"Don't be sorry. If I get that far out of line again, you have my permission to wash me out of the building."

Andy stared at Jack. She wanted to look away from him but found she couldn't. His eyes held her like an elemental lock.

The surprises just keep coming.

"So, are you really okay, Andy?" He sounded serious now, and earnest. More than that, his concern for her felt genuine, way down deep in her Sibyl instincts—and her basic female instincts, too.

"I'm fine. A little tired, sure." Andy brushed her hair out of her face and felt the burned tips of a few of her curls crumble to her shoulders. "Right before I came over, Dio had a bad dream, so I guess I'm obsessing about that."

Jack leaned against the door frame and folded his arms. His expression went a little flat. "A bad dream or a vision?"

"I keep forgetting how much you've studied about us—about Sibyls." Andy relaxed a bit, which surprised her. "Bela thinks it was a vision, but Dio doesn't usually have prescient dreams."

Jack's features darkened and his whole body seemed to tense. "Then the threat must be powerful. Mother Anemone in Greece told me that even the least prone air Sibyl can have prescient dreams if they're really in danger." His intense gaze gripped her even tighter. "Them, or somebody they care about."

Andy glanced past Jack, in the direction Neala had taken. "But what she saw didn't make any sense."

"It upset you." A statement. Absolute certainty.

Tears welled in Andy's eyes, sudden and unwanted. "Yeah."

Jack let his arms drop to his sides, and he looked like he might be struggling with himself—over what to say? Or what to do?

Panic clawed Andy at the thought of him coming close to her when she wanted to cry, at the thought of him pulling her against all that muscle and holding her when she felt so jumpy and vulnerable.

He stayed where he was, holding her in his own way, with those deep, forceful eyes. "How about I take you guys off patrol tonight, get another group to sub for you? You get some rest . . . then let me take you to breakfast in the morning? Around ten? We can talk about the dream then, after you've had a good night's sleep."

The thought of not having to go out on patrol all night nearly made Andy sag with relief. She didn't mind tamping down squabbles between paranormal groups or stopping rituals that had gotten out of control—but the mind-numbing grid search for the Coven drove her half insane. She felt a touch of guilt about whoever would pick up their slack, but not that much guilt. They had done their share of cover patrols in the last year.

"Thanks. About patrol, I mean." She rubbed one hand against her cheek to wipe away a stray tear. The rest of what he said sank in more slowly, but she caught up after a few seconds. "Wait—breakfast? Are you asking me out?"

This time his grin nearly turned her into a puddle where she stood. "I'm taking you to breakfast to share information." He paused. "I'm hoping breakfast is tame enough that I'll get a yes."

Andy couldn't help remembering washing Jack out of this very townhouse with a blasting tidal wave she'd thrown at him, furious and out of control. Um, twice. Maybe even three times.

Hadn't she broken his leg or arm once?

She couldn't even remember.

The way he was smiling at her, she wondered if *he* remembered. "You like to live dangerously, don't you, Jack?"

"I like to live." The grin faded into something more intense. "I've remembered that since I started getting to know you."

The heat that crept through Andy moved slowly this time, warming her like water in a pot, ready to boil. This didn't feel jittery or silly or even experimental. It felt serious enough to scare the hell out of her.

"Breakfast," she heard herself whisper, her heart beating so hard she had trouble forming the word. Her legs started moving, carrying her toward him, straight at him, but he stepped to the side when she got to the door. Being polite. Maybe being smart.

She walked a lot closer to him than she had to, moving past, letting herself touch him ever so slightly, just brush against his clothes, her fingertips coursing across his knuckles.

Warm ocean waves.

A rising tide, breathtaking and frightening.

Rain on a hot summer afternoon.

The sensations surged through her all at once, making her go slow, making her savor the few seconds they were separated by nothing more than fabric and breath and the whisper in the back of her mind that she'd better be careful, that she'd better watch out or this man just might flood her landscape and change everything.

He watched her, saying nothing, making no move to force her or rush her or demand anything at all from her. His brown eyes asked her out all over again, hope burning in those warm depths, and she surprised herself by finding voice enough to say again, "Breakfast." Then, "Okay. I'll see you at ten tomorrow."

13

Jack was nervous.

He didn't like nervous.

Something about Andy made him worry about everything. He wanted it to be good, wanted it to be right, wanted everything to please her, even something that should have been inconsequential, like where he took her for breakfast. New York wasn't his town, and she knew it a lot better than he did. Good thing he didn't have Sibyl energy, so computers didn't crash and burn every time he sat down near a keyboard. An Internet search and some advice from the Lowell brothers had done the trick.

His truck was in OCU's storage garage downtown, so he had borrowed Riana Dumain Lowell's black Jeep and made it to the brownstone at half past nine. Being late—out of the question. He sat outside for fifteen minutes, barely moving, keeping his eyes on the front door like he was staking out the place. Wasting time. He could be reading case files or making notes. He could have waited another few and gotten some reports finished, but when he got up this morning, he had only one purpose, and that was getting this Jeep to this curb on time.

Damn, it had been a long time since he felt this kind of focus, this kind of purpose, without . . . without everything that usually held him back. He felt new. He felt like before. Before Afghanistan. Before the nightmare with his bastard of a father in Atlantic City. Had to be some kind of magic, though he knew Sibyls and most paranormals would laugh their asses off at that assertion. *There is no such thing as magic,* the Mothers had taught him. *There is only elemental energy—and those who control it.*

The brownstone's front door opened and out came Andy, wearing faded jeans with some sort of beaded pattern on the legs, a turquoise top with lots of ruffles and spaghetti straps, and a pair of yellow-framed sunglasses so big they looked like something she'd won at a carnival. Her curls spilled to her shoulders, red and riotous, refusing to stay in place as she jogged down the steps.

Jack laughed out loud.

Maybe the Mothers didn't know everything about magic.

This woman made the whole world look black-and-white, like she was the only thing in color, the only thing real and worth watching, and he did like watching. The creamy curves of her bare arms heated him all over as she spotted the Jeep and headed to the curb. Jack leaned across the front seat and opened the door for her, and she got in so fast he glanced up to be sure nothing was chasing her.

She slammed her door, then laughed at his raised eyebrows and waved a hand at the brownstone. "I snuck out. Move your ass before you get me caught."

Jack cranked the engine and pulled into traffic, glancing over his shoulder to be sure the brownstone's front door was still closed. "They wouldn't approve? If they think I'm kidnapping you and send some kind of earthquaking fire tornado thing to crush Riana's Jeep—"

"No, no, it's not like that." Andy shoved her pretty curls behind her delicate ears. "They'd give me shit. Especially Dio. I just didn't want to hear it."

Jack tried to pay attention to his driving, relieved he didn't have any major car repairs to worry about—for the moment. "You know, sharing a floor with Dio Allard and coming out alive every morning, that's pretty impressive."

"I'd say her bark's worse than her bite, but that would be a total lie. Really, though, she's not that bad. Not to us."

Jack kept his eyes on traffic even though he wanted to be staring at Andy, because the rest of the world really did look slow and dull compared to her. "Your fighting group, you're all pretty close."

"We have a lot in common." Her words carried a little sadness, but also pride, and Jack liked that. All good fighting units, military, law enforcement, Sibyl, or otherwise, needed cohesion. Andy's group was lucky to have her because she probably understood that from lots of different angles. He hoped they knew that. He hoped Bela and Camille and Dio appreciated her and let her know her importance on a regular basis.

"I like the jeans and your overshirt," she said. "Dark green looks good on you. Where are we headed?"

His grip on the wheel tightened. "The Village."

"A surprise? Imagine that." She laughed, and he enjoyed the sound. Energy filled the Jeep, vibrant and humming and active. If this was Andy after a good night's rest, he wanted to see her after a week of resting and playing and . . .

Yeah.

Let's leave that one alone for a few.

Andy put her fingers on the Jeep's window and let out a breath, sunlight shining off her giant sunglasses. "I love summer. Don't you?"

It had been a long time since Jack had thought about stuff as simple as which season of the year he liked best. "I'm not sure. I've moved around a lot, and some of the places have been more extreme than others."

I don't have a home. Never have, never will.

That part he kept to himself.

"New York City's great," Andy said. "All four seasons are so different from each other—but summer's the best.

The warm air, the people everywhere, the flowers and trees in Central Park. Wouldn't trade it for anything." She settled deeper into her seat. "I'm from the South originally. Trust me, it gets way too hot to live during June and July. August and September can be a bitch, too."

Jack wove into the far lane to give the buses some room. "I've spent time in Atlanta, Birmingham, and New Orleans, so I'd have to agree."

"Bet you have been a globetrotter, with what you've done for a living. Is there anyplace you're curious about that you haven't seen?"

"The South Pacific." Jack surprised himself by giving up that private fantasy so fast. What the hell. Andy inspired openness. Who could resist a woman in turquoise and beads—and yellow sunglasses? "Fiji, the Solomon Islands. I like to dive, so I've always figured that would be a little piece of heaven to me."

From the corner of his eye, he saw her grin.

"Hundreds and hundreds of uninhabited tropical islands. I like the way you think."

"Hope so." He turned left and hunted for a spot. There. Right in front of their destination. How lucky was that? Unless, of course, she hated the place.

He parked, got out, and came around to open her door, but Andy had already bailed out of the Jeep. She stood on the sidewalk staring up at the neon marquee above the storefront window. In glowing blue letters illuminated day or night, according to Nick and Creed Lowell—the sign read JOE'S BAGEL BAR.

Andy's expression remained unreadable for a second as Jack grimaced at the grimy windows and the ancient-looking booths he could see inside. Maybe Creed and Nick had yanked his chain. Maybe this was a mistake.

"I can't believe you brought me here," Andy muttered. "I haven't been here in a month of Sundays. Since—well, since I started flooding living rooms and shit." She pulled off her shades, her green and brown eyes sparkling in the bright sunlight. "I *love* this place."

Jack felt relieved—for a few minutes. Once he got inside and started trying to build his own bagel brunch sandwich with Andy directing him, things got a little hairy.

"Artichokes and roast beef? You sure?" He eyed the fixings on the other side of the glass as the servers worked.

She shoved her tray down the cafeteria-style bars in front of the display, having the servers load just about everything onto her poppy-seed mega-bagel. Onions, tomatoes, six different kinds of cheese—even anchovies.

She eats like she dresses, free and vibrant. Doesn't give a shit what anybody thinks—including me. His military side screamed for him to slow this down, to restore some order, but he ignored that. Maybe he could get used to a little less order.

She directed the servers to put two different kinds of mustard on his bagel, and he had to smile. When she told them to add three different kinds of peppers, he didn't say a word. He was beginning to think every minute he spent with Andy could turn out to be an adventure.

They took seats in a booth near the door, light from the dirty windows filtering over the mounds of sandwich Andy had created for both of them. Andy dug into hers without hesitation, making happy noises as she chewed.

Jack reminded himself that he'd been a soldier before he'd ever joined the Army, that he'd faced psychotic family members, death, demons, and shit that would kill most people, no questions asked. How dangerous could one sandwich be? Even if it looked a little funny.

He mashed the two halves of whole wheat together, picked it up, definitely did not let himself smell the thing, and took a bite. Chewed. His eyes watered. If he opened his mouth, he'd spit flames like a fire Sibyl.

Andy watched him, grinning around her mouthful of bean sprouts and mushrooms and a bunch of other stuff he hadn't even been able to keep up with. After she swallowed, she said, "Food shouldn't be boring."

"Nothing's boring around you. I'm getting that." Jack ate another few bites and washed it down with the sparkling water she'd picked out for him. The lemon she'd added took the sting down a few notches, and the flavor—not bad. "Do you know how to cook?"

"I wish. I make a mean sandwich." She hoisted another bite and scarfed it down. A hefty note of garlic wafted across the table.

Jack didn't say anything about the fact he actually knew his way around a kitchen. Maybe he'd surprise her with that little fact someday.

"Why did you ask me out?" she asked suddenly.

Direct question. Deserved a direct answer. "I think you're . . ." He hesitated. What word? Beautiful? Amazing? Interesting? All of them would fit. He settled for "Exciting." It didn't come near all the layers of her he could see, but it was a start.

Mischief glinted in her eyes. "Was it the underwear? Tell the truth."

No, sweetheart. Not that much truth. Not yet. Jack's whole body reacted to the memory of her standing on the beach with nothing but wet lace hiding what he wanted to see. "The underwear got my attention, but you already had my appreciation."

"From what, all the broken bones I gave you?"

He shrugged. Just a leg, an arm, and a wrist. Bones healed. "Nah. It's the way you walk. Hot." He waited for her to laugh, and she did. "Really, it was the notes you wrote in OCU files. You're a strategist at heart. You see patterns and details most people miss. I respect that kind of brilliance."

This seemed to catch her off guard, and she looked down at her bagel creation.

Jack tensed. Was he treading ground Sal Freeman had

walked? He didn't want to be a reminder, not because he thought he couldn't find his own way with Andy, but because he didn't want her sad.

"Complimenting my body and my brains." She glanced at him and smiled. "You're working hard."

"I have to keep up."

"Letting this be anything like a date, it's a big step for me."

"I know."

Her eyes seemed to shift more to brown, darker with a seriousness he wasn't used to seeing from her. "Especially with you. When you headed off to spend time at the Motherhouses, you were the most arrogant fuckhead I'd ever met. What changed?"

He gave her *hot, brilliant, exciting*—and he got *fuckhead*. Figured. "They reminded me I wasn't the only person on earth who had been fighting evil my whole life. That I wasn't the only arrogant fuckhead who'd lost people who mattered, or the only guy who cared how the battle ended."

Andy chewed on this along with another bite, then her smile started to creep back into place. "I was pretty sure one of the Mothers would kill you."

"I wondered myself, especially in Ireland—but I think I got more lumps and bruises in Greece."

Andy pointed a bit of carrot at him and nodded. "Dio aside, most people think air Sibyls are sooo sweet until they piss one off, you know?"

"The same could be said for water Sibyls, at least the modern variety." He watched as she popped the carrot into her pretty mouth. "I read a lot at the Motherhouses, but I didn't find out until just recently—you were the one who killed the Leviathan demon and ended the war with the Legion cult."

The seriousness came back to her eyes. "Everybody

had a hand in that. The fucker was already down and re-strained by the Keres—you know, the Fates from Greek mythology. They're all about fate and doom and death and vengeance. They're the ones who contained August. I just pumped a few darts into his big demon brain to finish him off. It was—" She broke off, and he could tell she didn't want to explain why she'd been the one to take out the Leviathan.

Jack took another bite of his sandwich, managing the pepper juice and mustard on his tongue. Why wouldn't she tell him something like that? Unless—well, hell. Yeah, it probably did have something to do with Sal Freeman. He had to let her know that it was okay to go there, that she didn't have to try to shield him or please him or pre-tend Sal had never existed. Soldiers died in battle. Good soldiers. Better soldiers than him. Jack didn't feel any need to compete with the memory of a dead man.

"You don't have to censor with me. Not ever, not about anything." Pepper juice dripped from his sand-wich to his fingers, burning along his skin.

"That's a pretty big invitation." All serious now, no play.

"It's a real one, and it's always open. For example, that dream Dio had that upset you so badly. Start with that."

For a time Andy gazed out the grimy window, watch-ing New York City pedestrians troop by, heading God only knew where, for a thousand different purposes. When she did speak, her voice went soft. "She dreamed about Tarek coming back from the dead. Some people brought him back by sacrificing Neala and me, and he had more power than ever. As much power as the Leviathan I killed. In Dio's dream, Tarek killed her. Well, tore her apart. Those were the words she used."

The thought of Andy and Neala being murdered made

Jack tense so fast, so deep inside, he barely managed to keep his expression neutral. "Was her dream a vision?"

"The Mothers don't think so." Andy brought her gaze back to Jack's face. When he saw the tears glittering in the corners of her eyes, he wanted to hold her until all the pain and danger faded to nothing. "We reported it, but Mother Anemone already got back to us and said it's probably metaphorical. That it means we're tangling with forces as powerful as the Leviathan."

"I don't like that." Jack meant all of it, especially the part about Andy and Neala being sacrificed, but he knew she would focus on the Leviathan part. He expected her to say something sarcastic, something full of bravado to chase away her own tears.

Instead, she seemed to steel herself. Then, staring straight into his eyes, she said, "The Keres gave me the honor of slaying the Leviathan because in their eyes, it killed my mate and I had the right to vengeance."

Jack took that in without flinching. His own instincts told him that this got to the center of Andy. This was what he needed to know, what he most needed to understand about her if he wanted any chance to know her better. And he definitely wanted that chance.

"Did you consider Sal Freeman your mate?"

"Yes." No hesitation. No game playing. He saw sadness sink across her face, but also acceptance, and maybe something like distance. Like she'd been working on this thing and she'd managed to get a little perspective.

"I've never had a lover murdered, but I lost some people in my family—and so many friends in Afghanistan I thought my soul might bleed out on the sand." Jesus. Had he said that out loud? He'd never told anybody anything like that. The truth of it punched him in the gut, and his throat got tight as he made himself finish. "I wish I'd gotten to kill the Rakshasa who took out my men in the

Valley of the Gods, but I'm damned glad Camille and your fighting group made that happen."

He hadn't meant to get so forceful, but he wasn't sorry he was talking to her. Talking seemed easy with her. He had a sense of her water energy, something relaxing, something soothing, totally at odds with her eye-grabbing appearance. Another layer, deeper than all the rest.

"What happened in the war—do you think it's your fault, Jack?"

Shit. Who was getting to the heart of things now? His damned heart. Direct hit. "It was my unit."

He expected her to argue, to try to use some modern mental health shit to talk him out of that, but she said, "You were right, back on the beach when you came to talk to me on Kérkira. If I hadn't suddenly discovered my Sibyl water talents, I would have accepted command of the OCU." She pushed some of her curls behind her ear. "Commanders are always responsible for everything, fair or not. When people march out and die on your orders, you don't get the luxury of whining that it's not your fault."

Jack didn't know what to say back, couldn't quite find the words, but *thank you* came to mind. He hadn't expected her understanding, but getting it felt damned good.

"The past can hold on for a long, long time," she said. The pain in her voice made him want to hold her, make it go away—or at least ease it as much as pain like that ever got eased. "War scars people. Duncan and John, they have their issues from battle. Hell, I was active duty four years in the Marines and saw my share of crap— but nothing like what you faced. You went through a lot in Afghanistan."

Jack got down a little more of his sandwich before he said, "We all did. I'm nothing special."

"The Rakshasa. The Valley of the Gods. That was special. Outside the ordinary, I mean." She was half through with her own sandwich, and the other section looked completely different from the one she'd finished. "I've never commanded as many men as you, but I've lost officers on the streets when I was in charge—so I get it. And I'm sorry, Jack."

"Thanks."

Her smile made him feel everything from sadness to elation in a few quick seconds. How did she *do* that? Had to be magic. Had to be.

"So, you want to do this date thing again sometime?" Andy's smile flashed, more tentative, a little self-conscious, and Jack felt like she had her hand on his heart, squeezing.

"Oh, yeah. What about tonight?"

She shook her head. "Patrol. And if we shirked off a second night, somebody might graffiti our front door."

"Tomorrow night?"

This time he got a nod. "Tomorrow night will work."

"Want to meet somewhere so you don't have to deal with your quad?"

"Gotta face them sooner or later. I get to pick the restaurant."

"And the time after that, it'll be my call."

"You're that confident we'll have a third date?" More smiling. Jack hoped she never stopped.

"Yes." He finished off the last bite of his sandwich, relieved, but also a little disappointed. He'd gotten used to the jarring taste, and if they finished, they'd have to leave. "But before that—I had an idea about the sketch that was giving you trouble."

"I'm listening." Andy dug into the rest of her sandwich, not too fast, taking her time, and Jack wondered if she didn't want to leave, either.

"We know all of this is mob-connected, and we're suspecting some sort of demon conversion, right? So it makes sense that the demon might be somebody we've run into before."

"A known criminal." She considered this. Seemed to like the prospects. "Somebody on the books."

"Maybe." He thought he could look at her forever, even in a dive eating freaky bagel sandwiches. "I pulled a bunch of mug shots for you to search through when you have time. You might see something that helps you line up the face on the sketch."

"Sure. How about when we leave here?"

She kept at her sandwich, a little faster now. Good. He didn't have to think about taking her home yet. He'd have her for a few more minutes, maybe a couple of hours—and maybe they'd make some progress on the case, too.

When she'd polished off the last sprout and crumble of cheese, Jack paid the tab and the two of them walked into the sunlit morning. It had to be close to noon, or maybe a little after. Damn, time moved too fast.

They reached the Jeep, and as he reached to open the door for her, Andy put her hand on his arm. Her soft skin resting against his, the connection of her fingers gripping him, made Jack's body come to full attention all over again.

"That was nice. A nice start." She rose on her toes and kissed his cheek, her wet, full lips lingering along his cheekbone.

His mind filled with her sweet scent. The buildings around them, the Jeep, the crowd surging down the sidewalk—everything faded away from Jack except Andy and her fingers on his arm and the way she moved her lips on his face. He felt like a man under a spell, unwilling to move because he might shatter the magic.

Her mouth whispered down his face until she found his. Her kiss came gently, tentative and sensual, and she tasted like ocean and woman and a thousand spices he couldn't name. She gripped his other arm, balancing herself but getting closer, her breasts brushing against his chest.

Animal instincts flooded Jack. He couldn't hold back even if he wanted to, not with her this close, not with her lips on his. He pulled loose from her grip and caught her before she could tip backward and slip away from him. Then he kissed her like he wanted to, slow and deep and long, and only a tiny part of his brain logged the fact that he hadn't been hit with a tidal wave.

Yet.

14

Somewhere between the last bite of garlic and cheese and the sunlight on the sidewalk, Andy had lost her mind. She'd touched Jack. She'd kissed him.

And now—

Now he was bending forward, tilting her head back, and taking what he wanted.

His lips covered hers, firm and hot, and pepper spice scorched her senses as he held her closer and tighter. The pressure on her mouth turned insistent, commanding her to give him everything, to keep absolutely nothing back for herself, nothing that might save her sanity. The world ceased to exist save for the burning taste of his lips, the rough demand of his tongue. Her mouth moved against his, and she slid her hands under his shirt to find the hard ridges of muscle defining his waist.

She wanted him naked.

She wanted him, period.

She wanted the hard proof of his desire out of those jeans and in her hands. What she could do to him . . . what she would let him do to her . . .

She got wet in every way just letting herself imagine. Water soaked her clothes, soaked his, and he kept kissing her out on the sidewalk in front of anybody who cared to watch. Wild as she was, she'd never done anything as public as this in her life.

When Jack ended the kiss and gazed down at her, Andy didn't want anything but another kiss, so she took it, and another after that, until they were both half drenched with random water she'd pulled toward them.

"Somebody's gonna think we're auditioning for a wet T-shirt contest," Jack murmured against her ear, making Andy shiver from the deep, delicious sound.

"You'd win." God, her voice was nothing but a shaking rasp. "Maybe tonight would work out—if you don't mind dates at four in the morning when I get off patrol."

The tension in his muscles let her know he was thinking about it, that he wanted to take her up on it, but he kissed the top of her head and said, "No. Work, then rest. I want you strong and ready because I'm going to wear you out. Still on for tomorrow night, though?"

I might die here, and I think I'd be happy. Andy liked the feel of his face in her hair, of his hands on her body. Every second with him made her want another second, then a minute, an hour, a day. She could get used to this way too fast.

"You're a tease, Jack Blackmore."

"And you're beautiful." His hot breath tickled her neck this time, driving her nearly crazy.

Her body ached from wanting him, but she managed to keep her act together enough to say, "I'm still picking the restaurant tomorrow night."

He pulled away from her again, this time letting her go as he smiled at her. "We'll see about that."

Andy wanted him back right away, wanted him next to her, rubbing her, holding her, stroking her. Her mind heaved and the sky seemed to give off colored light. Kaleidoscopic New York, and she hadn't even needed a shot of Jack Daniel's to see the world in living color.

It's been so long, part of her mind thought while her mouth came up with, "There's no sense fighting me for control."

"The fight's half the fun."

That smile. It really could kill a woman. "Tease, tease, tease."

Andy got in the Jeep breathing like she'd run five miles

on a sandy beach. She knew her face had to look like a freckled cinnamon drop. As Jack got in the car, she realized the water stains on his clothes lined up with hers.

Oh, they were so not walking into OCU headquarters with matching water spots.

Her face got even hotter. "I'm going to dry us off, okay?"

Jack turned the key but didn't move the Jeep from its parking spot. "If it involves touching me, don't do it while I'm driving."

Andy made herself look straight ahead, but the second he pulled into traffic, she slipped her hand toward his leg and rested it on his knee as she drew the water out of their clothing and shunted it onto the Jeep's floor. "Am I a distraction, Jack?"

"You're way more than that, sweetheart." He waited until he was dry, then nudged her fingers off his leg.

"I'd kill most men for calling me sweetheart."

"You've already tried to off me a few times, and I'm still here."

The iron crescent moon around Andy's neck gave a sharp tingle against her damp skin, and she lifted her fingers to it. Weird. That had happened before with Sibyl distress calls and emergencies, any power dark enough or strong enough to fire through projective metals and surfaces.

She reached out with her water energy, but didn't feel anything beyond people and dogs and asphalt and concrete.

The tingling got worse.

Something snakelike and wrong slithered through her mind, muttering, almost like it was searching for her, calling out for her.

Andy . . .

She heard the sound. Just a whisper, but she was pretty sure she wasn't imagining it.

Andy . . .

Close. In front of her.

What the hell was this, some psychotic demon ghost about to make a grab for her throat?

Andy's heartbeat changed, skipping instead of pounding. She picked up more wavy wrongness around them. Unnatural energy, like darkness rippling across the lit surface of their world.

Andy . . .

"Jack, I think you should stop the Jeep."

He put the brakes on without asking why.

At the same moment the Jeep jerked hard to the right, screeching across pavement and straight toward a line of parked cars by the sidewalk.

"Jack!"

"Tire." His voice rose over the squeal of other cars and cabs peeling away from the Jeep.

Andy heard a loud pop. The Jeep jerked even more violently. She held the panic bar so tight she felt like her fingers might crack. Jack swore and fought the wheel as the Jeep smashed past a Toyota Prius, knocking the little blue hybrid sideways before hopping the curb and blasting through a gate into somebody's private alley.

Jack rode the brakes hard. They spun. Smacked off something. The hood flew up. Airbags deployed with a chest-splitting crack, and for a second Andy saw nothing but white powder and cloth. She heard nothing but fluid hissing out of hoses and the bang of the Jeep's hood as it crashed down.

Stopped.

After all the motion and squealing of tires, Andy's senses buzzed, making noise in the relative silence. She fought with the airbag, clawing it and pushing it off her. Where was the street? The back of the alley?

She was facing the street out her passenger window.

The crunched front of the Jeep sat about five feet from an alley wall. Behind them, another stone wall.

Three men—three very big men—seemed to materialize at the ruined alley gate.

Andy's necklace burned her like steam off an iron. Wrong. Darkness. These men were all wrong. Every nerve in her body fired, and she wanted to claw her way through the Jeep's metal roof.

"These aren't friendlies," she said to Jack, grabbing her SIG out of its ankle holster.

"Neither are those." Jack jerked a thumb toward three more men heading toward them, alley-side. They were each carrying a MAC-10 "spray and pray" with a sound suppressor.

Jack drew his Glock, but Andy couldn't quit looking at the submachine guns.

A thousand rounds per minute, her mind informed her, the words jamming between her ears. "Fuck."

The three assholes at the alley mouth pulled out matching MAC-10s.

Andy moved even as Jack yanked her down to the Jeep floor and covered her with his own body.

The charm around Andy's neck sizzled into her skin and the Sibyl tattoo on her right forearm seemed to catch fire as bullets ripped into the Jeep from both sides.

Glass shattered. The *thump-thump* of holes punched in metal nearly deafened Andy. The Jeep rocked and pain blasted into her left leg. She bit her lip instead of crying out, but when fire lanced her right arm, she figured they would die right here, and quickly. She couldn't see anything but black carpet and torn leather and metal and now light popping into the Jeep from hole after hole as the MAC-10s chewed it to pieces.

She yanked on her elemental energy, not caring how much water came or how hard. The Jeep rocked all over again as water sprayed through the shattered metal and glass, and the gunfire cut off. Andy heard the whooshing roar of waves underneath them. The sudden silence outside made the clang of a manhole cover hitting alley walls twice as loud. Something exploded. Another manhole cover bashed stone. Water mains gave up everything she asked them to send her, and she knew she was rupturing several of them. Thank God. Panting, trying to ignore the agony in her arm and leg, Andy drew the water forward, pulled it all, every bit, and hoped she was turning the alley into one big psychotic waterslide.

"Cover your weapon," Andy warned Jack just as the Jeep slid and spun in the current and water flooded through the ruined windows on her side.

As the big waves passed, Andy thought she heard screaming. From farther away, sirens cranked into the background noise.

The Jeep went still again.

"Out," Jack said, and she knew they had to move. If the shooters were still standing, they'd reach the Jeep in seconds, cram their MAC-10s through the jagged glass, and shred them like so much bloody paper. Andy had to get a fix on these bastards and drown them properly.

"One . . . two . . ." Jack hesitated, then grunted, "Three."

His weight shifted off her and Andy didn't let herself think. She ignored the throbbing fire in her arm and leg, shoved open the Jeep door, and fell out shooting, splashing as she landed in the waterlogged alley.

Gunfire erupted on Jack's side of the Jeep, and Andy didn't hear anything but the noise, couldn't smell anything but gunpowder and water—and something like a wet, moldy cat.

Her eyes focused.

One shooter on her side down. Two more coming at her fast, weapons pointed.

Human, her brain said. *But not.*

Whatever. She pumped three rounds into the one closest, then the one farthest away.

They staggered—and kept coming.

They looked big, too big at the shoulders. Built like men, but enhanced. Disproportionate. Their faces seemed too square, like cartoon thugs, but those MAC-10s weren't funny at all.

"Shit!" She lowered her SIG and strafed the first shooter's ankles. The bastard tumbled onto the wet pavement, yelling his head off. Andy dropped the second shooter the same way, at close range, using her bullets like a sword and nearly cutting his feet right off his legs. Just in case the big bastards did have demon blood, she shot them both in the head, and crowned the one lying in the wet alley behind them, just for good measure.

"Jack!" Why was she yelling? She couldn't hear a damned thing. And the shooters—the ones she had pumped full of bullets—were starting to move.

"Jack, goddamnit, are you alive?"

Andy tried to lift her right arm to line up her shots to kill the assholes all over again, but the damned weapon wouldn't budge. Her left leg had gone dead on her, too. Water poured into the alley from every direction, bashing against the shooters and Andy and the Jeep. Nothing contained the waves, so they moved on through. Damn it! If she could fill the alley, she'd have a fighting chance since she could breathe water and maybe the shooters couldn't.

Don't drown Jack. Be careful. Be careful!

But she couldn't see him, couldn't sense him, still couldn't hear shit-all. No idea if Jack was still alive. Andy let out her rage in a massive scream—and she heard the answering, thunderous roar of a wind funnel storming across the streets of New York City.

"Cover and anchor!" she yelled in case Jack could

hear her, and she rolled against the Jeep and wrapped her good arm around the front tire, turning her face away from the alley mouth and the weird, writhing shooters who absolutely were trying to get up despite being shot in a dozen places, including their big, thick heads. The third shooter, the one who hadn't charged her yet, had already made it to his feet.

The sky darkened to near night, and wind blasted down the alley, pushing Andy's wet hair away from her face and staggering the struggling shooters.

A big tornado came screaming into the alley, blasting gate and shooters and Jeep alike as it whirled to a stop and vanished, thunder crashing over the spot where it had been.

Dio hit the ground less than three feet in front of Andy, knives drawn and teeth bared.

Andy rolled over and lifted her SIG with her left hand. The shooters were up, all right, but they were moving back. Turning. Now they were running, splashing through puddles and sluices. Three more bashed around the Jeep and ran past Dio.

Andy would have brought more waves, but she couldn't muster the force. Too much pain. Too much blood mixing with the water all around her. Everything felt like congealing ice except the hot spots in her arm and leg. Everything smelled like copper and burned powder.

Dio planted three-sided African blades in the shooters' backs—and they kept running. Dio hit them again, and still they kept moving.

"What the hell are they?" Dio's yell barely trickled into Andy's numb ears.

A shadow rounded the back of the Jeep, and Andy almost shot Jack between the eyes before she realized it was him. He was bleeding from the chest and neck, and his eyes—dear God. Andy had never seen a human male with eyes so cold and furious.

He shot at the retreating figures and Dio kept bury-ing knives in them until they pelted out of the alley. Each blade and bullet hit its target, Andy knew, but the shoot-ers spilled onto the sidewalk, scattering civilians. Nobody could take a safe shot now, not without risking friendlies.

Seconds later, two black leather blurs rocketed past the alley. Bela and Camille, charging after the shooters on foot. A few more leather-clad women hurtled by. Sibyls. Andy realized that all over the city, wind chimes would have jangled in Sibyl houses, and anyone with the tattoo of the Dark Crescent Sisterhood would have heard her in-stinctive, automatic call for help.

Emergency sirens got louder.

"You're hit," Jack muttered, his deep voice cutting underneath the growing chaos. He sounded as furious as he looked.

"So are you." Andy tried to pull herself to sitting but couldn't do it.

He didn't answer that, and the expression on his face didn't change.

New cold washed across Andy's wet skin.

Jack wasn't really with her, was he? New York City, the ruined Jeep, the acrid tang of Dio's weather-making energy and the howl of her barely contained wind, the wet alley—none of that was getting through to him. The look on his face and the icy blue fire in his eyes told her he had gone somewhere else, somewhere *other*.

Before she could say anything to get him back to here and now, he scooped her off the ground. The pain from sudden movement nearly made Andy scream, and tears exploded from both of her eyes. She wanted to hit him, but then he'd drop her and everything would hurt that much worse. Instead, she grabbed his arms and dug her nails in as hard as she could.

Jack didn't seem to notice. He turned like he intended to carry her out of the alley.

Dio blocked his path. "Hold on, Blackmore. Help's almost here."

"She's hit. Got to find a medic." Jack's voice came out flat, robotlike. No inflection. Barely any volume.

Dio's wind shifted and she looked at Andy, hands and eyebrows raised. The implication was clear: *Should I blast him on his ass?*

Robo-Jack walked straight at her. "Get out of my way."

Andy sensed on a soul-deep level that Jack wouldn't hurt her, but she didn't feel confident that he wouldn't hurt other people. Not at all.

"It's okay," she told Dio. "I've got this."

What a fucking lie.

Dio frowned at Andy, but she stepped aside and Jack kept walking, carrying Andy toward the streets, toward the crowds and sirens.

Her leg and arm hurt so badly her head swam, but she made herself lean into Jack. "Listen to me. We need to wait for the OCU."

Nothing. He kept walking. His breathing sounded labored, and his blood flowed down his shoulder, soaking into Andy's jeans. Her acute senses picked up his heart rate. Irregular. Way too fast. She sent energy through him on instinct, pacing the beat as best she could. Her thoughts moved to his wounds. Bullets. Two through-and-through at the neck and shoulder, two still lodged in his upper right forearm. More energy left her as everything Sibyl inside her took over, making her want to heal him, *need* to heal him.

Her vision flickered.

Jack stumbled.

"Sorry," Dio said from behind them as marked cars, unmarked cars, and ambulances screeched to a halt on the street outside the alley. Andy felt the impact as Dio hit Jack hard enough to knock him down.

Jack grunted with pain, and Andy felt him falling. Felt herself falling. Sharp bolts of agony made her senses dim before she hit the pavement, but she was all too aware of Jack's warm weight beside her.

Heal him, her mind demanded, and her water energy flowed out of her, working, trying, pushing harder until somebody tore her away from him, crammed a needle into her arm, and turned out her lights.

(15)

Failure.

It pounded Griffen like blows to the gut. It stabbed him like shattered bone in the lungs. It festered like rotting thorns in his heart.

He hated standing here in the quiet warehouse next to his second in command and his chained, smug sister. His jeans felt too tight. His black sweatshirt felt too heavy, and it only added to the heat of his rage. Rebecca gave him a smirk as she eyed the proof of his missteps, the six blood-covered fighters back from the failed ambush on Andy Myles, but she didn't say anything. Neither did the twelve men in his coven—the ones handling the fighters and the ones standing quietly, as if showing support. That, at least, was a small miracle.

Rage flared through Griffen, and he punched the first fighter in the face. The big fuck went to his knees, unable to keep his balance because of his badly damaged ankles. The bone and flesh near the fighter's feet had healed—but badly. No more blood, no more exposed tissue, but very little function, either. The other five fighters who had blown the ambush stood next to their handlers, quiet and subdued. Dried blood crusted their clothing, but at least they were whole. For the moment. Of course, two had been blinded, but eyes could be replaced.

"We should put this group down, adjust the formula, and make a new batch." Donovan Craig had the black hood of his sweatshirt down like Griffen, and his reddish beard and hair made him look like an angry lion. The scars on his face, knuckle marks from years of scrumming, pulsed crimson like his temper. "They can't heal if the flesh is torn completely away. You can see it's a weakness."

"Of course I can see." Griffen didn't even try to keep the snarl out of his voice. In all their sparring sessions getting ready for the ambush, these fighters had taken wounds. He realized only now that the wounds had been to their torsos, to the thicker portions of their bodies, where flesh could easily rejoin and knit. The fighters had healed without so much as scars to show for their damage, and he had assumed they were ready to face bullets and blades.

Failure.

Griffen wanted to kill something. "Work on the formula if you want," he told Craig, "but I don't want to spend any more time in research. These will do. We can armor the weak points."

Craig's frustration bubbled straight to the surface, revealing itself in his next comment. "These fools let you down. Give it more time, Griffen. Give us more time, and we can produce stronger fighters."

Griffen glanced at the lab door. They had an endless supply of demon essence, but a limited pool of "volunteers" unless they started snatching goons off the street. Always a possibility. They could keep refining the process, especially now that they understood the problem of detached flesh, and that the eye tissue was weak and lacking in the same restorative powers as the rest of the enhanced body. When that bitch of a Sibyl had used her SIG to nearly shear off one of the fighter's feet, she had blown away so much tissue that the ankle couldn't coalesce. Unlike the original Rakshasa, the Eldest, these fighters didn't draw their own essence back to themselves. If it got lost, it was just gone. The fighter on his knees probably needed his feet amputated. What good was a superwarrior who couldn't walk? Prosthetics might make a difference, but the time needed to learn to use them—not worth it.

Griffen let air out of his filled lungs. Slowly. Centering and focusing. What happened, happened. He needed a teaching case anyway. An example to solidify his absolute control over all the fighters.

"We're in motion now," he told Craig. "We'll make do with what we have, and if you come up with something better, we'll add fighters as we go."

Really, though, he wanted to shoot these six for being imperfect. For failing. He wanted to watch their blood pool underneath their shattered heads, but too much time and money had been poured into their creation.

Rebecca pointed to the fighter on his knees. "Let the old man out of his cage. I want to watch."

The joy in her voice made Griffen give her request a moment's consideration, but he knew that would be a bad idea. "No. Leave the creature alone. We have much better uses for him."

And our energy's low right now. We can't risk losing control of him. That much, Griffen didn't say, because it would only remind everyone of another one of his failures. To Craig, Griffen said, "Put the fighters up. Except this one on his knees. He's finished."

Rebecca grinned at the kneeling man, her blue eyes glittering as the Coven quickly moved to put five of the six fighters back into their cells.

The sixth remained on his knees beside his lone handler, eyes forward, expression dull. The elemental energy the handler used to contain the fighter felt like cotton in the air to Griffen, but it had little effect on him.

He drew the Glock he kept in an ankle holster. It had a full clip of hollow-point ammunition specially treated to be effective with his new creations. A man couldn't be too careful.

Bloodlust rose like a blush to Rebecca's pale face, highlighting the sharply tapered tips of her ears. She looked more otherworldly than ever, and Griffen sensed something about her. A readiness. A coming of age. He'd been feeling it for months, but right now in this moment, she seemed . . . completed, somehow. Like the next phase of her life was about to begin, whether or not he allowed it.

I have so much to live up to, Griffen thought, wishing his father had survived the murderous assault of the Sibyls. Bartholomew August could have advised him, could have guided him, but now Griffen had to carry on without that assistance. He could do it, of course. And he would do it.

The Coven returned in full, ringing Griffen and Rebecca and the kneeling fighter. Griffen gestured for the fighter's handler to rejoin the circle, and he did so, leaving the containing blanket of elemental energy in place to keep the fighter subdued.

As the circle expanded to receive its returning member, Griffen said, "The men in my Coven do their best not to look at you, Rebecca, but some of them can't help themselves." Griffen caught a few quick glances as he spoke, and he sensed pulses rising. A second or two later, the guilty men managed to look anywhere but at him or at her. Good for them. His men would control themselves because they knew their higher purpose lay with the work of the group, that the group would suffer if he had to execute some of them for going where they didn't belong. His sorcerers knew better than to cross him—and besides, Griffen figured they didn't want to die at Rebecca's hand.

"Men look at me. So what?" Rebecca didn't so much as glance at Griffen. She was too captured by his weapon and the kneeling fighter.

"So maybe you're ready to branch out into more serious relationships. Not the juvenile dalliances you've enjoyed in the past, but liaisons with a purpose."

"I'm not interested in marriage."

Griffen held up the Glock, let her study it, let her desire to see it in action grow. He knew she could imagine the tang of the gunpowder, the shocking crack of the shot, and the aftermath. He handed her the gun.

Rebecca took it without difficulty despite the elemental cuffs around her wrists and the chain binding her to him. Her smile widened as she crammed the muzzle against the fighter's head. With no preamble or warning, she pulled the trigger. The explosion kicked the man's head away from her and he flopped to the floor like a useless bag of rags. Gore spattered the concrete beneath the fighter, and Griffen finally got the blood he had craved, the payback for the immense ineptitude the fighters had shown in the failed ambush.

Rebecca offered Griffen the Glock, handle first.

He appreciated her good safety awareness, though he knew the barrel had to be hot against her sensitive fingers. He never worried that she would shoot him, because she knew he had bound his essence to the elemental cuffs. If she decided to be treacherous, his death would send a killing pulse through the metal, and he and his sister would die together.

"You shouldn't focus all your energy on one Sibyl," Rebecca said. "Broaden the field. Sibyls grieve their losses like all sentimental humans. Death hurts them. If we do enough damage, we could rip the fabric of the fighting groups."

"You have a point, but you know why I want Andy Myles dead." Griffen holstered his weapon and faced his sister as she sighed. "You know why I want her to be first."

"To disrupt and weaken her dangerous fighting group, the one that poses the most threat to us." Rebecca sounded like she was reciting, but at least she didn't imitate Griffen's voice. "To make an example. To get revenge." Her eyes still danced from the excitement of killing, but her tone grew serious, almost emphatic. "Our father never made vengeance his first priority."

Griffen gave this a moment's thought and had to concede that his sister was correct. "Bartholomew August focused on winning battles and winning wars, and carrying out his higher purpose."

Rebecca's nod came too quickly for her to sense the trap Griffen had laid.

"We have a higher purpose, too, Rebecca," he said, and he knew she couldn't argue.

Her gaze roved around the circle of the Coven, but the twelve men who worked for Griffen remained silent and impassive, the hoods of their black sweatshirts obscuring their expressions.

Rebecca seemed to debate with herself, then settle on the truth of Griffen's words, as he had been hoping she would.

"What do you have in mind?" she asked, sounding as interested as she did frustrated.

"It's time you think about destiny. About passing on your power and abilities to a new generation. It's the charge our father left both of us, and we should both be thinking in that direction."

"I'm not interested in marriage," Rebecca repeated, anger and fear creeping into her tone.

"Marriage isn't necessary," Griffen told her, relief sliding through him as he spoke. He felt the rightness of what he said even as the words formed. "I'm happy to bring you males and let you do what you want with them after they've served their purpose. Not all of them will be disposable, of course, but some won't be missed."

Rebecca reacted to this with hesitation, then with increased interest. Griffen could feel the bond between them strengthening, feel her weigh and accept this option, and he felt pride in himself—and in her.

Yes.

This would be much better than what he had been planning, marrying her off to an elementally powerful male who could control her. It meant he would have to be the one to supervise her for a while longer. She wasn't all that much trouble, not really, not when he considered the amusement she provided.

And with the men, those poor bastards.

She would be the consummate killer, slaughtering the spent mate before he even understood that he had bedded a black widow, a mantis—a predatory female who disposed of inconvenient lovers before moving on to the next.

Rebecca raised the elemental cuffs that kept her in check—to a point. "And these?"

Griffen knew he had to offer her something in return for her level-headed acceptance of reality. She really had grown these last months. She had changed, and perhaps it was time to see if those changes made her more stable.

He fished in his jeans pocket and brought out the key.

Moving as one entity, the Coven circle widened, giving ground to Rebecca even before Griffen set her free.

"Come here," he said. "We'll see how this goes."

(16)

Jack . . .

The cold violence in that voice cut Jack worse than any blade.

His chest ached. His lungs burned. Sweat plastered his T-shirt to his chest as his father's voice punched through the motionless air.

"We can still work this out, boy. You're only seventeen. You don't know everything yet."

Jack threw himself around a corner in the massive casino vault, scraping his jeans on a wooden crate. He had to get away from that voice. Had to find a place to hide. Concrete floors. Metal walls. He stumbled past stacks of locked metal boxes, costumes on mannequins, sculptures, paintings—nothing big enough to hide inside. Nothing safe enough to hide behind. His heart beat so loud and fast he knew his father could hear it, and his mother's Luger shook in his hand.

"There's no way out of here, Jack." His father switched to a friendly voice. "You're my only son. You don't have to run from me."

Lie.

Jack barreled into a dead end and edged behind the vault's last wall, shoulders to metal, still shaking. His breath came so hard his father could probably track every rattle and wheeze.

Have to take care of him. For Mom. For Ginger. He had to get them out of this, because Ginger was talking to the feds and Mom was probably talking and Jack knew—*knew*—what his father would do. Jack had watched what his father did to his own sister, Jack's aunt, after she talked, right here in this vault. He had seen it last year, and he wished he hadn't.

"Jack." Dino Amore, known to the bosses who hired him as "The Hand," sounded less friendly now. Dino never left evidence and he never missed a target, and he'd made enough money by killing people to buy this little off-the-boardwalk casino in Atlantic City. After Jack saw his father shoot his aunt in the head, he'd been listening to his father's calls, spying on his father's meetings, trying to find anything he could turn over to the feds to get his father arrested and put away forever. He'd read FBI transcripts from other calls and meetings, and he knew the truth. His father loved nobody. His father loved nothing. Jack and Ginger and their mother—they were just social cover for The Hand and the dangerous crew who did his bidding. And now, with all the increased pressure from the feds, The Hand's family had become inconvenient and dangerous.

"Do you want to know where they are, boy? Your mother and your sister? Show yourself. Talk to me and I'll take you to them."

God. Tears jumped to Jack's eyes. *Are they already dead? How did he find them?* Jack felt like something was standing on his heart. He couldn't stop sweating, and the Luger in his hand wouldn't stop shaking.

No way his father had found Mom and Ginger. Jack had hidden them too well. The FBI—they'd already be picking them up at the location Jack had given, saving them, getting them out of Atlantic City and away from New Jersey and The Hand and his men, forever.

"It took balls to call me, Jack." The Hand switched tones again, this time sounding like he did when he really, really wanted Jack to agree with him. "To tell me the truth about what you know, what you plan to do. I know you want to let me change your mind. Why'd you set up this meeting if you didn't want to talk to me?"

Because as long as you're alive, Mom and Ginger won't be safe. Your little crew might look for them, but they won't find a thing. You—you'd never stop.

That's why Jack planned to kill his father, to hit the worst hit man in New Jersey mob history, but now that the asshole was almost here next to him, almost face-to-face—

He's my father.

Jack lowered the Luger and held it against his right leg.

The hand that clamped on Jack's left arm felt like solid iron. Cruel grip. Bruising, down to the bone. Was that emotion in his father's frozen black eyes? The vault lighting and total panic played havoc with Jack's senses. Was his father's smile loving—or triumphant?

The cold barrel of the Heckler and Koch 9-millimeter against Jack's temple gave a firm answer to that question.

The Hand held his gun on his left, but that didn't matter. He could shoot either way, and he was deadly at any range, much less point-blank. "Where are they, boy?"

Jack drew a sudden breath. His eyes focused on the concrete wall a few feet in front of him, on the draped paintings leaning against that wall.

He doesn't know where they are. Mom and Ginger are still safe. I'll die, but they'll be free.

He stopped shaking and tried to yank his arm free from his father's grip. His father held fast.

The Hand didn't fire. Instead, he smiled. "Balls, like I said." He lowered his pistol, but not all the way. His fingers dug into Jack's skin. "These people you think you're friendly with, they've been confusing you. Ginger and your mom, too. Take me to them. We'll work this out."

For about three seconds, Jack wanted to believe him. He wanted to pretend he'd never heard his aunt gurgling as she died with his father's bullet in her brain, that he'd never seen his father wrap her in a rug and carry her out like so much trash. Nobody had ever found her body.

Nobody would ever find his.

The world seemed to narrow to a few feet in a casino vault. Jack's senses spun to high alert.

Maybe it was the flash of brutal glee in the bastard's eye. Maybe Jack saw his father's shoulder flex as he raised the 9-millimeter.

Jack shot his father in the face, just below his left eye.

The Hand's bullet hit Jack in the side.

Jack fell, screaming and digging at the fiery, painful wound.

The Hand died on his feet before he ever fell, looking truly surprised, and—

Jack was back in Afghanistan. Back at the sweltering, blood-soaked mouth of the Valley of the Gods. He could smell the cat-piss stench of Rakshasa demons everywhere, only this time, he knew what they were. He knew the fuckers had killed his men.

He knew they were coming for him just like The Hand. He was losing everything all over again. His family, his home. There was nothing. He had nothing. He *was* nothing. The life in him died. The will to live snuffed out. He gripped his weapon and stared at the swirling sand at the valley's entrance.

He wanted only one thing now. Blood for blood. He wanted killing and he wanted death and he wanted . . .

Something else.

His grip on the hot stock loosened, and the rifle's tip dipped.

He wanted . . .

Someone else.

For a few seconds, his hands seemed different. Older. Maybe stronger. No sunburn.

"Blackjack."

The nickname punched into his awareness. His men used to call him that, in the war. But his men were dead. Most of them. John Cole had made it, and the few guys he'd held back with him from that expedition into the Valley of the Gods—Duncan Sharp and some younger guys. And back at operations, Saul and Cal would be waiting for him to check in, wouldn't they?

God, I fucked this up. It's over, and I fucked it up completely, just like Atlantic City.

Jack hadn't died in that vault, but he'd lost his last name, his past, his home, and the mother and sister who'd gone into the federal witness protection program. Splitting the family was safer than sending them all together, and Jack was just a few months from adulthood. He'd already enlisted, so three months after The Hand died, with his shiny new Blackmore identity and credentials, Jack walked into basic training, an education, a career, and a destiny that finally seemed sterling and planned—until Afghanistan.

He felt like his guts were sliding out of his body, and the taste of sand and sweat filled his mouth.

He turned his head, glanced away from the valley, and saw a light that looked nothing like the ball-scorching sun he dealt with every day. Blue light, soft and cool, like the inside of a building. Maybe like water.

Andy.

His eyes flew open. "Did I get her out?"

He grabbed the first arm he saw. Saul. Saul with his tattoos and his long ponytail and his dark, worried eyes. "You carried her out, man. She's good. She's cool. Better than you."

Damn, this place stank like antiseptic and cleanser.

Cotton sheets didn't feel too bad, but the mattress felt like something from a cheap motel.

Hospital bed. Needles in one arm. Bandages—neck, arm, leg. Jack took stock of himself on autopilot, registering John Cole's big square face and Duncan Sharp's hometown-boy mug a few feet from him. Duncan and John were standing side by side at the foot of his bed.

"You got old," he told them both. "And Saul, you got weird. I was . . ." He stopped himself, not sure what to call it, so he just said, "Dreaming."

Saul waited until Jack let him go, then nodded once, gazing across Jack and out the hospital room's only window. "We all go back to the Valley now and then."

Jack's awareness cranked around slowly, but wound itself tighter and tighter until everything lined itself up again and he could settle on the only thing that mattered. "Andy?"

He looked straight at John Cole, then at Duncan, who said, "You've been out three days, and she's a Sibyl. Can't even tell she got shot."

Jack was beginning to realize he felt like he'd been chewed up by something with teeth the size of freight cars. "You shitting me? I know they heal fast, but—"

"She's fine," Saul said. "I swear on my brother's life."

"I lost track of—I thought I was—that we were back in—" Jack couldn't say it. Closed his eyes and tried to erase Atlantic City and Afghanistan from his mind's slate completely. He remembered seeing Andy had been shot. He remembered picking her up, trying to get her out of the alley. But it was a bloody, foggy haze. "Did I embarrass myself?"

"You got a little turned around about where was where and what war you were fighting," Saul said, "but I think you did yourself proud by the lady."

Jack opened his eyes, and the white of the hospital walls felt blinding.

"I *know* you did yourself proud," John said. "Asshole. Always have to be the hero, don't you?"

They were being too nice to him. Now Jack was positive he'd let everything go to shit. Everything he owned hurt like a bitch, and now he was getting sick to his stomach, wondering if Andy really was okay.

Motion at the door caught his eye, and he recognized Bela Sharp in street clothes—jeans and a stylish tank. Camille Cole was with her, also wearing jeans, red hair dusting the shoulders of her yellow shirt. Behind them came Dio Allard and a little bit of wind.

Bela and Camille went to their husbands and gave Jack friendly smiles, but Dio stopped at the hospital room door and just glared at him. She had pulled her blond hair back so severely that her gray eyes tilted up at the corners. Made her look twice as mean.

"Talk," she said, and the wind in the room blew so hard Jack's IV pole rattled. "Say something so I can go back to the townhouse and tell her you're awake and fine. It's the only way I'll be able to keep her still and resting."

"Awake and fine," Jack reported even though he thought his right shoulder might bust off his body and crack into pieces. His chest, gut, and arms looked like somebody had covered him with bruise tattoos.

Dio gave him a once-over, then something that looked almost—but not quite—like a smile, and she left without saying a word to anybody. Air seemed to be sucked out of the room behind her, and Saul said, "That woman's got amazing energy."

"You have no idea." Bela sounded like she wanted to groan, but Camille laughed a little, enough to loosen the mood in the room.

Jack had a flash of memory—Dio roaring into the alley, riding a tornado and dropping out of the sky like a knife-throwing Harpy. She might be the world's meanest air Sibyl, like Andy kept saying, but she was damned useful in a fight. He wished he could pull off a trick like that tornado. He found himself glad she was the one heading back to check on Andy. Hell, it was probably taking five or six Sibyls just to keep Andy contained in the brownstone. She'd want to be out hunting the assholes who'd fired on the Jeep.

Maybe she'd want to come here. See me.

That was pushing his luck.

But he remembered kissing her, he remembered her kissing him back, a million years ago before all the bullets started flying.

"We had six big bastards shooting at us," he told Duncan, John, Saul, Bela, and Camille. "MAC-10s. A planned attack. They took out our tires to be sure we crashed in an alley, then they came at us from both sides. Riana Lowell's gonna be pissed about her Jeep. Looks like somebody took a can opener to it."

"Riana's out for blood," Bela confirmed, "but not yours. Andy says the gunmen looked human?"

"Yeah, but off. Not quite right." Jack tried to lift his arms to give proportions, but stopped when pain jagged through his chest. "Shoulders were too big, and they ate bullets like candy—heart, head, it didn't matter. I slowed them down by aiming for their eyes."

Camille pointed at the tiled floor. "Andy tried to shoot through their ankles. Low man wins and all that."

"Is she really okay?" Jack addressed the question to Bela, because he figured that, as the head of the fighting group, she'd be most likely to tell him the truth.

Bela's exotic face got tense, but her words came out gentle and kind. "She's fine, even though she gave up a lot of energy to help you."

Jack gazed at her, then at Camille. "You mean the waves in the alley? The water she pulled from all over New York City to try to drown them?"

"That, and she used her power to do some deep healing." Camille pointed to his bruises and bandages. "It's why you didn't die and why you're already awake and on the mend. Andy doesn't know how to regulate her healing energy yet, or even how to call it on purpose, so it cost her."

Jack wanted to smack something. He didn't like the thought of Andy risking herself to make him feel better, not even a little bit. He'd taken bullets before and gotten better pretty quick on his own. They'd have to talk about this, he and Andy, as soon as he saw her.

And at the thought of seeing her, the rush of stubborn anger faded as fast as it had flared, and he just felt worried again. "After it was over—I'm sorry if I wasn't . . . myself."

Bela shrugged. Her expression seemed casual, but her dark eyes blazed into him, completely intense, like she wanted to be sure he knew she meant what she said. "No harm, no foul."

Jack glanced at the door. "It was Dio I knocked past trying to get Andy out of there. I'll apologize to her when I see her again."

"Not necessary," Camille said. "Dio didn't hit you with a knife or a lightning bolt, so I'd say you're good."

Bela pointed toward the hospital room window, in the general direction of the brownstone. "We got some blood from the freaks in the alley—yours and Andy's, too, but a good measure of theirs. They are mostly human, and the DNA matches files on Klopol Pashka, Ari Demelov, and Shada Nour."

"Seneca's clan. Ari Seneca, Foucci's biggest rival." Jack turned his attention to Saul, then to John and Duncan. "That should have been obvious, given their past association with the Rakshasa and Griffen's sorcerers—and who they've been killing. But our sources and observations indicate there weren't any Seneca people left in the city. Not after the slaughter in Central Park last year."

Camille touched the crescent moon charm around her neck "The DNA matches those profiles, but those men have been enhanced. More like a gene splice than demon conversions." She held the charm for a few seconds, her eyes unfocused. John slipped his arm around her waist, which seemed to help her say the rest of what she needed to tell him. "The demon essence looks like Rakshasa. Jack, it looks like it came from an Eldest."

For a long moment Jack sat very still, fending off the sneaking tendrils of his war nightmare. The blood. The Valley of the Gods. "That's not possible. The Eldest are dead."

"Yet we've got an air Sibyl dreaming about Tarek coming back from the grave, and now we've got enhanced criminals with Eldest demon essence." Bela's no-nonsense voice seemed to fill up the hospital room and all of Jack's mind. "The Coven's upped their game. Who knows what they're capable of doing? Until we've got a better explanation, I think we better assume that at least one Eldest made it out of Camille's molten metal bath, and a few of Seneca's men survived and were willing to get changed into something . . . other."

Jack didn't want to go there. Not yet. Not at all. His head started to ache because he was clenching his teeth, so he loosened his jaw enough to say, "Supermobsters. Just what the world fucking needs."

"Supermobsters." Duncan glanced at his wife, then at Jack. "Great. Look, we've got to take those bastards down in a big hurry, before they take over."

Saul keyed on this, getting serious, which Saul rarely did. "A crime family with supernatural foot soldiers could consolidate enough power to pose a serious risk to the entire NYPD, not to mention the public."

"Stop right now," Dio hissed from somewhere in the hall outside Jack's room, "or so help me, I'll blow you all the way to Oz."

"Don't make me put a dart in your ass, sweetcheeks." Andy's voice rang clear and menacing in the hospital quiet, and the sound of it made Jack sit up straighter. He ground his teeth against the pain of shifting his weight and waited, watching the door. Hoping. He wanted a look at her. Needed to see her up and moving. Somehow that would make everything square again, at least for the moment.

From the corner of his eye, Jack noted that Bela was smiling. The expression seemed sincere even though she was also rubbing her temples. "I knew peace and sanity couldn't last forever. Andy must have taken off from the brownstone and headed here before Dio ever got home— but obviously Dio tracked her down."

Wind blasted down the hospital hallway, rattling carts and sending paper medication cups dancing past Jack's door. A split second later came the unmistakable sounds of a sprinkler tearing loose, water splashing everywhere, and raised voices from the nurses' station.

"Excuse me," Bela said, hurrying out the door. Camille went right behind her. Jack had no elemental power, but he could have sworn he felt energy humming through him, buzzing all around him.

"Probably our cue to get the hell out, too," Saul said, and he and John and Duncan followed the women into the hallway.

More raised voices shattered the hospital's peace. Dio, followed by Bela. The guys said something. Then Andy spoke.

Jack kept his eyes fixed on the hospital room door.

She stormed into view a second later, her red hair and blousy white shirt damp and her freckled face red like a sunburn. Her jeans slung water with every step, and her sneakers squeaked like chalk on a blackboard.

"They're fucking nuts," she bellowed, pointing down the hallway. "There's *nothing* wrong with me, and I *am* ready to work."

"You look perfect to me," Jack said, vaguely aware she might kill him, then have her regrets later. "And your accent gets thicker when you're angry."

More water trickled down from her shoulders, but the frenetic red eased out of her cheeks as she faced him. For a moment she just looked at him, like she might be counting toes and fingers and making sure all his body parts were where she expected them to be.

"You talk smooth yourself," she said with normal volume. "But you'll take their side."

Jack had done his own limb counting, but he still couldn't relax. "Anything broken? Everything moving like it should?"

"Good as new." She walked toward him, raised her arms over his bed, and flexed her lean, well-toned muscles. Warm water rained all over his bedsheets. "Oh. Sorry."

He examined her still-outstretched arms, the gentle

curve of her neck, and the swell of her breasts. "I'm not sorry."

"I was worried about you." She lowered her arms. "I'd have been here sooner, but—"

"But you have good friends who look after you, one of whom makes a mean tornado." Jack couldn't keep his eyes off Andy, but he figured if a threat like Dio showed up in the doorway, Andy would react, so they could both duck in time.

"Something like that." She kept looking at him, her gaze steady.

He gestured to the nearest chair. "You can sit, but it's a hospital chair. Your butt might cramp."

Andy's expression changed several times in the next moment of silence, settling on concern and frustration. "I know you're sore as hell. I wish I could do more for you. I could try, if you'll let me."

Jack wished he could push himself out of the hospital bed and take her in his arms to make sure everything still felt right. To make sure everything was still the same between them. "No. You need all your energy for yourself right now. I've taken my share of bullets and I bounce back, no magic required."

"I'm not magic, Jack."

"That's debatable."

Andy glanced down at her hands and curled her fingers into fists. "I should know more about the healing I'm supposed to do. Sometimes I think I'm getting it, or part of it, and the rest of the time, I don't have a clue. I don't know what I'm supposed to do."

Jack could tell the uncertainty and confusion ate at her, and he understood that. She was used to being on top of any job she tackled, used to competence and certainty. He understood that. He also understood that it felt like shit to be up against something you couldn't even define, much less conquer.

He lifted the arm closest to her, the one free of needles and tubes, and reached for her hand.

She caught his fingers, then pressed both of her palms against his knuckles. So soft, but what a grip. Strong woman. He liked that, and the physical contact solidified the fact that she really had come through the shooting in one piece. He looked at her, surprised by the fact that being with her made him feel stronger even if she didn't do anything special to enhance his healing.

"Practice on yourself and your fighting group." Jack kept his hand still so she wouldn't let him go. "I'll be on my feet fast enough. Always am."

She massaged his fingers, and Jack had no idea which kind of magic created the heat creeping up his arms. "You talk to Bela and Camille and the guys about what we saw? Did they tell you about the supermobsters?"

"Yeah. I think we came out pretty good, all things considered."

Jack shifted his hand so that he caught hold of her fingers instead. He gave her a gentle squeeze, just enough to get her attention. "The rest of the OCU and the other Sibyl groups can handle hunting for them. I don't want you back on the streets yet."

"Told you you'd take their side." Andy frowned, but she didn't pull her hand away from him. "When I go on patrol again isn't your call. I don't work for you, remember?"

Jack knew he should step carefully, but he found himself worrying a little less about offending her. This was too important to him. "I was hoping you were working *with* me."

She hesitated. Gave him a look probably designed to piss him off. It tickled him instead.

"You use that smile like a weapon, Blackmore. It's not fair."

"Is it working?"

"No." She moved her eyes to the wall. Back to his. Showed him she had her own weapons-grade smile. "Yes, damn it. But you missed our date."

Jack pulled her closer to his bed. She didn't resist. "Yeah. I stood you up. Are you going to tell me what I have to do to earn a second chance, or do I have to guess?"

Andy leaned down and kissed him, her soft red curls brushing his cheeks as her lips tasted his, as her tongue slid easily across his mouth. Jack closed his eyes and let himself have the sensation, have every bit of her softness, her smell. Still so new but already familiar.

Mine.

When Andy lengthened the kiss, when she pressed closer to him, heated but careful of his wounds, he tried to tell himself not to get possessive, not to take a chance on scaring her away, but he gave it up fast. He rested his good arm across the small of her back, holding her to him, enjoying each warm second of the contact. She raised her fingers and stroked his cheeks. Electricity. More heat. Every part of him responded.

Jack thought he might have to take the damned IV out himself if she didn't stop, because bullet holes or no, he couldn't take this much longer.

A second shy of the point of no return, Andy moved back, trailing her fingers down the bare skin of his neck and chest, giving him a little push back against the bed. "Easy. I don't want to set off any alarms."

"Too late for that, sweetheart."

She smiled again, and he watched her, enjoying her even as he felt her thoughts slip away from him again. Her gaze wandered, then she seemed to come back and pull her focus together. "You said I don't have to censor with you, right?"

Jack raised his arm and managed to touch her cheek. "I meant that."

"Then I have a question I want to ask you, not for public consumption." Her eyes went clear and her features sharpened. Work stuff again. He could tell. That was fine with him—a relief, actually. He'd never met anybody else whose mind worked on two tracks all the time—life, sure, but also the job, always the job, whatever case seemed most pressing.

"Shoot," he told her. "Ah, not literally, please."

She moved out of range of his touch, folded her arms, and turned to look out the window. Jack figured she had to be hunting for words, trying to pull something together in her own head.

She didn't sound tentative at all when she asked, "Did that attack feel personal to you?"

Jack's eyebrows drew together, and pain flickered in his temples. "I hadn't given that any thought. I assumed the assholes went after us because I'm OCU and you're a Sibyl, and they were ready to show off their new muscle."

"Maybe I'm off." Andy kept her arms folded and kept looking out the window. "Maybe we were just a grand example, a first volley."

"But you think it was more than that." Jack could tell from the rigid lines of her stance that she had gone deep into her instincts, police-born or Sibyl-bred, he didn't know, but he felt inclined to listen no matter what the source. "Is this all instinct, or did you see or sense something more specific?"

"I felt like they were coming after me." She let her arms relax, but she still didn't look at him. "Before the attack, I picked up some kind of strange energy, but I also thought I heard something. Maybe it's more like I heard it in my head, my mind. My name. Like those mobsters had been wound up and sent out with me as their goal—like Asmodai, remember? How the Legion created their demons, then gave them some sort of talisman to target people?"

"And they'd go until they destroyed the target, or got destroyed." Jack didn't like what she was saying, but he had to give it credence. "It doesn't hold totally, because they did retreat when overwhelming force arrived—but if you felt targeted, then we have to assume you were. Ever have any dealings with Seneca's family?"

Andy let out a little groan. "Not that I know of, but it's possible I arrested somebody's uncle's cousin or girlfriend or boyfriend or whatever. Who knows? I've been doing this for a while."

This felt too fucking familiar. Somebody he cared about in the sights of a soulless, heartless bunch of mobsters. Jack's head reached the pounding stage. He had to lean against his pillows for support, which pissed him off. "If they were targeting you specifically, that's another good reason for you to stay in the background."

Until I'm out of this friggin' bed. Until I can watch your six.

She turned to face him again. "I was thinking exactly the opposite. If it's me they want, then I'm the one who can draw them out. Only with a lot more firepower on my side this time."

"You. As bait." Jack's head got fuzzy, but he stayed upright and looked at her, even though her image seemed divided as he squinted against the burning ache in his head, his bruises, and the freshly healing holes in his neck and arm. "That's not happening."

"What if I wait until you're better?" Another smile, this one teasing, but Jack didn't think any of this was funny.

"We're not negotiating here, Andy."

The smile went away, replaced by a stern, stubborn look he recognized all too quickly. "No, we aren't."

Jack sat up straighter, clenching the sheets in both fists to fight back the misery in his body. A thousand orders and commands shot through his head, but just as fast his better sense told him each of those would just make her more determined to do something dangerous and get herself killed faster.

He started to tell her no way, no how, that he'd order the entire OCU to stand guard over her, but when he got his mouth open, he said, "Please. I don't want anything to happen to you."

Andy's face softened and she came toward him again, closer, until she pressed her hip against his bedrail and rested her fingertips against his shoulder. The contact soothed him, calmed him, eased the pain, but Jack kept his eyes locked on hers.

"That's mutual, you know." She leaned down and kissed him again, even softer this time, her lips warm silk against his. She smelled so good, so fresh, driving back the stink of hospitals and illness and stuff Jack didn't want to think about.

Jack moved his lips to her ear. "Not while I'm like this. If you have to do this thing, wait for me. Let me be there with you."

She shifted against him, and her lips touched his ear. Her breath whispered across his awareness. "I can make that deal, if it'll help you get better."

He relaxed, hearing the commitment. Not a promise, but good enough. "It helps."

"Fine. I'll lie low and be careful until you're full force again—not that I can't take care of myself, but just because I feel like doing you a favor. It's all the bruises. I always feel sorry for handsome men with a shitload of bruises."

Sweet God, if she didn't stop using her nails on his face, his neck, he'd do something that ripped a bunch of stitches—and he probably wouldn't care until he bled out on the antiseptic tile floor.

"I've had worse."

She kissed him again. "About that date."

"I'm listening."

Andy's eyes gleamed, no trace of work thoughts or doubts or anything other than total focus on him. "Ever had sex in a hospital bed?"

Every vessel, muscle, and nerve in Jack's body answered her, and he couldn't stop the wince and groan. Screw it. He had to sit up and get his arms around her, and right now.

She backed off before he could carry through with that slightly suicidal plan, leaving one finger on his chest. "Somebody's not ready to play, and guess what? It isn't me."

He bit back a groan, mixed pain and frustration. "Somebody's a tease, and guess what? It isn't me."

The pressure from her finger—nothing and everything, just like the waves of heat he could sense passing through her body, passing through his own. "I'm not teasing you, Jack. As soon as you're up for it, we've got unfinished business."

Jack wanted to tell her he was up for anything, and right now, but he knew he had started to lose the battle. Energy left him like it was leaking out of every bruise, and he couldn't keep his eyes all the way open.

Don't sleep. His lids tried to lift. Didn't make it all the way. *She'll leave. She'll be gone, and you'll dream.*

He didn't know which of those things would feel worse.

"Stay," he muttered as he drifted off even though he didn't want to.

From somewhere close, Andy said, "I'll be right here."

❨ 18 ❩

Andy . . .

The voice didn't sound natural. Wasps buzzing. Broken boat motors whining through peaceful waters.

Andy . . .

It sounded like—like a *they*. Like a lot of people saying her name all at the same time, only they were hissing it. Spitting it, somehow, like they hated her more than anything in the universe.

Murderer . . .

Andy squinted through the darkness. The water surrounding her felt too thick and dark, like she had chosen to wade through a pool of octopus ink. She tried to see, wanted to get a grip on her own feelings and instincts, but nothing felt clear. Nothing made sense.

Show yourself, bitch!

Andy whirled in the murk.

A knife flashed toward her—

Her eyes popped open even as she gripped her bedspread in the brownstone. Her breathing sounded like asthmatic wheezes as her lungs reached for water but found only air. She closed her eyes again and forced herself to relax. It took half her energy to make herself let go of the bedspread, but little by little she was able to breathe easy, then deep. Her buzzing, swimming head calmed, and the peaceful sand and coral tones of her bedroom came back into focus.

"I'm just too tired," she muttered to herself. Jack being shot, her time with him in the hospital on top of all her other responsibilities—and now an escalation in fighting between crime families that was running the NYPD ragged. Of course she was tired. That's all it was. A dream reflecting her exhaustion.

If she fell asleep, she'd probably have another one.

No, thanks.

Stretching to be sure she didn't topple over when she stood, Andy got up and went to the bedroom's front window. Sunlight streamed through the lace curtains, and she pulled them aside to get a better view of traffic and Central Park. In a spot two places down from the brownstone, an unmarked car with three OCU officers kept vigil on Jack's orders. He took her seriously, about the attack in the alley feeling personal, and after that dream . . .

Her eyes strayed over the park as she sensed elemental energies. Mostly flickers and streams, people with paranormal talents passing by as they enjoyed the summer day. Most of them had no idea they had any special abilities, but some probably did. Maybe a few were Wiccans or Pagans or practitioners of other older faiths, like Vodoun, that tied people more closely to the rhythms and energies of the universe.

A light, whispering touch of wind announced Dio before she walked into the room, and Andy welcomed the breeze as she came to stand next to her at the window.

"Were you dreaming?" Dio asked, her voice unusually quiet.

"Yes."

Dio kept her gaze straight ahead, not intruding. "I felt something, like an agitation. Maybe it was your dream, but Bela says the NYPD found four more dead mobsters—this time from another Russian crime family."

Andy's muscles burned from sudden tension. "Were they torn apart?"

"No." Dio sounded as tired as Andy felt. "Shot in the head, old-school. OCU isn't on this new case, but you know they're all tied together."

"Christ. We have to do something to stop this before there's a lot of collateral damage." Andy couldn't stop looking at her OCU bodyguards, feeling guilty about the manpower loss but increasingly relieved that they were close at hand. "In my dream, somebody was calling my name, like I thought I heard in the alley before the shooters showed up. And the time before that, with the projective trap, I heard the same thing."

The windows in the brownstone were bulletproof and elementally treated, so neither of them felt like they had to step out of view. Dio checked for the OCU car, seeming to take as much comfort in its presence as Andy did, and nodded. "At least we've got backup right here, even if we don't really need it. That dream just makes everything twice as weird."

Andy's gaze drifted back to the walkers inside the park, and outside on the sidewalk, too. Here and there, elemental energy made itself known, almost like a flash of color. Andy wondered how many of them did know about themselves, and how many remained blissfully unaware of the worlds within the world, the existence of truly paranormal beings.

"I used to be one of those people out there," Andy said, sounding sadder than she intended. "Clueless. Able to live without worrying about nightmare shit nobody should ever have to deal with on a regular basis."

Dio picked up her meaning immediately. "I can't imagine what it would be like to grow up human with no knowledge of Sibyls and powers and the creatures we have to fight, then have to get used to it all in just a few years."

"It's been a hell of a ride. And now something's after me."

Dio's knuckles paled as her fingers dug into the windowsill. "You're sure of it."

"Yes. I'm positive. The voice I'm hearing is faint and whispery, but it's real and saying my name. The two attacks were targeted at me."

"Then we should go after the Coven right fucking now—we should risk tracking them with our projective energy." Dio's fist banged against the windowsill. "If we could take them out, we could probably stop the mob infighting before a whole bunch of civilians get caught in the crossfire."

"I promised Jack I'd wait until he was strong enough to go with us. And Bela will never agree to us tracking anything, not after what happened with those coins." Andy sighed. "I'm not around enough to help her stop worrying."

"You're still doing it, you know." Dio's knuckles turned even whiter as wind moved faster in the room, blowing Andy's hair across her face and shoulders. "Stretching yourself so thin it's not healthy. All you've done this week is spend time with Jack at the hospital, stare at mug shots to help you with that sketch of Frank the mobster, and run back and forth between here and Motherhouse Kérkira to check on Elana and the adepts."

"I've played a lot of battle with Neala and Ethan—and I've slept a little." Andy didn't feel defensive because she was too surprised at Dio expressing concern outright like this. Still, she had to do what she had to do—be a fighter, a Mother, a godmother, and still enough of a cop to make herself happy.

"A few hours, maybe. With bad dreams. We're on patrol in a few hours, and you're exhausted."

Andy thought about arguing with her, but instead she pushed away from the window and flopped on her bed. She stared at her blank, boring ceiling and wondered if it was possible to clone herself.

"I know you can't help the fact you've been scarce lately." Dio's voice sounded atypically warm, almost friendly, which let Andy know that Dio's concern for her fatigue ran deep.

She sat up on the edge of the bed a little too quickly, and a head rush almost sent her toppling onto the floor. "I'm sorry."

Dio steadied Andy with a hand to the shoulder. "And you say that a lot."

Andy bit her tongue so she wouldn't say it again. Damn, but now that she had her full attention on Dio, she realized Dio looked like hell. Her blond hair, usually so neat and carefully combed, fell in disarray around her thin shoulders, and her eyes seemed unusually dull. Black circles beneath them made her look like she had on a mask.

I wonder what other details I miss, all day every day. And I probably don't look so hot, either. I think I've had on these same jeans for three days, never mind this stupid yellow blouse. With coffee stains.

Dio saw Andy studying her face and let out a breath. "I had another dream, too."

Wind stirred through the room, weak and cool, nothing like the quick, forceful bursts Dio usually gave off as a matter of course. The air around her smelled like rain, but salty. Almost like tears.

Andy got a little more worried. "Have you told Bela and Camille?"

"Why? Nothing's different. Same as last time but more vivid, like everything I'm seeing has gotten more possible." Dio didn't say probable, but the worry in her exhausted gray eyes made Andy wonder. Before she could ask any more questions, Dio cut her off. "Jack got to go home, right?"

"Yes. He's back at the townhouse." Andy felt a twinge

as she said this, because she hadn't let herself see him since he got released.

Dio's pretty face twisted into a confused frown. "Not to be rude, but why aren't you with him?"

Andy stared at Dio, unable to believe she had shifted her attitude about Jack, and especially about Andy dating Jack.

"I'm sorry I acted like an ass about all that before. I just—it's more change." Color crept into Dio's cheeks, then vanished as fast as it came. "It's me, and us maybe, I don't know. Losing you somehow."

The look Dio gave Andy was so open and guileless Andy almost went speechless. It took her a few seconds to recover her balance and understand what Dio needed to hear. "You're not losing me. You'll never lose me. And I haven't seen Jack because I didn't want to wear myself out and make myself totally useless to all of you. I've had to spend time on Kérkira and with the kids and on patrol and stuff." Andy tried to sound casual even though that didn't match her emotions about staying away from Jack. "Plus I thought it wouldn't be a good idea. He needs a few days to rest."

And I need a few more days to screw my head on straight about him.

All the hours of talking in the hospital, trading military stories and work tales, and going over strategies on their current case had made everything between them seem . . . normal. Calmer. More real. Somehow that bothered her more than the strangeness of suddenly liking the man, of finding him attractive instead of the most annoying person on earth. At least when stuff felt strange, she could hold back.

Now things seemed more complicated.

Dio eased down to the bed beside Andy, looking small and too thin against the rumpled spread as she pulled her legs to her chest and wrapped her arms around her knees. "You have a date scheduled, right?"

Andy shifted to face Dio, feeling her stretched-out jeans twist on her hips. "I'm taking him out next week."

Dio gestured toward Andy's closet. "Are you wearing that dress I want to steal? The dark green one with the killer neckline?"

Andy smiled at Dio, knowing that any dress of hers would hang like an oversized T-shirt on Dio's slender frame. "Plan on it, yep."

Dio's smile seemed relaxed enough, but a little sad. "He doesn't stand a chance." She blinked at Andy, and more air stirred in the room, a little warmer this time. "You're wondering what we all think of this. Of you and Jack."

Andy's heart fluttered. "Yeah. I guess I am."

"Bela and Camille think it's funny." Dio swirled her fingers toward the ceiling theatrically, like she was revealing some deep, dark secret to the heavens. "Weird, but fitting."

"Weird. Fitting." Andy thought she could live with that. She agreed with it, in fact. "And you?"

Dio lowered her hand and once more hugged her own knees. The air in the room moved faster, heating with each lap around the tiny space. "Am I that important?"

"Yes. You're practically my roommate." Andy felt her hair stir against her face and neck. *And I feel like I'm letting you down. Like you need healing more than anybody, and I don't know how to help you.*

Dio waited a few seconds, and the breeze in the room, confused and frenetic, told Andy how hard she was thinking about her answer. "Honestly, I don't know what I think. Before Jack showed up at Kérkira to ask you to come home, you still seemed pretty much hung up on Sal. You haven't even gone on a date since Sal died, and now, boom, you're with this other guy. A guy you hated a few months ago."

The bald assessment made Andy go tense inside. She found herself straining through Dio's words to make sure she caught all the meaning, all the intentions. "I didn't really know Jack back then."

"I'm not sure any of us did." Dio's breezes calmed as she spoke. "But I think he wanted it that way. Maybe that's part of what's worrying me. What else is he hiding? What else do we not know about Jack?"

"Good point, and good questions." Andy searched her instincts and came up with nothing concrete, but a sense that yeah, Jack was probably holding a few things back.

But who wouldn't be?

They weren't sixteen-year-old virgins. Both of them had pasts, had secrets, had parts of themselves they hadn't shared with anyone, or didn't plan to share unless circumstances—and the other person—happened to be just exactly right.

Still . . .

More flutters started in her chest and belly.

Were they good flutters? Anticipation of getting to know Jack even better—or worried flutters giving her the first hint that something might go horribly wrong between them?

"Sal's gone." Andy looked at her hands, wondering if she'd ever put that in words so baldly before, even to herself. "I think I've known that for a long time, but with Sal, I learned what it feels like to be serious, to be in love, to have a relationship mean something. That's why I haven't gone on dates since then. Dates seemed stupid."

"You don't want to do casual anymore." Dio's voice seemed to grow heavier with understanding. "You don't want to spend time with a man unless you know for sure he's got serious potential."

"Exactly. I mean, I could do fun and casual, I guess, but it's not what I want anymore." Andy looked at Dio again, and noted that her gray eyes had darkened and worry lines stood out on her tense face. "Now what's wrong?"

"You just admitted Jack's not casual. So things are probably going to change around here. Again. Even faster than I worried they would."

"I didn't—wait a second. Whoa. You're way ahead of me."

"No, I'm not. But if it makes you feel better to think so, just keep kidding yourself." Dio smiled, but this time the expression seemed forced and it faded fast. "Just be careful, Andy. Jack feels like a wanderer to me, a man with wind in his heart. That's air Sibyl for somebody who doesn't settle down. Somebody who doesn't stay in one place too long."

The flutters in Andy's midsection got worse. "I've wondered about that myself."

"Have you asked him?"

"The time hasn't seemed right, and I don't want him to think—I don't want to give him the idea that—"

"That you're developing serious feelings for him?" Dio's knowing look brought heat to Andy's face.

She smacked Dio's knee. "I thought fire Sibyls were supposed to be the ones all about truth and open communication."

Dio rolled her eyes. "Oh, for the sake of the Goddess. Our fire Sibyl works in the earth Sibyl's lab and does more research than I do. In case you haven't noticed, the roles in this fighting group get a little mixed up sometimes." She yawned and stretched, and unfolded herself from Andy's bed. "I think it has something to do with a water Sibyl being present—figuring out our flow and all of that."

"Thanks a lot," Andy said to Dio's retreating back,

glad that the wind in her wake felt warmer and stronger and more normal now, at least.

"Anytime," Dio shot back as she drifted into the hallway, heading for her too-neat room. "Somebody's got to do truth around here."

"This isn't the same area patrol reported and examined before." Bela's leathers creaked as she knelt on the Central Park grass near the path that led to the sidewalk across from the brownstone. The moon hung in the summer sky, glowing over her head like a round, white lamp and illuminating every sad detail of the dead rabbit she prodded with her finger. "This is fresh. We might be able to get something. I don't think natural material like leaves and grass can be used to make a projective trap—and I don't think the Coven's doing this, anyway."

As Bela made a hand signal to let Dio know everything was okay, that she didn't have to pull in closer from her surveillance and cleanup position, Andy and Camille stared at the dead grass around the rabbit. Nearby, Andy saw patches of dead leaves in trees that should have been rich with summer foliage. Dio was probably close to those trees, maybe in one of them, keeping a wide view of the fighting group and any potential threat. She'd let them know later what she picked up from the leaves. Andy knew that her group's projective talents were rare, that they could see things other fighting groups couldn't, especially when they worked together—but stuff like this could get unpleasant.

Get over it. Work to do. She closed her eyes and gripped her crescent moon pendant, doing a preliminary scan of all the water energy in the area. "Raw power killed the rabbit, and probably the grass and leaves, too. Elemental. Nonspecific. You're right that it's not the Coven, because this energy feels too old. Like, ancient. Whoever did this, their power seems . . . older than time,

but natural. Natural paranormal, I mean. Nothing enhanced. And I don't think they're demons of any sort."

Bela had hold of the charm around her neck, and Andy
knew she had done her own initial read of the earth and
earth energy, to see what it could tell them. "This isn't the
ground the creatures usually walk. New York's not their
preferred habitat, and it's costing them a lot of energy to
be here. To be here and not do more of this." She pointed
to the dead patches.

Camille went last, but she didn't handle the crescent
moon charm she had made for herself last year. Her ability to use her projective energy had gotten so strong she
rarely needed to focus her power like the rest of them.
"This all feels . . . familiar. I keep wanting to say it's fire
Sibyl energy or something like it, but I don't know what
that might be. Or I can't remember. It's poking the back
of my brain, trying to come forward."

Bela prodded the rabbit's carcass again. "Not human.
And not something we've encountered."

"Not something we *usually* encounter," Camille corrected. "Maybe—maybe it's something I sensed a long
time ago, when I used to run around in the tunnels at
Motherhouse Ireland. After Jack and the OCU and Sibyl
patrols reported seeing something like this the first time,
I searched the archives, and Dio did, too. We didn't find
much. I mean, vampires and some species of Fae cause
minor die-offs if they use the full force of their elemental
abilities, but this—"

"This is like a feeding," Andy said, settling into the
strange energy and understanding it a little more. "Like
whatever drained the energy from these things did so to
sustain itself. They did it with a lot of restraint, like drinking water in the desert."

"They didn't come here to watch us," Bela said. "The
patterns in the earth, the way they moved—our brownstone's not the focal point. It's here, and here, and right

over there." She pointed toward the trees. "Near some other energy, a lot weaker—residuals from perverted rituals. Griffen or some of his Coven."

"We've known the Coven has been trying to do surveillance on a lot of Sibyl locations, but they can't get past our elemental locks." Andy let go of her charm. "All they can do is spy on us, and I bet the die-offs match up to a lot of vantage points near Sibyls' dwellings."

"So whoever or whatever is doing this, they're watching our watchers," Camille muttered. "Why?"

"No idea." Bela stood, dusting off her hands. "I think the better question might be, are they friend or foe?"

"I'm betting they're neutral." Andy did what she could to put her instincts into words, trying to explain the flavor of the water she had sampled. "Nobody's side. Whatever purpose these creatures have, we're ancillary to it."

Camille frowned. "And if we accidentally get in their way?"

"Let's not." Bela folded her arms. "After we get back to the brownstone, put out the word. If Sibyls get a sighting on these things, don't take a shot. Leave them alone unless they make a move against us."

All the unknowns in this equation made Andy squirm. She'd rather have a better grip on what was leaving dead animals and foliage behind, even if it meant stirring up the creatures with unwanted approaches. "Shouldn't we try to make contact?"

"I don't think so," Bela said. "If they wanted to talk, they could have knocked on the door and said hello. There are things in the universe much older than Sibyls, and very few of them are actually evil—unless they're provoked."

"Problem is," Camille said, "provocation takes different forms for different beings."

Andy thought about the ocean, about the zillions of

creatures beneath the waves, and the octopus she'd startled. A peaceful little thing that had coated her in purple only because she scared it, and all it had taken to scare it was extra motion, maybe a few words. The tension in her belly eased a fraction. Maybe these beings creating the die-offs weren't any more menacing than the wart with eight legs. Maybe they were just . . . shy, or whatever.

"Maybe I should talk to Ona," Camille said.

Andy gave Camille a look just like Bela's—surprised and wary. "Ona doesn't give audiences, you know. She's on my island because she really doesn't like talking to other fire Sibyls."

Camille's smile always made her look gentle and wise. "She'll talk to me. Maybe not for long, but long enough."

"You're going to do that thing," Andy said, unease flaring through her all over again.

"If you can do without me for a bit." Camille gazed at Bela, waiting for permission.

Bela let out a fast, loud sigh. "Okay, fine. If you're sure Ona won't kill you."

Camille knelt and retrieved some of the dead grass. Andy had a horrible moment when she thought Camille might take the rabbit, but she left the carcass alone. She put the grass in the pocket of her leathers, gave them all a smile, gripped her crescent moon pendant, and seemed to melt into the ground.

The sight of it gave Andy shivers. "I still find that completely creepy."

"She's not really disappearing or dropping into the earth," Bela said. "She's just using ancient energy channels without having to do the dance or use a projective mirror to open them."

Moving almost instantly to where she wanted to go, which in this case was to Motherhouse Kérkira to have a confab with the world's oldest—and craziest—fire Sibyl.

The only other fire Sibyl on the planet who could use that little moving-with-no-mirrors trick. Ona was so unbalanced Andy figured Motherhouse Ireland had only let her stay in their castle so many years because Mother Keara had a soft spot for her. "It's creepy," Andy insisted. "It's creepy when she does it, and it's even creepier when Ona does it. Always popping up where you don't expect her."

"I wish I could learn how." Bela actually sounded wistful even though she was already shaking her head and waving off her own thoughts. "I know, I know. I'm an earth Sibyl. The channels only open for fire Sibyls—but you have to admit, that trick could be way useful and save tons of time across a life span."

"Dio's tornados are pretty fast," Andy grumbled. "That doesn't mean I want to ride one ever again. They make me puke. God only knows what melting across thousands of miles would do to me."

"Tornados are fast but messy," Bela said. "You know Dio doesn't like messy."

Andy thought about her old friend Merilee, the first air Sibyl she had ever known. Merilee's living space always looked like one of Dio's tornados had just blown through it, even now that Merilee had gotten married. Explosive messiness was an air Sibyl thing. A trait. Why didn't Dio have it?

She's too hard on herself. A perfectionist. If she can't do everything, if she can't do it just exactly right, then screw it.

Damn, that sounds a little too familiar.

"Don't look at me like that," Bela said, the defensive edge to her voice sounding remarkably like Dio. "There's nothing inside me that needs reading or fixing. Not tonight, anyway."

Andy stared at the stars for a second to take her focus off Bela and try to help Bela feel less invaded. "Okay,

okay, Ms. Touchy. Does this mean we're done for the night?"

"Yeah. We're history." Bela gave the we're-moving-on signal to Dio, wherever she was. "Camille can—you know—melt back home whenever she wants to."

Jack felt surprised.

Normally he didn't like surprises, but he had to admit this one filled him with a sense of wonder.

He had gotten Andy's handwritten, formal-looking invitation to dinner at Dylan Prime in Tribeca. He'd never been to the place, but Saul told him to dress nice and try the fondue. Good thing he had a few sport jackets and trousers. He had picked navy and tan to keep Andy from ribbing him about FBI colors, but now that he was here, he wondered if he should have gone even more formal.

This place—it was nice. Totally not what he had imagined from Andy when she insisted on selecting the restaurant. He'd have put his money on some hole-in-the-wall cop dive, which would have been fine with him, too. This pick showed him a whole new aspect of her. Surprises. She was good for that.

Jack straightened his tie, approached the host, and gave his name and Andy's. A minute or so later, he got escorted to a candlelit table near one of the windows looking out across the city. Completely exposed, but intimate at the same time. The host placed two menus on the table, along with an impressive wine list.

Jack sat in the comfortable chair and glanced around, impressed by the linens, the tasteful arrangement of the place—modern and open, yet private. Sound didn't carry, and no blaring music distracted him from the peaceful, tasteful ambience. The lights of the city glittered, warm and inviting in the hot summer night. He had to admit,

New York City had it going on. He'd thought he was a rough country sort of guy, meant to retire one day to the wilds of Colorado or Alaska, but New York had proven to be its own kind of wilderness—and pockets of high-end civilization like Dylan Prime made it seem even more attractive.

There I go, thinking about staying here again.

Jack's insides tightened. He still couldn't quite fathom waking up day after day in the same place for the rest of his life. Of having a home again. A *family?* Thoughts of it gave him a confined sensation, not quite trapped, but limited.

As for waking up day after day with the same woman, that didn't seem confining anymore. Not if the woman in question seemed as deep and mysterious as the ocean, as free as waves on the surface of a lake, and as tempestuous and unpredictable as the rain. Jack couldn't imagine Andy ever getting dull or confining. He could imagine—

There I go, thinking about her being mine again.

Motion near the host's desk caught his attention. When Jack glanced in that direction, he found himself standing before he fully registered the vision who had just arrived to meet him. That dress. Dear God. Dark green to set off her beautiful skin and the rich redness of her hair, and it touched her everywhere, hugging her full breasts, her tapered waist, her rounded hips, her slender thighs. Her arms and shoulders were bare except for her red curls, tamed, just barely, and pulled back from her face enough to accent the size and warmth of her eyes and the sexy curve of her glossy red lips. She had on dark green pumps that made her long legs seem even longer, and she seemed to float toward him across the quiet restaurant.

Jack couldn't move. He couldn't swallow. He knew he wouldn't be able to speak when she got to the table.

This version of Andy looked like a pinup from a

1940s calendar, full of charm and so damned beautiful anybody who looked at the picture would want to touch it. He sure as hell did. Right here. Right now. All his stitches were out and his bruises had faded. All his parts worked. He could handle it. The table was a little small, but he'd make it work.

Stay classy, his brain warned.

The rest of him wanted to let out a feral snarl and announce to anybody who might be looking that this woman was his. All his. Nobody else's, not ever again.

She reached him and stopped. Close. Close enough to touch, to hold, to kiss. *She's showing you a secret part of her heart, something she keeps to herself. Don't blow it.*

Jack took her hand, brought it to his mouth, and brushed his lips across her knuckles. Her sweet scent made him ache to get closer, but he pulled out her chair instead and helped her get settled at the table.

When he sat down, she smiled at him. He wanted to say something about how beautiful she looked. No, not beautiful. Stunning. He wanted to tell her she had surprised him completely. Again. In every way. And he was really starting to enjoy that about her.

"Do you come here often?" he asked.

How lame was that?

"About once a month." Her smile didn't falter, which relieved him. "A little treat I give myself. But before tonight, I've always come alone."

If she came dressed like that, he couldn't believe she left alone, but he didn't want to think about that. At the moment, if he found out she had lots of previous lovers who weren't already deceased, he'd be too tempted to make them that way.

"I'm glad you included me," he said.

"Have you looked at the menu?"

"I can't look at anything but you. Why don't you tell me about it?"

"Smooth," she murmured, and seemed pleased, sitting up straighter and treating him to an even better view of the dress's plunging neckline. "That's right. You're not a New Yorker, so you don't know." She made a quick gesture toward the main part of the restaurant. "This is the best steakhouse in Manhattan, in my opinion."

"Steak." His stomach gave a rumble. The way the place looked, he'd figured he'd be spending the meal sorting through weird French offerings—stuff that came on decorative plates in portion sizes so small they wouldn't feed a mouse. He hadn't cared, because he could always get a burger later. But steak? Damn. No burger necessary.

"The wine's spectacular, and the appetizers and desserts are rich and filling." Andy's Southern accent only added to the ambience. "You can't go wrong with anything you order. Are you a strip man or a filet kind of guy?"

Jack thought about picking up the menu, but he didn't want to shift his attention off her for fear she'd vanish like a dream when he looked away. "Since this is your spot, choose for me."

"A control freak like you, letting me run the show. I'm impressed." Her smile captured him completely, in fresh, new ways.

When the waiter reached them, Andy ordered farmhouse cheese fondue for the table, and French onion soup for both of them as appetizers. She chose a filet for herself with baby baked potatoes and grilled asparagus. Then she studied Jack for a few seconds, glancing at the menu, then looking back up at him. Weighing. Measuring.

"For you, I think the Carpetbagger will do, with the lobster and white truffle mac and cheese for an extra treat." After Jack selected a wine, Andy said, "The Carpetbagger is a big filet stuffed with oysters. There's spinach and mashed potatoes—and the sauce is made from Guinness and brown sugar. Like I said before, food shouldn't be boring."

Andy handed her menu to the waiter.

"And I'm betting you picked a dish named *carpetbagger* on purpose." Jack handed his menu over and tried to gauge her reaction. He was sort of glad to note she seemed surprised.

"There's the whole Civil War and North-South meaning," she said, trying to work it out. "Oh. But in general *carpetbagger* refers to an opportunist who shows up on the scene, loots, plunders, degrades the local culture, then splits when times get tough."

Jack tried to keep it light, but he needed to know where he stood. "Is that how you see me?"

She didn't give a flip answer or blow him off. Probably a good thing. Her eyebrows came together like she was sorting her thoughts, getting them in order, instead of trying to make stuff up on the spot. "I did at first. And now I've started to think you wanted me to. That you wanted all of us to see you as a carpetbagger so nobody expected you to be loyal, or put down roots, or finish what you started."

Her words felt like a fast slap, so sharp and on target that Jack's skin stung. "That's harsh." He swallowed, trying to shake off the stun-gun effect of that much honesty. "But there's probably some truth to it."

Andy put both of her hands on the table and laced her fingers together. The force of her gaze made Jack brace for a tough question or observation.

"A friend of mine told me you have wind in your heart," she said. "Is that the truth, or is that an image you're trying to uphold?"

Tough. Yep. "I heard that phrase about wind in the heart at Motherhouse Greece. It wasn't flattering."

What to do here? Defend? Lie? Explain?

Or just . . . answer?

"There's truth to that, too," he admitted. "Both things. The wind in the heart—and the image I keep."

Please don't ask me why.

She didn't, which gave him enough space to keep breathing and thinking and functioning. Jack wasn't sure he'd ever been out with a woman who had such a spot-on sense of when to lunge in for the kill and when to back off. Andy might be dangerous in a lot more ways than he had realized.

The wine and fondue arrived, and Jack got a few more minutes of reprieve as they sampled the rich, warm cheese. "This stuff spoils me for other dips and fondues," Andy said. "Definitely not boring, and it's hard to find any better."

"It's great." Jack took another bite. He didn't go to nice restaurants often, and he'd never really slowed down long enough to wonder why.

"I like the wine choice. Mount Veeder cabernet. Strong but not overpowering." Andy raised her glass, and the wine looked almost purple in her glass as she sipped it. "How are you feeling?"

Jack knew she meant physically, his body after getting shot. A lot easier to answer than questions about character or emotions. "Almost like new, which is damned surprising. That healing thing you do, it's pretty powerful, but I can't figure out why it worked on me."

She took another sip of wine. "We can do a little healing on non-Sibyls."

"The Mothers told me it didn't work well on people with no elemental talent—and they were pretty clear that I don't have any of that—but you've helped me twice, with the shooting and, before that, with my hearing."

Andy seemed surprised, then perplexed. Something else crossed her face then, a mix of confusion and shock, quickly covered by embarrassment. Maybe she'd just figured out why she'd been able to help him out with her healing talents—and she didn't like what she realized? But whatever it was, she didn't seem ready to share it. Instead, she said, "I guess water Sibyls are more able to help the nontalented. I'm still not good at healing. I need to learn a lot more, and I really need more practice."

Jack tasted his own glass of wine and enjoyed it. Strong, like she said, but not too strong. "You don't have time to do everything on your list. It's not possible."

Her smile looked a little sad. "Hardly ever."

"If you're a Mother, why do you fight?" He set his glass back down and waited, because this was one of the things he'd found most difficult to understand.

"Because I need my time on the streets, my time in a group to learn and understand and grow. One day I'll spend all my time at the Motherhouse, but not until I'm a lot older."

Jack thought about how long Sibyls lived and felt inadequate for a moment. Thirty years from now, Andy would still be lithe and beautiful, still fill out that incredible green dress like nobody's business—but he'd be an old guy.

Stay in today. You're thinking like you'll get to keep her forever.

Which is exactly what I want.

The thought was so sudden, so certain, Jack almost dropped his wineglass.

Andy was talking about mug shots. Something about not seeing too many faces similar to the one she had been hunting. "Most of them are too young. I think I'm going to start on the upper echelon of all the local crime families. The bosses. Though I can't imagine somebody high up agreeing to turn himself into a Frankenstein monster."

Reverting to work talk was exactly what Jack needed

to keep his sanity, so he went with it. "Unless the boss wasn't given a choice, or he didn't have an option due to other factors."

"Good point. I'll have Dio and Camille and the OCU search specialists poke around to see if any of the heavy-weight players had bad injuries, or maybe got sick or something." Andy's wine was disappearing faster than Jack's. "I know we don't have reports of any of them going missing—well, any of them that haven't shown up in pieces already. I think this was probably voluntary, even if the guy probably didn't understand what the out-come might be. His family and his people aren't looking for him, so it may be part of some plan."

Jack enjoyed more wine and more time looking at her. He liked the alertness and interest in her voice when she worked on her thoughts about cases. "You think any of this is related to the stuff dying in Central Park?"

"Not directly, but Camille thinks she knows which beings might be responsible for the die-offs. The Host. Well, their actual name is the Sluagh." She pronounced it "Slooa." "They're from around Ireland and Scotland, maybe Wales—all the old Celtic territory."

"What are they?"

"Something like the Keres, an ancient race who made a treaty with the Sibyls to survive. Mythical, and not to-tally friendly. They likely blended with humans at some point to give rise to fire Sibyls in the first place. Some people say they're a type of Fae, and other records call them fallen angels. In Irish fairy tales, they're the Un-seelie Court, or the Unblessed."

Jack downed the rest of his wine, reminding himself not to get too grim or serious—but shit. "Evil faeries. That's just great. What the hell are they doing in New York City?"

"We don't even have a guess about that. They've never been known to come out of hiding and leave the British

Islands. The Irish Mothers are going to attempt to contact the Sluagh still in Ireland to see if they can figure out why this is happening, but we don't think the Host pose a threat unless we engage them."

"Or unless you have what they want. They have to want something to come all this way." Jack went back to the dip, finishing off the silky cheese faster than he should have.

"They're watching the sorcerers, best we can tell. I can't figure what Griffen and his bunch have that could possibly be important to them." Andy glanced around, and Jack figured she was checking for the waiter to get them some refills.

He looked around, too, but no luck. The guy had made himself scarce. "Some stolen artifact? Or maybe Griffen's behind Frank and the supermobsters? Or both?"

"His group allied with the Rakshasa, but I don't think humans could come up with the technology to manufacture Rakshasa demon blood." Andy still had a bite of cheese dip on her plate, and she ate it with a floret of broccoli that came with the appetizer tray. "He's probably helping whoever's doing it, though, because we can't find any traces of where the supermobsters are hiding."

"What paranormal group would have the technology to manufacture Rakshasa blood? The Host?"

"Possible." She leaned back in her chair, leaving both hands on the table. "But that doesn't feel right. Not that I should be surprised, since none of this feels right anyway. The whole Rakshasa connection just doesn't make any sense."

A small knot of tension formed in Jack's gut, fighting with his cheese dip as he got to some questions that bothered him on deeper levels. "What about your connection to the Seneca crime family? Come up with anything on that front?"

"Not a thing. I've never tangled with those guys that I'm aware of, and OCU swears they're history, anyway. The old man pulled out and went back to the Balkans to regroup after we kicked his ass last year, and he had virtually nobody left except his sons and a handful of loyal locals."

"Some of whom are now genetically altered, demon-enhanced supermobsters."

The French onion soup arrived. Jack tasted his as Andy let out a low moan of satisfaction that got his blood boiling all over again.

"It's good," he agreed, surprised he could still talk when he wanted her so badly.

"Nothing like exciting food."

"And an exciting woman."

"You've got all the lines, Jack."

"Only with you, they're not lines. At least, I don't want them to be."

"I'm enjoying this, our teasing and playing. And those kisses before we got attacked—those felt special to me." Andy put down her spoon and stared at it instead of looking at him, and Jack knew another moment was at hand, a moment where he could take a step toward winning her or get a head start on losing her forever.

Don't screw it up, Blackmore. Whatever you do, don't screw it up.

"I guess I'm just wanting to know where we're headed. No bullshit and no lines. Where do I fit in your life, Jack? Somebody to warm your bed until the wind blows in your heart and you move on? The truth won't put me off. It'll just keep me realistic. I need that much."

Jack took a slow, deep breath. For a few seconds he tried to pick the best words, then tossed that idea and spoke from his heart. "I want you in my bed, but not just to keep me warm. You're more than that."

Andy's lips parted, and all Jack could think about was

kissing her. He could lean across the table, or move it—
or what the hell, just pitch the thing sideways.

"How much more?" Andy asked him.

He barely heard the words, barely kept his thoughts
together enough to answer her. "Right now in my life,
you feel like everything."

She didn't say anything in response to that, and she
looked away. A sobering thought pounded its way into
Jack's mind, and he voiced it before he considered whether
or not it was a good idea. "Will I be the first since your
loss?"

"Yes."

Jack's heart squeezed until he almost coughed from the
pain in his chest.

She sounded so soft. So scared.

Right that second, he wanted to cradle her and keep
everything in the world away from her—everything but
him. He hadn't wanted to be the first, but at the same
time, he felt a roaring, thundering sense of triumph that
he would be. Nobody else had her love, her attention.
Nobody else had a claim on her, and damn it, nobody
ever would.

Don't screw it up. Don't . . . screw . . . it . . . up.

"That's a big step, Andy."

She met his gaze again. Pain and anger flashed across
her face. "If you're not comfortable taking it with me—"

"Stop." Jack held up both hands, then made himself
put them on the table. "I know you'll have a lot of emotions, not all of them good, but I can take it."

Andy's bottom lip trembled for a moment.

Christ, was the woman trying to kill him? He was
gonna end up tossing away the table between them before this was over, he just knew it. He hated the piece of
wood for separating him from her.

*Yeah, go ahead and haul her out of here over your
shoulder like a caveman. She'll really appreciate that.*

"I'm sorry," she whispered. "I don't mean for this to be so complicated."

Jack had to use every bit of his physical and mental strength to keep his seat and keep his body still. He relaxed each muscle group as quickly as he could, then once more decided to speak from the heart instead of worrying about the words. "You're a woman with so many layers I can't even count them. Complicated goes with the territory."

Andy seemed to get hold of herself, to beat back the fear and old pain threatening to stand between them. She seemed to be relaxing, too, even though he figured they were both getting tense in new ways.

"If we take this to the next level, just be straight with me, Jack. If you start thinking about moving on, I won't cling—but tell me."

She stared into his eyes and he let her. He stared back. Here it was. He had his permission. He had his invitation.

Don't turn over the table and act like a caveman. Don't screw it up. Speak from the heart and *choose the right words.*

"We're taking it to the next level." Jack put his hands over Andy's, enjoying how small her wrists and fingers felt compared to his—and giving thanks for the way she looked now, like she wanted him to touch her, like she wanted him closer.

He lifted one of her hands and kissed it, letting the softness sink into his consciousness and keep him sane. "We're taking it to the next level tonight, and I'm going to be right here."

❨ 20 ❩

Andy stood in Jack's room on the second floor of the townhouse, taking in all the details. Spacious. A few leather chairs and a table near the fireplace, which was close to the door. A leather couch right in front of her. Big bed with a dark spread behind her. Nothing on the walls. Nothing on the dressers. They'd had "the talk" on the way here from the restaurant, about how Sibyls didn't need contraception or conventional protection because their elemental energy defeated disease, and they chose the moment of pregnancy. That was all sane and rational. And Jack, he was downstairs checking in with the OCU so they wouldn't be interrupted. Also sane and rational.

Andy standing here in the middle of Jack's private world, barefoot, the straps of her heels dangling from her fingers—that didn't feel sane and rational at all.

What the hell am I doing?

She didn't want to look at the bed. She realized she was shaking. This was wrong. It had to be wrong because it wasn't Sal.

Sal's gone. Jack's real and he's here and he's now.

Handsome man. Smart and kind and understanding, despite the fact he worked not to show that softer side of himself to anybody. Damned sexy, too. And if she told herself the truth, the feelings he stirred in her—way different from what she'd shared with Sal. That relationship had been warm and peaceful and close. Safe. Yeah. *Safe* was a good word.

And Jack?

He's got wind in his heart. . . .

Behind her, the bedroom door opened and closed.

Andy's skin tingled. The room seemed to fill with Jack's cedar-and-earth smell, with his male energy and the desire he radiated whenever he got close to her. She liked that sensation, and her fear doubled. Tripled.

She tried to put the shoes down and ended up dropping them.

Was it hot in here? She didn't remember it being this hot. She knew she was turning red all over.

Jack's hands gripped her shoulders, but he didn't turn her around. He massaged, firm yet gentle, working out the knots in her neck, then moving lower, to her bare arms, easing her hair carefully aside.

Why can't I stop shaking?

Her dress had gotten damp, top to bottom. She made herself breathe, did what she could to keep her water energy in check. Jack came closer and the feel of his muscled chest against her back blotted out her sense of the real world.

She leaned into him and closed her eyes. Felt his lips on her neck as he squeezed her elbows, her forearms. Kissing soft. Slow. Chills of pleasure covered her skin, and she kept shaking, only now she was pretty sure it was because she wanted Jack so badly.

"Are you sure?" he whispered into her ear, setting off a new round of delicious shivering.

Her breath came short and fast, but she managed a definite "Yes."

Invited, wanted, his palms slid from her arms to her waist, then up until he cupped her breasts. The soft fabric of her dress and the silk of her bra seemed like nothing between her skin and his powerful hands—nothing, but too much. He rubbed her nipples through the fabric and Andy moaned. Water pooled between her breasts as his hands moved again, behind her. Then her zipper opened and the damp dress slid off her shoulders and past her hips. The bra went just as fast, and he slipped it off her arms, freeing her, leaving her in nothing but her silk underwear. The fabric of his suit scrubbed against her back and legs, and she could feel his erection pressing into her.

Definite yes. Definite.

I need to quit shaking.

He kissed her shoulders. The stubble on his chin tickled and burned at the same time, sliding across the moisture she couldn't control. He cupped her breasts again, this time grabbing her nipples roughly as he bit her neck.

Andy moaned louder, getting wetter all over, in all the wrong places and all the right ones, too. She leaned into him even harder, rubbing herself against his muscles, against the bulge in his slacks. The hot spot between her legs throbbed as he kept rolling the hard flesh of her buds between his big fingers.

"You're too beautiful for words." The words came out low and jagged, and that only made Andy want him more. She pressed herself into his palms, teasing the fingers pinching her until bolts of pleasure shot all over her body.

"Harder. I can take it harder." She raised her arms and reached back, finding his head, his thick hair as he bit her neck again. The pressure on her nipples doubled, making her squirm, making her hotter, pain and pleasure, just enough, just right. His fingers turned to fire on her nipples, tugging, pulling, rolling, and his teeth burned everywhere they touched. The bulge against her back seemed to pulse. She wanted him inside her and she didn't want to wait much longer.

God, she was wet. Water dripped everywhere. She couldn't help moving and her knees brushed against the thick cushions of the couch in front of her.

"I want you." He kept nibbling but let his hands move

down, across her belly, between her legs. He stroked her through the damp fabric and she barely bit back a scream.

"I want you," he said again, more ragged, more insistent.

Heat washed across every inch of Andy's body. "Yes, please. I'm ready. I'm ready for you."

Jack's bass growl of need nearly made her come as he let go of her, turned her to face him, and kissed her like a man starving for anything she'd give him. His tongue probed hard and deep, demanding response, and Andy kissed back with everything she had.

She pushed forward, rubbing his shirt with her breasts as she shoved his jacket off his arms and got rid of his tie. The buttons were harder. Some popped loose as she pulled open his shirt, running her nails up his well-cut abs and pecs. The scars from his bullet wounds felt rough, but he didn't act like the wounds were tender. They seemed more healed than they should have been, almost like they were years old, like his other scars. More bullet wounds. A few knife or claw scratches. She'd known he would look like this, a warrior's warrior, but it still turned her on beyond all reason.

With a sigh, she let herself go flesh to flesh with him. So warm. So hard. He gripped her ass, rubbing, massaging, sliding her underwear down as she unfastened his pants, pushed them down, and reached inside his dark briefs.

Jack bit her lip and she bit his, sighing at how thick and hot he felt, how full and long. Naked together. Nothing between them now. Jack's hands seemed to be everywhere at once, and she wanted that, she wanted him now, right now, right that second.

He pushed her down on the couch, and her bare ass rubbed the soft leather as he settled himself, forcing her backward, forcing her legs open so he could kneel in front of her. Before she could absorb all the sights and sounds and feelings, he cupped both her breasts, bent over, lowered his head, and took one nipple in his mouth.

Andy gasped. Her back arched as furious pleasure washed through her body. His teeth. His tongue. His mouth heated her skin as he tasted first one nipple, then the other, and all Andy could do was hold the sides of his head and ache for more. His rough cheeks brushed across her breasts and he whispered, "So beautiful. Feel like heaven. And damn, you smell even better."

He moved his mouth lower, and Andy ached even more, hot between her legs, so excited and surprised she couldn't quite remember how to breathe. The feel of his hard muscle between her thighs and the leather against her bare skin nearly made her crazy.

Jack kissed a slow path down her belly, and lower.

"Red," he murmured as he kissed the edges of the curly hair between her legs. "I knew it."

And he kissed lower.

"God, yes." Andy kept hold of his head, pushing now, wanting his lips and tongue lower.

He was taking his time. Treating her like a delicacy. Making her blood pound. Every inch of her kindled to hot and ready, and each electric touch made her shiver.

Jack's tongue moved closer to her wet center. Andy raised herself toward his mouth, feeling water break across her whole body and flow down, soaking them both.

Jack's shoulders moved and Andy realized he was chuckling as she drenched him with her water energy. His hot breath between her legs nearly made her explode. "Please," she said, barely recognizing her own voice. She hadn't known it would be like this, that she'd want him so much—and he'd go so damned slow! "Please, please!"

Jack pressed his mouth tight to her throbbing folds. At the same moment, he slid one finger deep inside her, moving in rhythm with his mouth, and she had to cover her mouth to keep herself from screaming loud enough to bring half the OCU running.

He plunged his finger in and out, moving his tongue in circles and setting off ripples of pleasure. Chills covered her and she breathed harder, faster, keeping time with his thrusts.

Her first climax hit her so hard that a thin wave of water crashed against the wall of his room, soaking the plaster. She clamped her knees tight against his head. "Jack. Damn!" Her hips bucked outside her control as his mouth moved away from her depths. Up again. To her belly. Higher.

Andy arched backward, her head against cushions, and Jack kissed her neck, her chest, and moved down fast all over again. When his mouth fastened on her nipple this time, she did scream. He gripped her with both hands at her waist, pulling her into him as he nibbled and sucked on the swollen tip. Before he could torture her with the other nipple, she leaned sideways, pulling him down with her.

"I want to feel you. I want you inside me. Please, Jack."

The look on his handsome face turned positively wild as he lifted himself to the couch then stretched on top of her, spreading her legs with his knee, bracing his hands beside her head. His dark eyes focused so completely on her face that she thought he must be seeing everything about her, past and present and future, and she knew how good he'd feel. More than good. Better than good. She wasn't even breathing anymore, barely moving except to open herself, let him in, hoping he'd go deep and never stop.

He teased her for an instant, a second that lasted a year, letting her feel his width across her sensitive, waiting center. Then he sank inside her, going every bit as deep as she wanted, as deep as she could stand.

Better than good. More than more. Infinite.

"Oh, my God." It was all she could say. The rest was nothing but moans as she trembled and shook and took him, barely able to stand the thrusts, lifting her hips to meet each one. Filled and completed. She grabbed his shoulders, pulling herself up, moving against his rocking hips until her eyes closed and her water became a slippery heaven between them, slick and warm, and still he went deeper, possessing her completely.

"You're mine now," he murmured, and the sound of his voice, the raw possession in his claim pushed her closer to the edge.

Andy held back by sheer force of will. She wanted another minute. Two minutes. An hour.

"Jack." Saying his name felt delicious. The sound of their bodies moving, moving on the leather sofa spun through her senses. She felt released in ways she hadn't imagined, hadn't even known she wanted. Each stroke lifted her now, pushing her harder, pushing her faster.

"Come for me," he whispered, driving into her, sliding her on the couch. "Let me hear you moan."

Andy's orgasm took her like a fast-moving wave, starting in her center and washing outward, all over, from her aching nipples to her curled toes. She moaned and kept moaning, and Jack kept moving.

She didn't think she could take another second, but she wanted more, she wanted everything. Andy wrapped her arms around Jack's neck and held on as those dark, dark eyes blazed down at her. Black inside brown. Endless depths. He claimed her mouth again, setting her lips on fire with the rest of her. She loved how he felt inside her, loved how he looked at her.

She had to force her legs to work, to keep her thighs

tight around his waist. He broke the kiss. Looked at her again, cherishing, possessing, adoring her completely.

Andy tensed, fighting the next wave because this one, this one might drown her senses. As her breasts thrust upward, he caught a stone-hard nipple in his mouth, grazing his teeth across the sensitized flesh and making her scream. Another second, and she'd wash away completely.

With a bone-deep groan, Jack exploded inside her, filling her even more, catapulting her into an orgasm so hot and hard she couldn't feel anything but heat and shivers. Ecstasy hit her in waves, taking her sight, her hearing, every bit of her energy and resolve and reserve. She collapsed in a haze of satisfaction, feeling like she'd been set adrift in a warm ocean, and he held her to him, let his warm weight anchor her, easing her down, kissing away the tears she didn't even know she was crying.

"You're mine," she heard again as he moved himself gently off her, then picked her up, cradling her as he carried her to his big bed.

"Prove it," Andy murmured as he lowered her onto a mound of soft pillows.

He climbed into the bed beside her, tucking her in, pulling her close, then kissing her face and whispering, "You're beautiful," until she fell asleep and dreamed about coral palaces, crystal beaches, and endless blue waves on the sand.

(21)

Jack slept in a dark, velvety peace he hadn't known since he was a kid too young to understand the world had real problems. When he woke, he wondered if he'd dreamed about making love to Andy, but she lay in his arms like a gift he'd never deserve, soft and barely moving as her breathing pushed her chest into his over and over again. Her head tilted back against the pillow, giving him full view of each curve and freckle.

Beautiful.

He'd wanted to take his time. He'd meant to go slow and make her beg for every pleasure, but the sight of her standing in his room waiting for him to touch her, wanting him to make love to her—too much. He'd had no more control than a teenage boy.

They'd be lucky if the ceiling below his bedroom didn't collapse, too. He was pretty sure they'd let off quite a bit of water.

Rubber floor coverings? Maybe a first-floor room with a drain. Had to be some practical solution.

Her rich red curls lay across her bared breasts, and he couldn't stop staring at her, and he couldn't stop thinking this was what he wanted, what he'd always wanted—and what he wanted forever.

Jack brushed aside a curvy wave of hair, then rubbed one taut nipple with his thumb.

She gasped in her sleep, and her whole body shivered with pleasure.

Take your time.

Yeah, right.

He was already getting hard again. Hell, he'd woken up hard, and he knew he couldn't wait long to be inside her.

Andy stirred in his arms, blinked once, then leaned into him and kissed him, her warm breath brushing across his cheeks as her soft lips and tongue teased his mouth. He sensed her fingers reaching for his cock before he felt her grip, and that teenage boy problem came roaring back. He put his hand over hers before she could stroke him again. "Careful. I won't make it three minutes with you touching me like that."

"Good. Then we can sleep and start over again." Her sweet voice tickled his senses, and as her lips found his again, he moved his hand so she could do whatever she wanted with him.

Her fingers felt like a dream on his hard shaft, dancing along the length like she knew each sensitive spot by heart. Jack had to jam his teeth together to hold back, especially when he looked into her heavy-lidded eyes and saw that she liked how he felt against her palm.

Another second. He could hold out. He could control himself.

Or maybe not.

"Enough." He rolled over and took her with him, and she kept hold of his hard length, then guided him in, smooth and flawless. She was so tight and wet he almost lost it all over again.

Andy moaned and arched toward him, offering herself, and he moved deeper inside her, trying to force himself to go slow, to make her moan a little longer. He could sense her power rolling like tides through the air, and he liked that, liked her strength—and loved the vulnerable softness on her face, the pink in her cheeks, the way her mouth parted and her throaty moans as he drove himself deeper, deeper, giving her everything he could.

Afterward, he lay in the soaked sheets, holding her to

his chest, enjoying the feel of her nails on his chest as he kissed the top of her head. "Any regrets?"

Her sigh sounded almost like a purr. "Waiting longer than I had to."

"Well, we did get shot."

"There's that. What time is it?" She lifted her head enough to squint at his bedroom window. "Is it still night, or have we moved into morning?"

"Day, by the look of the light through the blinds." He pulled her to him again, and she let him even though he could feel her muscles tensing beneath his caress.

"I'm supposed to be on Kérkira training adepts."

"Can they wait?"

"They'll have to."

Jack wished he could make her life more sane, more reasonable. That he could somehow craft time and hand it to her as a gift, or find some way to truly help her bear the burdens she'd been handed. He tried to find some way to express that, to pick exactly the right phrases.

"Let me be the one," he said before he got a good handle on what he was trying to offer her. "The only one for now."

Andy lifted her head again, and some of the sleepy relaxation faded from her pretty eyes. "Excuse me?"

I'm sucking at this relationship thing already. But he'd started, and he knew he needed to finish. "I don't know you as well as I should, not yet—but I intend to learn everything you'll let me about who you are and what you want and what you need. Will you give me that chance?"

She gazed at him, unblinking, definitely fully alert now. "It's not me who comes and goes like the wind."

"You have it in you." He met her stare. "Don't tell me you haven't thought about disappearing since you found out about paranormal creatures—since you learned you were a Sibyl."

Her lips pulled into a frown. "Okay, fine. More than once. So?"

"So don't disappear from me." He brushed her cheek with the back of his knuckles, enjoying the warmth and softness. "I want to see you, and I want us to be exclusive until we figure this out."

Andy propped one elbow on his chest and one beside him on the bed, keeping herself eye level with him. She shifted from frown to smile, then back again. "You're awfully damned full of yourself, you know that? I've never given anybody that kind of power over me."

"I don't want power over you. I want you. All of you."

Be mine. Have my children.

Fuck, he had to get a grip.

"Exclusive." She let out an exaggerated sigh, the kind that went with her sunglasses-and-big-shirt persona.

"That's about the only thing that's nonnegotiable. You're mine until you decide you're not." Jack wanted to roar that part from the nearest rooftop, but he steadied himself and kept going. "If you make the call that you're through with me, I'll respect that—but I'm not a man who can take other men poaching on his territory."

Her mouth came open. For a few seconds, she seemed too stunned to say anything at all, and he figured he'd made a misstep—but he couldn't help it. He had to be honest.

"You should hear yourself," she said, a lot less warmth in her voice. "I'm not territory, Jack."

His gut tightened. "I didn't mean it like that. I don't—" He paused. Calmed himself. She hadn't moved away from him, so all wasn't lost. Not yet, anyway. "I don't think of you like that. As a nonperson or something I own. I don't always say things the best way. Not—not in circumstances like this."

Her eyebrows lifted. "Have any of your circumstances ever worked out?"

Jack refused to let the sarcasm in her tone goad him, so he answered simply, "No."

She closed her eyes. "Now I'm just being mean, and I need to stop. You're allowed your male instincts. I can feel them bursting out of you, honest and whole and pure."

When she opened her eyes again, she looked away, and he could tell there was something she wasn't saying.

"What?"

Another sigh met his ears, this one not dramatic at all. "There's something you need to know, and you might not like it very much."

Shit.

He waited. Tried to be ready.

"You know the whole emotion-sensing thing I'm supposed to do with my quad? Well, I'm not so good at it where they're concerned, but it's happening with you." She faced him again, and he saw guilt and worry fill her eyes.

The weight of her meaning settled on his insides like a cold weight. "You're reading my feelings?"

"Yes." More guilt, and now helplessness, too.

"For how long?"

"I'm not certain. Maybe since the beach, but definitely since that day in the warehouse, right after you touched me."

That simple contact had been powerful for Jack, too. What she was saying made sense to him, made him happy in a weird sort of way, like she was admitting a deep connection even if she didn't realize that.

"And what am I feeling right now?"

She laughed. "Horny. And triumphant. And vulnerable." She leaned closer to him and kissed his cheek. "I'd say we're on the same page. Now you have to tell me—is that too much for you, Jack?"

Good question.

Jack realized that a few months ago, he would have backed away in a big damned hurry from anybody who got a bead on his emotions—especially a woman. But Andy? Somehow with her, it didn't feel invasive. It felt as right as having her naked body stretched against his and her soft, lovely mouth only inches from his own.

Aware that he might be doing his own admission of a deep connection, Jack surrendered with no fight at all. "For you, I'll be an open book. Now, do we have a deal on the exclusive thing?"

Andy's eyes flashed, but not with anger. She kissed him again and whispered, "Deal. If you make me regret it, I'll feed your balls to an octopus."

22

Rebecca had known for years that she didn't need as much sleep as her brother.

Lately, she hardly slept at all. Why anyone would waste the vibrant night hours—that confused her.

Night had a voice. Sometimes it sang to her, sometimes it whispered, but the darkness always reached out to her and touched her in ways she couldn't explain. The hours between darkness and dawn gave her an excited focus and energy she didn't quite know how to manage.

She tended to get in trouble at night, when her brother slept, when the Coven took turns standing guard over the warehouse in pairs and keeping track of Sibyl movements and activities. They had been especially active this last week, since the head of the OCU got out of the hospital—and since Rebecca got out of the prison her brother had designed for her. Her wrists ached as if remembering the elemental cuffs that had bound them for so many months after the last time she ran away from Griffen. At night, of course.

She wasn't even sure why she'd run, or what she had been looking for, but it didn't matter. Griffen always found her. They each had inherited different gifts from their father, and one of his was recognizing and tracking specific energies.

Hers, apparently, served as a beacon Griffen could follow to her whenever he liked. She didn't think she'd try running again, at least not until she knew where she was going.

Rebecca took care to stay well away from the watchmen as she moved through the ground floor of the warehouse. She didn't need light to see. Not anymore. For the past few years, she'd been able to see in the dark like most people saw at noon on sun-filled days. Seeing in the daytime—now, that was getting trickier. Bright light burned her eyes, making her head ache and her skin and insides feel like she had some terrible, feverish infection. She had taken to wearing sunglasses almost all the time, but she had them off now so she wouldn't miss any subtleties or detail.

She bypassed the small apartments holding sleeping fighters, bound into their quarters with elemental locks that dulled their senses and lust for action and blood. She ignored the off-limits lab in the corner where the—thing—was, and went instead to the heavily barred cell built into the farthest corner next to the lab.

In the stark, bare space inside, the old man sat staring at nothing. His abnormally large and muscled body heaved with the force of his breath, a symptom of the lungs he'd damaged during his human years.

Couldn't fix all of that, Griffen had explained. *Damage done before the injection can't be reversed. Only new damage.*

Rebecca knew the old man had expected to be young again, that he had imagined himself fit and full of fresh air as he joined with Griffen and the Coven to take control of the more powerful crime families in New York City. He'd been played, of course. Griffen had promised him these things without having a clue what that injection would do. The first few rounds had killed recipients outright. The next few attempts at revising the formula—not pretty or appetizing, though she had at least gotten to kill the misbegotten creations Griffen couldn't stand to look at, much less study.

Her brother thought she liked killing, but in truth, she

sought death, or being around dying things. The bigger the animal, the more its death energy fed her.

Sometimes she thought she'd starve, but sooner or later something around her would die or, like Griffen's pitiful experiments, present itself to be slaughtered. She'd do the killing, but only for the sight of the blood and the deep, strengthening flow of nearby death.

When this creature in its cage finally died, his final throes might sustain her for months. The old man's lined face had a sour tightness that might have made her laugh a few years back, or even a few months ago. Now the creature just looked sad. She pitied him, but she also needed him. That knowledge came from instinct, and lately her instincts had become much stronger and more accurate.

Rebecca breathed in the stale, motionless air around the creature's cage. Ammonia, sweat, and despair. The stench made her wrinkle her nose, but she held back comment. She hadn't come here to anger the thing. She'd come to help him remember his anger—and what to do with it.

She leaned as close to the bars as she could get without actually touching the metal and whispered, "I know you can speak."

She had expected the old man to ignore her, but his comeback was fast. "Leave me."

His resonant, raspy voice disturbed Rebecca's composure. He sounded very much like the thing in Griffen's lab, and she despised that thing for what it had done to her when it walked the earth free and in control of its own destiny.

It took a few moments to get herself back in control, but when she could think again, she went right back to her task. "You and I, we have a few things in common."

"Go away, girl."

Rebecca's gut reacted to the voice again, and she had

to hold back a scream of pure rage and hatred. This time, it took longer to bring herself back under good management, and she did so only with great force of will.

"We don't belong," she said to the creature when she was sure she could speak rationally. "Not in this world."

This brought silence from the monster, and Rebecca watched as the big creature glanced down at his massive hands. Demon claws extended from his fingertips, and the smell of ammonia grew stronger.

She coughed, but kept herself in check. When she touched his cage bars with her fingertips, she almost gagged at the stifling elemental energy. The locks seemed heavy and cruel, like they had been designed to crush the monster's essence instead of just control him for the safety of the Coven.

"This is terrible," she said aloud, shoving back at the energy enough to realize it might prove too powerful for her, too. Just the single contact had bled out some of her will.

The monster nodded, agreeing that the locks were unpleasant.

Gratified, Rebecca reached for the cage door, quite capable of working the elemental energies keeping the actual mechanical locks in place. She almost unlatched the bars, but hesitated, then had a storm of second thoughts.

Instinct again. Given her recent experiences, those instincts were likely correct.

Rebecca stepped back from the bars. "If I let you out of that cage, you'll kill me."

The old man didn't answer at first. He just kept looking at his clawed fingers. After a time, he nodded once.

Rebecca folded her arms. "Why?"

Silence ensued for a time, but the creature did at last manage an answer. "Because you are there. Because you breathe."

The reasonless reason didn't distress her, but it also

didn't tell her what she needed to know. "Is it the killing you like, or the death?"

The creature raised his head enough to look at her, to study her, as if he might be seeing her for the first time. He seemed to be considering her question, and she could tell when he settled on the correct words.

"The pain. I like the pain and the fear. It . . . fills me."

Interesting. So the thing craved dark, violent energy, much like death—especially death from attacks and wounds, like the Rakshasa from whom the creature took its supernatural power. Death from murder had the most explosive energy of all. Now Rebecca knew they were headed in the right direction. "Does it have to be people?"

She could tell the creature didn't understand what she was asking, so she figured out a new wording and tried again. "Would the pain of animals satisfy you and help you grow stronger?"

The old man studied her for a longer period of time before answering. "Some."

Rebecca got closer to the bars but held herself apart from the locks coursing through the bars. "Enough to free yourself from my brother and the Coven?"

"Perhaps."

There it was. A possibility. Maybe one day a solution. Instinct drove her questions almost completely now, and this time she asked, "Could you clean the mess from the animals so nobody would know you were getting them?"

"I could." The creature's calm certainty reached her even through the dense energies containing him, and Rebecca knew he was telling her the truth.

Now it was her turn to trade truth for truth, and to see if they could reach a bargain. "If I do you this favor, one day I'll want a favor in return."

The creature in the cage didn't hesitate. Once more Rebecca received a single nod. She knew for a fact that the monster had struck many such deals in his human life, and he understood that if he failed her, one or both of them might die. If Griffen didn't kill the monster for his deceit and betrayal, then Rebecca surely would.

They had an agreement, then, her and the creature. And what fed him would in small ways feed her, too. Not so much the pain suffered by the creatures, but the power of their fear and panic, the energy released during their deaths. She had no idea why she wanted to grow stronger, why she needed so much energy from other creatures, but her rampaging instincts urged her not to ask such questions. It didn't matter, anyway. Not yet. When the time came for her to understand, she'd know the answers—and she'd know what to do.

Wordless and silent, Rebecca slipped away from the cage and into the darkened warehouse. Tonight she'd deliver her new friend some rats. Tomorrow, whenever she could escape Griffen's stifling supervision and protection, she'd go in search of larger game.

23

Andy . . .

She tried to see who was calling her, but smoke and fire blotted out everything except the bars in front of her face. Cage bars. She grabbed them. Heat rattled through her fingers and hands, up her arms.

She realized she was naked, and she started to sweat. Everything smelled like sulfur. Her eyes watered.

Andy . . .

August's voice drifted through her awareness. Seductive and powerful. The sick sound of it made her heart race so fast she worried her chest would explode.

Andy let go of her cage bars as a figure stepped out of the swirling clouds of smoke. The stench of sulfur got stronger, with a spike of stagnant seawater and raw sewage. She coughed and squinted at the tall, thin man. His features seemed blurred but generally normal.

He came a few steps closer, and Andy registered his black silk suit just about the time she heard whimpering in the cage beside her.

She glanced at the barred floor—and all the blood in her body stopped rushing. Her breath caught so hard she pitched forward into the bars before she recovered and scrambled to grab Neala away from the flames licking toward the bars. The little girl had been wrapped in a blanket, and her red curls lay limp against her pale face. She moaned but didn't open her eyes.

"It's been a while," the oily-voiced man said.

Andy gripped Neala and turned toward him, shielding

the girl's face with her hands like that would keep August from knowing who she was, or doing whatever he chose.

The tall man had red eyes now. A dart wound opened in his forehead. Black blood trickled down his face, which was rapidly growing scales.

"Vengeance is a dish best served hot," the demon snarled.

It lunged for Neala.

Andy screamed.

"Look at me." Jack's voice sliced into everything, ripping the world in half. Flames exploded, sizzling into Andy's skin everywhere at the same time, immolating her, burning Neala—

"Look at me, sweetheart." Jack again.

The flames faded into sparkles. The red-eyed man vanished. Neala disappeared, too, and Andy opened her eyes. Sweat and water covered her whole body, and she shook as she lay in Jack's arms. He held her gently, gazing down at her with brown eyes full of worry.

"You're safe. I'm right here, and nothing in this room will hurt you." His voice seemed as magnetic as the voice from her dreams, but without the menace.

Andy took slow breaths, letting her pulse slow as she made a quick check. Leather couch, hardwood floors, big bed—Jack's room in the townhouse, the same room where she'd spent every night of the past two weeks. His firm embrace helped her calm down from the dream, but then the content started to piss her off.

"Great. Now I'm dreaming about dead demons, too."

"Rakshasa?" Jack kissed her forehead.

"Worse. Bartholomew August."

That made him draw back and stare at her. "The Leviathan? The demon you killed near Mount Olympus, with the Keres helping?"

"None other." Andy pressed her head hard into her pillow. "He wanted revenge, of course."

"That must have been terrifying."

"I'm not scared of him. I killed him. What was awful—"
She broke off, not wanting to say the rest aloud, but
knowing she should. Jack brushed his lips across her forehead again and gave her the long seconds she needed to
get out the true horror. "Neala was there. He wasn't just
killing me. He was cooking Neala, too."

Jack didn't offer any lame comforts or try to reason
with her. He just turned her over, straddled her waist,
and rubbed her shoulders more expertly than any professional masseur. Now and then he kissed her back, her
neck, her head, until all the pieces of the dream faded
from her senses and her temper eased.

Andy let him spoil her for another few moments, then
turned over and gazed up at him, pressing her palm to
his cheek. "Thanks."

"Like I've said before, I have my share of nightmares."
He took her hand and kissed it. "And I'm feeling a little
guilty because I've been keeping you from a full night's
rest for nearly two weeks."

Andy blinked at him, trying to absorb that. Time had
been moving so strangely she hadn't been keeping up.
Each day seemed too full—and yes, each night, patrol or
no, turned into another blazing hot session in Jack's big
bed. When she was with him, she couldn't stay focused
on anything but him, and when she was away from him,
all she wanted to do was find him again and end up like
this, lying beneath him and staring into his brown eyes
for hours.

I might be going insane. No, not might *be. I'd say it's
pretty definite.*

"When I'm tired, that's when I have the worst of my
dreams," he said. "The kind I can't shed for a few hours
after I finally get myself awake. The Rakshasa in the
Valley of the Gods. Other times . . ." He trailed off and
seemed to debate with himself for a few quiet moments.

When he met her gaze again, the stark vulnerability she saw startled her. "I had a difficult childhood. Not all of it, but the last few years turned out to be a serious bitch."

Andy sat up in the bed, pushing him up with her and covering herself with the sheet. He settled himself beside her almost shoulder to shoulder, hands clasped, and she waited, knowing he had something he needed to say. Something major. She got a fluttery sensation in her belly, like when Dio had warned her that Jack was a man with wind in his heart.

Was he about to tell her one of the reasons he blew in and out of places with no more care than a summer storm?

"My father was a bad man," Jack said, and just getting those words out seemed to hurt him.

Andy thought about touching him, but decided against it. "How bad?"

Jack frowned. "The worst. A hired killer. We lived in Jersey, Atlantic City, and the casino he bought, he funded by carrying out mob hits. My mother and younger sister and me, we were just cover for the sociopathic bastard."

Andy could tell there was more, something much worse, and Jack was still arguing with himself about telling her. She risked laying her fingers on his forearm. "You don't have to censor with me."

He looked around the room, at the walls, the ceiling, everything but her. "Some things I censor with everyone."

She scooted closer, her hip against his, her leg pressing into his thigh, and she kept her hand on his arm. "Except me."

His expression changed, and now Andy saw something like fear and worry. Maybe shame. "My aunt—his sister—talked to the FBI, and he killed her for it. I saw him do it, and that's when I realized what he was."

"Jesus. How old were you?"

"Seventeen. For a while, it messed up my brain, but then I knew what I had to do. I started spying on the asshole, collecting whatever evidence I could."

Jack stopped talking again, and his eyes had gone dark. The lines of his face hardened. Rage and despair rolled off his skin like little tides, and Andy didn't so much as take a breath, because she knew he didn't need to stop.

"It got close to my eighteenth birthday, and I was going to turn over what I had to the FBI, but Mom and Ginger beat me to it. They had made their own realizations about him and started talking, and he found out, and I knew what he'd do to them. I got them out and told the FBI where to pick them up, and then I went back and took care of him."

This time when he stopped, Andy knew he'd gotten out the worst of it—and it was bad.

Dear God. He had to kill his own father. He was just a kid, and he had to do something like that. No wonder he seems detached so much of the time.

Jack's stubbornness and lack of social graces when she'd met him—all of that made more sense now. He needed that persona, that gruffness, because he didn't have wind in his heart, like Dio thought. He had too much agony for any normal man to bear.

Andy tightened her grip on his arm, wanting to do so much more, wanting to give him something that might ease that kind of pain, but she knew that would just push him away. Instead, she let the police officer still living in her soul say what needed to be said. "With a man like that, your mother and sister never would have been safe as long as he lived."

Jack nodded. "He would have found them himself, or paid somebody to do it." He stared at the ceiling for a long minute, then added. "When we faced off, I couldn't shoot him—not until he tried to pump a round into my head."

Shame. Definitely the emotion now. Shame mixed with regret and self-doubt.

Andy wanted to cry for his pain, couldn't stop the tears from coming to her eyes, but she held back the rest. "You hesitated because you weren't like him. You had doubts—and still have them—because you've got a heart and soul and mind. You're not a stone-cold son of a bitch."

"Thanks." His hand covered hers, and finally, finally, she sensed a little relief mingling with his frustration and distress.

"What happened to your mother and sister?"

"I don't know. We got to see each other one more time, then we had to go our separate ways to keep my father's associates from coming after us."

"Witness protection."

Jack didn't answer that question, which was answer enough. He'd had to kill his father, then surrender everything about who and what he was, who he had planned to be, and lose his mother and kid sister, too. To keep them safe, he let them be dead to him, even though he knew they were probably alive and well somewhere, living out their days without him.

She thought about what he'd asked her to do in the hospital, about using herself as bait to draw out the su-permobsters. *If you have to do this thing, wait for me. Let me be there with you.*

That meant more to him than she'd realized at the time, but she knew it now. He needed to fight beside her, needed it at a soul-deep level, because Jack couldn't stand to lose anybody else who meant something to him. If it came to that, he planned to go down shooting to save what he cared about, just like he'd done when he was seventeen.

He's taking a huge risk, letting me come this close. The jolt of understanding that she wasn't the only one laying everything on the line to see what might grow between them woke Andy in entirely new ways.

Jack's emotions washed into her again, from the hurt to the worry to the warmth and caring, and she dropped her sheet, moved into his lap, and kissed him. Somewhere between the third and fourth kiss, she whispered, "I love you."

He didn't flinch at the words, and the stream of feelings flowing between his heart and hers only got warmer and stronger.

"I love you," he said, his voice low as he held her tighter. He captured her lips with his, kissing her as he eased her to the pillows again and covered them. Chest to chest, leg to leg, their bodies became one creation under the single, soft sheet. He kissed her until she couldn't stand it, until her whole being ached for more and she wanted to beat his shoulders and beg him to give her relief.

Finally, finally, he lowered his head, pulled her tight nipple into his mouth, and stroked it with his tongue.

All the water and blood in Andy's body surged at the same time. She arched backward into the bed, pressing her breast into his mouth, doubling her own pleasure and raking a razor's edge of erotic pain. His hand swept up her belly to squeeze her other nipple, soft, then hard, soft, then hard, and her hips bucked. She rubbed herself against his hard length, throbbing with each touch, letting water slide across her skin as she held him tighter.

He had her now. He had her completely. Captive heart. He might as well hold it in his hands.

His soft growl of pleasure made her moan. "You want me to beg, don't you?'

Another growl, this one deeper and even more stimulating.

Jack shifted his weight and moved his hand away from her breast. Down, lower, into her curls, into her folds, cupping her and pressing against the wet center, and all the while, his teeth and lips and tongue teased her sensitive nipple.

Andy cried out from the hot pleasure, feeling completely owned and possessed and loving the sensation in ways she'd never imagined. He stroked between her legs, circling and pressing and giving gentle pinches until she thought she'd have to start screaming and keep screaming until he got himself inside her and made the ache stop.

"Jack." Her voice had gone ragged. She couldn't control the words.

And he let go of her nipple. Moved his hand. Moved his whole body down, his bare chest scrubbing across her belly, her sex, giving her new shivers, more shivers, until he settled between her thighs. That's when he took hold of her ass, pressed his mouth against her aching core, and made her moan out of control.

He tasted her, teased her even more, each of his low rumbles of pleasure traveling like wild waves through her body. Andy closed her eyes, lost and immersed like she was falling to the sea miles and miles under the heavy, hot waters above. Her body thrashed almost outside of her awareness, and Jack kept sucking and kissing, moving his lips and tongue like he'd never in his life known anything so good.

Andy's breath got more and more shallow. She couldn't take it, but she had to, she wanted to. So incredible. "Don't stop. Please. Don't stop."

She pushed herself against him, letting the shocks of pleasure drive her even deeper into the unbelievable sensations. Her whole essence seemed to blossom out from the center as she moaned and pressed her legs against the sides of his head.

Jack kept up the pressure, easing and starting back, the right place, the exact right touch, and her orgasm didn't end. Couldn't end. She knew she was screaming now, her head moving back and forth as she made herself ride each pulsing second. Melting. Her mind, her skin, her bones. And he kept it going until she whimpered. Begged some more. She had no idea what she was saying, if she was even forming words.

Jack shifted again, moving his body along hers until he braced his arms beside her head, until his hard cock pushed into her throbbing channel.

Andy let out a fresh groan as he drove inside her, powerful and demanding. He really was taking her, making her his own, and she opened wide to let him, wrapping her legs around his hips and taking him as deep as any man could go. She opened her eyes. Saw the crazed desire in his brown eyes, the warmth in his expression.

"I love you," he said. "I love you."

Pushing her, faster, deeper, so right, so satisfying.

Andy moaned as the waves of her orgasm closed over her head, sweeping her away to a world where she could be his forever, with absolutely nothing else to worry about.

24

Jack felt crazy.

He could get used to crazy.

Hot and endless and total—and crazy. Those were the only words he could find to describe the last three, almost four weeks of his life. Here he was again, dressed in jeans and a black shirt, open at the neck. He had gotten used to the look. He had gotten used to the relaxed feel of dressing more like his real self. A lot of his rules had gone out the window. Andy was allergic to rules, and Jack had begun to wonder why he had so many in the first place. He couldn't stay away from the woman even after she proved to be a rotten influence on his self-discipline—and he definitely couldn't keep his hands off her, work hours or not. Their tendency to end up in bed . . . or on couches . . . or even on his desk was probably what drove her to flee the townhouse for the brownstone and use an innocent child as a buffer while they tried to get a little work done.

Well, not really. Cynda had to go out shopping. She'd be back any second, but Andy said she'd watch Neala, and told Jack Neala would help her keep her mind on the task at hand—which today happened to be more mug shots, pictures of captains and bosses, further up the criminal food chain.

Jack had spread the books of photos on the big wooden table in the alcove at the back of the brownstone's living room, and he tried to relax on the leather sofa while Andy whizzed through the photos.

Sitting across from him in one of the leather chairs,

Neala in her lap, Andy glanced at each picture, then pushed them aside. In the projective mirrors on the walls around them, Jack could see her from all different angles, and he enjoyed each one—even the views from the darker mirrors, with lots of swirling mist.

"That's him." Andy shifted Neala onto one knee, used a little water to squelch the fire the little girl had started on Andy's jeans, and stared at the photo she had picked. "That's Frank the monster. I should have thought to look at boss pictures first. I'm sorry my schedule has been so scattered."

"Ari Seneca. What the he—" Jack glanced at the little girl on Andy's lap. "Um, heck. What the heck would drive him to let somebody turn him into a science experiment?"

"We took down his empire. We cut his men to pieces and left him with nothing, and whatever we didn't take, the Rakshasa probably did. He didn't have enough left to rebuild his syndicate for his sons."

"So he thought he didn't have a choice, and now he's let himself get turned into God knows what." Jack smacked his hand against the picture. "He's taking out all his rivals, and he's terrifying whoever isn't dead yet. That's one way to get business back on track."

"I'm still not sure he's driving this anymore." The sleeve of Andy's blousy white shirt flared as she moved her arm and tapped the picture. "He might have thought he'd be running the show, but I'm afraid he's just a big, dangerous flunky now, working for whatever mad scientist brought him back to life. We need to draw him out, Jack. Him and his friends. We need to understand how they created him."

Jack's tone got edgy before he could control it. "Don't start that again."

Neala twitched at the gruff sound, and half the mug shots of crime bosses burst into flames. Andy hit them with a big splash of water just about the time a knock sounded on the brownstone's front door.

Cynda opened the door and poked her head inside, her short red hair brushing against her cheeks. "Here I am. Thanks—wait a second." Her gaze narrowed at Neala. "Do I smell smoke?"

Andy held the little girl tighter as Neala hid her face. "It's okay. She was just reminding Jack not to be a jerk."

Cynda stepped into the entryway and frowned as the sensitive wind chimes above her head gave a jangle, set off by her strong fire energy. "No flames in the brownstone or the townhouse. No fire inside, period. You burn enough stuff by accident without destroying things on purpose."

"Soo-oorry," Neala said to her mother. To Andy, she said, "Battle? Can we play? Please?"

"Not now, honey. Maybe next time we get together." Jack watched as Andy kissed Neala's cheek. "Go with your mom and I'll see you soon."

"Promise?" The kid plied Andy with an adorable pout.

Andy poked out her bottom lip in an imitation of Neala. "Yes."

Neala's pout turned into a giggle. "Promise about battle?"

Andy made like she was debating about this, then said, "Yes."

"No Ethan. Just us?"

"I'll think about that." Andy gave Neala a little push out of her lap.

The little girl ran to her mother. Cynda gave them both a wave, then pulled the brownstone's front door closed behind her. Jack couldn't help thinking about how Cynda and her husband, Nick, found a way to juggle the OCU, Sibyl responsibilities, children, extended family, and God only knew what else. They had put down major roots, and every day they made it all work. Hell, they didn't even have the option to cut and run, and they didn't seem worse for it. On the contrary, they seemed happy and solid.

What would that be like?

Too late, Jack realized he was staring at Andy.

She lifted one eyebrow, a smile pulling at the corner of her mouth. "Why are you looking at me like that?"

Busted.

Might as well come off with the truth. He leaned back on the sofa without taking his eyes off of her pretty face. "I like watching you with Neala. You're a natural with kids, and she has red hair like you."

He let that sink in, and when she didn't start to freak, he added, "Do you want children of your own?"

"I—ah, yeah. You?" She said it casually, but she broke their staring game and started an intense study of the floor. This had major importance. Another thing he had to answer well and right.

Honest. Just go with honest. I think she can take anything if I'm just straight with her. Yet another thing to love.

"I've always wanted kids," he said, "but I never took the time to do it. Guess I figured I'd let my chance pass me by."

Until we happened.

Okay, way too soon for thoughts like that. Or maybe not. Crazy, and definitely liking it.

Andy kept her eyes on the floor. Her fingers came together in her lap, and she seemed tense and soft all at the same time. "I thought the same thing." She looked up, straight into his eyes. "Until recently."

That echo of his own secret thoughts hit Jack hard. He knew she tried to give him his privacy, tried not to read his feelings, but right now he wished she would. He wanted her to experience every second of the rush of tenderness and affection and desire. He didn't hold an ounce back.

Her face flushed. "You . . . want me to have your babies." She stood and turned away from him, fanning herself, and once more he couldn't help thinking how beautiful she looked in all the mirrors, from all the different angles.

He stood. Moved toward her. The only thing he could think about was touching her, but she backed away from him, still waving her hand in front of her face. "Oh, God, Jack. Look, we have to work. We have to get things done—other than sex. You know that, right?"

Jack paced her, more or less pursuing her around the table, past her chair and the next, toward the couch. "If you say so."

"I say so." She kept backing away from him and pointed her finger at his face. "And I mean it. I know these supermobsters and the Coven have gone silent, but do you really want to wait for them to spring their next plan?"

He stopped in front of the couch and caught her by the waist. "Not sure we've got a lot of choice. Griffen knows how to hide his people with that energy-damping thing he does."

Andy put her hands over his, looking pissed even though he knew she wasn't. "You're only being conservative about baiting them because I'm involved."

He shrugged one shoulder. "There's truth to that. Sue me."

"When you got hurt, you asked me to wait—but you're healthy now." Her tone and gaze turned serious. "Very fit. I can attest to your stamina. It's time to let me do what I do."

Jack's gut did an instant churn. Anger blazed through him, but just as fast, he realized what it masked. Fear.

And he decided to admit it since she'd probably sense it anyway. "I still don't want to make you bait for a monster that pulls people apart—or any of his bullet-eating buddies."

Andy let go of his hands and put her arms around his neck. "You got any better ideas? Because I'm afraid if we let them have all the time in the world to put together their next plan, we might not get lucky and live through it."

Movement in one of the mirrors caught Jack's eye, and he turned his head toward the misty glass as Andy kept talking.

"I think you're being too cautious. I know you're worried about something happening to me, but I can take care of myself."

"Somebody's coming." He let her go as wind chimes started to ring all over the brownstone.

"What?" She sounded totally confused. "You can't sense elemental energies. How can you—"

Jack pointed to the large mirror, the one now bright and full of rapidly swirling mists. "Doesn't that one connect to Motherhouse Ireland?"

"Shit. Yeah. It does." Andy swept photos and ash and water off the communications platform. "You better step back. Whoever's coming through doesn't seem to need help on this end, so it's probably a Mother."

The wind chimes jangled and clanged.

Jack moved a few feet to the side. Staying out of the way was a wise choice when it came to the Mothers, especially the fire breathers who wore the green robes of Motherhouse Ireland.

Less than a minute later, the mist in the mirror parted to reveal a stone chamber and a tiny woman so close to the glass she looked like a gray-haired, wrinkled blur. The wind chimes got more and more frenetic as she got closer to the glass, and closer. Jack's skin tightened, and he knew he was picking up bits of the powerful energy surging as the woman stepped into the projective glass, into one of the ancient energy channels coursing through the planet—and out of the smoking mirror on their wall. She landed easily on the table, like she'd done nothing but hop from one spot to another in some children's game.

Her fierce green eyes blazed at Jack before turning on Andy, and he noted the Irish hand-and-a-half sword on her back, crossed with a Chinese great sword that had to be almost as tall as the woman herself. Her hair hung in fuzzy ropes all around the blades, and there was no mistaking who had come calling.

"Mother Keara," he said by way of greeting as the smells of wildfire, smoke, and sword oil filled his nose. Little by little, most of the wind chimes settled to silence.

Andy gave the formidable Mother a nod. She obviously didn't share the sudden, wary tension that consumed Jack the minute he saw the woman. Mother Keara didn't make social calls, so Jack's autopilot took him to immediate red alert.

Mother Keara glanced around the brownstone's living room, then asked Andy, "Where's yer group?"

"They went to the townhouse to take report for tonight's patrol." Andy gestured to the front door. "I was here looking at mug shots, trying to get a bead on Frank—on the enhanced mobster who pulls people apart."

Mother Keara's green eyes narrowed. "Did you?"

"Yes. It's Ari Seneca, a Balkan crime lord." Andy reached down to a pile of photos and pulled out a picture, but when she tried to hand it to Mother Keara, the old woman waved her off.

Smoke rose from Mother Keara's shoulders as Andy tossed the photo on the couch. "I know who that one is. Good-lookin' in his day, smooth talker—and a first-rate bastard running cons and guns and money in two nations, across a long span of years for a human. Why would he let such be done to him?"

Andy blew a cloud of smoke out of her face. "We don't have an answer for that."

Jack would have responded to the question, but he knew better. Where the older Mothers were concerned, it was best to speak only when spoken to, especially if you had no natural ability to repel earth, fire, or giant gusts of air. It still struck him as odd to watch Andy speak to Mother Keara like an equal, with none of the automatic deference younger Sibyls usually gave their elders. Even with all his worrying about how much she expected of herself, Jack realized he still let himself forget that she was a Mother in her own right.

Quietly, carefully, he edged around the table until he was standing beside her, facing Mother Keara directly. Something was wrong, and Jack had an instinct that the something involved him.

Mother Keara gave him a quick appraisal, then nodded like she approved of his existence. "I came to give a report of my own. With the others gone, I'd do just as well to give it to you, Jack Blackmore."

Jack gave her a polite nod and waited, mouth closed. He was surprised, then gratified when Andy's hand brushed his. She wasn't making any secret of her association with him—that had to be a good thing, right?

Mother Keara paid the gesture no mind. She stood on the big table giving off smoke like a messenger from hell, and her voice came out strong and forceful as she said, "We have made contact with the Host in Ireland, but our efforts came at a high cost. One of our Mothers is in the infirmary, though we expect she'll recover soon enough."

Andy frowned. "Do the Sluagh know why some of their ranks have come to New York City?"

Mother Keara's face puckered. "They do, but damned if they'll be givin' us any easy answers. Queen Gwynneth lay ill, but she received us long enough to say her warriors are off searchin' for what rightly belongs at the Unseelie Court."

"That's cryptic," Jack muttered, wishing he'd had a chance to interrogate the faerie queen, or whatever the hell she was.

Mother Keara folded her arms and gave off even more smoke, along with a few stray flames. "The Host seem to be believin' things were unfairly stolen from their kingdom. Queen Gwynneth wouldn't let on what those things might be."

"They can't have their own children, right?" Andy's frown deepened. "Camille said they used to steal humans to mate with—people they thought nobody would miss."

"Aye, but the treaties we forged centuries ago put a stop to that," Mother Keara said. "We don't keep watch on the Host, and they let humans be unless the humans go willingly to the Unseelie Court and ask to be admitted."

Her tone suggested only an idiot would make a move like that. Jack tried to take in that explanation, and got stuck on one point. "If one of your Mothers got injured just knocking on their door, so to speak, what are the odds any human would survive that experience?"

"Slim to none, unless the Host happened to be in a grand and charitable mood." Mother Keara's smile probably would have terrified small children.

"Do the Sluagh think we—the Sibyls or the OCU— know where their stolen objects might be?" Andy asked. "Do they think we have them?"

"No. We got that much out of the old hag." Mother Keara's scary smile shifted to a glare. "What they're about has nothing to do with us—at least not at this time. By treaty, if the Host has issues with the Sisterhood, they'll be bringin' those issues to us at Motherhouse Ireland first. We'll hear them out and set plans for resolvin' the problem."

"So we just ignore them." Jack didn't much like that solution. It seemed too passive and risky. "Even when they're operating in our own backyard." He gestured to the brownstone's front window. "Or the park right across the street from our front door."

"Until they give you reason to do otherwise, yes." The old woman's green eyes got impossibly brighter as she glared at him. "Do *not* engage them. Not for any reason. These aren't simperin' demons, man. The Host have abilities that rival our own, and they drink elemental energy like humans breathe air. I wouldn't advise gettin' within a league of any of them."

Jack's mind shifted to the next difficulty. "What do they look like? If I'm going to put out a general order for the OCU to avoid contact even if these creatures are sighted, how do I describe them?"

Mother Keara gave this a moment's thought before coming up with, "Much like Astaroth demons, only with darker skin and hair and eyes. They have only one set of wings, thicker and more powerful, but they retract. In human form, they're tall, dark-haired, and muscled—and quiet. They only move at night, and you'll not be noticin' them unless they choose for you to do so."

Jack nodded. Not much to go on, but enough to give patrol officers a hint about what to avoid.

Andy didn't seem satisfied. "What about all the dead leaves and grass and animals? Usually when creatures create a die-off, they're not peaceful."

Mother Keara gave a sharp laugh. "I never said the Host were peaceful. But what you're callin' a die-off, that's a natural consequence of touchin' one of the Host. Weaker life forces get drained right away. They don't do it on purpose, and the stronger among them can control that effect for a time. In the end, though, living things around the Host tend to become dead things."

She focused her attention completely on Andy. "The Host may be formidable and dark, but they've proven honorable over the years. They'll be keepin' their part of the treaty if we keep ours. Spread the word to the city's Sibyls, if you will."

Andy agreed, and Mother Keara moved back to the center of the table. She turned a single circle, then a second, surprising Jack with her spryness as she did the dance most fire Sibyls had to do to grind open the ancient channels. It didn't take her very long, maybe half the time it took Cynda at the townhouse—and other fire Sibyls took even longer.

Wind chimes started to ring. The projective mirror on the wall brightened, and a few steps later, Mother Keara walked right off the table and seemingly into thin air. Jack had that skin-tightening sensation again, then watched in the mirror as Mother Keara walked across the communications platform back into Motherhouse Ireland. The smoke in the mirror swirled behind her, obscuring her tiny form, and then the mirror went dark.

"First time I saw that, it bent my brain for days," Andy murmured, staring at the sleek black glass.

"I can imagine." Jack tugged Andy's wrist and turned her to face him. "You came to all this even later in life than I did. You've had to get used to a lot that would drive most people insane."

Andy stared into his eyes as he bent to kiss her.

"If you start that," she whispered, "I really might lose my mind."

"In a good way?" He kissed her, and she melted into him, deepening the embrace. Jack liked how her loose shirts left plenty of room for his hands to find bare skin and roam. He really liked the soft moans she made when he ran his fingers along the small of her back, and—

The chimes over the front door gave a loud jangle.

Jack groaned and broke the kiss. "Tell me that's your energy."

"Not mine. Sorry." Andy pushed back from him and straightened her clothes as voices rose outside and got louder.

25

Jack ached to take Andy back into his arms, but the front door burst open and Bela came in talking to Camille. Loudly. "No. No fucking way—no projective energy. I'm positive the Coven's been busy refining their traps. They've probably dropped false leads and clues all over the city just hoping to snare us."

Both women were dressed in jeans and T-shirts instead of battle leathers, but that did nothing to soften their severe expressions.

"I don't like being helpless." Camille flexed her fingers like she wanted to get hold of her scimitar. "And I'm sick of looking night after night and finding nothing. We've done this before, the entire time we've been dealing with the Rakshasa. Poke and hunt, poke and hunt—and we got nothing until we used our projective talents."

Dio brought up the rear, dressed like a fashion model in her straight skirt and form-fitting blouse. Wind swirled through the house as she entered. "It pisses me off, too. There's got to be something we can do to find the Coven before they make this mess any worse." When she spotted Andy and Jack, she said, "We've got more dead people. Some of the Giotto crew shot it out with a few Bellagia family men in a convenience store in the Bronx. Three assholes down—and the store owner, too."

"Damn it." Jack glared at the ceiling for a second to calm himself, and he felt his face going red at the edges. "I knew this would start happening if we couldn't move on the Coven."

Andy looked like she might get sick all over the floor,

but she pulled herself together pretty fast. "Nobody knows who started the killing, so every crime family in New York City is freaking the fuck out. A lot of people are going to die. Camille, can you figure out some new way for us to throw projective energy in the Coven's direction so we can at least *look* for the bastards? Something they won't recognize or expect?"

Camille didn't answer right away because she was busy sniffing the air in the brownstone. "Who's been here? The whole place smells like really old fire Sibyl."

"Mother Keara brought us a message." Andy pointed to the chairs, and as her fighting group took seats around the communications platform, she relayed what she and Jack had learned about the Host.

When Andy finished and sat on the couch beside Jack, Camille said, "I don't like it. The Host are too dangerous for us to just let them wander around town unchecked. What if they accidentally touch a human child—or even somebody's dog? Knowing our luck, they'll start killing mobsters, too, and we'll have full-blown gang Armageddon in the streets."

Dio lounged back in her chair, her expression showing only mild concern. "If the Host really do honor their treaty like Mother Keara said, that won't happen. And if they're anything like the Keres, they mean what they say, and they never break their word."

"I don't like it, either," Bela said, "but it seems like it's a risk we'll have to take for now."

Jack leaned forward. "Unless we figure out what they want and make sure they get it. I could put a few teams on researching that and ask the Astaroths to help, if you think that might make a difference."

Everyone paused, and all eyes moved to Camille, since the Host had connections to the fire Sibyls—and because Camille tended to be the academic in their group. If anybody could spot a flaw in a plan, she could.

"I think that's an excellent idea," she said. "The Astaroths won't be at risk for an energy drain, and Jake Lowell has taught his crew to be very diplomatic. Maybe they'll make friends."

Andy smiled brightly. "If they don't start an interspecies war. Think you two could convince your husbands to pitch in? Bengals should be safe from the Host's influence, too."

Camille and Bela both agreed, but Camille's attention had shifted to the photo lying on the couch next to Andy. She pointed at it. "Who is that?"

"Oh! I almost forgot." Andy picked up the photo. "Everyone, meet Frank."

"No shit." Dio studied the picture and obviously recognized the man. "Ari Seneca himself. Damn, he must have been whacked to let somebody do that to him."

"I wonder how much of his actual mind and essence stayed intact." Bela took the photo from Andy. "With paranormal genetic experiments, it could go either way—but it would be good to figure that out. Might help us guess what he'll do next."

"Either his emotions are ruling everything, or his handlers have absolute control," Andy said. "What I sensed from the remnants at the warehouse crime scene added up to betrayal and fury. I don't think what's left of Ari Seneca has any control left to him at all."

"Even if we could get the word out on the streets that he's behind the first bunch of killings, I'm not sure it'll stop all the conflict." Dio let off a frustrated burst of wind. "The other gangs wouldn't be happy until they got him, and if they went after him, we'd just get more piles of body parts. Our best shot is to find weapons to bring him down—him and his supermobster friends."

All eyes went back to Camille, and Jack asked the question. "You got anything new for us?"

"I've adjusted the elemental locks on our bullets and blades to make them more lethal to the supermobsters, at least the kind that attacked you and Andy in the alley." Camille pointed toward the weapons closet under the stairs. "When we shoot, we need to use the new hollow-points I've treated, direct hit to the head or do a lot of damage on the extremities—tear away flesh until they're down, then make the head shot. I think our blades will cut them now, so beheading's an option, too."

Jack wanted to believe it would be that simple, but he'd been dealing with demons and paranormal monsters way too long. "And if all of that doesn't kill them?"

"My best guess is, we handle them like Rakshasa," Camille said. "Elementally treated metal to the heart, beheading, and burning. I don't think we have to scatter the ashes so completely, though. I don't think they can reconstitute."

Jack filed that away to share with the OCU as soon as they finished with this meeting, but another question kept nagging at the back of his mind. He eyed Camille, then Andy, not sure if he should ask it, but in the end, he had to know.

"Which one is it?" He realized he was clenching his fists and made himself relax.

Camille gave him a blank look like she had no idea what he was talking about, but Andy picked up on the question right away. "Which Eldest survived, Camille? I know Motherhouse Russia would have checked, and so would you."

Flecks of red formed between Camille's freckles. "Oh. That." Her breath came out slowly, like she might be steadying herself. "We think it's Tarek."

Bela's jaw locked. Tarek was the demon who'd infected and almost killed her husband—and one of Jack's best friends.

Dio and Andy also looked thunderstruck. Dio's dreams had new meanings now, even though Jack wasn't mystic enough to figure them out.

His fists clenched all over again because he couldn't believe any of the Eldest—least of all *that* bastard—had gotten out of Camille's molten ore bath alive. "How?"

"No idea." Camille looked as frustrated as Jack felt. "The Sibyls and the OCU worked the aqueduct in teams. Each demon kill got logged before the remains got scattered, and Tarek's checked off as dead."

"He must have gotten out before we moved in and started recording," Bela said.

"Or somebody took him out, or helped him escape." Andy seemed suddenly tense, and Jack knew she was running through a mental list of who could have pulled off something like that and lived through it.

Bela reached out and patted the arm of Dio's leather chair. "Knowing that Tarek's not dead, what do you make of your dream now? I mean, he doesn't have to come back to life if he's already here, right?"

Dio gave this some thought as eddies of wind stirred against the tile floor. "It still feels real to me, that he needs a ritual to regain his full strength."

For a few moments, nobody said anything. Then Andy let out a sigh, and Jack knew he was in trouble. She was moving to decision mode, and he had a gut-level instinct that he wouldn't like where that took them.

"We can't wait for a Rakshasa Eldest to show up on our doorstep," she said. "He could be busy making another army of half-breed Created to take us on, along with however many supermobsters he's got at his disposal."

Bela rubbed her face with both hands. "But we could look for a month and never find a hint. No matter what, I won't agree to us using projective energy to hunt them. That'll just get us killed."

Andy's expression conveyed her increasing worry and frustration. "Then we need to draw them out, like I've been saying. Get them to take a chance."

"Yeah, right." Dio crossed her legs at the ankles and tapped her fingers on the chair. "Just exactly how are we supposed to do that?"

"Dangle something they want right under their noses," Andy suggested despite the look Jack gave her. "Me."

As Andy's fighting group sat silent, contemplating that little bit of insanity, Jack thought fast. "I think it makes more sense to pull the Sibyls and the OCU out of the center of the city. Go to your safe houses, and we'll form grids and launch tactical sweeps. Hard target moves. Big show of force until we flush them out."

Camille shook her head. "They could stay ahead of us by moving around and slipping in and out of places we've already searched."

"We can hit the informants hard." Jack pushed his fist into his palm. There had to be another way other than Andy's plan. Had to be.

"If there are any informants who know anything," Andy said, "which there won't be, the Coven will just kill them when they realize you're tightening screws."

"If Tarek is behind all this, then he'll want us to take a chance like this." Dio glared at Andy, and Jack decided he liked Dio more than he realized. "It's playing into his hands. He'll draw us in and cut us down. Cut *you* down."

To Jack's great relief, Andy looked thoughtful instead of pissed off at Dio's challenge. "I'm not sure it's Tarek or Seneca's people who have a grudge with me. It may be Griffen or one of his Coven. That makes more sense, and that's where my instinct keeps going."

"Does it matter?" Dio fired back, her gray eyes wide and angry. "Dead's dead, no matter who kills you."

Yeah, Jack liked Dio—and by the look of the expression on Bela's face, he was about to like her a lot more, too.

"Andy, I don't think we can risk you so deliberately and totally, not without the consent of the other Mothers," Bela said. "It's one thing to take chances on routine patrol, but this—well. You're one of just a few water Sibyls in the world right now."

"Elana can do what I do." Andy folded her arms and glared at each one of her group, one at a time. "And even if she couldn't, I'm not just a Mother, I'm a fighter, and in my heart I'm still a cop. The risks I take are my call, nobody else's."

Before Jack could even begin to find an argument for that assertion, Bela's cool voice took over the room. "You might be a Mother, but this is my quad. I'm your mortar, and it's *my* call, and I'm saying no. For now." Her gaze shifted to Camille even though Andy was sputtering for a comeback. "Earlier, Dio had a point. We need a new way to use projective energy, or maybe some new elemental protections. Care to join me in the lab?"

"I'm game." Camille was on her feet in a second, and so was Dio.

"Don't look at me," the air Sibyl said. "I'm not going near that stuffy underground dungeon. I'll check with the Astaroths, if I can find one. Their archives are even better than the ones at Motherhouse Greece, and if there's anything we haven't found on projective talents and protections, they're the ones who'll have it."

Andy sat, apparently speechless, as her fighting group dispersed without making eye contact with her. Dio jogged up the stairs without so much as a sideways glance, and Bela and Camille scuttled off through the kitchen, heading for the downstairs chamber that housed the lab.

Before the swinging door between the living room and the kitchen even stopped swinging, Andy got to her feet and glared down at Jack. "Did all of you work this out ahead of time? I'm not some rookie who needs coddling and protecting—I have special skills, and these Coven assholes seem to want me, personal-like. It's crazy not to use that to our advantage."

Crazy. The word echoed through Jack's mind as he held up both hands, palms out, hoping he looked clean and innocent and completely nonconspiratorial. He stood. Slowly. No point in riling Andy into a mini tidal wave that might smash the brownstone's front window.

"You're probably right," he said.

"Damn straight I'm right." She jabbed a finger against his chest even though he still had his hands raised in a peace gesture and he'd just agreed with her. "And don't forget, you asked me back here because I'm a strategist, and a damned good one—so why do you keep arguing with what I propose?"

"Give them a little more time to find an alternative to hanging you out in the wind. Please? At least something to better our odds?"

Andy kept glaring, but at least she stopped poking him. Her palm flattened against his shirt, and he wondered if she was about to push him through the living room wall. She hissed out a breath through her teeth, and her red cheeks faded to a slightly less hectic shade of furious.

"It's hard to argue with you when you're not being an asshole."

"Thanks," Jack said. "I think." With all the bad news about more gang shootings, he knew he should be all business, but she had her hands on him, and Andy's touch short-circuited his better sense.

"I still think I'm right," she muttered.

"Noted."

"I still think we're going to have to do this my way. Soon. A few days. A week tops. We can't keep slow-footing because you're all scared I might get a hangnail."

Jack tried to keep any hint of frustration out of his voice. "You took a bunch of bullets in the last attack. A lot more than a hangnail."

"They didn't even leave marks." She moved her hand across his ribs to his shoulder, right above one of his new scars. A funny look crossed her face, like maybe, just maybe, she might have realized that putting herself in danger could have consequences for other people in the world, too. The fight seemed to drain out of her then, and she just stood there with her hand pressed tight and warm against him.

"So, earlier we were talking about babies." Jack risked putting his hands on her shoulders. "Since you can read my feelings so clearly and you know exactly how much I like that idea, what do you think about having my children?"

Andy's mouth came open. "I—" She blinked at him. "I—you. Now you *are* being an asshole."

He put his arms around her. Pulled her to him and lowered his face toward hers. "I think we'd make gorgeous babies, if they come out looking anything like you."

She kissed him, then whispered, "Asshole," one more time for good measure.

Jack didn't care. For the moment, his world had up and turned perfect while he wasn't paying attention, and that was just fine by him.

(26)

Sunlight streamed onto the beach as Andy walked with Elana, barely enjoying the waves and definitely not enjoying the heat. "Jack's not listening. I've spent almost a week trying to convince him to let me try one of my plans. He's dead set on going after one of Seneca's heirs instead."

"Jack's stubborn." Elana navigated the rocky terrain like she had every step memorized. "And he's concerned for you. I imagine by now he's desperate to make some progress—any progress—before more killings touch off riots and gang wars."

Andy didn't want to acknowledge how right Elana was, so she kicked a little sand and some stones instead.

"As for you," Elana continued, "you're not confident enough in your own instincts, and you aren't giving the truth enough value."

Andy bit back a bunch of smart remarks, but in the end, she couldn't completely control her own mouth. "I'm confident. It's just that nobody else is—and what the hell do you mean about truth? I tell the truth."

"Some of it." Elana shrugged. "What you let yourself know and accept. The rest you look away from because you fear it."

"Okay, old woman. Knock it off." Andy kicked a few more rocks. "I don't fear anything."

Elana stopped walking and turned her scarred face to the sea. "Why do you think you can heal Jack Black-more? Why is it, do you suppose, that your talents work on him when they would have little or no effect on another human with no elemental abilities?"

Uh-oh. Andy looked at the water, too, but she didn't find it relaxing at all. "I—I haven't given that much thought."

"Come now. Is that the truth?"

"Go to hell, Elana."

The old woman laughed at her. "Your own feelings for him make a connection between the two of you. A true connection, soul to soul. If you can let yourself evade one obvious truth, why not others?"

Andy found herself too choked up to say anything, so she didn't bother trying. She focused on easing a few of the bigger waves she'd accidentally summoned, helping them crest early, then watching as the foamy water swirled around her bare feet.

"It's been too long since we occupied our rightful place in fighting groups." Elana sounded sad—and a little anxious. "They'll learn, Andy. And, I'm sad to say, so will you. To disregard a water Sibyl's intuition is to court disaster."

Images of Bela's smile, Camille's grin, and Dio's bright, stormy eyes flashed through Andy's mind. "I don't want any disasters. God, that's the last thing we need."

"Then you must listen to yourself, and you must make others listen. It's not always possible to accept truths in your own good time, or to allow others that luxury. Truth—and destiny—have their own timetables."

Andy heard the words, and she heard truth, both what Elana said and what Elana meant, but how was she supposed to figure all that out *and* make everybody do what she sensed was best? She stared out at the sea, feeling its peace, its power, its immense relentlessness. The sea never had to convince anybody of anything. It just flowed where it wanted, how it wanted, and washed over anything that stood in its way.

For all my bluster, I'm more like a windswept puddle than this ocean. Andy bit at her bottom lip. *I've got to find my own inner force.* Aloud, she said, "Jack's plan isn't all bad. He's got some good points about going after the visible remnants of the Seneca empire. How can I argue with that?"

"It may not be that your plan is superior to his, or his to yours." Elana still seemed patient, but she was clearly worried, and the light off the blue water made her hair twice as silvery. "You may simply be sensing that you and your group should not take the direction he's encouraging."

"But why? What reason can I give?"

"We don't always know the reason. We just feel it here." Elana placed her hand over her heart, then let it drift down to her belly. "Have you had more dreams?"

"Just one, about a quiet place in the ocean and floating on waves so warm I never want to leave. It was peaceful, not some portent of doom."

"But the rest of your dreams, and your air Sibyl Dio's nightmares—do you still see monsters from your past, rising to kill you all?"

"Yes." *And Neala.* Andy didn't say that aloud because she didn't want to make it any more real.

"How does your group feel about the dreams?"

Andy started into descriptions about Bela's beliefs, Camille's theories, and Dio's ideas, but Elana stopped her. "I didn't ask you what they thought. I asked you how they felt."

"I—nervous, I guess." Andy tried not to look at Elana, but she couldn't help it. "Don't give me that shame-on-you expression. My group doesn't want me poking around their emotions. They tell me almost every day."

"Do it anyway. Force the issue. Force all the issues just as your fire Sibyl forces issues of communication and your earth Sibyl makes decisions about directions the group will take. Force it like your air Sibyl forces protection in emergency situations and never fails to record the necessary details. This is your duty, Andy, and it matters."

Andy watched the waves wash into the tidal pools, then watched the water eddy off down dozens of grooves in the rocks and sand. "Everything connects. Everything returns to the same source." Elana planted her foot across one eddy as if she could see it in great detail. Trapped water washed against her foot, then pooled, backing up the outflow for that tiny branch of the system. "Not much water retained. Not much effect on the source—though in truth, we never know that. It could be a tipping point for temperature or salinity or nutrients needed by a weak species that feeds a stronger species. Chain reactions could begin. The effect on the whole might be tremendous."

"Or it might be nothing."

"Yes. But no matter what, the effect on the water in this pool"—Elana pointed to the moisture beside her foot—"is intense. Possibly permanent. This water may never rejoin the source, at least not in its current form."

"I get it, I get it." Andy wanted to sigh, but she managed not to do it. "My quad is like the tiny branch you dammed up with your foot. If I don't take care of what I'm supposed to take care of, bad things could happen."

"To them. You. Maybe everyone."

"No pressure." Andy hugged herself and started walking away, wishing she hadn't come here this morning at all.

"Plenty of pressure," Elana called from behind her. "All the pressure in the world."

Less than eight hours later, Andy decided Elana was unrealistic, cracked, or just plain crazy.

There was no reasoning with Jack about him being wrong and her being right. The man was too damned stubborn for words. She really didn't think this raid was a good idea, but Jack wanted it, and Bela, along with most of the OCU and the Sibyls in the city, thought hitting one of the few remaining Seneca family strongholds might gain them some valuable information. God only knew Andy wanted movement on this case, but everybody might be getting a little too desperate for progress. Sometimes yanking the tiger's tail wasn't the best strategy—literally or figuratively.

Not that anyone's listening to me.

Elana would tell her to make them listen—but how?

And what would happen if she couldn't?

The warm night air seemed to stick to Andy's skin as she followed Bela and Camille into the basement of the big office building. Her sensitive Sibyl vision made the night bright, but the darkness still seemed too close. The taste of stagnant water in her mouth reminded her every few seconds that this course of action felt strange. Not really wrong, just—off. Like it shouldn't be. She gripped the crescent moon pendant around her neck and thought about Elana disrupting the flow of water on the beach in Kérkira.

Where would this lead?

Don't be stupid. You can't always have your way, and disaster won't always follow if you compromise.

Anyway, they had new advantages. Camille had remade their charms with new elemental properties. Now the jewelry was supposed to give them some basic protections from projective energy traps and make it harder for anybody to track their specific energy signatures. Good idea if it worked, but they hadn't had time to test them, and to Andy, her charm still looked and felt the same.

Dio slipped into the basement behind Andy and closed the door. Before she slid into the shadows to watch their backs from a distance, she muttered, "I don't like the look on your face, Andy."

Andy didn't answer, but Bela must have heard Dio because she stopped, turned, and said, "Talk to me."

Andy faced Bela and Camille and whispered, "Won't do any good."

"Andy." Bela sounded wounded, and Andy felt like a bitch.

So much for managing her group's emotional flow. Andy sucked in a deep breath of the stale air in the quiet basement. Some sort of telemarketing firm used it in the daytime, and her sensitive vision picked out rows and rows of desks, chairs, and phones. The remnant emotional energy in the place felt frenetic and a little desperate. "Sorry, Bela. I didn't mean that you wouldn't listen or care. I meant we're committed to this course of action, and I had a chance to voice my objections earlier. I got overruled."

"Okay, but that's your my-instincts-are-bothering-me look." Bela studied her with dark, worried eyes. "Do you sense something wrong in the building?"

"No, not really." Andy rubbed her leather-clad arms with her palms to fight the chill from the old, rattling air conditioner servicing the building. "I just feel like we're off course here. Right ocean, wrong current."

"And?" Camille glanced around the basement, then back at Andy. "We have three minutes. Say the rest of what's on your mind."

Andy frowned. "I think Jack's doubting that Tarek's alive, and I don't doubt it."

"I don't, either," Camille said.

"I think he's got plenty of tricks up his furry demon sleeve." Andy let her concerns out in a rush, feeling stronger and more settled with each word. "I think we might be about to get our asses kicked—or do something that leads to that outcome down the road."

"We've got five OCU SWAT units and four Sibyl patrols converging." Bela looked at the ceiling over their head.

"We've already arrested the lookouts—three humans, headed to the precinct for questioning. All we're going to do is bust a crooked stock trading operation Seneca's son is still managing off the third floor of this building and question the guy if we can. I don't think there'll be any ass kicking tonight. Not our asses, anyway."

Andy fidgeted with her own elbows. "Maybe not. If it's that simple. If everything works like we think it will."

"We've got good surveillance," Camille said. "It's fifteen guys, all human, and Ari Junior. No demons. No projective traps."

"That we know of," Bela allowed. "But we won't need projective energy for this raid. Even if we did, I think Camille's new protections would give us time to react if we encountered any unusual elemental protections or energy snares."

"I know, I know." Andy let her arms fall loose and tried to shake out her tension. The emotions bouncing out of her group ranged from irritation to impatience to worry, and she didn't know how to get a better read, a deeper read, much less redirect the energy or even put it to good use. She didn't even want to bring up sensing feelings since it made the people closest to her so uncomfortable. "Honestly, maybe I'm just ticked because everybody went with Jack's plan instead of mine."

Bela's angst shifted to something like sympathy. "Yeah, well, I can understand that. Before he showed up and took over, this would have been your call."

"It wouldn't have been my anything." Sadness trickled through Andy, top to bottom. "When I started really accepting all of this and becoming a Sibyl, I would have had to give up my station and status with the OCU and the NYPD. That's not Jack's fault."

"I don't think he's being overprotective, just so you know." The sympathy stayed on Bela's face. "Just . . . reasonably protective."

She didn't address Andy's sadness and confusion about the loss of the life she had known, but Andy didn't fault her for that. That topic was too broad and huge to address in a handful of seconds in some strange basement when they were supposed to be on a raid. And she had no business letting all that emotion distract her, either.

Time to pack it all away. Time to go to work.

Camille slid her hand to the hilt of her scimitar. "We have to move."

Andy reacted immediately, falling into the raid time schedule. She walked with Bela and Camille to the stairwell they had located on structural maps provided by the OCU researchers. No structural alarms had been detected, and Andy didn't sense any elemental alerts, either. Bela gave an all-clear signal, followed by Camille. One at a time, earth first, fire second, then water, they slipped into the stairwell and climbed toward the third floor. Behind them in the basement they had just vacated, Andy heard the rustle of OCU officers moving in to take their initial positions.

Andy sensed other Sibyls nearby and on the move. Her pulse picked up and her breathing got faster. Her muscles felt loose and ready, and her hand dropped to the hilt of her dart pistol. They reached the third-floor stairwell door. Bela pushed it open. Waited. Waited a little longer.

Another Sibyl group was arriving from the western corner of the floor, having come up a separate staircase. Two more groups were on their way down from the roof, covering the north and south doors. OCU squads waited for the all-clear on each staircase, and one squad had the elevator covered.

When the Sibyls got into position, Bela quietly opened the door to lead Andy and Camille into the hallway. Andy tapped twice on the metal railing before she left the stairwell, getting their OCU SWAT team in motion.

Once she got into the hall, Andy detected no stray elemental energy on the third floor. All the other Sibyls seemed to reach the same conclusion, and Maggie Cregan, who was closest to the elevator, pushed the call button to bring up the main OCU raid team. When she turned to rejoin her fighting group, she gave Andy and her group a startled look. Her gaze moved over them like she was searching for something, but whatever it was she didn't find it.

Andy didn't have time to figure out what was bothering Maggie. If it was serious, she'd let them know later. For the moment, Andy was just glad they hadn't run into any unexpected disasters.

In the center of the main hall, the wooden doors to Seneca Trading were closed, but light spilled under them, illuminating the old tile of the building's hallway. All the hall fixtures had been switched off, likely by a computer program at the close of business hours, and the other offices on the floor weren't occupied at this time of night. Even though the American markets were closed, Seneca's group used this time to contact and pressure clients, work world markets, and deploy illegal programs designed to influence trading activity and swing activity in their favor. The SEC and other monitoring agencies had gotten wise, but the FBI's organized crime division had argued for the takedown and gotten the go-ahead from different agency coordinators. Then, thanks to Jack, the assignment had fallen to the OCU. Whichever suspects they didn't keep, they'd hand over to the various regulators who wanted them.

The soft ding of the elevator's bell cranked Andy's anticipation to fresh heights. The bad taste in her mouth had drained away. Now she swallowed the tang of adrenaline, and the hammer of blood in her ears let her know she was ready. She zipped down her face mask and saw most of the other Sibyls doing the same thing.

OCU SWAT swept past her wearing typical gear—
boots, black fire-resistant coveralls, and body armor.
Black gloves, black face covers, black Kevlar helmets,
and night vision goggles completed the ensemble. Their
assault rifles had been loaded with the new elementally
locked bullets Camille had designed, and a few carried
flashbangs, Stingers, and tear gas grenades in case the
situation went seriously south.

Jack and Saul Brent had suited up, and they moved
with the main raid unit. Jake Lowell, wearing nothing
but jeans and a nice blue shirt, brought up the rear.

"Nothing like this," Andy whispered to Jack as he
passed.

His carnivorous grin felt like a reward.

She tensed as the raid team surrounded the wooden
doors. They didn't knock or announce. They just swung
their big battering ram.

With an explosion like a small bomb, the doors splintered and burst inward. OCU poured inside the stock
trading office, yelling, "NYPD! On the ground! On the
ground now!"

Jack and Saul and Jake disappeared from view.

Shouting erupted, and gunfire, and all the Sibyls in the
hallway drew their weapons. Maggie's sword caught fire,
and so did two other swords. Camille's scimitar didn't
flame, but the damned thing looked terrifying enough, its
curved blade gleaming in the low lighting.

Four men in jeans thundered out the ruined front doors,
looking both pissed and triumphant until they came
face-to-face with all the women in leather with their
knives, swords, and big, burning blades.

Three of the men ran back inside, preferring the police
to the Sibyls. The fourth man wheeled toward Andy's
group, but Bela warned him off with a quick "Wouldn't
try it."

He raised his hands and backed slowly into the office as Bela, Camille, and Andy advanced on him.

Andy walked through the doors beside Bela and Camille and quickly located Jack and Saul and Jake putting cuffs on swearing, furious men. Two men lay on the floor, clearly past medical help thanks to expertly placed head shots. They still had pistols in their hands. Some of the men getting cuffed had obviously been disarmed, and OCU officers were picking up discarded weapons.

"None of our people down," Bela said, and relief eased the battle energy surging through Andy's veins. She caught the scents of smoke, blood, leather, and wood, and the room smelled like victory to her.

She turned her attention back to the man they had stopped outside the office, and her jaw locked as she processed how much he looked like the monster she'd seen in her vision in the warehouse. Broad shoulders, dark hair, oil-black eyes. Yeah. This guy was nothing more than a younger version of his father.

"Ari Seneca, Jr." She smiled at him as she made sure her dart pistol was leveled at his face. "We need to talk."

He kept his hands in the air. With a heavy but understandable foreign accent, he said, "You have the gun. Or whatever it is."

Bela searched him quickly, first with elemental energy, then with her hands to rule out any plastic weapons or other items they might not easily detect. He stood very still and didn't stare at any of them even as Bela locked a pair of elemental cuffs on his wrists just to be sure he didn't have any secret elemental abilities.

He's not too surprised by Sibyls, Andy thought, and she could see the same realization on Bela's face, and Camille's, too. Wind stirred in the hallway outside, and Andy sensed the air Sibyls getting closer now that the main operation had succeeded.

"Secure," the OCU raid leader called, and Andy gave Junior another big, friendly smile.

"Time for phase two," she told him as she grabbed him by the elbow and steered him toward the office's conference room door. "A little chat with us before we hand you over to the people who *really* want to lock your ass up forever."

A few minutes later, Andy, Bela, Camille, and Dio had settled into seats at a long table in the stock office's conference room, along with Saul and Jake. Jack stayed out in the main area, supervising arrests, coordinating with other agencies, and overseeing the arrival of the OCU's computer crime techs. Andy put Ari Seneca, Jr., right next to her, and even though she no longer had her weapon drawn, he kept a respectful demeanor.

From directly across the table, Saul started to speak to Junior, but Jake, who was sitting next to Saul, stopped him with a single shake of his head. "Let Andy do it."

Saul cut Jake a look. "But Jack—"

"Has never seen Andy work." Jake's expression had a hint of fangs, and Saul went instantly quiet. He gave Andy an all-yours gesture, then folded his arms and leaned back to watch.

Andy turned to face Junior, who studied her with his mean black eyes for a few seconds before saying, "I want a lawyer."

"Good for you." Andy smiled, and hoped she was still keeping it sweet. She made no move to stop questioning or grant the man's request, because Sibyls functioned outside normal law enforcement protocols and procedures—and because she didn't give a shit what Junior wanted.

He seemed to understand this, and his meaty face darkened a few shades. "I have rights, yes? Lawyer, please."

Andy ignored him. She kept herself relaxed in her chair despite the fact she was almost knee to knee with her suspect. "Where's your father, Junior?"

Junior seemed to debate going silent and repeating his demands for a lawyer, but the sight of Dio picking her nails clean with one of her African throwing knives might have changed his mind.

"My father disappeared months ago," he said. "You know as well as I do, he's dead."

Andy waved a hand at the conference room with its decent chairs and nice oak table. "So you've taken over the few operations still profitable in this country and sent everyone else back to the Balkans?"

Junior went sullen again. "I do not know what you're talking about."

"We don't think your father is dead." Andy kept her eyes locked with his. "We think he's different."

For a moment Junior didn't move. Then he tried a jowly smile of his own. "Now you speak in riddles."

Andy glanced at Jake.

Jake stood and walked slowly around the conference table, passing Dio, then Camille, then Bela until he was standing on Junior's other side.

"Look at me," Jake said.

Junior didn't move. "I want a lawyer. I have asked three times. Nothing you do will convince me—"

Jake turned the man's chair to face him, then vanished.

When he reappeared, he started his transformation into his Astaroth form. He took his time, too, probably to be sure Junior appreciated the pearl-white skin and scary eyes, the length of his claws, the size of his double set of wings, and just how sharp his fangs looked in the conference room lighting.

Junior sat transfixed, shaking like a man seeing a ghost for the very first time. His cuffed hands started to tremble, and he swallowed twice, really fast, as Andy turned his chair to face her again.

"Where's your father?" Jake asked Junior from over

the back of the chair, allowing a full measure of demonic resonance to ring through his voice. "And why did he let himself be changed into something like me—only worse?"

Even with all her training and learning, Andy couldn't help thinking that Jake sounded like an entire legion from hell when he talked like that.

"My father is dead." Junior's voice shook as he spoke, and Andy had a sense that he was telling the truth as he knew it, or wanted it to be. She nodded to Jake, who backed off and let himself go human again.

"So tell us where Daddy's body is and we'll get you that lawyer," she said to Junior.

"No, no. You fail to understand. Somebody might have killed my father, but even if they let him live, he would be dead by now. When he disappeared, he was very sick."

Interest stirred deep in Andy's gut. Okay, now they were getting somewhere. "How sick?"

"Dying. He had lung cancer. We tried the best hospitals, even experimental drug and radiation treatments—but the tumors in his lungs kept growing. When my father vanished, he had weeks to live. We assumed, my younger brothers and I, that he walked away to make it easier on us. To show no weakness to our enemies."

Junior looked down at his knees, and for a moment he seemed genuinely saddened.

Andy glanced at Jake and Saul and her group. At least now they understood why Seneca had let himself be used as a demon biology experiment.

"Interesting that you mentioned enemies," Andy relaxed again, staying tuned to both sets of instincts—her police experience and her Sibyl intuition. "Before he died, your father made some unusual friends, didn't he?"

"I knew something of that," Junior admitted, "but I believed little of what he said. He told me of—of women like you, and men who had abilities beyond those of normal humans. At first I thought his mind might be slipping, but he showed me a few things." He glanced up, his black eyes bright with pride and determination. "He wanted to ensure the vitality of his family. For that, he faced fear. He was willing to take pain and risk everything, and now he is dead."

Translation—Seneca wanted to make as much money for his sons as possible, and leave the syndicate in a powerful position. "And now he's dead. But if that's true, don't you think it's odd that right after he vanished, thugs from your rival gangs start getting butchered? That all your criminal buddies are so terrified they're taking potshots at each other?"

"Odd? No." Junior seemed genuine with that answer, too. His cuffs rattled as he shrugged. "Fortunate for me, yes. But I have no knowledge of any of that, or how it has happened."

Truth. Except the part about it not being odd. Junior thought it was odd, all right. In fact, it scared him shitless, just like it did everyone else.

"You had, what, six armed men to protect a bunch of computer hacks?" Andy leaned toward him again. "You've been worrying maybe you or your crew might be next. That's why you brought so much extra muscle to where you were running a stock-trading scam."

Junior hesitated, then gave it up easier than Andy had imagined he would. "The murders of Foucci's men were beyond anything I have seen or even imagined, even in a nightmare." His eyes flicked to Jake Lowell, now seated across the table again, polite and human and watching with interest. "It would take a monster to handle human beings in such a fashion."

"We think that monster might once have been your father," Jake said. "And we don't think he can control himself or distinguish friends from enemies—or family.

Want to tell us where he might be holed up, just in case we're right?"

"I don't believe what you're saying." Junior stared at Jake, but broke the eye contact pretty fast. "My father has not become some devil who can tear men apart with nothing but his hands."

There was no conviction in his words anymore, and he'd really started to shake.

So he did know. As much as he let himself acknowledge, anyway. Junior had also figured out that the killing might be indiscriminate, or out of his father's control, and he'd done what he could to protect himself from things he didn't understand.

Andy knew she didn't have to spell out the simple bargain—help us, and we'll keep him from killing you. It went unspoken, and Junior's slump-shouldered posture suggested he was ready to lay everything bare if they'd just get him out of this nightmare.

Andy gave Saul a nod, and Saul slid a piece of paper over to Junior. "Here's the list of Seneca properties we know about. We'll be raiding each one of them within the next hour."

Junior read the list. "My father is not in any of those places. I have been to all of them in the last month."

Taking your cut of Daddy's business, Andy thought. "Any properties we don't know about? Think carefully, Junior." She waited for Saul to slide a photo across the table, this one a full-color shot of the Foucci crew reduced to body parts and blood. "Because you could be next if you don't help us put a stop to this."

From the corner of her eye, Andy saw Jack standing in the conference room doorway, watching. He seemed pleased. She could sense that emotion, along with leftover exhilaration and something like pride and admiration.

Stay focused . . .

Junior rattled off the addresses of three properties that

weren't in Seneca's records. "They're in my wife's sister's name, Tamlyn Jones." He gave her social security number, birth date, phone number, and address of record. When he finished, Andy could tell he didn't have anything left to offer. She stood and dusted a few wood fragments off the front of her leathers.

"He's done," Andy told Jack, and Jack moved in to take charge of the man and get him to whatever agency had the strongest claim to prosecute him.

As Junior got to his feet and made his way toward the door with Jack, Jack glanced back at Andy. The look he gave her said they'd talk about all this later—after a lot of touching, kissing, groaning, and definitely, definitely not talking. Not with words, anyway.

Good thing she didn't need her focus anymore, because it evaporated like water droplets in the desert.

"No disasters," she muttered to herself. "Nothing unexpected. Guess I'll have to admit the son of a bitch was right after all."

Saul and Jake went out the door behind Junior, and Bela and Camille and Dio came to a stop beside Andy.

"You're still law enforcement," Bela told her, "even though you're a Sibyl, too."

"You did good with Junior," Dio told her. "Smooth. I was impressed."

Before Camille could add any praise, Sheila Gray, Maggie Cregan, and Karin Maros filled the conference room doorway.

"What the hell's going on?" Maggie asked, her strange green eyes bright with confusion and maybe a little fear. "We can't sense you. It's like you don't exist. You're all like those coins we found, the traps that nearly killed us behind that closed-down storefront restaurant. You're giving off absolutely nothing."

Andy saw that the other Sibyls from the raid detail had crowded in behind the East Ranger group. Apparently all of them had been surprised by the same thing and they wanted answers.

Camille's lips tugged into a smile, unusual for her around a group of Sibyls. She was usually pretty shy, especially with her successes. "Guess my charms work," she said to Bela. "Maybe we should have warned everybody before we field-tested them."

Bela gave this a moment's consideration before blowing it off by rolling her eyes. To Maggie and their audience, she said, "Camille and I have been experimenting with elemental treatments to repel projective traps." She touched the copper crescent moon pendant around her neck. "They're also designed to mute our signatures so hostile creatures can't track us directly."

"Well, Camille's right. They definitely work." Karin sounded impressed, but *impressed* didn't describe the other expressions Andy could see. *Wary, worried, angry, suspicious*—those would be better words.

"If you got taken or got in trouble, we Sibyls couldn't track you, either, no matter what kind of energy we used." Sheila's calm voice cut across the currents of agitation flowing between the Sibyls outside the conference room. "You should take that into consideration before using those charms on a regular basis."

Andy wasn't sure, but she thought she picked up a note of condescension in Sheila's warning, and it irked her. They'd heard crap like that before from the Mothers when they all began to explore their projective talents, then again when Camille first started crafting her charms to help them with their projective energy.

Real Sibyls don't need jewelry to fight battles. . . .

"Yeah, thanks." Andy took Camille by the elbow. "We'll keep that in mind if we get snatched or dropped down a storm drain. I thought we were the big bad trackers, anyway."

Bela started for the conference room door, and Sheila's group stepped out of her way. All the Sibyls moved enough to make a path for them, but Andy sensed their stares as well as the curious gazes from OCU officers and technicians as she steered Camille through the crowd. Behind her, Dio's wind energy picked up to dangerous levels for an indoor setting, and light fixtures and the pieces of the broken office doors started to rattle.

Not soon enough, they made it to the stairwell and started out of the building the same way they came in for the raid.

"I can't believe there's still so much prejudice against projective energy and improving the science we're using."

Camille's voice sounded young and vulnerable, making Andy feel even more protective.

"People can be assholes," she said. "Even Sibyls."

Camille sighed. "They have a point about us not being able to sense and track each other."

"I can sense all of you just fine." Dio's tone screamed *don't listen to those uptight bitches*. "And we *are* the ones who would be doing the tracking. They're just weaker in the elemental detection department than we are."

"Or maybe since we're all wearing the same charms except for the differences in the metals, we aren't blocked from detecting each other," Bela suggested.

Andy waved that off with one flick of the wrist. "I like Dio's explanation better."

They banged open the basement door, spilled into the dark space, and Andy had about two seconds to freeze, to choke, to realize the truth.

Here it was. This was it. The unexpected complication.

The disaster.

A wave of energy unlike anything she had ever experienced drove Andy to her knees.

It hit her hard, over and over, punches she couldn't withstand, but couldn't surrender to, either. The energy beat her, pulled against her, sucking her essence just like a projective trap—worse than that. Infinitely, horribly worse.

She tried to scream.

No sound.

She tried to breathe.

No air.

She pitched forward, barely catching herself on her palms. Some part of her mind was aware that her entire group had gone down with her. Fighting. But losing.

The charm at her neck trembled against her skin, then burned her as water coated her leathers. She didn't know where the water was coming from, but she had a horrible feeling it was rising out of her own pores.

Life fluid.

Leaving me.

She tried to pull it back and couldn't. She thought about Bela and Camille and Dio. Tried to reach out to them with her energy. Nothing happened.

The charm got hotter. God, she wanted to rip the thing off before it branded her.

Water poured off her skin now.

The charm burned her until she cried out—and this time, she heard the sound. Light flared and the ground shook—

And nothing.

The energy bruising her inside and out vanished with a dull, listless thump, almost like an explosion in reverse. Andy gasped deep and fast, gathering air, summoning her water energy, pulling her body's fluid and essence back where it belonged. Almost instantly, she made contact with Bela, then Dio and Camille, offering what power she could to help them, but they all seemed okay— or at least as okay as she was.

Andy blinked at the dark basement, but couldn't see anything near her. She couldn't hear anything, either, but she smelled something sharp and earthy. Juniper, maybe, or some other type of evergreen. Her mind followed the scent, and the charm around her neck stayed hot as she rocked back to sit on her ass and grip the metal as her projective senses flooded around the room, searching, pushing at everything—

There.

Near the door.

Four of them. No, wait. Five. Six.

Whoever or whatever they were, they must have sensed her probing them, because they stopped moving.

"I know you're there." Andy forced herself upright.

She staggered, but still managed to draw her dart pistol and gather more of her elemental energy. Water trickled into the basement through the floor, the walls, the ceilings. In a few seconds she'd have enough to hit the bastards with a cold blast like a fire hose if they didn't start acting friendly.

Wind energy blended with her water, and Andy knew Dio had gotten to her feet. She heard the whisper of throwing knives drawn from Dio's belt. Then came the whisper of a wicked, curved scimitar leaving its scabbard, suggesting Camille had shaken off the attack. The basement floor trembled again, and this time it was Bela who drew her serrated blade.

"You've got three seconds to start talking before we wipe the floor with you," Andy said, punctuated by Dio's menacing battle snarl.

One of the figures moved. Slowly. Carefully. As if deliberately trying not to incite Andy to fire or Dio to eat them.

Why couldn't she see the thing better? Man-shaped, definitely. Tall and heavily muscled, but her usually keen Sibyl vision seemed to have deserted her. That, or the man-thing was made out of darkness and shadows.

It raised its hands, and a purple-black light kindled between its palms.

Andy started to squeeze the trigger on her dart gun before the thing could take them out with whatever weird fireball it was making, but Camille yelled, "No! Wait."

The light over the man-thing's head expanded until his features became more distinct, from his long black hair to his black jeans and shirt. He had arms like the most dedicated gym rat ever, and all the bare parts she could see had tribal markings that glowed black in the weird illumination. Those thighs—damn. The guy could probably crush skulls with his legs, and without much difficulty.

"His ears are pointed," Andy whispered to Camille. "Like the Vulcans from *Star Trek*. What the hell is he?"

Camille lowered her scimitar, then sheathed it and said something in Gaelic. Andy had no idea what it was, but the man nodded, spoke a few words in return, and a few seconds later, he grew wings. Big black ones. They had feathers, but not ragged bits of fluff like the Keres— real, with rounded tips and darker patterns etched into the black down at connecting points. The light he had made hovered over him now, and Andy saw the creatures with him. Four more men came to stand beside him, and one woman. They looked enough like each other to be relatives, except the five newcomers weren't showing their wings. Every last one of them seemed so dark and beautiful that their appearance nearly moved Andy to tears.

"Everyone," Camille said slowly and carefully, overe-nunciating like she needed to be sure she got every detail correct, "meet the Host."

"Oh, shit," Dio muttered, and her wind energy whipped down to nothing.

Andy lowered her dart pistol, but she didn't holster it. Just because these creatures had some treaty with the fire Sibyls didn't mean they weren't dangerous. The Keres could have easily killed her and everybody else who tres-passed on their mountain back when she killed the Leviathan. Who knew what the Host might do if they didn't get what they wanted?

"This is Mikeal." Camille gestured to the Host show-ing his wings. "He's like their captain. Prince, really."

"I'm not bowing," Dio said in tones so low Andy barely heard her. Bela didn't say anything, but Andy re-alized she hadn't sheathed her sword, either.

"We didn't intend to harm you." Mikeal was the one to bow, fast and graceful. "We didn't realize you were so close to us. Why are you invisible to our senses?"

Camille held up the charm around her neck. "I crafted these for my fighting group to keep our energy signatures muted. They're elementally treated to block your ability to pick up our essence. We have enemies trying to find us, so I wanted to keep us safe."

Mikeal studied Camille for a few long moments, then gave Andy, Bela, and Dio similar scrutiny. As he spoke, his wings retracted, leaving him looking more human. "You have much of the old powers in you. All of you do."

"We're different from most Sibyls, yes." Camille smiled at him.

Mikeal didn't smile back. His attention shifted to Andy. "You are unique among your fellow warriors. We have encountered nothing like you in many, many centuries."

"I'm a water Sibyl," Andy told him. "One of the few."

"Our people are accustomed to existing on the edge of survival." The female member of the Host sounded almost sad. "We appreciate any creature in your position, fighting against extinction, but unwilling to cower in some distant cave just to stay alive."

Andy wondered if that gave her special permission to ask questions. She decided to take a risk and find out. "Why are you here?"

Andy meant why were the Host in New York City, but Mikeal offered a more literal answer. "We have been tracking a group of sorcerers—those who pervert energies for their own purpose. They came here tonight after you did. They entered through this door. I believe they intended to trespass farther into this building, but something put them off. They fled."

"In disarray," the Host woman said, obviously disgusted by such a display of cowardice.

"The Coven was here." Andy heard herself say the words, and gooseflesh rose across her neck. An almost-disaster. Was that what had set her instincts off about coming here tonight? "Do you know what they wanted? Do you know who or what they were after?"

Mikeal's expression remained stony, made twice as severe by the strange lighting. "That we cannot tell you. We have no understanding of their purpose, only their whereabouts now and again, when we can detect their energy."

Andy thought about asking him why he was tracking the Coven to start with, but opted for a less direct, hopefully more respectful approach. "What did you come to New York City to find?"

Mikeal didn't answer, but Andy didn't detect any malice in his silence. Whatever they were after, he considered it Host business and Host business alone.

"If we knew, we could try to help you," Camille said.

Mikeal lowered his head in a quick gesture of thanks, but he said, "We don't require assistance."

Dio laughed. "Of course not. That's why you've been poking around here for weeks murdering grass and squirrels."

Camille and Bela flinched at Dio's disrespectful tone, but Mikeal and his soldiers smiled. Maybe they liked insolence.

Good. Andy allowed herself a measure of relief and holstered her pistol. *Then we'll all get along after all.*

Mikeal's eyes tracked Andy's every movement. When she finished and folded her arms, he addressed her. "Explain the term *Coven.* Please."

"The Sibyls are actively searching for thirteen men and their followers." Andy watched the guy, thinking how much he looked like law enforcement, never mind the pointy ears and tattoos. It was something in his expression, his eyes, the way he held himself. "Sorcerers, like you said, because they pervert natural energy for their own purposes and kill innocent people. They refer to their organization as the Coven."

Mikeal nodded. "And the leader of this Coven, he goes by the human name Samuel Griffen."

"Yes." Well, well. The Host had themselves some good intel. "You're ahead on that one."

"Does this Samuel Griffen have a charm like the ones you wear?" Mikeal pointed to the crescent moon at Andy's neck. "Is this how he hides himself and his people from our detection?"

Andy glanced at Camille, who took the handoff smoothly. "Not exactly. Griffen crafted charms for his group out of Rakshasa demon teeth, but they have the same effect—muting elemental energy."

The Host exchanged looks of satisfaction, then dark, hungry anger. Andy realized they must have been deeply frustrated by their fruitless pursuits, and confused and maybe even doubting their own abilities. Now they had an explanation and an understanding of why they had been failing. They'd probably be making some changes and maybe getting some results.

"If you would surrender your charms, we would consider it a favor," Mikeal said, and Andy caught the strange tone in his voice. It sounded formal. Almost ritualistic. The juniper smell in the basement got stronger.

Camille immediately removed her necklace. When Andy and Bela and Dio hesitated, she glared at them. "I can make more. Please, don't insult them."

"Okay, whatever." Andy took off her charm. Bela and Dio removed theirs, too, and they all handed them to Camille.

Camille held out her hand, dangling the four necklaces. "May I approach safely, Mikeal?"

He bowed, then gave his companions a quick look. The woman and the other four men put some distance between themselves and Mikeal, fading into the shadows of the basement so completely that Andy went back to thinking they might be made out of darkness.

Mikeal beckoned for Camille. She walked toward him and held out the charms. He took them from her, and seemed to be careful to avoid touching her skin. "Thank you," he said. Then his dark eyes seemed to gleam with a light Andy didn't like at all. "Our bargain is sealed. We will repay you."

With that, the impromptu light he had created vanished, and so did he. Andy heard a few rustles, then the building's basement door banged on its hinges.

It took Andy's eyes a few seconds to adjust, and when she could see normally again, Camille was still standing where Mikeal left her, staring after him with her mouth slightly open. New dread bloomed in Andy's chest, and her skin got cold as she reached out to her sister Sibyl with her water energy.

Surprise. Concern. Fear. Fascination. All of those emotions bubbled out of Camille before she realized Andy was sensing them and shut herself down.

"Don't *do* that." Camille shivered, rubbing her hands against her leathers. "It makes me feel like a little girl when you tap into my feelings so easily."

Andy didn't apologize. She pointed to the basement door where traces of the Host's dark energy remained. "Mind telling us what you just did?"

"They owe us a favor. That's all." Camille glanced at the door, then back to Andy. "What Mikeal asked, it wasn't exactly a request I could refuse given their old-fashioned views on polite cooperation and exchanges of information. They would have been deeply insulted and they might have challenged us to a battle."

"Old-fashioned," Bela said. "As in draconian? Sadistic? What?"

Camille shook her head. "It's not like that. Old-school chivalry would be closer. Look, I'm sorry. I really didn't want to put them off, not when they were talking to us so freely."

"That was freely?" Dio's sarcastic tone echoed Andy's thoughts.

"Yes. And they'll repay the favor when and how they see fit. The Host are pretty fanatical about their honor." Camille glanced at the door again. "Let's get back to the brownstone. I need to make us new charms—with some more adjustments to the elemental locks."

"Yeah, those didn't work too well against the Host, did they?" Andy asked, drawing a look of wide-eyed surprise from Camille.

"Are you kidding? We surprised them." Camille spread her arms wide, encompassing the whole space of the basement. "We caught a full blast of their projective energy. By all rights, we should be burned to husks on the basement floor."

"That's good to know." Dio blew the basement door open behind Camille, making her jump. "Lovely image and all, but I am so over this place. Going home now. Anybody joining me?"

(28)

Jack got back from booking and processing the jerks the OCU had rounded up in the raid sometime around three in the morning. The minute he got to his townhouse bedroom and saw Andy, he knew something was wrong. She was all curled up in his leather chair, pale and staring at the bedroom door when he came in, and his gut clenched.

"What?" She stood and he made it to her in three steps. He put his hands on her shoulders. "Talk to me, sweetheart. What happened?"

"I—" Her bottom lip trembled, then she closed her mouth and looked unbearably, endlessly tired.

Jack wrapped his arms around her and held her tight, wishing he could pour his strength and energy into her like she had done for him. He'd give her everything he had, if he could only find a way. As it was, the best he could offer was holding her up as she told him what happened at the warehouse after they parted company. The Coven showing up, maybe to screw up the raid or go after Andy and her group. The Host tracking them and spooking them off, then almost shriveling Andy when they got surprised.

Christ.

Jack thought about the dead leaves and dead animals in Central Park and held Andy that much tighter. He felt huge to her small, rough to her soft. His bedroom room seemed unnaturally quiet as he felt her breath ripple across his neck.

Just like that, she could have been gone. Nothing but

ashes on a basement floor. That godawful image made his own breath come too short. Rage pounded through him as he tried to figure out who to kill first, but some part of his overheated brain kept hold of the fact that Andy needed him—and that he needed her to be okay. He realized he had started touching her, running his hands along her back and hips and arms just to be sure she really was whole and healthy.

"I'm fine," she murmured as he kissed her, but he couldn't accept that even as he savored the press of her warm lips against his, even as she bit his bottom lip and made him half insane with sudden, desperate need.

He'd almost lost her *again*, and this time, he hadn't even been there to make a difference. A tiny bit of treated metal and a whole lot of luck had saved her life. She moved against him, unbuttoning his shirt and jeans as he unzipped her leathers. Jack pushed the stiff sleeves down from her shoulders, freeing her arms, barely stopping their kisses long enough to get the damned suit out of his way.

Crazy.

Yeah, that word was more and more his reality. He had to have her. He had to have her right now, and he'd take her hard, make her crazy, too, make her scream, make her promise never, ever to put herself in that much danger again.

"I need you," she whispered, blasting his body to a new level of heat and want. She gave herself up to him so easily, so completely, letting him take control and finish stripping off their clothes. Jack kissed her head, her face, her ear, her neck. He nibbled the soft flesh above her collarbone, tasting the light salt of her skin and drinking in her exquisitely feminine smell. Vanilla. Oceans. Woman. All natural. All sweet. More intoxicating than any liqueur. The sight of her bare breasts, her tight nipples, and the red triangle of hair below made him wonder if he'd gone demon himself. She made him hurt. She made him burn. He could turn into a beast like some crazed werewolf. If anything ever happened to Andy, he would transform into something other, something dark and soulless and full of murder. No question about that now.

"Beautiful," he said into her ear, molding her body to his, stroking her everywhere he could reach. "You're more than beautiful. You're everything."

"I love how you feel, Jack."

Damn. He was already so hard he thought he might explode, and the sound of her sexy voice nearly made him come unhinged.

Jack managed a single "I love you." Then he lifted Andy off her feet, carried her to his bed, and spread her out beneath him, straddling her hips and gazing down at her supple muscles, at her creamy skin, at the way her eyes had gone smoky brown and her pretty lips parted with pleasure as he caressed her shoulders and arms.

When he cupped her bare breasts and closed his fingers around her hard nipples, she moaned.

"You're mine." His voice sounded like a harsh rumble to his own ears, but he didn't care. "I want you now. I want you always. This almost-getting-killed shit, it has to stop."

Andy didn't argue with him.

Jack's senses stayed on high, his arousal like a force of nature. When she looked him in the eyes, he could see it. Yes. She'd be his. She'd give herself up, keep giving herself up, open herself to him in every way he demanded, every way he dreamed—

Don't screw this up.

Jack pinched her nipples again and she lost her mind, arching her hips and rubbing her sex against him. Too much. He almost lost it, but bit his lip hard to keep himself under control. Each brush of her heat against his cock sent shocks through his body. Each moan drove him that much closer to the edge.

His.

This was how life was supposed to turn out. This was his future now: her body, her essence, her pleasure fueling his. No lines, no boundaries. No point where he stopped and she began.

Andy raised her hands to his hips and dug her nails into his waist. Then, fast as a flash, she slipped those fingers forward and caught him in a tight grip, pressing him down against her soft hairs and belly. Before Jack could form a rational thought, she stroked him from tip to balls and back again, and then he didn't have a rational thought to form.

He groaned. "You drive me out of my mind."

Gazing up at him, keeping her eyes locked on his, Andy caressed him another time, then another. Jack's head snapped back, and he heard himself say her name.

"You're mine, too, Jack." The squeeze she gave his hard shaft melted what was left of his brain. "Don't forget that."

She felt like silky heat beneath him. So soft. So good. She gripped him at the base and pulled her hand along his pulsing length.

"I want you inside me," she said. "I don't want to wait any longer."

Jack couldn't speak. He answered her by moving faster and rougher than he intended. He stretched himself on top of her, holding himself just high enough to spare her his weight. His lips crushed hers as he pushed her legs apart. Too hard. Too strong. She didn't seem to care. She kissed him back like she was starving, and when the tip of his cock rubbed against her swollen folds, he couldn't wait.

So ready. So open for him. She really did make him crazy.

"I want you, Jack," Andy whispered. "I want to be yours."

Jack drove himself inside her, and she took him deep, wrapping her legs around him like she was staking her own claim.

"You feel perfect," he told her, his chest tight, every nerve he possessed waiting to fire as he sank deeper, deeper into her warm depths.

"More." She moaned again and he gave her more, moving himself in and out of her tight center, trying to stay slow, but going too fast, then faster as she rose to meet him.

When he looked at her, her eyes were still open and that doubled the force of his thrusts. Her lips stayed parted as he pumped harder, faster, deeper, wanting her to scream, to go as crazy as he felt. Her nipples scrubbed his chest, and Jack felt their sweat mingle as they slid together. Vanilla and ocean and sex, too, ripe in the air.

When Jack kissed Andy, she gripped him tighter, drove him harder. When he let her breathe, she moaned until the sound made his body vibrate.

Hold on. Wait. Give her more.

"Beautiful." He pushed her, stretched her, shoving them both toward that just-right mix of pain and ecstasy.

Andy screamed, just like he wanted to hear. Her channel clenched around his cock, forcing him over the top with her as she drained her feelings, her emotions, her pleasure into the wild sound Jack craved almost as much as he craved her. He couldn't stop moving and neither could she. Her nails stung his back as she held on, and he rocked her, rocked her, until she went limp in his grip, until he had nothing left and she pulled him down on top of her and held him there.

Jack didn't want to fall asleep. He didn't want to take his eyes off Andy for a second, but as he rolled to his side and held her, her easy breathing took him with her all over again. Seconds later, darkness claimed him, and he slept with only bits and pieces of dreams he couldn't remember.

Sunlight nudged Jack's eyelids, and when he woke, he instantly knew Andy wasn't with him. He sat up fast, threw off the sheets, and got to his feet, grabbing his jeans and stepping into them before he processed that she was sitting in the leather chair again.

"Sorry," she said. She stretched, and he realized she had on nothing but one of his white T-shirts. It fit her like a dress—and she looked too sexy for words. "Didn't mean to startle you."

"You . . . okay?" But he knew she wasn't. He fished through everything he'd said to her before and during their lovemaking, trying to be sure he hadn't crossed any lines.

Andy let out a sigh. "Yes and no. I dreamed about dark water. A quiet place in the sea or some ocean I've never been to. Makes no sense, but it felt important. And that's the story of my life right now. I can't stop sensing things and I can't stop thinking and I can't seem to get anything sorted out."

Ah. Jack's muscles relaxed a little. He knew what that felt like—not the sensing weird stuff, but the rest of it. Which helped him find a clue about what to do next.

When he got over to the chair, Andy stood. She slipped her arms around his neck and kissed him slowly, lingering over his lips and tongue like he tasted better than the coffee and breakfast he'd been about to offer her.

Jack decided to hold her for a few minutes before he suggested they leave their little sanctuary in his bedroom, and as he rubbed her shoulders and back, she sighed again.

"Something inside me—I knew we shouldn't have raided that warehouse, but I didn't know why." She pulled back, staring into his face with no accusations or I-told-you-so's. This wasn't about who had been right and who had been wrong. "The raid itself didn't seem like a problem, just—I don't know. The direction. The peripherals? It worked out okay, but I think that was because luck intervened, or God or the Goddess or whoever takes care of total idiots who don't know how to use their own instincts, or help other people understand them."

"I'm sorry I pushed that plan." Jack frowned as he smoothed her hair, once more stinging inside from the idea that Andy almost got dead from factors he hadn't anticipated. "The Coven could have ambushed you. The Host could have cooked you and left you for dead, and it would have been my fault."

Her eyes glistened immediately, and her chin drooped as she closed her eyes. "No. It would have been mine. That's the problem."

Jack pulled her into his arms again, then sat and eased her into his lap, cradling her and letting her cry, her face pressed into his shoulder, her fingers trailing along his chest and opposite arm.

When her shaking eased, he moved until he could see her face and run his thumb across her cheek and chin. "Put it into words if you can, sweetheart, because I'm not following how any of that was your responsibility. You tried to talk us out of it nonstop."

"Tried, but failed." Her shoulders flexed as she balled her fists. "I'm supposed to pay attention to flow, to understand how to make sense of my instincts and use them for the health of my fighting group, and I think for the health of our missions and purposes, too. And I don't know how." She thumped her fist against his bare chest once. "I'm not sure about what I'm sensing. I'm not confident about it, and half the time I can't even tell what's my bull-headedness and what's my gut, you know?"

"You're expecting too much of yourself. You haven't been doing this Sibyl stuff since you were born."

More tears pooled in the corner of her eyes. "Is that going to matter when I get somebody killed?"

"The bad guys do the killing, not you." Jack brushed away her tears. "Even with all your instincts, you can't see the future any more than I can. Any more than I could in New Jersey, when I whacked my old man and lost Mom and my sister forever—or talked you into the raid that almost got you killed." His own words punched him in the guts. Truth was truth, but—yeah. Damn. "Sometimes you just have to take your best shot. Try to do the right thing and hope for the best."

Andy kissed his fingertips as they slipped across her lips. "What you did in New Jersey was right. I don't have any doubts. And now I'm pretty sure the raid itself was right. That wasn't the problem. If I'd been tuned in enough to this flow crap, I might have been able to pin-point the trouble spots and been more prepared."

"Maybe we should just listen to your gut from now on. Period."

"And if we do that, how do I get you to back off and let me do what I have to do?" Her eyes glistened, stab-bing at his insides.

"I don't know. I don't want to lose you." He touched her lips again. "I can't let that happen."

This time she bit his thumb when her pressed it to her mouth. When she turned him loose, she said, "Then we may have a few problems."

"Enough." He did his best to smile at her and keep his worries to himself. "Seems to me the next steps are straightforward enough."

Her eyes shined at him again, but this time the right way. The happier way. "I'm listening."

"Breakfast. Coffee. Lots of it. Then we'll look at whatever intel's come in about the three buildings Junior coughed up in your interview last night. What does your gut say about that?"

He took a little risk and pulled her closer. *Definitely better shining in those pretty eyes now.* He liked that. A lot.

"I think we need to scour those buildings," she said, "top to bottom."

"See?" He kissed her quick and lived through it. "Not so hard for us to agree."

"Yeah, but it'll be hard to do breakfast. It's already, like, five in the evening on Kérkira. I've missed morning and noon training classes. If I miss evening, too, Elana will kill me."

Jack kissed her again even as she pulled away. "What a life you live," he called after her as she headed out of his bedroom, aiming for the townhouse's communications room.

"Oh, yeah," she yelled back, her sweet voice echoing down the hall. "I'm a real globetrotter."

The whistling came next, that old basketball theme, "Sweet Georgia Brown."

All Jack could do was listen and laugh.

29

Rebecca blinked in the early-morning sunlight, immediately estimating the time to be between 6:30 and 7:00 A.M., as New York City measured its passage. She was growing ever more accurate with figuring time, and with estimating and predicting other natural occurrences and forces like outbursts of dangerous weather, how much it might rain on a given day, and how many sparrows had hidden themselves along a leafy branch in Central Park.

She had no idea why she could do those things, but the skill was proving useful. For example, somehow she knew her brother would wake in the next handful of minutes, and he'd go immediately to her quarters to check on her. For "safety," of course. Because he "cared."

It would be safer if he found her where he expected her to be, at least for now.

Despite her great care to slip quietly from the man's bed, Donovan Craig woke with a start. His big hand shot out and captured her wrist, squeezing the delicate bones just hard enough to make her gasp with pain.

"Sorry," he murmured, thick beard twitching around his lips as he turned her loose. He sat up, giving her a full, delicious view of his scarred and muscled chest. His usually gruff voice sounded chagrined as he said, "Didn't mean to grab you like that. You startled me."

Rebecca shrugged and massaged her wrist, drinking in the pain. Then she pulled on her clothing, enjoying the big man's look of disappointment. She liked him best of all the Coven. He had decorated his earthy-smelling private cell with stone crosses, intricate metal knot sculptures, and colorful prints from his home country. The sight of those crosses and knots and pictures gave her strange comfort, as did his Irish accent. His wild, passionate lovemaking fed her need for energy in ways she hadn't thought possible, save for standing near death and letting the darkness take over her senses. She felt renewed and strong from their night together and pleased by the flickers of adoration in his gaze.

"I have to go back to my room." She allowed herself to pull in the energy of Craig's lust for her, thrilled yet again that she had discovered so many new ways to meet her need to absorb energy from other creatures. Death and torture, after all, could be messy and inconvenient. Sex always seemed to be possible and readily accessible.

"Don't worry about your brother." Craig's voice became a possessive growl. "I won't be lettin' him cage you or chain you like he did before."

None of the Coven would stand for that, Rebecca was fairly certain. She gave Craig a grateful smile anyway, as she had come to learn some of what men needed. She wasn't a child and hadn't been for many years, no matter what her brother thought.

"Griffen's not what he once was," Craig added, pulling Rebecca back toward the bed and treating her to another burst of hot, satisfying lust.

"He's obsessed with vengeance." She kissed Craig's rough mane of hair. "He'll find his way out of that dark forest soon enough."

Craig let her go. "Before he destroys everything we're building? If I don't miss my guess, you're far more powerful than he ever was. Am I wrong?"

Rebecca studied the man's dark eyes and considered his question, then gave him an honest answer. "I don't know."

"You are. I can see it. Everyone can, except Griffen. Whatever blood you've got running in you, it's stronger than all the concoctions he's mixing."

Rebecca bent down and kissed Craig's whiskery mouth. He wasn't the first man she had been attracted to in the Coven or elsewhere, but he was the first of Griffen's group she had allowed to touch her. A good choice. A strong choice. If her brother did force her to act to bring him under control, Craig would be both powerful and loyal in the fight.

"I have to go," she told him again as she separated her body from his. He didn't argue as she let herself out of his cell, but she had figured he wouldn't. Craig wasn't ready for outright conflict with Griffen, either. Rebecca didn't know why they were both avoiding that course of action, but she had a sense it was the right choice, at least for the moment.

She blended into the shadows still lingering in the warehouse, padding back to her room so quietly she didn't disturb the mice and cockroaches she sensed scuttling behind the old, damaged walls. They kept to their own paths, and she resisted the urge to take energy from them. It wasn't necessary. She was full for the moment, brimming over, after her time with Craig.

Keeping her movements quiet and economical, she covered the last few feet to her own cell and let herself in without a single noise.

The hulking figure of Seneca waited on the single chair in her room. He lifted his monstrous head and studied her with his flat, glittering eyes. Rakshasa-like claws and fur tufts extended, he smelled like ammonia and death—but the air of despair that had clung to him until she convinced her brother to release him from his barred prison had dissipated.

Rebecca moved immediately to a small, covered cage she kept at the foot of her bed. She worked the elemental lock that had been keyed to her energy, reached into the darkness inside, and snatched the larger of two field rats she had stored within the bars a few nights ago. Without comment or recrimination, she carried the writhing, snarling creature to Seneca, and he took it from her with an almost dignified gratitude.

Before he could begin twisting and breaking the rat's limbs, Rebecca backed away from him and sat on the edge of her bed. She didn't need this energy. Seneca could have it all, and she knew he appreciated her generosity, her understanding—and her silence until he finished torturing the creature to death. When he had taken from the rat every bit of pain and terror the animal had to offer, Seneca quickly and quietly consumed the carcass, dusting away his mess until not even a hair remained.

He folded his hands in his lap, and Rebecca saw the claws on his gnarled hands retract. "You take chances with your brother's temper," he said in a low voice as, down the hall, Griffen's door banged open.

Rebecca glanced at her own door, waiting for Griffen's entrance but feeling nothing. "I'm not afraid of him now."

Seneca grunted, giving away his trepidation. "Why?"

"Because his men are becoming my men, and you're my friend." Rebecca didn't smile at Seneca because he didn't need tokens from her. He only needed rats and rabbits and squirrels—and her respect.

He grunted again. "I have no friends."

Griffen opened Rebecca's door, and she noted that his jeans and black hooded sweatshirt needed a wash. He could use a wash, too, with his greasy blond hair and food-flecked chin. Her brother had begun to slip in ways she hadn't expected, but she still didn't fear him. Perhaps she was being careless, but she didn't think so.

Griffen's cold blue eyes shifted to Seneca for a second, then flicked back to Rebecca. "You really have done a great job with him. He's so much more useful and controllable now."

Rebecca tensed at the way her brother spoke about Seneca, as if he wasn't even in the room. To spare the

monster his dignity, she got to her feet and moved out of
the room, knowing that her brother wouldn't try to stop
her, that he'd follow her—so she led him where she
wanted him to be. Downstairs, to the center of the training floor, where most of the Coven was assembling to
work with Griffen's genetically enhanced fighters. In the
farthest area of the room, Craig made an appearance,
leading two of the fighters with him and making a good
effort to keep his greedy eyes off Rebecca.

Keeping each gesture casual, Rebecca greeted some of
the men, then turned back to Griffen, who was trotting
along behind her like a dog. "Do you have a plan to capture one of the creatures we ran into in that basement
the night the Sibyls raided that stock operation? The
winged things who seemed to be made of shadows. I
think they were fascinating."

Griffen slowed, then stopped walking, facing her a
few feet away. He seemed to give her words some consideration, but quickly waved them off. "They were interesting, yes. But they're distractions. No real concern
of ours."

Rebecca saw the Coven members eyeing Griffen. They
had all experienced what Rebecca experienced near that
basement—blasts of dark energy beyond anything they
had encountered in the past. She kept her tone even and
kind and tried to sound very innocent and curious as she
said, "I believe they're important. And powerful."

Griffen gave her what he probably thought was an in-
dulgent grin. "See, that's why I'm the oldest. Because I
have perspective. I can keep focus."

The Coven went about its work, training the fighters
to take better stances and level their weapons more
quickly.

Rebecca watched each man, though she felt certain
her brother would think she was ignoring them. "What
if their blood could enhance your formulas, Griffen?

Maybe their genetic structure is just the ingredient you need to make the injections stronger and more stable."

She could tell Griffen was listening even though he wanted to dismiss her again, so she plunged ahead, letting herself go a little breathless. "Imagine, all that dark power binding with the Rakshasa talents. Sometimes the universe provides. Puts things in your path. I think the creatures were brought to your awareness for a reason."

This type of plea played to Griffen's belief in his own importance—maybe even better than she had thought it would. His eyes got brighter, and he focused on her more completely. "Would their power be controllable, you think?"

Rebecca let her gaze stray to the upper level, to her door, where the dark figure of Seneca stood silent and watching, waiting for any command she might give him. "Anything is controllable if you understand what it needs."

Griffen nodded. Thought for a few moments. "Yes. I see. If we had a better formula, we could kill Sibyls faster."

Rebecca held back a sigh.

There it was again, his incessant obsession. She had grown so weary of it, and she could see in the eyes of Griffen's men that they had, too. Like Craig, they weren't ready for outright rebellion. Not yet. But it wouldn't be much longer. The way they looked at her, with interest, with lust, and sometimes with surprise and admiration— they were coming to respect her.

"I believe I can track the creatures," she told Griffen, increasing that respect on every face in the room, save for her brother's. He had become too distracted to notice such basic, important elements in his world. "If we take a few fighters with us, perhaps we can shoot one from the sky as it tries to fly away from us."

This time Griffen's grin was more bloodthirsty than condescending. "I like the way you think, Rebecca."

Do you, brother? Rebecca let her smile be kind even though she was finally feeling a few emotions like disgust and a bone-deep dissatisfaction. She let her expression remain sweet, young, and innocent as she regarded the man who had once kept her chained and behind bars to soothe his own fears.

Then you're twice the fool I thought you were.

30

The wood and stone gym smelled like rubber and wet puppies, courtesy of the room full of nattering girls rolling in every direction.

"Any dreams?" Elana asked as she and Andy positioned two eight-year-old adepts for a round of hand-to-hand fighting and made sure their pads were secure.

"Just the one about the ocean," Andy said as she stepped off the training mat. *Last night, after Jack made love to me for hours.*

"Your quiet spot?" Elana's white eyes seemed brighter than usual. "Yes, I had the same dream. I think it's of great importance."

Andy turned to stare at her just as the two adepts started punching it out, using hand pads to block each other's blows. "But what could it possibly mean? What good are these dreams if we can't interpret them?"

"I don't know that any interpretation is necessary. The dreams may be quite literal." Elana gestured at the girl on the right. "You. Savannah. You're pulling your punches. Do you think a demon will do that? Hit her, for the sake of the Goddess. Let your partner learn something that might save her life one day."

Andy watched the girls reposition and start over, wondering if she could ever be as perceptive as Elana. "If I follow your logic about the dreams, evil minions are going to kidnap Neala and me and use us to bring dead demons back to life, and then what? I'm going to get buried at sea in that quiet spot?"

Elana didn't even treat that like a joke. She just looked

perplexed. "I sensed no death in my dreams. Only possibilities."

"Yeah, right. Look, if you don't mind, I'll worry about my water dreams after I take care of the kidnapping-demons-rising-from-the-dead nightmares, okay?"

Elana clucked. "Savannah's still throwing sissy punches." To Andy, she said, "It's about time for you to go home, my dear. Instead of dreams, try to focus on the emotional needs of your fighting group."

Andy traveled back to New York City through the townhouse communications platform. Jack and the Brent brothers weren't there, and Jake told her they were out distributing architectural diagrams of their next target to Sibyl fighting groups and grabbing an early dinner. Grateful for the few minutes of to-herself time, Andy walked back to the brownstone through the park, letting herself enjoy the slight coolness of the late-afternoon breeze. Fall would be coming soon.

Maybe I'll get to slow down enough to notice it.

Once she got back to the brownstone, she went straight upstairs and took a quick shower, then spent a few minutes studying herself in the foggy bathroom mirror.

"Still have the red hair, and it's still curly." No huge bags under her eyes, but she could definitely use a few nights of uninterrupted sleep. Overall, she didn't look that much different than she used to, back when she was just an OCU officer rousting fortune-tellers and telephone psychics running scams. All the new roles—Sibyl, Mother, close friend, advisor, lover—none of those changes showed on her face.

Do they show on my heart? Can Jack see them all?

She thought maybe he could, that he could see all of her, even when she couldn't. It amazed Andy that he never seemed to blink at all the different parts she was supposed to play. He worried, but he didn't try to control her or stop her, just to help her. That was something special about him. One of a lot of special things.

Her fingers traveled to the bare hollow at the base of her throat. She felt a little naked without her crescent moon pendant, and she wondered if Camille had managed to create new ones yet. The air in the bathroom stirred, and remnant steam swirled across her cheeks and eyes. Andy pulled the moisture deep into her depths, enjoying the soothing sensation of the fresh water even as she caught another jolt of air energy.

She pulled on her blue jean shorts and cotton top and opened the door, still toweling her hair.

Dio stood outside dressed in a stylish, matching shorts outfit with beaded seams, arms folded, like some impatient kid waiting for her turn in the bathroom.

"Something's bothering you," Andy said, immediately aware of Dio's low-level agitation.

Dio looked surprised, then yawned with a bit too much drama. "Just the same dream. It keeps me awake. I never get enough rest—but nothing like what you're going through."

"Yeah. Right." *Don't push her.* Andy couldn't help glancing at the clock on the hall wall. One o'clock in the afternoon. She had been in Kérkira for four hours, and now she had at least eleven more hours of work to do here, at the townhouse, and tonight out on the streets. This living across time zones was enough to melt anybody's brain. "Have you gotten briefings from the OCU today?"

"Jack and Cal and Saul think one of the properties looks more promising than the other two. We'll probably start there, maybe as early as tomorrow night. He brought schematics over this morning, and we've been looking them over."

Dio made a mighty effort to conceal any evidence of real emotion, but she didn't fool Andy. Andy made a tentative reach with her water power, intending to offer Dio some energy and find out why she was being more evasive than usual about her feelings, but Dio stepped back from her and held up both hands. "Wait a minute. Don't—don't go doing that."

"It's my job." Andy didn't sigh, but only because she refused to allow herself that indulgence. "I'm supposed to sample your feelings, to sense your emotions. Flow. If you need energy, I give you energy. If you need clarity or relief, I help you find it. It soothes you, and it strengthens the group, so it helps me, too. Christ, am I sounding like Elana now?"

That brought a rare smile from Dio, and her strange gray eyes brightened a shade. "A little. But I can handle that. I think I can handle you giving me energy, too. It's that other thing you do, where it feels like you're brushing across my heart or something. That gives me the willies. Am I supposed to know when you do it?"

Andy tossed her towel back in the bathroom. "Of course. It's not a secret."

"Oh. Right." The brightness faded from Dio's eyes and she fidgeted with the beads at the bottom of her shirt. "I'm not sure I can get comfortable with that. I really don't want you to do it."

"Why? Have I not earned your trust?" Andy realized she sounded more wounded than she felt. Maybe. "Am I not here enough, not spending enough time here or with you or doing whatever the hell I'm supposed to do to help you get comfortable? Come on, Dio. Elana busts my chops for not trying hard enough to assume my role in the quad, and y'all bust me when I do try. Give me a break here?"

Dio's eyes widened until she looked seriously distressed. "It's uncomfortable. I can't help it—it feels invasive or something." She frowned. "Maybe it's just too new."

A new wound opened somewhere in Andy's depths. "Like me?"

"I didn't say that, and I don't see you that way." Dio waved off Andy's words like a cloud of steam. "Yes, having water Sibyls back is different, and I guess we all have to practice letting you take on all the duties you're supposed to have in the fighting group." Another frown. "I think I could tell you how I'm feeling, but I'm not sure I want you to know stuff I don't even know myself. Does that make sense?"

"Yeah. A lot of sense." Andy had to admit she had never considered that possibility, but with Dio, she should have. "Maybe it wouldn't be like that. Maybe I'd just help you put words to things you haven't been able to express yet. At some point, you're going to have to let me try to do what I'm supposed to do." She put on her best Elana expression, but the accent she came up with sounded like something from a cheesy Saturday-afternoon horror flick. "If you don't, terrible things might happen. Doom, I tell you. Dooooooom!"

Dio punched her and laughed.

Then she frowned. She clenched her teeth and closed her eyes like Andy was about to make her bend over, grab her ankles, and submit to a really painful, embarrassing medical procedure. "Okay. Give it a try."

"Christ, Dio. I'm not planning to stab you or anything."

Dio's posture didn't change.

Andy stared at her, trying not to laugh, then tried to relax enough to actually make an attempt to help Dio's energy. It took her a few seconds, but she managed to reach out again and share a small measure of her physical reserves, letting her water power mingle with Dio's air power until Dio visibly relaxed. Then Andy moved her concentration to the water blended all through Dio's body, to how the water moved, and what the patterns told her.

"Tired," she said aloud. "And frustrated. Excited we might get somewhere with this next raid. It's all a mix."

Dio kept her eyes closed, but she still seemed relaxed, so Andy pushed a little farther. Pain, not far below the surface. Self-doubt. Lots of worry. Her own emotions welled, because she hadn't realized she and Dio had so much in common.

Then . . . *fear*.

The cold taste of it flooded through Andy's mouth and made her teeth chatter. Imbalance. A wrongness Andy couldn't quite grasp, like she was sensing a small earthquake changing the course of a determined river, or a huge pile of toppled trees damming up the pure flow of a mountain stream.

Dio opened her eyes, looking peaceful and surprised, but also a little confused. "What? Did you find something I need to know about?"

Not good. What am I supposed to do now, Elana?

Andy didn't want to wreck this first experience for Dio and freak her out, and she was a little freaked out herself. "Pain, self-doubt, and worry," she said, deciding most of the truth was better than a lie, and filing the rest to discuss with Elana later. "Not too far below your surface, but I don't think that's any big surprise to you."

"That pretty much describes Bela, Camille, me, and you. It's why we're a match. Too many losses, strange abilities nobody understands—and not enough of a grip on how we're supposed to use all of our impressive talents."

"I was busy figuring out how to make you comfortable with everything I sensed, but you're the one making me feel better." Andy wanted to hug Dio, but that was usually a no-go. Today was no different. Dio backed up another step, probably on instinct, seeming barely aware that her shoulders were pressed against the hall wall.

"We should go downstairs and make Bela and Camille

sit still for one of your little, um, readings. Wouldn't that be a start to what you're trying to do? Get a baseline on all of us, or something like that?"

"Yes. And get you comfortable with me lending you emotional energy and helping you with emotional healing."

Dio's expression shifted like she had been slapped, but she covered quickly. "How about we take baby steps, okay?"

"Baby steps it is."

Dio led the way downstairs, and she and Andy found Bela and Camille seated around the communications platform, studying copies of old surveys and reconstruction plans on a property in the Garment District.

"That's not too far from where we examined the pile of bodies." Andy squinted at the schematic. "What's the word so far?"

"Hey," Dio said, trying to interrupt, but Andy stopped her with a pointed glare.

"Jack thinks an all-out hit would be best," Bela said. "Just leave skeleton patrols in the city and pull the rest of us in to join up with the bulk of the OCU forces. He even wants the demon allies and Bengal fighters to join in, just in case we run into paranormal forces we don't expect."

"Or supermobsters." Camille stretched and yawned, then made a shooting motion with two fingers.

Dio raised her hand.

"Yeah," Andy said, ignoring her. "Especially them."

"Andy wants to read your emotions now," Dio announced.

Bela looked up from her schematics, eyes wide. "Excuse me?"

"Hey." Dio propped her hands on her hips and let loose with slapping breeze. "I fucking had to do it make her happy, so you do, too."

Bela's gaze moved to Andy.

Andy stared at the ceiling for a second, then did her best to find her courage. "It's my job in this group. I need to practice, and I need you all to get comfortable with it."

"I see." Bela sounded thrilled.

"Do you have to look like I'm about to squish your boobs in a mammogram? It's painless. I swear." Andy raised her right hand.

Bela looked at Camille, who said, "Oh, no. You first. I insist."

With a loud, long exhale, Bela capitulated with a shrug. Then she closed her eyes just like Dio had done. Andy didn't bother to try to reassure her. She just got on with it, picking up Bela's low-level irritation about having to go through this, followed rapid-fire with fatigue, distraction, and several different layers of worrying. No surprises on the first level, but deeper down, Andy found a few things that made her lift her eyebrows. So much of the pain and unrest she often sensed clinging to Bela had dissipated, maybe even healed over and flowed out of her. She didn't have the same murky pit of self-doubt that Dio had, that Andy knew she herself had. And there was no sense of that . . . *wrongness* Andy had sensed in Dio, either.

After a few seconds, Bela muttered, "So, do I need a straitjacket?"

"No, you need to tell me how you do it." Andy drew back her energy. "How do you stay so calm inside and out? I always thought it was a mask you wore."

"It used to be." Bela's dark eyes went misty. "And then I got you guys in my life, and Duncan, and I think I've found my footing again."

Now Camille seemed curious instead of disgusted and terrified. She got up from her chair and came around to stand in front of Andy. "What about me? Am I better, too?"

"Happiness," Andy said aloud, almost overwhelmed by the warmth of Camille's inner fires. "That's the biggest emotion you feel, more often than not." And that was the truth. Andy picked up lots of distraction, probably Camille's busy mind devising science experiments with ores and metals. She also got worry and anticipation about the upcoming raid, but no matter what, happiness kept coming up again.

Camille had no wrongness in her, either. None of that unbalance she had picked up in Dio. Maybe she needed to try another read on Dio now that the air Sibyl wasn't so terrified of Andy's awareness brushing across her emotions.

"Okay, good," Dio said. "We're all sane. Can we plan a raid now? Jack will be back soon, and if we haven't come up with deployment patterns, he'll be all about doing them himself."

Then again, maybe I'll give Dio a fresh read later. No need to push my luck. Andy took a set of diagrams from the stack on the table and plopped onto her end of the couch.

Camille gestured to a pile of metal charms on the table, with strong-looking chains attached. "New necklaces. I stuck with the same metals, so everybody claim their poison."

Andy picked up her new iron crescent moon and fastened it around her neck. When it touched her skin, she felt a slight tingle as it keyed to her, then a settling as the elemental protections flowed across her skin.

Oh, yeah. These were strong. Almost like a casing designed to repel elemental attacks and elemental suppressions.

"Who are the extras for?" Dio fished her silver charm out of the remaining pile, and Andy saw that, like before, it had a rune signifying wind etched into the widest part of the moon. She pointed to the rest of the charms, all of which seemed to be made out of silver, too, though none had runes.

"The Astaroths." Camille slipped her gold charm over her head and let it dangle at her neck. "They've been chatting with the Host, and they're definitely helping with the search and the next raid, so I wanted to be sure nobody keyed projective traps for them, either."

"At least Astaroths aren't afraid to try extras and enhancements." Bela finished putting on her copper charm. "Would that our sister Sibyls might be so adventuresome."

We have armor, Andy thought, enjoying the silky feel of her charm's protective energy. *Armor nobody can see.* Then she realized Elana wasn't totally off her nut with all her talk about how finding flow and working with flow would help Andy settle down and focus. She felt better than she had in a while. More relaxed herself. More energized. More like she was paying attention to all the little bits and pieces she needed to understand and balance.

Finally. A sense that she was getting somewhere overcame Andy, and she smiled. The patterns and angles of the building plan she had picked to study took on fresh clarity, as did the list of available Sibyl groups and OCU officers. Now it was time to get somewhere in the real world, too, and find the stupid Coven and their supermobsters before bad went to worse and everything in New York City went to hell.

31

Jack did not like this.

Did. Not. Like it.

Andy's group moved across the pavement with her out of position and in the lead, cloaked in a night so dark even the city's endless lights had trouble driving it back. He watched the four women through night vision goggles, itching to get closer. For this to work, he had to stay back. They all did, all except Bela and Camille and Dio, who could accompany Andy without anything seeming out of the ordinary.

He had left enough Sibyl and OCU patrols on the streets to keep down suspicion and control minor disturbances, but the rest of New York City's Dark Crescent Sisterhood and all additional OCU officers and allies had been pulled for this operation. They had crowded into the closed factory with him, and they had taken vantage points at all available windows. Jack's mouth ran dry as a desert. With each step Andy took toward the Garment District property, a new twist formed in his gut. He kept his hand on the third-floor doorknob, ready to pound down the fire escape stairs at the first sign of anything going wrong.

Pretending to be doing a routine sweep, Andy and Bela halted their group near the front door of the warehouse. Andy gestured, and they moved out south, around the building's edge toward the service entrance behind.

From their position at a right angle, Jack had a clear view of that entrance, too. No people he could see, friendly or otherwise.

The Sibyls nearest him, Sheila Gray's triad, tensed.

Andy reached the service entrance, and she and her group made like they were inspecting it. They had their weapons sheathed. They intended to make themselves targets.

Any second now . . .

Maybe they were wrong. Maybe nobody would notice or care about the Sibyls getting so close. Maybe nobody had any special interest in Andy at all.

Jack's fingers tightened on the doorknob. His heart rate doubled in a few seconds. A quick glance told him everybody was ready to move.

The back doors of the warehouse's service entrance burst open, knocking Andy and Bela on their asses. Dio and Camille didn't go down, but they got swarmed in a big damned hurry. Ten men at least. Not as big or as bulky as Jack expected.

Elemental cuffs flashed as some of the men secured Camille and Dio and the rest mobbed Andy and Bela. Jack's jaw clenched so hard he might be cracking teeth.

"Not yet," he told himself, told everyone in the room. "Hold. Another few. Hold."

Fuck, this was killing him.

The men dragged Andy and her group through the service entrance doors, which had been standing open the entire time they had been capturing their prey.

The second the doors slammed shut, Jack gave the signal to move out. He yanked open the door and charged out, and Sibyls and OCU officers flowed down the fire escape like a black-clad army.

32

Andy's eyes adjusted quickly to the low yellow lighting in the warehouse as the men who had captured her
shoved her down beside Bela. Camille and Dio hit the
ground next, both on their knees, both wearing matching expressions of disgust.

Grimacing, Andy moved her wrists in the elemental
cuffs and quickly took stock. Looked like some sort of
small rooms against the far wall, with a barred cell in the
corner and a white door next to that. The twelve men
who had attacked them had on jeans and black sweatshirts, and they felt powerful—though not as powerful as
Andy had imagined the Coven to be.

Something about this felt a little off. Not horrible. Just
slightly sideways.

The Coven stepped back from them, ringing them like
they planned to start some ritual.

Andy carefully used her water energy to check for
other signs of life in the place. She was surprised by how
little she noticed the power dampening she should have
experienced from the cuffs. In the past, getting slapped
with a pair of elementally treated metal shackles made
her feel like she'd been kicked in the head—fuzzy and
unfocused—but thanks to Camille's new charms, they
barely fazed her. Apparently, the charm's protections kept
the elemental bindings from actually making contact with
Andy's skin. Such a subtle difference, but so important.

Bela and Camille and Dio were making their own
checks of the place, Andy could tell. They all could target their projective energy in narrow beams, making it

unlikely that the Coven would sense the working of their power.

One living being behind the white door—but that signal's not strong. It wasn't human, either. She couldn't get enough of a read to figure out what it was, but she marked the spot in her mind.

"We've all been looking for you," said one of the men in hooded sweatshirts. "Master Griffen says you hide almost as well as we do."

"Shut up," said another man, and Andy realized how young the two seemed to be. Nineteen? Twenty at the most. She also realized from what the first man said that Griffen wasn't present.

Damn.

Where the hell was he, then?

Was that why the other rooms in the warehouse were empty? He had his supermobsters out with him?

That, or they were never here to start with.

Her pulse picked up.

Not good. Maybe this situation was more than sideways. Maybe they were about to be completely fucked.

Air stirred around Andy, and she understood that additional protections had just arrived. Good. Not soon enough, as far as she was concerned.

"You're, like, what—twelve?" Dio asked the Coven member nearest to her. "What are you doing playing at witchcraft?"

He kicked out at her face, but she easily dodged the blow.

"Don't," the guy nearest Andy commanded. He sounded like he was in charge. "We need them alive and unmarked. Griffen will want to do this himself—including dishing out all the pain."

Bela cut Andy a quick glance, and her meaning was clear. *Where is Griffen? And who are these boys?*

Nobody had come here to kill kids.

A huge, splintering boom scattered the boys as the OCU and the Sibyls broke down the service entrance doors and stormed into the warehouse. Andy leaped up as Jack got to her and unlocked her cuffs, then lunged past her to help Saul Brent catch hold of one of the boys.

"I'll kill you!" the kid shouted. "I'll kill you all!"

"Watch them," Andy called to Jack. "They're young but they've got skills."

"An under-Coven?" Bela rubbed her newly freed wrists as Duncan hooked the cuffs he'd taken off her to his belt.

Dio let Duncan unlock her cuffs, then threw them to the nearest OCU officer. "Too young for that, even. Put these on their ankles. The more protections, the better. I'd double-cuff every last one of them."

John Cole removed Camille's cuffs, and she pointed to the boys. "They're like adepts. Maybe Coven members in training, but they're not cohesive enough to be the real group, or even the backup group."

Jack's voice dropped low, but Andy heard the concern and irritation when he asked, "How many backup groups do you think Griffen has?"

A burst of wind knocked a kid down so the OCU could grab him, and Dio said, "Where the hell is Griffen? That's the better question."

Saul Brent shoved a blubbering kid forward, and without his hood up, seriously, the kid did look twelve, though he could have been a scrawny fifteen, max.

"Killing cops," the kid snarled. "That's where he is. Cutting down cops and Sibyls, and tearing up a few more Russian assholes so the crime families will all kill each other."

Andy filtered some of that, then all of it. She grabbed the kid by the collar, tore off the sprinkler over his head, and let frigid water douse him as she tried to find out what she needed to know. "The Coven's out after our patrols?"

The kid's teeth chattered, but he gave her a hateful smile as he nodded.

Andy shoved the boy back into Saul's grip and spun to face Jack, her gut twisting.

"Shit," he said. "We're all here. There's nobody to cover them."

"Go," Andy told him, and seconds later, Jack, Saul, Duncan, and John were on the move with all the Sibyls and every officer save for two small OCU squads. She watched him go as he led them back out of the warehouse to fan out across the city and locate every police and Sibyl patrol and bring them in to the townhouse. Camille, who could dance with no communications platform, sent a warning message that left Andy's tattoo tingling against her skin. A few of the remaining officers led the handcuffed boys out of the warehouse.

"We've still got something in that room." Dio pointed to the closed door at the back of the room.

"Yeah." Andy stared at the door. "Kinda makes me nervous."

"Whatever it is, I don't think it's very strong," Camille said. "That or it's got even better ways than we do of hiding its powers."

Bela told the OCU officers to take positions around the warehouse floor and keep them secure, and Dio backed off to keep a good view as Bela, Camille, and Andy approached the white door.

They each used their energy to sample the room on the other side, but felt nothing out of the ordinary. The creature inside didn't react to their probes or the presence of elemental energy.

"I think it's asleep," Andy said, straining for more energy traces but coming up with nothing.

"Maybe unconscious." Bela shifted the earth beneath the door frame while Camille heated the heavy metal hinges. A few seconds later, the door fell away.

Camille glanced into the space. "It's a lab."

Andy sniffed at the alcohol-antiseptic stench and frowned. "More like a hospital room, or that's how it smells."

"Dear, sweet Goddess," Bela muttered, pointing to what looked like a hospital bed impaled by a metal post." What *is* that?"

Andy's pulse thumped harder.

Hospital bed . . . post . . . something was really wrong with that picture, especially since the bad energy was coming from that exact spot.

She went in first with Bela beside her, both of them with weapons at the ready, easing across the floor toward a creature in a bed, hooked to a respirator, intravenous tubes, and other lines and machines Andy couldn't even identify. Camille headed right, toward several glass refrigerators full of what looked like shot needles. Dio came to the doorway, still hanging back, but Andy felt the shift in her air energy when she saw the "patient" trapped in the bed before them.

"Tarek." Dio's identification carried across the room, a whisper on a light breeze. "Is he alive?"

"I don't know what you'd call this." Andy couldn't believe the metal rod, floor to ceiling, seemingly fixed in place and running straight through the Rakshasa's heart. "But *alive* wouldn't be the word I'd choose."

The four of them inched forward, circling the bed, studying everything. Andy just couldn't make sense of the mess she was seeing.

"I don't get it." Bela poked at Tarek's clawed foot with one finger. "I just don't understand."

"They're keeping him alive, but elementally restrained," Camille said.

"That's not restrained." Dio shivered. "That's tortured."

They changed positions one more time, and Andy looked up when she heard a noise at the lab door.

A blond man with cold blue eyes stood staring at her. Andy had a chance to process the jeans, the black shirt, to form the name *Griffen* in her mind.

"Well, well, well," he said. "Thanks for saving me a lot of trouble, bitch." He raised his pistol and fired before Andy could even begin to move.

The shot should have hit her right in the face, but the air in front of her flickered and an Astaroth demon rippled into view. Jake—no doubt the only reason Jack had been willing to leave Andy alone with her group to manage the warehouse raid scene—changed to his human form, then back to demon again, shedding the wounds and effects from the bullets. One of Camille's silver charms gleamed at his neck, right before he vanished again.

Griffen swore and opened fire again, this time in a wider arc. Andy whipped out her dart pistol and summoned all the water energy she could control as the rest of her fighting group spread out across the warehouse floor. The men pouring into the space behind Griffen— these were no boys with strong potential. These were grown men with real power, and they immediately used that power to cover the room with a crushing set of elemental barriers, forcing all the Astaroths to become visible. Six of the winged demons lifted into the air, fangs bared as they snarled at the sorcerers.

"Cover!" Bela shouted, and Andy and Camille and Dio leaped with her into one of the apartment-like rooms. They grabbed furniture and turned it over, dropping behind the heavy wood as the real shooting started outside.

Andy could see enough through the door to know that the twelve OCU officers were emptying their clips at the intruders. Most of their shots fell useless to the warehouse floor as the treated bullets slammed into energy stronger than anything Andy had anticipated. The Coven got out of the way, and in came five broad-shouldered, bullet-eating supermobsters, already covered in so much blood Andy knew people had died tonight. Probably officers. Probably Sibyls.

Her insides twisted and she wanted to throw up.

Griffen, who was still firing wildly at the demons darting down to slash at him from above, accidentally shot one of the mobster brutes. The big man dropped to his knees and fell face-first to the concrete, down from a single shot.

Andy grabbed Bela's forearm and pointed. "We need that gun."

Bela, who had her serrated blade on the ground beside her, hand still firmly gripping the hilt, lifted her weapon and bared her teeth. "We can't go out there until the bullets slow down. We won't be much good full of holes."

The four remaining supermobsters opened fire with their MAC-10s, and the OCU and Astaroths retreated, shouting to coordinate and get out the service doors alive.

Bela tried knocking down a wall with her earth energy, but the protections on the building were too strong, even with their repelling charms. Andy made an effort to summon a wave from a nearby water main, but she failed. "I've got nothing here. Dio, can you make a funnel?"

"I think so." Dio's voice already had the deep echo of mad wind rushing to answer her call. "It'll get us to the main doors, but the protections on the entrances will probably crush it as we pass across them."

Bela gave an up signal with her right hand. "Let's go."

As one, they stood and Dio raised her arms. Thunder exploded in the warehouse, and seconds later, a tornado spun furniture away and the wind sucked them into a tightly whirling cone.

Andy's stomach lurched, and she knew she'd have to fight to keep her dinner. "I hate this!" she yelled as Dio fired them out of the room, knocking bits of plaster in every direction.

They flew out of the lab, across the warehouse, and straight to the front door. As Dio predicted, the funnel blew apart before they made it outside. All four of them hit the ground tumbling, but free of the warehouse. Andy rolled to her feet just in time to hear Dio scream.

The sound seemed to split the night, unearthly and horrible and mind-chilling.

She spun around, pistol up.

Too late.

Dio crashed to the pavement, blood spraying in every direction.

The monster Andy had seen in her brief vision from the warehouse full of corpses stood over Dio's flailing form. With a detachment beyond horror, Andy realized the creature was holding an arm.

"That's enough." A female voice cut through Dio's moans, battering Andy's ears with its supernatural calm, with its absolute coldness. "They aren't worth risking you. Let's go."

And they walked away, just like that. The blond-haired girl and the monster carrying the arm.

Dio . . .

Andy threw herself toward her sister Sibyl, reaching her at the same time as Bela and Camille.

Don't think. Don't look at it. Just stop the bleeding. Andy pressed her hands against Dio's empty shoulder socket. *So much blood.*

Dio's gray eyes blinked twice, then went wide and closed. Her breathing stayed ragged even though Andy knew she'd gone into a healing trance against her will, her body's last-ditch effort to save itself. Earth and fire energy poured into Dio from Camille and Bela. Both of them sobbed and tried to help press the wound. Andy opened her mind, her heart, and poured her own essence into Dio's, as much as she could, as much as Dio's energy would allow.

The world around Andy swam and shimmered. Her elbows and knees got wobbly at the center. She thought she saw Griffen and his Coven marching toward her, then she thought she saw Jack and Duncan and John and a bunch of Sibyls drop out of the sky as what looked like a small army of Astaroths came swooping down. The golden glow of Curson demons filled the alley, making Andy's vision prism as Bengal fighters roared and charged into view, their tiger-like appearance a jolt after seeing Tarek's shell of a body riveted to that hospital bed.

Everything turned into snapshots.

Jack, slugging it out with Griffen.

Jack, going down. Something sticking out of his leg. A lot of somethings. Looked like syringes.

Then Griffen and the Coven were gone.

Then there was nothing but noise and clattering and shouting and flashing light. More officers. More Sibyls. Sibyls everywhere. Energy poured toward Dio and Andy grabbed it all, channeling it with her projective talent and using it for Dio's healing. Was the bleeding slowing down?

"Motherhouse Greece," somebody shouted as Camille started opening communication channels. "Now, now!"

Then, "Him, too. Take him to Russia. It's his only chance."

Jack . . .

Andy tried to keep herself upright, but she'd lost too much energy. She fell forward, still pouring everything she could into saving Dio, wondering if anything would make any difference.

33

"What am I now?" Jack stared straight into Mother Yana's weathered face and wolfish blue eyes to be sure she told him the whole truth.

"Human, so far as ve can tell." She put a pipe in her mouth and puffed once, filling the small wooden room with the smell of cloves.

Jack shifted on his cot, bending his right knee to work out the stiffness. "My damned leg felt like it got burned off. It's still not working right."

"Ve examined the contents of each syringe that affected you. They contained veakened versions of the formula used to turn Seneca into a monster, though vithout the Rakshasa element. I'm certain the serum did not come from the Eldest who is hostage to these madmen."

"What, then?" Jack had to work not to start all his *w*-words with *v*-sounds. He'd been here too damned long already.

"*Who* would be the better question. The blood in that serum, it vas human, at least in part—though it did have unusual qualities." Mother Yana beckoned for Jack to extend his arm. When he did so, she crammed her smoking pipe in her mouth, extracted a small blade from her brown robes and sliced across his wrist.

He didn't feel the cut—and the blood barely had a chance to form a small ribbon before his skin started to heal. By the time Mother Yana put up her knife, the wound had vanished completely.

"Impressive, no?" She removed the pipe from her

mouth and grinned, showing yellowed teeth. "Do not think you're invincible. A serious blow or enough vounds might be enough to bring you down. You vill not fall to age, though. The aging of your human cells has ceased."

Jack took a deep breath of clove and had to work not to cough. No more aging. That was . . . big news. Under better circumstances, he'd probably give a shit. "Anything else?"

"No changes in body proportion, no elemental talents ve can detect. Not even a small patch of tiger fur or scales or any hint of demon essence."

Mother Yana leaned closer, and the light from the torch behind her head made Jack wince. He pointed at the bulb. "The light looks bright."

"You may find all of your senses a bit stronger, but not overly much. All in all, you vere fortunate, Jack Blackmore. These enhancements should serve you vell, should you persist in courting Sibyls. Fewer broken bones, fewer near-death experiences. You might even be able to see them in the dark."

Courting Sibyls. Yeah. You had to go there, didn't you?

Jack's heart ached as Mother Yana walked out of his sickroom and left him alone to cough out her clove smoke and think about Andy. He knew she was still at Motherhouse Greece with Bela and Camille, where she had been since last week's raid went to hell in the worst way. Griffen and his Coven had managed to slaughter nine OCU officers across the city, murder four Sibyls, and wound two more officers before they retreated back to the warehouse. Then the fuckers got clean away, and somehow they spirited Tarek out of that warehouse with them. Saul thought the real under-Coven had smuggled him across the roof while Griffen and his bunch fought their way out the back. Jack had tried to take the bastard on and gotten a leg full of syringes for his trouble. The EMTs pulled nine needles out of his thigh, but only three had dumped their contents into his body.

But Dio—God.

Mother Yana had told him that Andy and her group were all sitting vigil over Dio, who still hadn't opened her eyes. When she did, if she did, she'd realize her left arm had been torn away at the shoulder.

"Don't screw it up." Jack glared at the wooden ceiling over his bed. "Yeah, you did real good following that little rule."

He hadn't planned that raid alone, but he was responsible for it. Now people were dead and Dio was hurt so badly she'd never fight again, if she even survived. He'd let his officers and the Sibyls down. He'd let Andy down so badly she'd never want to look at him again, and he couldn't blame her. This fucking fantasy he'd had of a wife and kids and a permanent home to call his own— what kind of crazy shit was that?

Fresh, helpless rage pumped through Jack. He felt seventeen again, standing over his dead father, knowing he'd never see his mother and sister again. He felt the desert in his heart, and remembered the sight of his tortured, mutilated men in the Valley of the Gods.

This kind of wreckage was his reality. His hallmark. His unmistakable fucking trademark. This kind of wreckage was his *life*.

He banged his fist against Motherhouse Russia's dense petrified wall. From outside in the hall came the low growling of a huge gray wolf, and soon enough, three of the big bastards stood in his doorway glaring at him, tongues lolling.

"Fuck you," Jack said to the wolves, and he got up and got himself dressed. No use hiding out in a place he had no right to be. Might as well get back to New York, get his shit packed and put in for transfer, and do what he could to help Saul and Cal and the Lowell brothers get the OCU past this new damned disaster he'd caused. Maybe they'd do the world a favor and shoot him on sight. Maybe that was better than he deserved.

34

Andy stared out the thick-paned windows of the crystal palace hidden on the slopes of Áno Ólimbos—upper Mount Olympus, near Litochoro, Greece, also known as the City of the Gods. Motherhouse Greece glittered in the afternoon light, a multicolored splendor in the clouds and mist, and Andy understood how ancient villagers might have believed Zeus and Apollo lived on these very slopes. Everything about the place seemed polished and pristine. Even the air smelled like scoured marble with the faintest hint of saltwater and evergreen.

Everything seemed so delicate and breakable—and extreme. Rooms in this Motherhouse were either opulent or thoroughly functional. The little antechamber next to the infirmary fell into the latter category, plain and purpose-driven, with reclining chairs, several benches, and nothing else save for a worktable sporting a notebook, a pencil, and a single light. It was a place made for meditation and silent waiting, and that's just what Andy, Bela, and Camille had been doing since Dio stabilized. She remained in a combination of coma and healing trance, recovering from massive blood loss and the amputation trauma, but she had taken in all the healing energy her fragile body could accept. They couldn't do anything now but stay close in case she woke.

Andy breathed in the too-clean air. Here in the little antechamber, waiting for Bela and Camille to get back from a quick check-in with the OCU, she had never felt so alone and so far away from home, wherever home really was. And Jack . . .

"Jack," she whispered, leaning her forehead against the window and touching the warm, sun-drenched glass with her fingertips.

Her memories from the battle after Dio's injury kept coming back to her in the same fast snapshots, no order, no detail, but she remembered the syringes. Motherhouse Russia had assured them he was healing fine, that he had virtually no supernatural effects from whatever formulas he'd been given. Andy felt torn in half, not seeing him, not helping to nurse him back to health, but she had to be here. No way would she risk Dio waking without her sister Sibyls ready to run to her bedside—God forbid there be some complication that might demand what little enhanced healing she could offer.

He'll understand.

The Mothers would have explained everything to him, and she knew Jack would do the same thing for one of his officers. She'd expect nothing less of him, and he'd expect nothing less of her. If they had any shot at a life together, they had to accept the fact that they each had so many other demands.

And that was what she wanted, wasn't it?

Tears slid down her face, warming fast in the sun.

She wanted a life with Jack. She wanted his children, and her quad, and her work with the OCU, and her duties on Kérkira. She wanted it all.

Did she have to feel guilty about that?

The antechamber's outer door opened and closed, and Bela and Camille came in, dressed in clean jeans and T-shirts, and carrying bags with fresh changes of clothes and what looked like briefing reports. Jake had probably compiled them for Andy, or maybe it had been Merilee, Jake's wife. Air Sibyls were always compiling something.

At Andy's quizzical expression, Bela handed one of her bags to Andy. "Got some stuff from the brownstone. Riana said she'd do our laundry."

Andy looked down at her own filthy jeans. "Good. These could about walk back to New York City on their own." She knew the adepts at Motherhouse Greece would gladly wash their clothes and give them robes, but for some reason it felt better for friends to do it. "What's been happening?"

Camille dropped her bag beside one of the chairs and flopped into it. "A lot of unrest and popping off between the crime families, but no civilian casualties and no new supernatural attacks."

"You know it's coming, though." Bela sat and folded her hands on top of her knees.

"Something even bigger this time." Andy muttered. "Something an even bigger level of awful."

Bela's eyebrows drew together. "Is that instinct or pessimism?"

The words stabbed Andy deeper than any blade, and more tears rolled down her cheeks. She looked away from Bela and Camille, letting the sunlight on the mountainside blind her. "I don't know. Bela, I really don't think we should trust my instincts ever again."

After a long moment of silence, Bela came back with, "That's ridiculous. Nobody can see the future."

She sounds like Jack. Shit. Just what I need. Andy tried not to cry harder. "It felt like the right course, but it all went to hell anyway."

"We busted their stronghold." Bela's reflection moved in the window, and Andy thought she looked frustrated. "We disrupted their plans and we got a lot of info on their protections and what they've been up to with Tarek. We even got twelve boys and young men out of the Coven's grasp, maybe before it's too late for them. The raid was good. It was good, Andy, and we did it right."

Andy shrugged to stop herself from saying something too awfully sarcastic. "We just happened to go in the night the Coven launched their own attacks, right?"

"That's a little too coincidental for me," Camille said. "John agrees. He's talking to the Lowells and the Brents. We've got a leak somewhere in the OCU, and they're going to find it."

Andy took those words like another kick to the gut. One of their own, passing intel to the enemy? She rested her cheek on the hot window, letting the sensation jolt her back to full focus. "We need to be in New York City, but I can't. I can't leave her. I won't."

"Our place is here." Bela sounded definite about that, but Andy caught something else in her tone and turned to face her.

"What?"

Bela looked at Camille, who quickly took a turn at staring out the window. When it got obvious Camille wouldn't be saying a word, Bela leaned back in her chair, met Andy's gaze, and said, "Jack left Motherhouse Russia last week."

Andy's heart did a quick tumble-flip. "Did he come here? Did Mother Anemone turn him away?" Damn it, she wanted to see him so badly she could almost feel his strong arms around her. She'd kill all the Mothers in Greece for not letting him get through the front door— because if he'd made it through the front door, she knew he would have bullied his way through all the crystal and glass until he found her.

"He didn't come here." Bela's dark eyes mirrored sadness and discomfort. "He went back to New York."

Andy's mouth came open. All the muscles in her gut ached at the same time, and she had to squeeze her arms tight against her chest not to sob out loud. "But . . . I wanted to see him." *Talk to him. Feel him holding me.* "Is he okay? Is there something I don't know? Because if those syringes turned him into something with horns and scales or fur and fangs and nobody told me, I'll—"

"He's fine." Bela stood and held up both hands to

slow Andy's tailspin. "No lasting negative effects from the serum he received. Those must have been test batches, too weak to do any real damage. That, or they were made with some kind of DNA other than Rakshasa."

Relief competed with confusion, leaving Andy oddly empty and disoriented. She kept looking at Bela, waiting for more information, the rest of the story, some reason Jack wouldn't have come here to see her when he was able, knowing she couldn't come to him.

Bela didn't seem to have any more information.

"He didn't really talk to us." Camille kept her gaze firmly fixed on the window, staring at a point somewhere over Andy's right shoulder. "Kinda got the sense he was avoiding anything to do with us, actually."

Anger. Disappointment. A hollowness she couldn't even begin to describe. Heat crackled all through Andy, and she fought to keep a grip on herself and her rational thinking. Jack probably blamed himself for what happened to the Sibyls and OCU officers on patrol with no backup, just like she did. He might even blame himself for what happened to Dio—just like she did.

But she didn't know that, did she? Because he hadn't shown up here to say *hello* or *I'm sorry* or *kiss my ass*.

"I can't deal with this," Andy muttered.

Bela looked like she wanted to cross the floor and give Andy a big hug. Bela tended to be a hugger, but right that second, Andy felt too raw and nervous and confused to tolerate any affection from anybody. She thought about Dio, about how many times Dio had stepped away when people tried to touch her.

Christ, was this what you were feeling, Dio? Is this what you've been hiding from me? Andy wanted to cry all over again. How could she let Dio walk around with so much pain and never even realize it?

"I think I really let her down," Andy whispered, and then Bela had her, hugging her fiercely, and she didn't let go even when Andy tried to pull away. The contact made her shake, made her hold on, and worst of all, it made her feel, it made her ache, then it broke open the gates and made her tears flow.

When Camille joined the party, Andy cried even harder. Elana's voice echoed through her mind. *Do it anyway. Force the issue . . . This is your duty, Andy, and it matters.*

"My duty," Andy muttered against Bela's shoulder, then pulled back and wiped her nose on the corner of her T-shirt. "God, I have to get better at all this. I have to get a grip on what the hell I'm supposed to do."

Camille and Bela stood with her and didn't argue. They didn't seem angry or let down at all. Maybe a little confused like she was. Definitely tired and concerned and full of caring—

I'm reading their feelings. Just like that. Fast and easy. The realization startled her into backing away from both of them. She glanced from Bela to Camille, and they looked at each other like they understood what had surprised her.

"Man, that was easier than it should have been," Andy said, trying to figure out what the hell was happening.

Camille looked a little guilty. "Reading our feelings, you mean?"

"You could tell? I didn't do it on purpose. It just happened."

"Maybe we've been fighting you a little on that point," Bela admitted, her tone as sheepish as Camille's expression. "It's time we stopped. You have jobs to do in this quad just like we do. The least we could do is help you."

The door between the infirmary and the antechamber rattled, and Mother Anemone made her way quietly into the room. Andy's mind and emotions cleared like they had been wiped clean by a giant eraser. She suddenly saw nothing but the Mother's misty green-blue eyes and the way her blue robes clung to her tall, thin frame like she hadn't eaten in a week. Her ash blond hair escaped its leather bindings in every direction, making her look rumpled and disorganized—not at all her usual self. When she spoke, she took care to address her words to all three of them.

"Dio woke a few moments ago. Her mind seems to be intact, and she's aware of what happened to her." Mother Anemone stopped like she wasn't certain what to say next. Her light Greek accent sounded unusually heavy, and her voice immeasurably sad. Andy had difficulty reconciling that with her own joy that Dio had finally opened her eyes.

"Are the other Mothers changing her dressings?" Andy took a step forward, followed close by Bela and Camille. Her heart beat harder than she could remember from any battle, and she didn't think she could wait another second to see Dio, to finally talk to her again and make sure her favorite prickly air Sibyl was still firing on all cylinders. "When can we go in?"

The sadness in Mother Anemone's voice transferred to her face, and the frown made Andy's fists clench.

"She doesn't wish to see you," the Mother said, "and before you try to push past me, you should know I can't allow that, and there are enough Mothers present for us to stop you. Please don't press the issue."

The heart of Áno Ólimbos rumbled, and flames actually crackled from Camille's shoulders and arms. It started raining in the antechamber even though Andy hadn't been completely aware of her pull on all nearby water. The notebook and pencil clattered off the work desk, and the desk chair chattered across the floor until it hit a big puddle and splashed around in the same spot for a few seconds. Then it caught on fire.

Mother Anemone stood in the middle of the earthquake, firestorm, and semi-flood, her powerful air energy wrapping around the three of them like a parent's gentle but restraining caress. Other air energy joined hers, driving all the smoke and rain out of the antechamber and lessening the mountain's menacing growl. Andy realized Mother Anemone must have gathered every air Sibyl Mother in Greece in the infirmary to back her up in case it came to a fight.

A fight we could win—but at what cost?

Hating herself for capitulating but knowing on some level it was the right course to follow, Andy forced herself to dial back her water power a few notches. She breathed and relaxed and made herself absorb as much of the water as she could. Camille's flames died almost as fast, but Bela's earth energy rolled out of her, relentless and nearly desperate.

"I know this must be terribly difficult." Mother Anemone's tone shifted to quiet and careful. "Perhaps it's better if the three of you leave, at least for a time. When Dio's ready for your company—if that comes to pass— I'll send word immediately."

"We can't just go," Bela clutched at the edges of her T-shirt as her earth energy finally dissipated and the mountain stopped its shaking. "How can you ask us to leave her?"

Mother Anemone's smile seemed as kind as always, despite the firm edge to her stance. "It's not me who's asking that of you, my dear. That's why you must respect the request."

She left the rest unsaid, but Andy felt it like a sledgehammer to the heart.

Dio.

Dio wanted them to go.

Camille hung her head, and Bela looked nearly destroyed. Their emotions blasted through Andy like a tsunami of grief, intensifying her own pain and indecision, but somehow, she left herself open to the flow until it left her shaking and spent and biting at her bottom lip. She knew Bela and Camille sensed her sympathy, her empathy, that they felt stronger knowing that someone understood exactly what was happening in their hearts and minds.

"Bela?" Camille asked, giving the decision to the quad's mortar.

Andy waited, trying to get ready for anything, because if Bela said they were going through the Mothers to reach Dio—well. They'd just be going through.

"We'll head home," Bela said, not sounding happy about it all. "But only for now. As soon as we rest, we'll be back, and you'll tell her we're here. You'll tell her we didn't want to leave, too. I won't have her thinking we've abandoned her, no matter how big an ass she decides to be."

Mother Anemone nodded once. "As you wish. I'll walk you to our communications room." Her relief was obvious as she headed toward the chamber door.

"That won't be necessary," Camille said, beginning a furious dance to open the channels only she could access with no platform and no mirrors—and three times faster than any other fire Sibyl on the planet, especially when she was pissed. "You first, Bela."

She grabbed Bela's hand, and the two of them melted into the floor.

Mother Anemone's fingers moved to her throat, fluttering like she might be struggling to swallow. She gave Andy a furtive glance. "I apologize. I'm aware of her powerful projective skills, of course, but a sight like that still unnerves me."

Good, Andy had time to think before Camille reappeared and grabbed her by the arm, twirling them both even as she started the transport. Andy felt herself yanked into one of earth's ancient energy channels, pelting back toward New York City with all the speed of the rage and sorrow she knew her entire fighting group felt—Dio included.

35

Jack let himself into the brownstone with a key he had gotten from Duncan Sharp. He still had the location guarded by two cars, one out front and one covering the private alley in back, but he and John and Duncan had been taking turns checking the inside and making sure the women hadn't left notes about needing something when they didn't have time to come by the townhouse.

When he got in the door, he found himself facing Bela, who was standing on the communications platform with a look on her face like somebody had just stolen her favorite kitten. Half her shirt was wet and the other half had been scorched. She had soot and water and tears on her face, and both her fists were clenched.

Not good.

Jack's gut did a funny twist. He grabbed his phone and punched the emergency button to bring Duncan and John on the run. His next thought was Andy, and he slammed the door behind him and rushed forward, startling Bela so badly she took a fighting stance. The floor beneath Jack's feet started to shake, and all around him, plaster cracked. Mirrors crashed off the walls, splintering and spraying glass as they hit the tile floor.

Cursing to himself over his stupidity, Jack pulled up and let Bela see who he was. "Sorry. Didn't mean to scare you. What's happened? What's wrong?"

Bela stared at him like she didn't quite know him, but she relaxed her stance and the room stopped shaking.

Right about then, the air in the room shimmered, and the hair lifted off the back of Jack's neck. His ears popped like he was sliding down the side of a mountain way too fast, and he heard a crack like somebody just snapped the world's biggest whip over his head. Andy and Camille dropped onto the platform beside Bela, both breathing hard, both looking like they'd been caught in some kind of fire-and-water disaster. They were so focused on whatever was going on, they didn't even notice him.

Camille whirled to face Bela and lifted the gold crescent moon charm she wore around her neck. "I don't agree that we should have left her."

Bela's frown turned epic. "What did you want to do, draw weapons on the air Sibyl Mothers?"

"Anything would have been better than leaving." Camille sounded beyond pissed, and a little smoke drifted up from her shoulders. "As for the Coven, we can find them. With these new charms, I know we could do it."

Andy seemed set on the same thing. She bounced her fist off her own iron crescent moon charm. "They'll never see us coming. We can tear them apart before they know what hit them."

Bela hesitated for about three seconds, then jumped off the platform and headed for the closet where Jack knew the fighting group stored their gear and weapons. He stood there like an idiot, just occupying space between the alcove and the front door, and it slowly dawned on him what he was seeing.

A unit that just lost a soldier.

Shit. Had Dio died? Something sure as hell happened, and now the warriors left behind were slamming on armor and steel and getting ready to take some vengeance. Furious. Blinded by grief. Ready to take chances no sane fighter would take.

A move like this ended one of two ways—total victory or absolute defeat.

Sorry, sweetheart, but this just isn't happening.

"Andy," Jack called into the clatter and rustle of sword

belts, dart guns, and battle leathers getting thrown from the closet under the stairs. Like a fast-speed ballet, the women shed their jeans and T-shirts and stepped into their protective suits, and almost as fast they were strapping on their weapons. Jack wanted to stride across the floor, take Andy in his arms, and hold her until she came to her senses and remembered her years of police training and experience. He wanted to hold her no matter what the outcome, but he wasn't the kind of man to go where he didn't think he was welcome.

All three women seemed to process his presence at the same time, and they turned on him like a pack of rabid dogs. Bela and Camille both grabbed the hilts of their swords. Andy didn't try to draw her dart pistol, but she glared at him for a full three seconds before she really seemed to register who he was.

He half expected her to snarl instead of speak, but she still had enough grasp of language to form words. "Jack." Toneless. No emotion at all. "What are you doing here?"

The sound of her voice warmed him, but it also shook him. She looked so pale and drawn he knew she hadn't rested well since the raid.

"Don't do this." He kept his voice level and tried to talk to her rationally, to her intelligence instead of her rage and sadness. "You've got no intel and no plan, and the odds suck."

"We're going."

Jack shook his head. "You'll have to kill me to come through this door. If you manage that—and my resilience might surprise you now—I've got officers covering front and back with reinforcements on the way. Duncan and John will be here in five flat, maybe sooner if they come like Bengals instead of humans. I dialed them 911." He dared to shift his gaze to Bela, then Camille. "At least talk to your husbands first. If they can't sway you, then we'll all give you cover and support."

Camille's answer had a little smoke behind it. "We don't need help, thanks."

"Everybody needs help." Jack tried again with Andy. "Think, sweetheart. Revenge ops are for two kinds of cops."

He waited.

She waited, too. He could tell she didn't want to answer. Then she let out an angry breath and finished the axiom. "Morons and idiots. Which one are you today?"

Some commotion broke out near the front door, and the chimes over Jack's head rang like somebody had bashed them with a baseball bat.

"It's John and Duncan." Camille sounded relieved, but also pissed. "Better let them in before they claw down the door."

Jack didn't turn his back on the women. He managed to get to the door, reach behind him, and pull the door open right about the time a very furry John and Duncan scrabbled up the front steps. They were through the foyer and halfway to the alcove before Jack finished signaling his patrols to stand down and call off the reinforcements, and all the way to the alcove before Jack saw human skin showing under the fur from their speed-enhancing demon essence. They had probably blasted through the park so fast human eyes never saw them.

"What happened?" Duncan spoke first, reaching Bela and taking her by both shoulders. "Is it Dio? Did she get worse?"

John had Camille by then, hugging her even though she was giving off sparks, which was very atypical for her. "No, honey. Tell me she's not—"

"She's not dead," Andy said to Jack. Her blank expression cracked open enough to show him an agony so acute it broke his heart. "She's awake, but she refused to see us. The Greek Mothers more or less threw us out."

Jack knew he couldn't sense emotions like Andy could, but he felt the weight and depth of her pain like it was his own. If he could have drawn it out of her like a poison, he'd gladly have taken the burden for her.

"I know you want these bastards, but this isn't the way," Duncan said, keeping Bela tight against him.

"Shut up," Bela told him, but without much conviction.

John didn't say anything to Camille, but Jack saw that she'd stopped flaming and sparking and trying to push him away from her.

He wanted to offer himself to Andy in any way she'd have him. He wanted to take control, to make her accept his support, but instinct held him back.

Instinct or cowardice?

Andy stared at him.

He felt seventeen again, looking his bastard of a father in the face, not able to pull that trigger even to save Ginger and his mom.

You always clutch in tight situations, don't you?

He didn't get a chance to say or do anything before everything fell apart even worse. Bela pulled back from Duncan, head hanging, all traces of fight seemingly squeezed right out of her. She faced Andy and Camille and said, "We left her. I let them drive us away. What kind of mortar am I?"

Camille's sparks started up again, and Andy's jaw went rigid. Jack could feel the energy souring, sense the women teetering on a dark edge. If they fell over, they'd tear themselves—and each other—apart with their own grief and frustration.

"Go to your Mothers," he suggested, desperate to do something to head off the disaster. "See what your options are. You can't take on Motherhouse Greece alone, but maybe Mother Yana and Mother Keara can reason with them and get you back in the door."

And maybe you'll benefit from a few days to recharge, to get your heads together. Somewhere neutral and away from here.

He left that part unsaid, but he could tell Duncan and John caught his meaning.

Fresh pain splashed across Andy's pretty face, and he added, "You can talk to Elana and Ona. They'd be powerful backup if you have to fight your way in, right?"

Andy didn't answer him.

Camille let go of John and ran her hand through her red hair. "I'm not best buddies with Mother Keara, but I do okay with the rest of them. John and I will go to Ireland and I'll try."

"Get them on board," Andy said, sounding so broken Jack felt like she might physically fracture right before his eyes. "Elana and Ona and I, we'll be waiting."

In an uncharacteristic moment of panic, Jack wondered if he'd suggested the wrong thing. If he'd screwed everything up by urging the women to part company. But he knew in his gut he had the right idea. They weren't thinking straight. They'd be safer if they cooled down in their neutral spaces. An army regiment couldn't protect them any better than a house full of Mothers and elemental adepts.

Maybe that'll even keep them safe from themselves.

Which was better than he could do.

It didn't take long for Camille to open channels, this time using the mirrors like most fire Sibyls did. Duncan and John shifted into demon form, getting furry all over again because projective energy and traveling through those ancient channels would strip them down to their demon essence anyway. Camille tried to send Andy to Kérkira first, but she said she'd go later, after she packed a few things here. Duncan and Bela went instead, then

Camille and John departed without saying anything else to Andy.

When everybody was gone, Andy just stood on the big table, staring into the smoky mirrors and shaking her head.

Jack couldn't take it anymore. He had to do something. He walked to the table, almost climbed up and took hold of her, but she saw him coming and moved away.

He stopped at the platform's edge and made himself look her in the eye.

"I'm sorry," he said, hoping she knew he meant he was sorry for everything, from the raid disaster to Dio's injury to not knowing what to do to help her now.

"Don't." Andy waved her hands and looked at her feet, obviously fighting to control herself. "I can't right now. Don't even come close to me."

Jack took the words like cuts to his heart, but he respected what she said and stayed put beside the table.

"I'm sorry," he told her again.

"It's not all your fault, you big asshole. It was my raid, too. And Saul's, and Cal's, and Jake Lowell's. We all put it together, and we all let it fall to hell. It doesn't help that the only water Sibyl involved was a huge piece of shit who doesn't even know what she's doing."

Jack's fists tightened at those words. "You did everything you could."

"Yeah. That's a big comfort, isn't it?" Andy's laugh only cut him deeper because he'd covered with laughter so many times himself.

"Let me do something, Andy. Please. Anything. Just tell me."

"You've given me plenty of space already. How about a little more?" She pointed toward the front door.

Jack didn't move even though he wanted to get the hell out now, more than anything. He didn't so much as twitch because he didn't like the mood she was in or the thought of what she might do when he didn't have eyes directly on her. He could see her hunting down the Coven on her own and going down in a blaze of bullets even as she cut to pieces as many supermobsters as possible.

She let out a breath. "Look. I'm going to sleep for a few hours, pack some clothes, and get hold of Ona and Elana to transport me to Kérkira, okay? If I go out, I'll take the patrols with me, but I can't see me going anywhere but the store or headquarters. I'm not going to do something stupid, Jack. That ship has sailed."

He kept right on staring at her, not trusting his own instincts any more than he trusted what she was saying. "Is that a promise?"

"I don't owe you any promises, but yeah, it's a promise."

He made himself relax, and tried one more time to connect with her. "I'm—"

"Not again, please."

Jack closed his mouth and gave up.

She let him get to the front door before she asked, "Why didn't you come to Motherhouse Greece when you got better?"

Shit. Was that what I was supposed to do? He turned and studied Andy, her posture and her expression, and realized fuck yes, it was.

"I didn't think I'd be welcome."

Way to blow it, you stupid jackass.

"You would have been welcome," she said. "I could have used the visit."

"You told me not to apologize again, but I'm sorry. I thought I was doing the right thing and giving you the time you needed."

She didn't look like she believed him, but she nodded.

"Just about the time I think I'm getting a grip on under-standing everybody's emotions, I realize I don't know shit about anything. It sucks, you know?"

Jack really did understand that concept, but he figured she wouldn't appreciate him agreeing with her.

She got off the platform, walked slowly to the stairs, and climbed them until he couldn't see her anymore.

Jack let himself out of the brownstone, then locked the door behind him. All the way back to the townhouse, he wondered what he should have done differently, and by the time he got to his office and started working on pack-ing more of his stuff, he knew the answer.

Just about everything.

36

Later that day, Elana sat with Andy on the edge of Andy's bed in the brownstone.

"I don't get it." Andy dug her fingers into the edge of the mattress, feeling the soft cotton of the spread giving beneath her stabbing nails. "You're always bitching because I don't spend enough time at Motherhouse Kérkira, and now you're telling me not to come hang out for a few days?"

"To hide? No." Elana patted Andy's knee. "And even if you intended to renew yourself and plot some deranged assault on Motherhouse Greece, Kérkira is not a restful place for you, any more than this brownstone or anywhere else in your life. These places won't offer you the soothing you seek."

Andy briefly wondered how Bela, who had never been happy at Motherhouse Russia, would find any solace there. And Camille—she hated Motherhouse Ireland, but that's where she had gone. Motherhouses might not be ideal sanctuaries, but they served as second homes for Sibyls, so Andy supposed her quad would be as happy in those spaces as any, especially since Motherhouse Russia and Motherhouse Ireland had no Dio-shaped holes in the fabric of their energy. There was slim to no chance that the other Mothers would gainsay what Motherhouse Greece had decided, Andy knew that—but maybe Bela and Camille would be persuasive. Maybe somebody would have an idea they hadn't considered.

So why do I keep feeling like it's me who's supposed to fix this?

"Where am I supposed to go?" she murmured, but Elana didn't answer. Motherhouse Greece popped into Andy's mind, but she didn't think she could take on all the Greek Mothers by herself.

"You should go to the place where you're most at home," Elana said, sounding way too confident that such a place existed.

All Andy could do was stare at the old woman. "That's nowhere. I don't have a home like everybody else. Not since my life became so changed."

"Home may not be a physical location for you." Elana's smile had a softness to it that probably saved her from a lot of cursing and screaming. "Not now, anyway. Home may be a person."

Andy stopped looking at Elana and studied her boring ceiling instead. "You're not even bothering to be cryptic now."

"Why aren't you with him right now, when you need him more than ever?" Such a simple question, and so hard to hear without bursting into tears. "Are you angry with him?"

"No. Yes. A little." Andy sighed. "I acted like a bitch to him earlier because I just couldn't stand to feel another thing, especially when I'm confused about my own emotions. My flow's all . . . crooked."

Elana kept one hand on Andy's knee, and the contact seemed like the only thing holding her on the planet. "Then I suggest you start by straightening yourself out before you try anything else. Your course of action from there should become clear."

"That doesn't solve the problem of me being such an ass to him when we got back from Greece."

"I imagine he feels that was his fault, and that he deserved it. From what I've seen of him, he's as good at taking responsibility for the actions of the entire universe as you are."

Andy brought her full attention back to Elana. "Wait a minute. You keep telling me I *am* responsible for whatever happens in the universe."

"For your part of it, yes." Elana took her hand off Andy's knee and shrugged. "But don't take me so literally."

Andy couldn't help glaring at the old woman even though she knew Elana couldn't see her doing it. "I might have to kill you one day."

The smile she got for that threat had absolutely no softness at all—more like hungry amusement, or worse yet, carnivorous glee.

"You're welcome to try," Elana said, and she never stopped smiling.

Less than an hour after Elana left, Andy had taken a shower, pulled on a pair of jeans and her favorite yellow blouse, tied her hair back, and asked one of the patrols outside the brownstone to give her a lift to the townhouse. The other car stayed behind to loop the block and keep an eye on things. A few times on the drive, Andy thought she had a sense of . . . something. Some sort of energy making contact with her. She touched her iron crescent moon pendant and let her senses expand, but no images came to her, and no sense of any real intrusion or attempt to overcome the charm's protective capacity. Only her own quad could track her as long as she was wearing her necklace, at least as far as she understood Camille's explanation of how the protections worked.

She realized she was probably picking up the building tension in the city, the ramping up for war between crime families and the agitation in the paranormal communities because of the strange murders, or maybe even the presence of the Host. Word got around, no matter how tightly the OCU tried to control information. If they really did have a leak in the ranks, who knew what stories had already hit the streets.

The two OCU officers who had driven her to the townhouse parked their car in one of OCU's reserved curbside slots. They walked with Andy through the gate and up one of the two staircases that carried through the big white columns that marked the building's entrance. She glanced up at the American eagle stamped in bronze across the stones directly over the door. The bird was still hanging around, wings outstretched as usual, gleaming in the afternoon sun

At least one thing still seemed normal in the world.

She pushed open the door, and almost instantly she heard Neala's eager "Aaaandy!" ring across the polished herringbone hardwood floors that covered most of the downstairs. A puff of smoke barely preceded the little girl hurling herself into Andy's outstretched arms.

Make that two things normal in the world. She gave Neala a big hug and carried her forward, into the big main entry room of the townhouse, where she could see all the halls leading off to the different sections of the ground floor. Maybe if she kept paying attention, she'd find even more—like the harried look on the face of the young fire Sibyl adept who was trying to work on Neala's training. The young girl, probably little more than twenty years old, had brown hair and matching eyes, and Andy wouldn't have been surprised if she already had a few gray hairs thanks to Neala's wicked intelligence and stubborn insistence on having her own way.

"Battle now?" Neala asked, but before Andy could answer, she saw Jack and Saul Brent wrestling a handcuffed OCU officer down the nearest hallway toward one of the interrogation rooms. The guy was struggling pretty hard, and the patrol officers with Andy went to lend a hand.

"No, honey. Not today." Andy hugged Neala one more

time, grateful for yet another dose of normalcy. Then she glanced at the adept, her heart beating like it used to when puzzle pieces to a case started snapping together. "Did Jack and Saul just catch the leak in the OCU?"

The adept gave her a clueless shrug and apologized. She must have just arrived from Motherhouse Ireland for today's tutoring session, and she probably had no idea what was happening in New York City.

"Battle?" Neala asked again, drawing Andy's focus back to her pert, freckled face and her pouty frown. Smoke drifted away from both of her little shoulders as Andy set her on her feet. "Pretty, pretty, pretty please?"

Andy glanced down the hallway toward the interrogation room. "Sorry. Like I said, I can't today."

"Ethan's gone with Uncle Creed. Mom's gone. We can have *fun*. Please?" Neala was getting cranked up, but she wasn't over the top yet.

Andy hated to disappoint her, but she just didn't have the energy or patience. "No, Neala. I have too much to do this afternoon. It'll have to be some other time."

"You actually do have lessons, you know." The adept sounded frustrated, but also like she intended to be kind and permissive if Neala didn't try her too awfully much.

Good luck with that, Andy thought.

"Boring." Neala pulled away from the adept's grip and flounced off through the main hallway. The adept had to run to keep pace with her, and the smoke in the air got a lot thicker before the two of them headed downstairs toward the gym.

Andy started for the interrogation room, then thought better of it. The friction between her and Jack might disrupt what he was doing, and if that officer was their leak, Jack needed all his concentration and attention to do his job. It would be better if she waited for him in his office. She reversed course just about the time the interrogation room door opened and Saul Brent came jogging out, ponytail bouncing with each step and his T-shirt and flexed biceps revealing rows of tattoos.

Saul sent an officer up the stairs, obviously with information to hand over to the Sibyl running the communications platform today—OCU's version of Sibyl dispatch. Then Saul headed for the main dispatch room near Jack's office, and Andy followed him and listened as he and the dispatcher worked out changes in patrol routes and groups, fast and efficient, and communicated them to OCU officers out in the field.

When Saul finished, he spied Andy and gave her a smile, but the expression didn't hide the simmering anger Andy didn't have to be psychic to sense. Saul gestured toward the interrogation room. "Little bastard's name is Simmons. We narrowed a list of possible suspects, then set them up with some false intel that gave him away—but not before he handed the Coven our schedule for the rest of the week. We just shook stuff up to keep everybody safe."

"Simmons." Andy didn't even think she knew the guy, which felt weird. Once upon a time the OCU had been so small and close-knit she knew everybody's birthday, social security number, and identifying marks. "How did he get compromised? Or more importantly, why did he sell out? Was it money?"

Saul leaned against the dispatch room door. "Not money this time. Power. He has some low-level elemental talent. From what we got so far, Simmons was part of your OCU SWAT team on the Seneca stock-trading raid. The Coven apparently breached the basement to do their own operation on Seneca and his thugs, realized we were there, and took off—but not before Griffen picked up Simmons's elemental skills. He approached Simmons later and offered to train him to reach his 'real potential' and 'full power' and made out like Simmons would be superstrong and all that bullshit assholes like Griffen use to beef up a stooge. Griffen told Simmons he'd help him in exchange for a little information, of course."

"Of course." Andy took this in, feeling cool blasts of surprise and the sensation of eddies of water beginning to swirl together into one big, clear pool.

If we hadn't done that stock-trading raid, Griffen might never have noticed this Simmons guy. Then the next raid on Griffen's HQ wouldn't have been compromised, and Dio—

Andy swallowed hard and broke off that thought before it killed her. "I've been telling the OCU since I got changed into a Sibyl by that little freak Legion flunkey that we need to screen OCU officers for elemental talents. We need to train the ones with paranormal abilities ourselves, because if we don't, our enemies will."

"We've got to get a plan together for that and get it implemented. Yesterday." Saul pushed himself free of the dispatch door and pointed down the hall. "Want to help us with Simmons? The guy would probably tell you just about anything to get Jack out of his face."

Andy's muscles twitched and her feet actually started to move before she got hold of herself and gave Saul a thumbs-down. "Thought about it, but I should sit this one out."

Saul's expression told Andy he thought she was blaming Simmons for Dio's injury. That was fine with her. If she got face-to-face with the bastard, she couldn't promise she wouldn't want to beat the hell out of him, or take his arm just so he'd know in real, living color what he'd done to someone else.

"I'll wait in Jack's office," she said. "When you're finished, let him know that I'm here."

"Okay." This time, Saul looked surprised, which confused Andy. Jack had never acted like he shared much of his personal life, even with his friends, so the fact that Saul might already know they had a sort-of fight perplexed her.

But . . . she supposed if Jack opened up to anyone, it would be Saul, or maybe John or Duncan.

"Later," Saul said.

Andy watched as he jogged toward the interrogation room, wondering how upset Jack had been when he got back to the townhouse. Guilt tugged at her insides as she headed into his office—and stopped cold in the doorway.

"What . . . the . . . fuck." Her accent sounded double-thick as her words seemed to echo through the cleaned-up, boxed-up space.

All of Jack's shit was in boxes. He was packed.

He's just changing offices again, the nicer part of Andy's mind tried to tell her, but she ignored that optimistic voice because she knew it wasn't true. He was gearing up to get out of New York City, and by the looks of this office, he'd been working on that a lot longer than the short span of time since he left the brownstone.

He'd come back from Motherhouse Russia without saying a word to her, and he'd started getting his crap in order. Probably already had the transfer arranged. So, what—he was just going to let her show up at some point in the future and find him gone?

Her face felt so hot she wondered if she could channel fire and burn something down. "The asshole's running out on me."

The one thing she had asked him to do was tell her if he got ready to run. Didn't he promise he would? Just a little notification.

Fuck.

Who was she kidding?

This felt like a huge betrayal. She'd thought they were closer than this. He'd told her he loved her. She'd told him the same thing. The time for running should have been long past over, unless—

Unless he didn't love her like she loved him.

The heat on Andy's face moved all over her body, and

two seconds later she started to drip from her elbows and knees. Sprinkler heads started rattling, and the water main to the townhouse gave a low, stressed groan.

Christ. Reality sucks.

Andy didn't know whether to cry or wash away the wing of headquarters where Jack was questioning Simmons. Smoke drifted through the door of Jack's office, but Andy ignored it. She had to get the hell out of here. Screw Elana. She'd go to Kérkira for a while. She had to go somewhere. It was way friggin' obvious she had no home here, not with this man.

And I thought . . .

The emptiness opening inside her hurt too much to bear.

She turned around and walked fast out down the hall, then through a thick cloud of smoke in the main entry room and an even thicker cloud of smoke by the front doors. She was all the way down the steps, out of the gate, and half a block away from the place before she took another breath, before the tears started falling and her head started aching and shit, but she was drawing way too much water in her wake.

She stopped on a small side street and turned to send some of the rushing stream of water back to where it came from, and she thought she saw a movement at the building's corner.

Andy frowned. Squinted. Saw nothing. Sensed nothing. She walked straight back to the exact spot where she thought she'd seen the flicker of motion, but all she saw was pedestrians trundling past on their way to wherever.

At least the mistake distracted her from crying like an idiot and making impromptu rivers—but her head pounded and her heart ached, and she wanted to get back to the brownstone in the worst way.

Running seemed like a good idea, but she hadn't gone ten steps when she heard running steps behind her.

This time she whipped around without even slowing—and she definitely caught a quick blur of movement. Something ducking, pushing through a tall wooden gate into a private alley.

She had her SIG and her dart pistol, one in each ankle holster, and she drew them both before sprinting straight to the alley.

The gate's latch was locked from the inside.

"Whoever you are," she shouted, "whatever you are, you picked the wrong day to fuck with me."

She kicked the wooden gate with all of her stored anger and sadness, and sharp pains ricocheted up her leg. The wood splintered and gave. So did at least one of her toes, but Andy didn't care. She ground her teeth and used her sneaker to shove the gate open hard, intending to smash anybody hiding behind it. The wooden panel banged against the fence and tore loose from its top hinge as Andy plunged into the alley. A tiny figure tried to leap away from her into the shadows, but Andy tracked it easily, grabbed it, brought both weapons to bear—

Dead center on Neala's little freckled nose.

"Shit!" Andy jerked the weapons skyward as Neala let off a giant puff of smoke and set the broken gate on fire.

"I just wanted battle," the little girl wailed as Andy jammed her weapons into their holsters, then dropped to her knees in front of Neala. "Play at your house?"

"I had no idea you followed me. That was so dangerous!" Andy grabbed Neala and hugged her tight. "Your mother's going to kill us both, you know that, right? Where's your tutor from Motherhouse Ireland? You didn't hurt her or lock her up in some closet, did you?"

Neala pulled back and started to answer, but her eyes went wide and her mouth came open, and little flames coursed all across her shoulders and arms.

Dread spiked into Andy like so many knives.

She yanked Neala to her again, but before she could turn to see what was behind them, something sharp jabbed into her arm and burned like hell.

"Wha—" Andy tried to ask, doing all she could to keep hold of Neala.

She never finished the word before she hit the pavement.

37

Simmons looked like a six-foot sniveling weasel with a black crew cut.

Jack hated weasels.

He really wanted to kill this quivering animal, but he couldn't let himself beat a man chained to a chair no matter how much damage the fucker had caused.

The whole room smelled like sweat, and Simmons had buckets pouring off his forehead.

"Want me to unhook you?" Jack asked, trying to sound polite.

"No." The asshole's answer came out too fast.

"Too bad." Jack leaned forward and folded his arms on the small stretch of table separating him from this jerk he wanted to choke so badly his fingers ached. "Tell me what else we need to know before I go get some Sibyls, and maybe an Astaroth or a Curson."

Simmons shook his head and slung sweat. "There's nothing. That's everything." His black weasel eyes darted to the interrogation room door. Jack knew he was looking for Saul, praying like hell Saul would get back before Jack went right over the edge.

As if on cue, Saul came in without knocking, straddled the chair on the opposite side of the table, and gave Jack a where-are-we glance.

"Simmons here just told me the Coven caught some sort of winged creature a few days before we hit their headquarters. They're keeping it hostage with the Rakshasa in some kind of broken-down old morgue with barely patched-together walls and floors, and they've got more beds set aside, like maybe Griffen's planning to start himself a collection of supernatural hostages."

"Is he?" Saul asked Simmons, looking as dangerous as Jack felt.

"I don't know." The man was talking too fast, very nearly whining. "And I really don't know where the building's located. It's a shit-poor dump, though. I always meet Griffen in Central Park and he takes me there blindfolded. I'm supposed to see him today at two."

Jack glanced at his watch. About an hour. "Too bad you can't make that connection. Saul, you want to take him upstairs? I'm sure the Motherhouses will fight over who gets to contain him."

That really made the weasel squeal. "I don't want to go to a Motherhouse!"

"We only keep prisoners without paranormal abilities," Jack told him, enjoying his fear more than he should have. "You got talent, you go to the Mothers. Speak any Russian? Because the wolves at that Motherhouse don't understand English."

Saul unlocked the leg and wrist cuffs shackling Simmons to the interrogation room table, but before Jack could play out a full fantasy of kicking the asshole's ribs through the roof of his mouth, Saul said, "Andy's waiting for you in your office."

Jack blinked. He got a big-time head rush, like he'd just downed three shots of whiskey way too fast.

Andy . . . here.

Maybe he would have a chance to do some things differently after all.

He turned and banged open the interrogation room door and let Saul and the prisoner into the hallway, then made tracks to his office, brushing past about sixteen people trying to get his attention.

Until they had gotten their hands on Simmons, Jack hadn't been able to think about anything but Andy, about how he could earn himself a few second chances, if she'd even allow him to try. Now she was here. Now he could try again to talk to her, and this time he wouldn't make such an abject fucking mess of the whole situation.

He got to his office in about two seconds flat, and he realized instantly that Andy wasn't there. She had been, because he could still smell the light fragrance of vanilla and ocean. Her scent. So completely female and enticing. It drove him nuts, just the hint of it. He wanted to touch her so badly his arms and hands ached, right along with the rest of him.

Jack clenched his fists and glanced over his office, and reality slowly edged into his thoughts and perceptions.

She had seen the boxes. She knew he was planning to leave, and he hadn't had the chance to tell her himself. The night they first made love, he'd as much as promised her he'd warn her before he hit the road.

Fuck.

He hadn't realized she'd get back before he left. He'd been planning to set up a meeting with her after Saul let him know she and her quad had finally gotten back to the city, but she didn't know that. She probably thought he was the worst coward she had ever known, to run off before she even got to have her say with him, before she got to take her pound of flesh over Dio and everything else he'd wrecked in her life.

And was he a coward?

No.

But the little voice way back in his brain . . .

Yes.

Jack thought about Andy like he'd last seen her in the brownstone, exhausted and grieving and all alone. She'd told him to leave. Hell, she'd as much as thrown him out.

But why did I go?

She had been standing right there in front of him. That had been his chance, and he'd blown it all to hell. The old Jack would have stormed over to her, grabbed her, and tried to make her see reason about letting him give her a little support. He at least would have made damned sure she understood that he wanted to be there for her, whether she accepted his offer or not.

But he'd learned to be more respectful this last year of his life. Maybe too respectful?

"I'm screwing this sideways," he told himself. "Making it too complicated."

Because the simple fact was, no matter how badly he'd fucked the whole works, Jack knew he loved Andy. He loved her more than he had ever loved anything in his life.

Mine. The raw, primitive instinct overtook him for a moment, and he could see himself banging on the brownstone door until she answered.

Not a lot of finesse, but hell. Andy wasn't much on finesse, was she?

He turned and plowed down the hall toward the front door, almost slamming into a young adept in green robes. The girl was on her knees looking under chairs and tables, and Jack barely caught her before he fell over her and busted his ass.

"Sorry, sorry," she said as he lifted her to her feet. "Have you seen Neala?"

Jack focused long enough to stare into the adept's wide, miserable eyes. "Were you playing battle? Because if you were and you let her slip your supervision, you're hosed. You won't find her until her mother comes home. She can hide better than any kid I know, and she never, ever loses a game of battle."

The adept let out a short groan. "She was right with me in the basement. I turned my back for five seconds to stop some exercise balls from exploding—and poof. Do you think she went with that Andy woman she adores so much?"

"No way. Andy wouldn't take her out of the town-house. Too much risk." Right about the same moment, Jack saw the patrol officers that should have been Andy's escort back to the brownstone talking to Saul by the main steps.

His pulse slowed even as it beat louder in his ears. He stepped away from the still talking adept, jerked his cell out of his pocket, and punched the speed dial for the unit still stationed at the brownstone.

When one of the officers answered, Jack asked, "Any activity?"

"No, sir."

"Andy didn't come back there?"

"Haven't seen her, sir. Brown and Davis haven't called to tell us they're on the way, so we thought they were still with you at the townhouse."

Jack's heart beat harder. Louder. "Call immediately if she shows."

He hung up before the officer could acknowledge. About a minute later, Jack had established that Brown and Davis thought Andy was in Jack's office, just like Saul did.

Saul must have seen the look on his face because he came toward him fast, eyebrows raised.

"Something's wrong," Jack said. "Andy's not here and she's lost her escort."

Saul frowned. "It's a big townhouse. She's here some-where."

"No." Jack swiped his hand across his eyes and made himself say it. "She saw my boxes."

"I thought—you didn't say anything to her about leav-ing?" Saul's expression darkened. "You son of a bitch. I think I'll help the Lowell brothers tear you apart."

"She probably blew out of here pissed as hell." Jack felt tried and convicted by Saul's glare, and he knew he deserved it. "So pissed she might not have noticed she had a tail."

"Neala. Shit. Shit!" Saul slammed his fist into the paneled wall, cracking wood.

"I'm getting a raid together." Jack glanced at his watch. "Everybody who can hold a weapon. We've got exactly one hour before Simmons doesn't make his rendezvous with Griffen and the bastard realizes we're on to him. You hit the panic button and coordinate from here. Search any building that might have an abandoned morgue. And get Bela and Camille in the mirrors *now*."

(38)

Where is here?

Neala's voice. Tiny. Afraid.

Andy tried to wake but couldn't open her eyes. She wondered how she'd gotten to the bottom of the ocean, with millions of tons of water holding her tight against shifting layers of sand and silt.

You must be quiet, little one. That voice Andy didn't recognize. Female. It had secrets in it, maybe a lie—not in the words but in the tone. The creature sounded normal enough on the surface, but whatever she was, she was no more human than a slowly trolling shark.

And no matter what happens, you must not touch me, the shark-thing whispered.

But you have fire like me. Neala again. She sounded so real and so close. Andy fought harder against the weight of the water holding her prisoner.

The shark-thing kept its voice low and sly. *Our people are related, but my energy would swallow yours and leave you with nothing.*

Neala gave a frightened sniff. *You take my fire away?*

I wouldn't want to, but yes, little one. I could.

Andy fought the water even harder.

Lost the battle.

She drifted away in her own mind, and time passed.

Aaandy . . .

Neala's sweet little voice called her back.

No sense of the shark-thing this time, but Neala felt hot and real and near enough to touch. The child was so frightened she whimpered, and Andy caught the light

scent of smoke, enough to let Andy know the little girl
was giving off sparks and flames in distress.

Andy wanted to wake up and punch the shark-thing
in the face. How could she scare Neala like that? Neala
was just a kid. Andy shoved her mind to the surface of
the water. Currents shifted in her soul, threatening to
wash her farther out to sea, but she doubled her effort,
breathing hard through her mouth, grasping, pulling,
rising, rising—

Somebody slapped her in the face.

Andy's eyes popped open. Her cheek stung and her
left eye watered. She tried to jump up and punch the shit
out of the bastard who just hit her, but the most she
could do was strain against what felt like iron chains se-
curing her to some sort of metal table. She couldn't even
turn her head—but she could see the asshole who was
laughing at her.

Black jeans and T-shirt, stylish but plain. White-blond
hair, eyes like blue ice, and a tiger-tooth necklace dangling from around his neck, along with what looked like
one of Camille's golden crescent moon charms.

Griffen.

Andy had seen him before a couple of times, usually
from a distance. Easy to recognize with his sharp, pale
features. Now that he was up close, though—something
about those eyes made her think about the Keres and the
black moonlight of Káto Ólimbos—and the Leviathan,
right before she planted darts in its evil demon brain.

Her heart started to thump and squeeze in her chest.
Where the hell was Neala? And why couldn't she get her
mouth to work well enough to say anything to this bastard?

Perverted energy radiated off Griffen in twisted waves,
and Andy wanted to draw weapons she couldn't reach
and probably didn't have. She tried to use her elemental
powers, but the chains covering her chest, arms, legs,

and belly grew instantly heavier. Her head spun and she almost passed out again.

"Elegant elemental locks, aren't they?" Griffen's smile made Andy want to hit him five more times, right in the face. She realized she had a foul flavor in her mouth, some cross between dog shit and sour milk, and she gagged.

Griffen's smile got even bigger. "The drug I used to neutralize you, that was my own concoction, too. A tranquilizer mixed with elemental components. All natural, quite harmless in the long run, but yes, it does cause a wicked aftertaste."

Andy couldn't have said anything if she wanted to, and she couldn't spit at him, either.

Just wait, asshole. My muscles will work sooner or later.

"The locks have a projective component." He stroked the chain over Andy's breasts, and she tried to jerk her hands up to choke him. The best she could manage was a feeble thump and rattle.

"That kind of expenditure won't hurt you, even if it's useless," Griffen said. "If you use elemental energy, however, the chains will absorb it and take strength from it. We have your quad to thank for our improved technology. The necklaces you've been wearing." He touched his crescent moon charm. "Impressive bits of work. We were glad to get a sample to study."

He pointed to Andy's right.

She managed to turn her head far enough to a badly patched board floor with big metal plates over the rougher parts, paint peeling off walls, impossibly high ceilings with construction lights dangling from newly hammered support beams, a new-looking sink and counter, and another metal table. Old-fashioned, obviously heavily used, but polished.

Morgue table . . .

On it was a dark-haired, pale woman with pointed

ears. She lay so still Andy couldn't even tell if she was breathing, but somehow she sensed the woman's life force. Strong and dark and sneaky, and absolutely furious.

One of the Host. Shit. They caught one of the Host, and she had one of Camille's charms. Andy wanted to scream and curse. That's why Griffen had been able to find her. Bela had been right when she theorized that her quad would be able to track each other since they were wearing similar charms. Another bad twist from that stock scam raid. She never should have let her quad go along with that crap. If they hadn't been in that cursed basement, if they hadn't surprised the Host—

But that was in the past. She needed to be in the now, think in the now, and think damned fast. Andy realized her own charm was still around her neck, and it occurred to her that Griffen assumed the charm had the same properties as the sample he captured. He knew she couldn't use it without the projective chains draining her literally to death—or at least that's what he believed. She made a brief effort to send energy through her Sibyl tattoo, some kind of alarm or alert or beacon—but instantly knew it was useless, as the projective energy in the chains drained the message to nothing before it could be sent.

She moved her mouth again, and this time her lips and tongue cooperated enough to slur out a single word. "Neala."

"The child. Yes. We didn't bind her." Griffen's frigid eyes shifted again, this time to a spot behind Andy's head. "That would have been barbaric. We don't plan to hurt her, and we'll keep her in good enough health to serve our purposes."

Andy looked at his pupils, his teeth, even the metal wrappings on his tiger-tooth necklace, trying to catch any hint of reflection that would let her estimate Neala's location. She got nothing but soft, half-demented laughter, and another pat on the boob chain.

"I'm really glad I didn't kill you after all. You're one of the only fully functional water Sibyls in the world, so your blood might be worth something in the formulas I'm creating. I know Neala's blood will be of great benefit. Now, if you'll excuse me, I have an appointment."

Griffen slapped Andy again so hard she saw black.

Some time later, maybe minutes, maybe hours, she came back to herself again, her jaw aching from the bastard's latest blow. Whatever. That fucker would get his, and soon enough.

Tightening all her muscles against the pain and pinch of the chains, Andy tried turning her head to the left, then to the right again. She couldn't see Neala anywhere. She could fight her chains with her physical energy, but not her elemental powers. The second she tried even the slightest elemental manipulation, the energy bindings sucked her absolutely dry.

"You have been here for part of a day," the woman on the metal table whispered. "I believe it is early evening now. They're doing experiements with viral genetics. DNA-based, perhaps RNA. Griffen believes he can create injectable elemental powers—mix and match until he discovers the most effective and advantageous formulas, then alter the basic essence of the creature who receives one of his little potions. They've taken blood from me daily, trying to create the Goddess only knows what."

Andy didn't know what to say. She thought about Jack with the needles in his leg. Damn it. What had Griffen pumped into the man's body? The Mothers thought Jack was okay, no lasting negative effects—but what if his DNA suddenly misfired and turned him into a walking monster? Could that even happen?

She was no scientist. Guns felt better than beakers as far as she was concerned.

"Andy," she muttered. "That's my name."

"Siobhán," said the Host woman. "They have a Rakshasa, and me, and now you and the child. I think they're planning to continue renovating this pit, and I think they plan to collect more."

"Collecting." Andy stared at the ancient-looking elevated ceiling with the new beams and construction lights. Christ, but her brain didn't want to work. "Collecting more what?"

"More supernatural captures. They brought in more metal beds last night."

Siobhán's low, angry voice gave Andy the shivers, and so did the thought of freaks rolling morgue tables into this creepy, moldy vault. Where the hell were they, anyway?

Andy rotated her head carefully beneath the chains. "Where's Neala?"

"The child is in a newly constructed cell against the far wall, directly behind your head." Siobhán kept herself very still on her table. "She struggled against her bars and the energy trap drained her. She's sleeping. Her bed, at least, is not metal."

Tears threatened, and Andy jammed her eyes shut and took a deep breath. What a fucking idiot she was to get so caught up in her own mind, her own crap, that she hadn't noticed Neala following her out of the townhouse.

"I'll die to save her," she warned Siobhán. "When the time comes, don't get in my way."

"I, too, pledge my life to save the child. She is innocent. To do any less would be a crime against the universe."

Andy had no idea if the Host woman's pledge was for real, but it sounded like the truth. "How did they catch you?"

Siobhán gave a furious snort. "The cowards shot holes

in my wings. Automatic weapons fire. I couldn't heal myself fast enough to stay aloft, and my fellow warriors couldn't come after me for fear of meeting the same fate."

Slowly, slowly, Andy's thoughts gathered themselves and started flowing in a straight line. She started noticing details, like the slight damp chill in the air and the scents of mold and bleach and alcohol, with hints of freshly sawed wood. Siobhán's admission worked its way through her sputtering, fitful mind, and she muttered, "You and your people were hunting the Coven and you found them."

"Yes."

"Then they're the ones who have something that belongs to you."

"Yes."

"And you're still not going to tell me what it is."

Silence from the Host woman. Then, "Griffen believes me to be unconscious. I give him that appearance whenever he is present, even when he strikes me or takes my blood. Perhaps we can use his assumptions to our advantage."

Andy stared at the rickety walls and ceiling. "Do you have any ability to fight the bindings?"

"No, but you might," Siobhán said. "Your charm has different properties. I can sense them from here."

Andy rolled her head back and forth in frustration. "I've tried, but the chains drain me every time I use my elemental energy."

"Direct it through the charm only." Siobhán sounded excited, like she knew she was on to something. "Focus it like a beam."

More frustration. Andy knew what she meant, but she also knew she sucked at that. "My sister Sibyl Camille is good at focusing her energy. Me, not so much."

"I see." Disappointment filled the Host woman's voice. "Water is a difficult element to control."

"Aaaandy," Neala whimpered in her sleep.

Damn it. Andy wanted to break her chains in half. "I'm right here, honey. It's okay. You're okay."

Andy heard a few sniffles, then caught the slightest whiff of smoke. "A bad man with lizard eyes stucked me with a needle. You, too. Why?"

Andy thought about the syringes Jack had taken in the leg and wondered if he'd gotten a good dose of some mixture containing Siobhán's blood. "Because he's a jerk. But we'll get him. Don't you worry."

And now, somewhere in this lab, Griffen's storing syringes full of my blood, and Neala's, too. Asshole. What's he trying to do?

"Is the tiger sick?" Neala asked, obviously fearful. "I been sick before."

Andy managed to turn her head toward Siobhán, who directed her own gaze to a spot near the room's new stainless-steel door. "The Rakshasa Tarek is to your right, but behind you. The child has a clear view of him."

Andy's stomach lurched. She remembered the horrific sight of Tarek impaled on the bed in the warehouse, nothing but a zombie-demon hovering at the edges of life. She'd give anything if Neala didn't have to see that.

"I don't know where it will go, or what it might do, but I'm going to try to use my charm to direct my energy. Neala, if any of my water power touches you or hurts you, tell me. I'll stop." To Siobhán she said, "Same for you."

"Pain is no issue for me, Sibyl. Do what you must."

Andy sank into one of the relaxation exercises Elana had worked so hard to teach her. She let herself sink into the water in her mind, float there, drifting along like she did in her dreams about the quiet place in the endless ocean. A peaceful place. A safe place where she could finally be happy and have a home.

Without Jack . . .

An image of Jack's office in boxes intruded, breaking her concentration. She swore and went back at it, doing her best to erase Jack completely from her thoughts. About five seconds later, she opened her eyes, pissed as hell and blinking back tears.

Fuck him for leaving. Fuck him for lying to her. And really, really, fuck him sideways for distracting her when she most needed to focus.

Damn it, I'm a Sibyl, and before that I was a good police officer. I can do this.

She opened her senses to locate Neala, and tried to gain a feel for the bars around the child. Projective. Waiting to suck energy just like her chains. But theoretically, her charm should resist the projective trap. Maybe the resistance would be stronger since the bars weren't actually touching her.

I can do this. I have to. I will.

She let herself sink deeper, close to the bottom of that chasm that seemed to surround her when she woke from Griffen's nasty designer drug. She let herself sink into the quiet place in the ocean she had dreamed about so many times, let the memory of water's bliss flow into her. In her mind, she shaped it, pressed it, coaxed it into the thinnest of streams, and she directed her energy to the charm she wore.

The little bit of iron at her neck vibrated and got hot, but Andy sensed no reaction from her chains. She envisioned the tiny sliver of her water power rushing between the heavy links crushing her against the table, touching nothing but air.

The charm shivered and bucked against her skin, and the pressure on her chest and arms and belly doubled. Damn it. The elemental traps were trying to spring.

Hold it steady. Hold it. Keep it going.

She changed the imagery in her mind to cell bars, to a cell door, to a locking mechanism. With no idea if she was even getting close to Neala's cell door, Andy lowered her stream of energy and directed it as best she could, imagining it splashing through a key-sized opening. She blended the elements of water and air and metal, wove them together like tying a knot with gossamer thread until she could taste oxidation and rust on her tongue.

Her crescent moon charm burned and shook. The chains squeezed so tight one of her ribs cracked, but she jammed her teeth together. Air squeezed out of her lungs. Sunbursts blasted across her vision and she got so dizzy she dug her nails against the metal table.

For Neala. Keep going.

Killing her. The chains. Squeezing her like some giant constrictor.

Rust. Work the water into the air, the metal.

Behind her, something rattled. A tiny child's voice snarled a few words a tiny child shouldn't know but probably had learned from her mom or her mom's friends.

"That's it, little one." Siobhán sounded eager. "Use your shoulder and ram it hard, but keep your fire tightly contained."

The rattling behind Andy turned into a loud bang, followed by a sharp cry and the sound of flesh hitting metal. Andy's heart crashed and her focus exploded. Pain seared her chest just below her throat. Hot shrapnel. Her charm had deflected just enough of the traps. It had absorbed all the projective energy it could before it broke into bits. The chains, God, the chains—

The chains were moving. The links across Andy's forehead slipped off, but the rest stayed stubbornly in place.

"Stupid locks." Neala sounded miserable and pissed as she smoked and jerked at the heavy metal. "They're stucked to you. And they bite me. Take my fire."

"Don't try." Andy's voice shook. "Don't use your energy at all."

"I break them!"

"Just get out of here, honey." Andy fought not to yell at the little girl. "Can you do that?"

"Nooo," Neala whimpered, and Andy knew the little girl was terrified at the thought of trying to run away by herself.

Breathe. Just breathe. "You can do it. Get to a police officer, get to a safe place."

"Scared, Andy. Can't."

Andy's composure finally snapped. "Damn it, Neala, run! Torch a wall and go straight to your mother. Burn down anybody who gets in your way and don't look back!"

"No!" Fire blasted along Neala's arms and she squealed and dropped the chains. Then she doubled up her tiny fists and bashed the thin edge of Andy's table. Her skin was so hot she softened the ancient metal, making a knuckle-sized dent.

Neala stared at the dent, then at her fists.

Andy was about to yell at her to get out of their prison again, but the next thing she knew, her jeans and shirt were on fire.

"Table doesn't bite," Neala muttered, her tone half psychotic in the huge, dilapidated room.

Andy bit back a scream and pitched all of her elemental energy away from the chains, toward the now molten and dripping table beneath her. It was all she could do to keep her ass and back from cooking like a pig on a roasting spit.

"Burn," Neala told the table, sounding as dark and angry as the Host woman chained behind her.

Siobhán laughed, adding to the absolute madness.

The table melted right out from under Andy, and she

crashed to the floor in a heap of chains and molten metal. The blisters forming all across her butt hurt bad enough to focus her completely. She scrambled to her knees, then her feet, shrugging out of the chains and drawing water from everywhere she could find it to cool herself down. Her shirt and jeans fell off in a heap of ashes, and she picked up the rags, tying them across the important parts even as she grabbed Neala's hand and rushed to Siobhán's table.

Andy faced the Host woman, once more struck by her unearthly beauty. "Can Neala free you without putting herself at risk?"

"Yes." Siobhán hissed the word, and the black light burning in her eyes made Andy grab Neala's shoulders. She started to pull Neala back, but the little girl scorched her palms. Andy yelped and turned loose.

Neala had already gone to work, softening then melting the metal beneath the Host woman's tall frame. As the molten heat bit into her jeans and T-shirt and the fabric smoked, Siobhán laughed again, holding herself rigid as if daring the fire to take her. Andy realized she was absorbing Neala's fire even as it melted the metal, taking it into her body and saving her flesh even if she couldn't save her clothes.

Seconds later, Siobhán hit the floor and came straight out of her chains.

The room's metal door banged open, and a red-faced Griffen barged in, clearly with no idea that some of his lab rats had sprung themselves from his maze. Andy turned on him and yanked hard on her water power, blasting him with jets from both hands and ramming him against the door. It banged shut just as Andy felt the warning tug of a projective trap beginning to drain her all over again.

That fucking tiger tooth around his neck!

She broke off her attack. Water splashed to the floor and rushed through the thousands of cracks in the aged wood and metal patches.

Griffen crashed to his knees, holding the tooth and coughing up gouts of the moisture he had swallowed.

Fury swelled through every inch of Andy. She looked left and right for a weapon, any weapon, but what she saw was Siobhán grabbing Neala and shoving the child behind her.

Neala screamed and sagged, wilting like a leaf in Siobhán's grip. In her half-burned rags, with her dark eyes wide and feral, Siobhán snarled at Griffen like a wild animal.

"Let her go!" Andy lunged toward Siobhán, but the Host woman moved preternaturally fast, dragging Neala like a ragdoll.

Griffen was talking.

Andy wasn't listening.

She pulled water to her again, getting ready to flood Siobhán and snatch Neala back from the crazed woman.

Without looking in her direction, Siobhán threw Neala at Andy, then leaped between Andy and Griffen.

Andy caught Neala to her chest. Limp. But warm. Breathing. Alive. She pressed her hand to the little girl's head, then turned in time to see Griffen, arms raised, start a phrase that would create a crushing elemental dampener.

Siobhán let out a banshee howl that stabbed Andy's ears. The Host woman lifted her own long arms, and seemingly every bit of the fire in the universe blasted out of her body.

The flames crackled across Griffen like a white-hot wind, burning every bit of wood and cloth and flesh that it touched. For three seconds, the sorcerer became a human torch, belching black smoke and a skin-scrawling stench that made Andy cough and press Neala's face into her neck.

Then he was gone.

Griffen was just gone.

A pile of charred bone and teeth and ashes.

Siobhán collapsed, and before she ever struck the metal-patched floor, Andy knew the Host woman had done just what she vowed to do—die to save Neala. Somehow, using Neala's fire energy, Siobhán had made herself a living bomb. Now, spent, she collapsed like she had no bones, not breathing, no sign of life registering at all when Andy checked with her elemental senses.

Have to deal with this later. Come back for her later. Her and what's left of Tarek.

Choking back bitter waves of shock and sadness, Andy forced herself to turn away from Siobhán's body. She drew as much water to her as she dared, then hurled a barely controlled tidal wave at the nearest wall. Old brick and wood and metal plates gave like children's blocks, tumbling away from the rushing stream of water.

Moonlight, Andy's mind registered as she wrapped her arms double-tight around Neala and ran through the hole in the wall into a dark, overgrown courtyard.

She didn't even get time to feel the exultation of escape before she had to pull up hard in the face of a curtain of elemental energy so thick and vicous it felt like boiling oil when she brushed against it. Strange, dark energy rippled off a blond-haired girl a few feet in front of her, distorting the moonlight but doing nothing to obscure Andy's view of the Frankenstein mobster, four enhanced fighters with MAC-10 spray-and-prays, and twenty-four men in jeans and black sweatshirts, each with their own tiger-tooth necklaces dangling dead center on their broad chests.

The blond girl, Rebecca, Griffen's psycho sister, glanced

from Andy to the ruined lab, where Siobhán lay dead in front of her brother's ashes.

Andy tried to get Neala closer to her body, to protect her as much as she could. She waited for the torrent of rage, for the blast of energy she wouldn't be able to withstand. Whatever came, she'd take it. She'd do anything not to let that horrid, body-ripping freak that used to be Ari Seneca get near Neala.

The creature just stared at her. Stared at both of them, like the fighters and what Andy had to assume was Griffen's true Coven and under-Coven. All of them, men and monsters alike, seemed subdued and under complete control.

Rebecca's control.

She nodded once, as if approving everything she had just seen and sensed in the devastated lab.

"Well done," she said to Andy. "Though I would have preferred you left that Fae woman alive. She was unique. It's sad when something unique has to die, don't you think?"

Andy didn't answer.

"It's time we stop such tragedies," Rebecca continued. "Now's as good a time as any, and you and the kid will be useful in our next round of experiments."

Andy's insides went cold. Her eyes darted around the courtyard. The ancient brick building surrounding them looked like a run-down medieval castle. All the doors but one had been boarded up, and Rebecca and her friends were blocking that exit. Andy figured she could run back into the lab, but she wouldn't get far. No way she could risk using elemental energy against the damping force the Coven had created. That much elemental blowback would crush her like a bug, and Neala with her.

She was still reeling through possibilities when four of the Coven took Neala from her, spiriting the still-sleeping girl into the lab. Four more took hold of Andy and started chaining her all over again, ankles and wrists, elemental shackles even more powerful than the last she had escaped.

When she had been thoroughly trussed, Rebecca came close to her, right in her face, her nose just inches from Andy's. Her expression seemed to be a combination of curiosity and sadness as she lifted a syringe. Amber liquid glinted in the barrel, and the needle looked long enough to hit bone.

"I'd say we'll make it painless," she murmured as she jabbed the needle into Andy's arm, "but that would be a lie. Will fast be good enough?"

39

As sunlight broke over the city, Jack maxed the OCU van's speedometer, rolling up pavement behind him on the Verrazano-Narrows Bridge between Brooklyn and Staten Island. He kept his gaze straight ahead and his mind clear. Andy and Neala had been gone a little over sixteen hours. Too damned long—but maybe it wasn't too late. He had what he needed now. All the resources. A good plan. A solid target. He'd get them back.

Goal one—Andy and Neala out safe.

Goal two—nothing left of the Coven but blood, bits, and bones.

He was going for broke. A total gamble. This time he wouldn't hesitate. He wouldn't lower his gun or leave his men lying torn apart in some faraway desert. This time Jack didn't intend to lose, and everybody he knew in New York City—hell, even people and demons and Sibyls he'd barely met—they were square behind him and thinking with the same mind.

The townhouse had been locked down with a single squad of regular NYPD officers standing guard. Every OCU officer not on medical leave followed in vans and Jeeps and SUVs, official and unofficial. Every Sibyl in the state was driving, walking, running, or pouring in through projective mirrors to meet them at the corner of Stanley Avenue and Castleton. Astaroth demons formed an invisible cloud above the caravan, so dense it blocked shadows as it moved, and Cursons and Bengal fighters hammered along below on the bottom deck, running as strong and as fast as Jack could drive.

If he'd had time, he would have called in favors from the National Guard. From the Army. From any damned organization that could give him bodies, weapons, and a chance.

Saul held the van's panic grip with his right hand and his cell with his left. "Shut it down," he barked to Homeland Security's local office after giving them FBI and NYPD clearance codes. "Shut it all down tight and keep it closed. Goethals, Outerbridge, Bayonne—all of it. Call MTA and stop the buses and the Staten Island Railway. Hold the ferry on the Manhattan side. No fly, no buzz, no news crews. Nothing moves unless it's ours. Come up with whatever cover story you want and we'll back it."

Five seconds later, he had a conference call going with the 120th, 122nd, and 123rd Precincts on Staten Island. "It might get loud and it might get nasty, but stay clear. Keep the roads empty."

Nobody argued. Everybody moved fast. The OCU was low-profile but it wasn't invisible, and no regular NYPD officer wanted anything to do with the crazy shit Occult Crimes handled.

Jack came off the bridge on two wheels and swept north by the most direct route he could follow. A group of leather-clad Sibyls was already waiting when he screeched to a stop at the rendezvous point and bailed out, fastening his body armor, then checking his stash of clips and flashbangs. OCU SWAT poured out of his van with Saul, and out of other vans before they even came to a full stop behind him.

Bela and Camille came toward him with Duncan and John and a group of Sibyls Jack didn't recognize at first glance.

"You're sure it's the Smith Infirmary?" Bela looked at the ancient, boarded castle rising toward the sunlit sky less than two blocks away. "Positive?"

"We checked the other options," Jack said. "This is the only one that makes sense with the descriptions we got."

"There's terrible energy here," said one of the smaller Sibyls, and Jack realized with a start that Elana had come, that the old, blind woman had suited up in leathers like she planned to fight alongside everyone else. "Strange and muted, but under the surface—terrible. We're in the right place."

Before he could say anything to Elana, he counted two more too-short Sibyls, one with thick white braids and the other with ropes of gray hair wreathed with clouds of smoke. Mother Yana from Russia. Mother Keara from Ireland. A taller Sibyl standing next to them had ash-blond hair pulled tight against her regal head. Jack knew Mother Anemone right away.

"Mothers don't fight," he said, more to himself than anyone, trying to wrap his mind around the sight of Mothers in leathers.

"Andy's too important to the future of water Sibyls," Elana told him. "We have to get her back. And Sibyls do not surrender their children, not ever. If we all fall, Sibyls from all over the world will come, wave after wave, until the child is freed."

Two golden Cursons lumbered into view, each with a Sibyl on their backs, and Jake Lowell landed with his wife, Merilee, a few yards from them.

"Get to them," Jack barked at Saul. "Keep them reasonable until we get Neala and Andy out of there."

Saul hauled ass toward Neala's parents and extended family, taking Astaroths and Bengals with him to add another layer of calm, rational persuasion.

Jack waited another sixty seconds for arrivals, then began positioning OCU squads and Sibyl units on the outer periphery. Most of the New York City Sibyls would form a primary assault line with OCU snipers and officers laying down cover if needed, and acting as a human protective wall with body armor and riot shields. Astaroths would handle the air attack, and Cursons would move in if the Ari Seneca creature or the supermobsters made an appearance. The Mothers—they could do whatever they wanted. Jack knew better than to say a word to them.

As for Jack, Bela, Camille, John, Duncan, and Neala's parents and family, they'd be the tip of the spear. Jack motioned for Saul to bring Riana, Cynda, Merilee, and their husbands into position with him and Andy's group. They'd make the breach and get to Andy and Neala at all costs.

All right, sweetheart. Jack narrowed his eyes at the weird-ass castle. *Here we come.*

"We've got surprise," Saul said to Jack as they lined up beside him. "We've got overwhelming force. We've got superior elemental power, especially with four Mothers in the game."

Jack gave Saul a glare to shut him up, but Saul wasn't finished.

"If I were a total idiot," he went on, sounding a little more tense with each word he spoke, "I'd ask what could go wrong."

Jack checked his Glock. "Who the hell knows. Let's go find out."

40

Andy . . .

This time, Andy's dreams didn't scare her. She didn't bother looking at any of the nightmare images. She treated them like a passing slideshow. Like practice. That's all they were, all they had been all along, just the universe giving her what she needed to get ready, even if she hadn't understood at the time.

With a calmness that almost scared her, Andy forced herself awake with complete understanding of where she was and what she had to do. The dog-shit taste in her mouth nauseated her, but she shoved it to the back of her awareness and took stock before she opened her eyes.

Somebody had put a robe on her. A man's robe. Big and black and heavy. Shackles cut into both wrists and her ankles, and she knew instantly the cuffs had projective traps built into the elemental locks. Her fingers brushed tiny, warm fingers, and immediately Neala gripped Andy's hand.

Andy slowly let her lids open, and she took in a new set of details. She and Neala were lying side by side in an elementally treated cage barely large enough to hold the two of them. Andy's right arm and Neala's left had been secured to the sides of the cage, and they both had intravenous lines running from their forearms out of the cage. Andy couldn't see what, if anything, those lines had been attached to, but she thought she knew.

At the moment, the lines didn't seem to be active.

"Scared," Neala whispered as Andy confirmed to

herself that they were in the makeshift laboratory. She recognized the patched, rotten floor, the new beams and construction lights running across the raised ceiling, and the peeling paint on the walls. Sunlight streamed in from around a makeshift tarp-and-board cover on the hole Andy had blasted in the wall the night before.

Andy squeezed Neala's fingers. "Don't use your fire."

The little girl sniffed. "Bars bite."

Andy couldn't use her elemental senses, but instinct told her the room had a full complement of Coven members. Rebecca's strange energy crackled now and again, and the raspy, heavy breathing of the Seneca monster was hard to miss. They were all talking in low voices, moving equipment, clearly setting some plan in motion.

Where are the assholes with the MAC-10s? Just about that fast, her law enforcement experience answered that question. *Probably on the perimeter outside the lab, along with whatever Coven members aren't in the lab.*

The sharp stench of sulfur made her eyes water, and in that moment, Andy knew her first moment of panic. Too much like her dream. Exactly like her nightmares. She got hold of herself by breathing, by working through one of Elana's shorter relaxation exercises.

The sulfur wasn't coming from the Leviathan demon, but probably from the chemicals the Coven had selected for whatever insane experiment they were about to run.

Neala's hand shook against Andy's. "That lady took my fire. She died like demons in battle. My fire killed her."

"She made a choice," Andy whispered, letting her voice harden to the sharpness of a fire Sibyl Mother and hoping for the best effect. "You had nothing to do with it. The bad guys killed Siobhán, not you."

Neala pondered this for a few heartbeats. "I should have kept my fire."

Andy channeled Jack before she even let herself think. "No way. She took it on purpose. Not your fault."

But this—what's happening to you now—is my fault. I could have changed the flow at so many different points.

Andy kept herself breathing evenly, trying to think, but for a few seconds, she couldn't help where her mind traveled. She realized she had been telling herself she wasn't afraid of feelings, her own or her quad's or Jack's or anybody else's. She had been telling herself she was taking steps toward being a full member of her fighting group. She'd let herself get close to Jack—but had she gotten close enough? Had she let him get close enough to her?

And what about Dio? I could have forced the issue with her before she got hurt, or when she sent us away from Motherhouse Greece. I could have gone after feelings more deeply with Bela and Camille at the house before they left, or even with Jack at the brownstone or the townhouse.

Fuck.

I ran away just as fast as everybody else, didn't I?

Andy gripped Neala's hand and tried to keep herself in the present, but she had to admit the truth to herself. If she had quit letting people push her away, if she hadn't fled from feelings and people right when she was about to get closer than ever, the flow could have changed. It would have changed, and she and Neala might not be chained up in this horrible place.

So many opportunities, and I wrecked them all—but I swear to God, it ends here.

"It ends here, Neala," she said aloud, "because I'm going to end it. We're going to play battle now, only we're not really playing. Do you understand?"

Neala's fingers went still in Andy's grip. "Battle for real?"

"Battle for real." God, she hated that the kid had to go through this. "That's right. And you'll have to fight better than ever."

A few more heartbeats, and then in a scared but also determined voice, "I burn things for you."

Baby fire Sibyls. Gotta love them. "I need you to stay safe and get home to your mother." Andy swallowed in spite of the massive lump in her throat over Neala's courage. "No matter what happens to me, no matter what happens to anyone or anything in this room, that's your job. Understand?"

"I burn things for you."

Once more Andy let herself be amazed by the strength of fire Sibyls, age notwithstanding. She shifted herself carefully in the shackles, and got a full view of the horror spread around them. The cage had been placed on two large metal tables that had been bound together. Two more metal tables had been lowered and placed beside them. On one table lay Siobhán's body covered in what Andy had to assume were Griffen's ashes. On Neala's side of the cage, Tarek's semi-alive figure looked pitifully small and thin. The huge pole had been removed from his furry chest, but a dagger protruded from his heart and his legs and wrists had been firmly shackled to his table's four corners.

Intravenous lines ran from Andy's wrist to a bottle with brownish liquid, probably the source of the sulfur stench, and the lines from Neala's wrist ran to a similar bottle on her side of the cage. The bottles had been hooked to intravenous lines in Siobhán's and Tarek's wrists.

They're planning to bleed us. Andy clenched her teeth. *Whatever's in those bottles will mix with the elemental power in our blood, and who knows what happens when it runs into that half-alive demon and that dead body.*

Her dream-images and Dio's nightmares made a ghastly kind of sense now. Blood rituals. Tarek rising from the dead. Bartholomew August coming back in spirit if not in body.

Couldn't happen. Couldn't be allowed.

Andy knew that when she summoned her elemental powers, the traps in the shackles and bars would attack her and her energy. The harder she fought them, the faster she would die, but she figured she could make enough of a shield for Neala to safely melt her way out of this hell.

In low, careful tones, she explained the nondying parts of her plan to the little girl.

Neala shook, tears streaming down her small, pale cheeks, but she nodded as Rebecca came to stand over them and stare into the cage.

Andy met the girl's cold gaze and kept her face expressionless. She hoped Neala was doing the same.

"We're ready to begin," Rebecca said. "As I promised, we'll make it fast."

The girl's blue eyes sparkled like hard diamonds in arctic sunlight. To Neala, Rebecca said, "Thank you for allowing our friend Tarek to regain his strength. I haven't yet decided what to do with him, but he's the only one of his kind now. He deserves better than a captive existence."

To Andy, she said, "I don't know what will come of this attempt, but I hope to bring back a creature with aspects like my own father."

Father. Of course. That bastard of a demon fathered who knows how many children with all kinds of elementally powerful women, trying to restart his race.

"Bartholomew August," Andy said aloud, wishing more than anything that she had her dart pistol and a few Keres to lend a hand.

"You killed him." Rebecca sounded more clinical than angry.

"I did and I would again." Andy quietly started her fight with the cuffs and bars, beginning to gather her elemental power but not yet attempting to send it outward.

"I should hate you for that like my brother Griffen did, and maybe I do." The girl's smile was way shy of sane. "In truth, I feel nothing about it. I feel nothing about so many things. Sometimes life gets confusing."

Andy forced herself to look the girl straight in the icy eyes. "Don't do this. Take your sideshow freaks and your brother's formulas and get out of New York City. You can carry on your father's work somewhere else, find the meaning of life—whatever. Just don't start by killing children."

Rebecca actually seemed to consider this, but too quickly she dismissed Andy with a flick of her delicate-looking wrist. "I don't think I have to leave. This is the only real home I've known, and I believe I can build what I need right here—a better lab, a proper collection of paranormal creatures, and several strong Covens to protect Ari and me while we develop genetic injections."

She reached down and opened the clamp on Andy's intravenous line, and Andy watched as her own blood rushed through the thin tubing into the brown liquid. The mixture instantly began to drip in the line leading to Siobhán's body.

Andy drew a slow breath through her teeth as Rebecca opened Neala's intravenous line, then turned back to the Seneca monster and the Coven members present in the lab.

Don't lose it. Keep focus. Hold it tight.

Which was hard, given that Tarek and the corpse on the table next to Andy started to twitch and jerk.

Time's up. Here goes.

Andy opened herself to the full might and power of her water energy. She didn't just crack the windows or edge open the entrance inside her essence. She threw open her inner floodgates, accessing every bit of flow and water she could find, sense, or touch.

Instantly, the cuffs threw off a stunning cloud of energy, dulling her mind and senses, crushing her awareness into so many bits and fragments. Then the strength of the elemental locks on the bars added weight and pressure.

Andy let go of Neala's hand. She shoved against the elemental locks and projective traps expanding across her senses and energy. The pain came so fast and harsh she knew right away it was killing her, but she kept right on turning herself into an utter, absolute mirror for the world's water. She'd draw it all if she had to. She was a Mother, after all. And a decent Sibyl and a good cop, and a good friend, and a woman who had loved some pretty fabulous guys. All of that and the soul-deep wish for Neala's safety gave her strength. All of that gave her definition and identity as she struggled to keep her own shape against the power trying to course through her essence.

"She's fighting the locks and traps." The Seneca monster's voice sounded like growling from a hound of hell.

"They'll hold."

Rebecca's confident assertion didn't soothe her pet beast. "Assuming is dangerous. Assuming gets you killed."

Shouting rose outside, and the Coven men reacted in a hurry. Andy's fast-blurring vision let her see them running out of the lab as the under-Coven rushed in to take their places.

Something must be going down. Something that required big elemental firepower.

Jack.

That thought gave her a major boost, and just as fast, Andy knew she was right. Jack hadn't run out on her after all. He was here, trying to do something to try to save the day. Maybe he'd brought help—though she'd need half the city and the Motherhouses, too, to get her out of this alive.

"Are we okay?" the Seneca monster asked, moving close enough for Andy to see the mottled, cobbled mess that functioned as his face. Saggy, wrinkled flesh. Lumpy jaws. Ridged forehead. Bristles of black fur jabbed out his cheeks in different directions, and his ears seemed more feline than human.

"We're fine," Rebecca assured the thing. "I don't sense anything amiss for us now or in the near future."

The monster seemed to consider this. "How near?"

God, it can think for itself, too. Andy knew that wasn't good.

"We'll get out of this lab alive," Rebecca said with all the conviction of a teenager who believed she could never die—and never be defeated. "No worries."

Tarek and the thing on the table next to Andy twitched again. Something groaned. Andy didn't want to look at whatever was trying to rise and find life beside her, so she stared into Neala's face.

The child's eyes fluttered, and her cheeks went pale.

Andy focused everything she had on their shackles and the bars holding them hostage.

"Ready?" she managed to whisper to Neala even though it took most of the energy she had left.

From seemingly far away, she heard Neala's mumbled answer. "Ready."

Andy clenched her fists and doubled her efforts. The shackles chewed into her skin, sucking away most of the water energy she pulled through her body.

Let it flow.

The bars burned her arm and backside, gripping her like long metal talons, pulling her into the bite of the treated steel. Blood streamed from her nose, from her mouth, from the wounds on her arms.

I can do this. I can. I absolutely can.

She was breaking the traps. Somehow, her energy was enough—or turning into enough.

She saw herself in the flow of the water. She saw herself *as* the flow, the source of its direction and strength.

Boards cracked and split under the cage. Patched metal shrieked and gave way. Water rushed up so hard and fast it battered Andy like fists, and she fought to keep the force of it on her side of the cage even as she struggled to wrap Neala inside the stream, to insulate her from the bars, to place at least a film of water between the shackles and her skin. Not much protection, not very much at all—but enough?

She heard the child whimper and splutter as the water tore out the intravenous lines in her wrist. Tarek let out a howl on his table, bashing claws and feet against the metal. Neala ignored him and burned her own wound until it stopped bleeding. Then she melted off her shackles and crammed her wrists and ankles into Andy's swirling water energy to cool them. The cage shifted on its tables, beginning to slide back and forth as waves sluiced beneath them.

Andy barely perceived the world around her. She had thought dying would be a lot harder than this.

She heard shouting, Rebecca and the Seneca monster.

"Breaking locks—"

"Don't be stupid—"

"She's breaking through them!"

Neala's smoke blended with droplets and fire turned some of the moisture into sizzling mist. Outside the growing maelstrom, nearly grayed completely from her view by the bulk of water between them, the Seneca monster loomed beside Neala. The girl screamed and leaped across the cage to Andy.

Andy couldn't move. Couldn't comfort the little girl. Couldn't even get a whole breath or keep her eyes completely open—but she could still call the flow, let it rush into her and through her and out around Neala, battering the elemental traps and locks.

The energy containing Andy and Neala shattered with

a great, yawing howl that seemed to come from the depths of the sea itself.

Mine, the oceans of the world seemed to scream, possessive and huge and endless, yet utterly feminine—a blind, rage-filled mother come to claim her own.

This one, she's mine!

Andy welcomed the sea's smothering embrace, breathing deep and drawing the salty spray into her lungs. Even more water poured through her, faster and harder. She became her own lake, her own river, her own ocean, expanding, expanding, and she thought about Dio, and how endless the world's air must feel, how Dio must have known this same feral exultation when she called tornadoes and brought weather crashing to earth at her whim.

Dio . . .

Jack . . .

Grief only opened Andy's essence wider. Water thundered into the lab, crushing and shoving and battering and pushing. Neala clung to Andy's neck and pressed her tiny body into Andy's arms, screaming and burning anything that lunged toward them through the water.

Off balance now, the cage heaved and washed off its tables, slamming them to the floor so hard Andy's teeth cut into her lip. Her body cushioned Neala's fall, and the cage door burst open.

Rebecca was nowhere in sight.

Neither were the men in black shirts and jeans.

The Seneca monster let out a bellow and half lunged, half swam straight at them. Neala shouted and scrambled out of the cage so fast Andy couldn't even tell which direction she went except for the slightest trail of steam as she fried her way through the sweeping, onrushing water, vaporizing a path as she made her escape.

Run, baby, run! Fresh joy surged through Andy, and the water she channeled took the path of least elemental resistance, out the open cage door and into the Seneca monster's misshapen, brutal face. Andy realized the water level in the room was actually starting to rise, that she must have flooded the space and floors below the lab, that she must be moving so much water in so fast it couldn't get out fast enough despite the gaping hole in the lab's wall.

Flow. Yes.

Andy knew her thoughts were breaking down, but she didn't care if the whole ocean washed through her now. Neala was out. Neala was gone. Neala never lost a game of battle. Andy hoped the little girl wouldn't stop running until she leaped into her mom and dad's arms—and even God couldn't help anybody who tried to go after the child then.

She thought about Dio again, about weather and windstorms and endless air and water, swirling across the world.

She thought about Jack and let the pounding waves beat away her pain and anguish. No matter what, she had loved him. No matter what, he had loved her, too. She was sure of it. With nothing in her soul but the pure, screaming ecstasy of her element, everything seemed so clear.

More water.

Still more.

Andy floated, and as she closed her eyes for the last time, she smiled.

41

Jack led his attack line through the ranks of Sibyls and OCU officers. Saul, Bela, Camille, Duncan, and John had one wing of their wedge, while Cynda, Riana, Merilee, and the Lowell brothers formed the other. Jack kept himself on point, weaving them through packs of Sibyls and OCU officers.

Something inside the building went off like a bomb, rattling the ground and tossing them all back a step.

Saul and Duncan went down, and so did Creed, Nick, and Riana. Jack kept his balance, kept his focus on the patch of courtyard he could see through broken-down windows and doors—Coven men, fighting back, trying to advance on them.

Behind them, water blasted into the air like some kind of volcanic mountain just born, rising huge and angry, straight out of the earth. The thing was monolithic and blue-black, and it was spinning so fast it almost looked still.

Officers shouted. Even Sibyls screamed.

Saul got to his feet beside Jack, his weapon temporarily lowered as he stared at the funnel lifting skyward. "What the living fuck is that?"

"Waterspout." Jack heard himself laughing as he started forward again. That was *his* woman. That was *his* warrior. She was alive and kicking major ass.

Bela whooped and Camille let out an excited cry. Then both of them yelled the same name, so loud it seemed to echo in Jack's soul.

"Andy!"

The Lowells and their wives were up and moving, and they all ran forward now, keeping the wedge formation.

"Keep it going, sweetheart," Jack shouted into the growing roar of the water tornado.

"Will it stop?" Saul called from behind him.

"I hope not," Jack hollered back at his friend. "Hold your breath if it scares you, little boy."

Saul hurried to keep up, calling him a few names and polishing off his fit with, "Fuck you, Blackmore!"

The circle of Sibyls around the Smith Infirmary regained their composure, tightened their ranks, tightened them again, and pressed toward the building. OCU officers got hold of themselves and laid down a withering carpet of cover fire, keeping the Coven men and their enhanced fighters holed up behind the infirmary's piles of bricks and stone.

From the corner of his eye, Jack saw the four Mothers in leathers change course and head straight toward the waterspout. At first they were running, but almost as fast, they started moving like they were walking into a hundred-mile-per-hour headwind.

At the same moment, Bela and Camille fell off the pace.

"Energy," Bela choked out from behind him. "Bad energy. Crushing us. Go. We'll break through . . . soon as . . . we can."

Jack glanced at the fury on Bela's face and the determination on Camille's. John and Duncan had gone Bengal, stripped to demon essence by the brutal energy Jack could barely sense, much less feel. They bared fangs, Cynda and her triad screamed with frustration, and the Lowell brothers, all in full demon form, roared and thrashed limbs, trying to push through and getting nowhere.

"Looks like we're it," Jack told Saul, and Saul nodded.

Adrenaline pumped through Jack until he tasted metal and salt.

He and Saul stormed forward and pressed through the

ranks of OCU officers laying down another round of cover fire. Immediately the officers opened a corridor for them, and Jack and Saul ran single file to stay clear of the bullets. They steered around the courtyard, where they could see the bastards in black sweatshirts and the big-ass altered mobsters with big-ass guns holding off the OCU and trying to advance on the Sibyls.

"Fucking mess of a place has to have a side door," Saul yelled, kicking at the first boarded window they came to. Jack kicked it with him and the wood split, revealing a bricked up window behind it.

"Fuck." Jack kicked it once more in anger, and they plowed toward the next bunch of wood.

More bricks.

Damn it.

The waterspout rained on them, light at first, then harder as they got closer. A minute later, Jack crammed his Glock in its holster to save it and shielded his face from the monsoon. He spotted a boarded door with a few holes in the wood, no bricks in sight.

"There!" he shouted to Saul, then lowered his shoulder and rammed his full weight against the wood. It gave too easily, rotten and wet, and he barreled into a ruined, graffiti-filled hallway full of bricks, bottles, broken glass, trash, and discarded needles from decades of junkies. He hit his knees and rolled forward, barely missing a few rusty old needles, and stopped just shy of a huge hole in the floor that went all the way to hell, as far as he could see.

Saul stumbled in behind him, and Jack was up, skirting the hole, then running toward the spout. He couldn't see the funnel anymore, but he could sure as hell hear it, picking up force as it gathered more and more water.

Don't stop. Don't let it stop, because that'll mean she stopped. He couldn't stand the thought. Couldn't live with it. No way.

"Metal door, three o'clock," Saul called, and Jack squinted in the building's dim light. He saw the door, too new, hanging open, partly off its hinges. From behind it came the angry bellow of whirling, flooding water. Like a thousand tidal waves. Like hundreds of rivers flooding at the same time.

Like Andy.

Jack drew his Glock and charged through the open door.

The ugliest creature he'd ever seen hulked in front of him. The big fucker looked something like Ari Seneca, but too tall, too wide, too muscular. Jack didn't give a shit who or what the thing was. He filled its face full of elementally treated bullets and blew right past it, trusting Saul to give the monster a run for its money and get out of the way before it could do him any damage.

The waterspout swelled through the room, pressing toward him, holding a deep well in its center. Furniture and bricks and people whipped past in the violent water, and now and then, way down deep in the center, Jack caught sight of bars and cuffs anchoring a floating, pitching figure in a black robe.

"Andy."

Jack rammed himself forward against the gut-bashing force of the water spout.

Shit. She didn't even look conscious.

His blood surged. He holstered his Glock again, spotted a broken chain on the ground, picked it up, and looped it around a jagged pile of stone and brick and bent metal until he got purchase and tension. His own anchor. He looped the other end around his waist and hooked a broken link into a closed link to secure it.

"Hold on, sweetheart."

No hesitation. No real thought.

Jack took a run and go and hurled himself into the

blasting funnel, trusting the weight of the chain to hold him down as his momentum carried him through.

Water flayed at his skin, scouring him like sandpaper as he dove forward. Bricks and wood and bodies bashed against him, and he lost perspective as he whirled and snapped in circles so fast he didn't know up from down, right from left. No air. Just water. Too much weight on his chest, his ribs—

And he was through to the center well, and sinking.

His chest burned. His eyes throbbed and ached like he'd been in a three-hour bar fight. He was moving, though. Knifing straight down and picking up speed.

Andy drifted in the currents below him, but the water flowing through her pushed Jack back so hard he had to swim like hell to get through it. Closer. His head started to spin. A little closer. A mile for an inch of progress. A foot. Almost there.

Andy . . .

She looked like a flower in a hurricane, blowing back and forth, back and forth, chained to some fucking cage like an animal.

Jack let out his last bit of air in a swarm of bubbles, and he swam harder. Her hand drifted past him, and he grabbed her wrist. Using her for leverage, he pulled himself toward her as carefully as he could.

Damned chains wrapped around her legs and arms. They weighed like a bitch, and the cage—

Jack's ribs and throat seemed to catch on fire, and he almost took a convulsive breath. Force of will. *No breathing, goddamnit. No passing out.*

He gave a big yank. The cage moved a half inch. No more.

Fuck! His cheeks puffed out and he gathered Andy to him. *Either we get out together, sweetheart, or we're both staying right here.*

His vision started to go gray as he fought not to breathe.

Andy's eyes fluttered. They opened. She looked at him and didn't seem to see him, didn't seem to know him.

And then she did.

The water around them blew apart like somebody dropped a depth charge in the center.

Jack felt like he'd been flushed down the world's biggest drain. His ears roared and popped as he plunged to the floor, doing all he could to roll so he caught Andy. They hit the floor together and he wheezed in a breath, coughing and holding her to him as all kinds of debris, human-type included, rained down around them. Jack had a sense that Andy was moving water big-time, sending it out, more or less throwing the weight of it back into nearby oceans and rivers and bays so it didn't flood Staten Island and New Jersey, too.

More bodies hit the busted floor.

Jack didn't know who all the dead guys were, but given their waterlogged sweatshirts and jeans, he figured them for Coven or under-Coven, or maybe both. No sign of Saul and the Seneca thing, but from somewhere down the hall came gunfire and clattering and lots of swearing. Saul was still holding his own.

Through a hole in the lab wall, Jack could see live Coven members and too-muscled mobsters up and moving. They seemed closer to the building, and the mobsters tried to lift their big guns, but they weren't doing too well. The earth kept rattling beneath them. Wind howled, driving against them and shoving them to their knees. Some of them caught fire. Arrows and throwing knives flashed in the sunlight as they rained into the courtyard, hitting targets with murderous accuracy.

Four seconds. That's all Jack gave himself to breathe before he rolled to his side and yanked the cuffs and chains right off the bent, battered cage that had been

Andy's anchor. He had her free in moments, and in his arms long enough to squish his hands against her water-logged robe and feel her warmth seeping through to his fingers, to sense the beating of her heart against his, in rhythm, just like it should have been. Then he pulled back and tried to help her stop the bleeding. So many cuts and wounds. He rolled up her sleeves and saw that the worst cut seemed to be on her wrist, which was torn open just below her palm. She yanked out the remnants of an intravenous needle and pressed the site with two fingers.

"Griffen's dead," she said, then bared her teeth at something Jack couldn't see.

Jack let her go, spun around, and drew his water-logged Glock all in one motion. The thing standing behind him—it defied all description.

Sort of female. Sort of male. With a few scales and something that might have been a wing pointing out of one arm.

Its eyes—Christ.

It had red, bleeding eyes straight from hell, with absolutely no trace of human in them at all.

Jack squeezed the Glock's trigger, praying it would fire, and the faithful weapon pumped six rounds right through the crimson centers of those satanic orbs.

The winged thing fell away from them, howling and waving its arms. It bashed into something even bigger as it went stiff and crashed to the floor. Something a lot more muscular, with golden fur, fangs, and claws big enough to slice a man open from nose to gut in one swipe.

Tarek drew himself to his full height, well over seven feet. The massive tiger's eyes flashed gold, then red, as he opened his fanged mouth and let out a roar that rattled the tumbledown hospital's piles of brick.

Jack's chest seized.

All these years of tracking these bastards, of fighting

from a distance, of trying to wipe them off the face of the earth and make up for what he and his men unleashed in Afghanistan—and here was the last surviving Rakshasa Eldest, up close and personal and ready to eat him.

"Time to die, asshole, once and for all." Jack fired, intending to pump an elementally treated bullet into the demon's chest, but this time, the Glock gave a wet click. Useless.

Every muscle in Jack's body went stiff. If the beast hadn't been disoriented, Jack would have died on the spot, or been turned into a Rakshasa demon by a bite or a claw wound. Tarek didn't seem to understand what was happening. He roared again, getting a clue faster than Jack wanted. He hurled the Glock at the demon's face.

The pistol bloodied Tarek's nose as Andy's arms circled Jack's waist, unhooking the chain he'd used to reach her in the water spout. She pressed the jagged metal into Jack's palm and he launched himself forward, ramming the metal into the Rakshasa's chest with all his strength.

Tarek grabbed at the hook, but Jack ducked away from him, grabbed Andy's arm, and yanked her out of the way just before Tarek's claws found her throat. As the elementally treated metal reached its target, the beast froze, and Andy and Jack both looked around the body-riddled room searching for something big enough, sharp enough—

"There!" Jack pointed to a dagger lodged at the base of the wall closest to Andy.

"That was in his chest before." Andy ripped the blade free and tossed it to him. "My water must have knocked it loose. It's treated, so it should work."

It was messy business, beheading a tiger-demon with a small blade, but Jack managed it as fast as he could. "We'll never get him dry enough to burn," he said as he got off the carcass and tossed the head a few feet away from the body.

Tarek's head burst into flames, and the demon's body went up like a torch, too. Jack had to jump back a few steps to keep from immolating right along with what was left of his enemy. The blood on his dagger caught fire, and the blade burned clean in a matter of seconds.

Andy washed the ashes of the Rakshasa's head and body in two different directions. Instead of looking relieved, she had gone wide-eyed. As she finished disposing of the demon, her mouth came open, her hands started to shake, and she turned a slow circle, squinting into the shadows.

Jack saw the little girl before she did.

Neala had wedged herself between some boards and bricks in the room's far corner. She was sobbing like a kid who had seen way too many monsters. He crossed the patched floor in a hurry, gathered her up, and carried her back to Andy, who wrapped her in her arms.

"Scared," the little girl said between big, gulping cries.

"It's okay," Andy told her. "I was scared, too. Scared's okay. Scared's just fine."

The lab's torn metal door rattled, and a thin blond girl stepped into the space. Drenched and bedraggled and obviously ten kinds of furious, she stared at him, then at Andy and Neala. At the same time, Coven members staggered in through the hole in the lab wall. They had their backs to Jack and Andy and Neala and the girl, but the supermobsters with the major weaponry didn't.

Neala let out a squeak, and all the barrels of the MAC-10s started to glow red and melt. A few of the mobsters tried to fire and blew big holes in their own chests. Andy washed them back into the courtyard before they could get off any decent rounds, and she blasted the Coven members next, sending them flailing and swearing through the wall, riding the crests of a dozen small waves.

"That's enough," said the blond girl. From all the descriptions Jack had studied, this had to be Rebecca, half sister to Griffen—species and elemental powers unknown. She marched forward, doing something with her energy that made Andy move back as she approached. Neala lifted her hands and screwed up her face, but no fire left the little girl's fingertips.

"You won't be burning me," Rebecca told Neala. To Andy, she said, "Hand her over before I crush you both. You know I can. You already feel your cells ripping. I'll make you explode if I have to, but I'd rather keep the two of you alive."

Andy said nothing, but she turned and used her body to shield the terrified, smoking, flame-spitting little girl. Jack started forward with the dagger. Whatever voodoo the girl had, it wouldn't work on him, he was pretty sure.

He raised the dagger, positioning it in his palm. He didn't want to stab a woman, even if she wasn't really human.

"Hand me the girl," Rebecca demanded, giving off what felt like a cloud of dark, bitter ugliness.

"I think not," said a quiet, powerful voice from behind Jack.

The sound of it punched through all the ugly in the air, and instinct made Jack leap out of the way as a huge gout of flame blasted forward and scorched the floor all around the girl.

Rebecca whipped around, her hands up, but when she saw her opponent, she hesitated. Her eyes narrowed. "What . . . are you?"

"Your equal." Mother Keara sprang forward, Irish hand-and-a-half sword drawn as she took a battle stance in her battered leathers. Her gray hair hung in wavy curtains around her wrinkled face, but Jack could see death in her bright green eyes as she said, "You'll be leavin' that baby alone now."

Mother Yana, Mother Anemone, and Elana came through the lab door and surrounded Rebecca before the girl grasped that she'd been outplayed. Jack realized the Mothers had to be containing her with their elemental energies, blending their powers together to form some sort of binding.

He edged around the group of them and got to Andy as five winged guys Jack didn't recognize came sailing through the hole in the lab wall. He put himself between Andy and Neala and the men, once more raising the dagger, but she put two fingers on his wrist and pushed it down.

"Fire men," Neala whispered, sounding awed.

Andy shivered visibly as she corrected the little girl. "The Host. The tallest one, his name is Mikeal."

The Host landed, squinting and obviously not enjoying the sunlight, but they never took their eyes off Rebecca. Their massive black wings cast shadows across the whole space, and a few black feathers drifted down to the mucky floor as Mikeal addressed Mother Keara in Gaelic.

She fired right back at him with words and sparks and smoke.

Jack had very little idea what they were saying, but he did catch the word *Sluagh* as Mikeal gestured to Rebecca.

"Oh, no way." Andy shoved Neala into Jack's arms and started forward. Jack barely managed to hold on to the little fire Sibyl and grab the shoulder of Andy's wet robe to hold her back.

"Her?" Andy shouted, water and blood dripping down her arms. "*She's* what the Host has been after?" She turned the full measure of her ire on Mikeal. "Host or not, you can't seriously think you're taking that murdering witch out of here alive. She and her pet monster nearly killed one of my best friends!"

Mikeal gave Andy a respectful bow. "Your friends the Astaroths and Bengals led me to believe you would be reasonable on this point, if we would only share with you what we had come to retrieve."

"*Which* Astaroths and Bengals?" Andy demanded, already plotting her own set of murders.

Mikeal turned back to Mother Keara instead of answering. The two of them bickered for a few moments, or maybe it was bargaining. Jack couldn't tell. They must have reached agreement, because the Mothers backed away from Rebecca and four of the Host instantly moved in and took hold of her.

Rebecca seemed too stunned to resist.

It was all Jack could do to keep a grip on Andy's robe, especially since Neala was busy burning holes in his wet clothes.

Mikeal took off and flew back out of the hole in the lab wall. Less than a minute later, he returned, this time through the lab door.

He had retracted his black feathery wings, and he looked mostly human now, like a normal guy. Well, a normal guy carrying a big, lumpy head under his arm and dribbling blood and gore behind him. Jack tried to turn Neala's face away, but the little girl shrugged him off, pointed her finger at the head and caught it on fire.

Andy twisted out of Jack's grip, but at least she didn't charge forward and try to throttle Mikeal. Not yet, anyway.

Mikeal put the Seneca monster's burning skull on the patched floor, right at Mother Keara's feet. The stench of scorched flesh and hair and sulfur filled the room as Saul came limping through the door, bleeding from his nose and at least five other places. His gun arm dangled at a weird angle, but he pointed toward Mikeal and the burning head with his good hand and glared at Jack.

"Why'd you send him? I didn't need any help. I had the bastard. I really did." When Saul finished, he sat down on his ass. Then he sort of fell over. Mother Anemone and Elana went to him and started to work on all his cuts and bruises.

Mikeal's lips twitched, but he didn't smile. To Mother Keara, in careful English, he said, "The perversion of nature is dead and your man has been returned to you." He turned his attention to Andy. "I ask your pardon, water Sibyl, but another one of our ranks was taken captive by the Coven—a female. Do you have knowledge of her?"

Andy lowered her head, and all the anger left her voice as she said, "Siobhán died saving Neala and me from Griffen."

For the first time, Jack saw a flicker of emotion on Mikeal's face. Dark pain. A moment of helpless rage. Jack had a sense that the man—the Host—whatever he was—was holding back a major amount of deadly elemental energy.

"Siobhán took my fire," Neala told the Host leader solemnly, like she understood that Mikeal had to be addressed as royalty. "She burned Griffen until his bones broked."

This seemed to give Mikeal what he needed. The tension left his face and fists, and he offered Neala a quick half-bow. "Then my sister met death well, little one, and you helped her achieve that greatest of honors. For that I thank you."

Once more, Mikeal focused on Mother Keara. "Our bargain is fulfilled, though we still owe debts of honor to some of your ranks."

Smoke puffed from the top of Mother Keara's head as she sighed. "Do us all a favor and go about satisfyin' those obligations some other time, hear me?"

Mikeal seemed surprised, but he said, "As you wish."

"Ve vish," Mother Yana confirmed.

Mother Keara twitched her gnarled fingers at Rebecca and the rest of the Host. "Go on with yer fighters now, and that—that whatever she is. Take her like we agreed, but we'd best not be seein' her ever again."

The Host didn't seem to have anything further to say on the subject.

Mikeal's wings reappeared, and on his signal, his fighters took off out of the hole in the wall in a rush of dark wings and feathers, dragging Rebecca into the bright New York sky and vanishing before Jack could wonder what would happen when people got a look at the bizarre human birds and their captive.

"What the hell did you just do?" Andy snarled at Mother Keara. "That little psychopath whacked a lot of people, and she let her monster tear off Dio's arm—and she just tried to kill me and Neala to resurrect a Rakshasa and her Leviathan father!"

"She's theirs." Mother Keara faced Andy with her thin arms outstretched. "The queen's daughter was stolen from them by that unholy Leviathan, and the girl Rebecca was the product of their union. August murdered the mother, but the Host has searched many years to find her offspring."

Andy stared at Mother Keara. "And?"

"And we have treaties. Agreements." Mother Keara sounded tired now. "She'll be more stable and manageable amongst her own. Whatever justice she deserves, the Host will see that she receives it."

"I don't like it." Andy dripped more water, but a little less blood. Jack knew her Sibyl healing had kicked into high gear, but he still wanted to check each wound himself, just to be sure she didn't need medical attention.

"Ve don't have many choices ven it comes to bargains with the older peoples of this earth." Mother Yana's soothing, earthy tones eased Jack's nerves a fraction. "Ve all have ties—fire Sibyls vith the Host, air Sibyls vith the Keres—and there are others like them that you vill meet and come to know. You vill also come to know their power, and the visdom of the bargain ve made this day."

"I hope so," Andy muttered, glancing at Elana and Mother Anemone, who had managed to brace Saul's arm and stop most of his bleeding. "And for the record, all of you look like freaks in those battle leathers."

"I heard that," Elana called as she tore a shirt off a dead Coven sorcerer to make a pillow for Saul until the medics could get to him.

"Fire men." Neala stared out of the hole in the lab wall. Jack managed to move his face before her next little jet of fire singed off his eyebrows.

A glowing, golden Curson demon appeared in the opening to the courtyard, and Neala yelled, "Daddy!"

Jack put the little girl down and she went running to Nick, who shifted to full human before she reached him. He scooped her into his arms, and Cynda ran to both of them and wrapped herself around them, spitting sparks and flames as Riana, Creed, Merilee, and Jake arrived. Bela came in next, followed by Camille, Duncan, and John. Bela's sword was streaked with blood.

"The Coven's history," she said. "We got them all and the supermobsters, too. Chopped them up and burned the pieces." Bela glanced at the bodies scattered around the lab, and at the still-smoking monster skull. "Looks like you took out the Seneca thing and the under-Coven. We saw Rebecca leaving with the Host."

Andy explained how Griffen died, and as she spoke, Jack felt her hand brush against his. He realized she was still shaking, no doubt exhausted, but also emotional from watching Cynda and Nick reunited with Neala, and seeing that Bela and Camille had come to her defense. Jack caught Andy's fingers in his and held them, wanting to do more, wanting to grab her and tell her how sorry he was, how much he loved her, but he didn't think now was the moment. She stared at him for a second, then went to her sister Sibyls and hugged them both for a long time. Jack couldn't hear everything that was said, but he caught lots of apologies and a few tales of Coven ass kicking that made him smile.

He felt strange, standing back as Andy interacted with Bela, Camille, Duncan, and John, and even stranger when he realized they were all looking at him. Waiting for something. For—

For me to join them.

Jack saw OCU officers and crime techs swarming into the courtyard, and he heard them moving through the broken halls of the infirmary.

The fight really was over, wasn't it?

He made himself move, made himself take the steps that would lead him toward a future he didn't have planned in any shape or form or fashion, save for hoping Andy would be its centerpiece.

Standing next to her in the family group seemed so natural it made his gut hurt, but it also made him happy in ways he wasn't sure he deserved.

"Elana tried to tell me, tried to teach me, but there was so much I didn't get. I think I get it now." Andy eyed Cynda and Neala, then blew Neala a kiss. The look on Cynda's face held a mixture of anger and gratitude that made sense to Jack, and seemed to make sense to Andy, too. Cynda and her triad left, demon husbands in tow, without looking back.

Andy watched them moving away for a time, then said, "If I had trusted all of you and reached out to you when you were in need—and if I had trusted myself and really stood up for what I knew inside—Neala never would have been at risk. She's a child and she trusted me, and I almost let her down big-time." Andy closed her eyes, then opened them again and Jack saw a sparkle in the rich brown and green depths. "Never again. So be warned, if we put this thing back together, all of us, I might not be so easy to live with."

She folded her arms and fixed her gaze on Bela. "And we will be putting it back together."

Bela didn't argue. Neither did Camille.

"Right now, and for the rest of your life, you'll be one of a kind," Bela said. "None of us except maybe Elana understands all of what you are, all of what you can do. Right now, we're all children who trust you."

Andy chewed at her bottom lip for a second, then raised her chin and faced Bela and Camille with Jack still standing silently by her side, hoping like hell he was doing the right thing, giving her what she needed from him.

"I'll get Dio back," Andy told her fighting group. "I don't know how, but I will. I swear it."

Both Bela and Camille looked away, and when they met Andy's gaze again, they had tears in their eyes. They hugged her, then took John and Duncan out of the lab, following after Cynda, Nick, and Neala and their group, winding their way out of the infirmary ruins.

Despite the Mothers and the influx of Sibyls and OCU officers and technicians, Jack finally felt like he had a moment alone with Andy. He turned and put his arms on her shoulders. Water ran across his fingers and dripped to the floor as he got lost in her wet red hair, her pretty freckled face, and those bright, beautiful eyes.

Do this right, Blackmore. For God's sake, don't fuck it up again.

Andy put her hand on Jack's chest, and he felt a rush of emotion, a bonding just from that simple touch. Nothing had ever stirred him like this woman, and he cursed himself a thousand times for not having handled things better with her every step of the way.

How could she forgive him? How could he even ask for another chance?

He tried to find the words, the right words this time, but she spoke first. Her question came out low and quiet, echoing both pain and hope and etching itself right across Jack's heart.

"Are you leaving?"

And then Jack knew the exact right word, and he said it with absolute conviction. "Never."

Andy's eyes drifted shut, and he covered her hand with his.

"There will be an us," she murmured. "There will be time for us to be together and work this out, but right now I'm the one with messes to clean up."

Jack gave her hand a gentle squeeze. "When you're ready, I'll be right here."

42

Andy stepped onto the communications platform at Motherhouse Kérkira still wearing the stupid black robe. Ona, the really old, really crazy fire Sibyl Elana adored so much, was waiting for her, holding out her most comfortable pair of jeans, her favorite oversized red shirt, a new holster and shiny new dart pistol to replace the ones she lost in the battle with the Coven, and a pair of sunglasses.

Andy realized Elana might have a point about Ona having a lot to offer, nutty spells and accidental genocide aside.

She took the clothes, got out of the wet, nasty robe, dried herself and got dressed. Then she allowed herself one artichoke and bacon sandwich with hot mustard, a single glass of wine, and exactly four hours to nap before she had Ona wake her.

When she strapped on firepower for her little journey, she didn't bother concealing the dart pistol under her jeans. She fastened it around her waist in plain view, enjoying its weight and feel. Shoving the sunglasses into place felt more like putting on armor than zipping up leathers ever had, and as Andy started out the door to head for Mount Olympus, Ona said, "Need any backup?"

"Thanks." Andy smiled at Ona even though the ancient fire-breather was almost as blind as Elana. "But I need to do this one alone."

The climb didn't take as long as Andy thought it would, but by the time she reached Motherhouse Greece, she really knew she hadn't eaten or slept enough, and her bruised bones and muscles bitched louder with each step she took.

The crystal palace shone like Oz's Emerald City in the very early morning light. Andy didn't announce herself, and the scrawny air adepts manning the entranceway got the hell out of her path when they saw her dart pistol and the back-the-fuck-off look on her face.

Andy never knocked on a door or asked permission from anybody about anything. She just kept moving, straight through the hallways to the infirmary and into the little waiting chamber where she'd wasted so much damned time doing all the wrong things. She didn't even bother trying the door between the chamber and the rooms where Dio had been staying. She just lifted her foot and kicked them open, letting them bang against the wall.

A sun-drenched hallway stretched before her, and six or seven air Sibyl Mothers leaped up from chairs and tables to block Andy's path.

"Move," Andy told them.

When they didn't get out of her way, she kept right on walking, drew her dart pistol, aimed it at the nearest giant window, and fired.

Glass shattered and wind instantly howled through the hallway as cool mountain air rushed into the closed space. Before the Mothers could tame the wind or do anything to stop her, Andy washed them out the opening, knowing that their air skills would keep them from falling thousands of feet to a rocky death at the foot of the mountain.

She stretched out her elemental senses and fixed on the right room in the little Sibyl-style hospital corridor, and kicked open that door, too.

Dio was sitting in her bed in a small room with solid crystalline walls and a floor-to-ceiling window looking down the mountainside. Her wispy blond hair spilled around her face like a child's curls, and she had pulled her single white sheet all the way up under her nose.

"Get up," Andy told her without holstering the dart pistol. She'd shot Dio before, and by God, she'd do it again if she had to—and Dio knew it. "You're coming with me."

Dio's gray eyes flashed. Her fingers gripped the sheet tighter and a steady, menacing breeze filled the tiny space. "Go away, Andy."

Andy blocked the breeze with a wall of water energy sans a ton of moisture—for now. "If I have to wash this crystal palace all the way back to New York City, I'll do it."

Dio blinked at Andy, clearly aware that she had crushed her air energy with the ease of a Mother who had years of experience. "Well, well. Somebody's been practicing."

"Somebody hasn't had a choice." Andy strode over to the bed, grabbed the sheet, and yanked it aside.

Dio had on jeans and a short-sleeved blue shirt with the left arm tacked shut. She wrapped her remaining arm around her knees and glared at Andy. "Touch me and I'll blow you the fuck away."

Andy cocked her head. "Okay, good. That's better. But I have to touch you, Dio. It's the best way for me to read emotions and restore flow."

Dio hit her with a major blast of wind this time, almost hard enough to make her stumble before she countered it with a full shot of water energy.

Almost.

Water splashed across Andy's arms, cool and familiar. A fair-sized wave doused Dio and her prissy white sheets, too.

Dio jumped up on the wet bed, slinging droplets in every direction. "Can you grow my arm back?" Thunder blasted across the mountain and lightning struck about a foot from the sickroom window. "Can you? Because that's the only damned thing I want from you right now. It's all I want from anybody!"

Andy stood fast in the sudden rush of air as the sharp tang of burning ozone clogged her nose. "You know nobody can give you that."

"Then piss off!" Dio's sharp, high scream barely punctured the next barrage of thunder.

Andy's heart ached, but she didn't move an inch. "No."

She waited for a fresh round of lightning to cut her in two, but the weather never came. Dio threw herself down on the bed and the air in the room got scary-still as she sobbed.

"Are you upset because I'm wanting to meddle in your emotions, or are you upset because I'm refusing to give up on you?"

Dio raised her tear-streaked face, still furious, and Andy knew the answer to her own question. So did Dio. Andy could tell even if Dio didn't grace her with an answer.

"I won't give up. Not ever." Andy dared to take a step closer. "So you might as well let me do what I have to do."

Sunlight bathed Dio's pale face in yellow and gold as she glared at Andy. "It's not like I can fight you off with one damned arm—and my weak arm at that. Go ahead. Grab hold of me and read whatever you want."

This time the pain in Andy's chest and gut made her wince. "I won't. Not unless you tell me I can. I want your permission, Dio."

Silence.

More glaring. It wasn't such a sharp glare, though. More like a nervous, worried stare. More like Dio trying to decide what she really wanted, what she really needed.

You need us. Andy wished Dio could read her mind

and hoped that reading the love and determination on her face would be enough. *You need yourself, your quad, your life.*

Dio's glare softened another fraction. "If I let you touch me and read my emotions, what are you going to do with them?"

Andy had asked herself this a few times and she still didn't have a solid answer. "I have no idea."

"Oh." Dio looked more scared than angry now. "So, what'll happen?"

Andy pulled off her sunglasses and tossed them on the little table beside Dio's bed. "I don't know."

"You're a big goddamned comfort, you know that?" Dio sat on the bed and dripped, but at least the thunder and lightning didn't start back.

"Trust me enough to let me try." Andy heard the plea in her own voice, but she wasn't sorry she sounded desperate. She *was* desperate. That was honest and right and true. She was desperate to do what she should have done when Dio first got hurt, desperate to help, desperate to start making things right, if that was even possible.

Dio tried to press her lips into a fierce frown, but her whole mouth trembled. A few seconds later she closed her gray eyes, and with a body-deep shiver, she nodded.

Andy saw Dio steel herself like she had done back at the brownstone what seemed like a decade ago, the first time she let Andy get a real sense of what she was feeling.

That was all the permission she'd ever get, so Andy knew she had to act. Trying to be definitive, trying to be confident, trying to trust herself as much as she'd asked Dio to trust her, she sat on the wet sheets beside her sister Sibyl. She let herself take one centering breath, then she wrapped both arms around Dio's slight shoulders and opened those floodgates deep in her essence just like she'd done in the infirmary—only without calling water to fill the empty space inside.

Feelings rushed in, a torrent of rage and pain and misery—and wonder and curiosity—and hope. Heart-gripping hope. Soul-stirring hope.

Andy closed her eyes, and that's when the images started.

Little Dio, running away screaming as older adepts chased her and pelted her with rocks and sticks . . .

Dio, older, in her older sister Devin's arms, her hands blistered and bandaged from lightning burns, sobbing her guts out to the only person who gave one damn what happened to her . . .

Andy saw it all rapid-fire. How hard Dio had worked to gain acceptance at Motherhouse Greece. How brutally other adepts had treated her because of her fearsome weather skills. How much Devin had loved Dio, and how the two had been each other's comfort and stability as the Mothers went about other business, leaving them to fight through the chaos on their own.

And finally, Andy saw the worst part.

Dio standing alone in the Motherhouse's bright little chapel, crying over her dead sister with not a single soul there to comfort her.

Oh, God. Andy let go of Dio and sobbed out loud, as much from fury as grief. At least when Sal died, Bela had stood beside her. Bela had given her a hug and a shoulder. Motherhouse Greece had given Dio exactly nothing. Fucking nothing at all.

Andy shoved herself off the bed.

Those Mothers she knocked out the window might have made it back up the mountain. If they had, she'd wash them every one straight to hell.

Dio caught her wrist and held tight, leaning back to offset Andy's weight and momentum. "Not necessary. It's old stuff—and no Mother and no Motherhouse is perfect. I get that, and you should, too, since you're running your own little operation at Kérkira."

Andy stopped pulling against Dio and sat on the bed again. When Dio let go of her wrist, she swallowed and took slow breaths until she stopped crying, until she could choke out what she needed to say. "I'm sorry. All that invasion—for what? What good did I do you?"

Dio's voice sounded unusually light when she answered. "Somebody else knows. That's good enough for now."

"Sorry." Andy wiped her face with her palms. "Not following."

"Before she died, my sister knew everything about me, what we'd gone through together and apart, and that helped me feel sane." Dio touched Andy's wrist again, two fingers this time, the slightest of contact, but so unusual for her that it made Andy stare. "Devin sharing everything with me helped me feel strong, because she knew, and I knew, and we had that bond together. I don't have Devin anymore, but I have you—and that matters. It doesn't heal the pain, but it makes everything hurt less. I'm not alone."

Andy shifted her stare from Dio's fingers to Dio's face. Dio was . . . smiling.

Sort of.

Her gray eyes had a clarity Andy had rarely seen, and Andy realized Dio's burdens had been lightened. Not removed, no—but definitely shared, like she said. Andy's energy had flowed through the hollow spaces and made them less empty. The water had gone where it needed to go and done what it needed to do.

"You'll never have to be alone again if you don't want to be," Andy said, making sure Dio understood she was giving a promise. "Motherhouse Kérkira isn't much to look at, but I don't plan for us to stay there long."

Dio's smile got a little wider. Kind of lopsided and cute, left mouth up and right mouth rebelling. "A crazy old fire Sibyl, an ancient water Sibyl, a bunch of water babies, and now me with all my thunder and lightning. It'll be a party, right?"

They got up together.

"Need to pack?" Andy grabbed her sunglasses and put them on.

Dio wiped water streaks into her blue shirt and jeans. "Nah. There's not a damned thing here I want."

By the time Andy and Dio got to the hallway, all seven of the air Sibyl Mothers had indeed managed to get themselves back up Mount Olympus and into the hallway between Andy, Dio, and the exit from the little hospital. The Mothers stood silent, dripping and glowering as Andy once more drew her dart pistol and took aim, this time at the nearest Mother.

"When Mother Anemone gets back from the States and we've all had a little time to heal and cool off, we'll be talking. Dio's going to fight again, and you're going to allow her to train to use her weather making in battle situations."

"Andy—" Dio nudged her in the back, but Andy gave her a look.

"Don't fucking argue with me. You been lying up here whining and worrying about how you'll pitch knives with one hand when you can aim lightning like a spear and drop tornados on people's heads. I've seen you do it."

The tallest of the blue-robed Mothers, a woman who looked a little like Mother Anemone, only not as elegant, especially with her dripping hair and torn robes, cleared her throat. "It's impossible to control that skill for combat."

"Hey." Andy got right up in the tall mother's face, bringing down a rain of mountain water on both of them. "Nothing's impossible. My life's been proof enough of that."

Water dripping off her big sunglasses, Andy used her

dart pistol to nudge the Mother aside. When the woman got out of the way, Andy motioned for Dio to follow. "Come on. I need a huge cheeseburger and a milkshake, some stitches in my left thigh, and about a week's worth of sleep."

They pushed through the crowd of Mothers, this time heading for the communications platform in Motherhouse Greece.

Ona was waiting for them when they got there, and Andy figured she'd done that melting-from-place-to-place thing Camille had learned from her—especially when she saw the four air adepts and the scrawny fire adept that tended Motherhouse Greece's communications room cowering in the corner.

As they climbed onto the platform, Dio asked, "Did you really make a waterspout on Staten Island big enough that people saw it all the way in Jackson Heights?"

Andy rolled her eyes. "Man, news travels fast around this place."

"I've been making the Mothers keep me informed. The ones afraid of storms were especially helpful."

Ona appeared on the platform in front of them and did a few movements, clearing all the smoke out of one of the large projective mirrors on the wall.

"The spout was big," Andy admitted.

"If I'd been there to give it some wind, they could have seen it in Eastchester and Co-op City." Dio plunged into the mirror, making tracks to Motherhouse Kérkira.

"Blah, blah, blah," Andy muttered as she jumped through the glass after Dio, not at all sorry to leave Motherhouse Greece behind.

43

A little over a month later, Andy sat in the conference room of a long, old-fashioned frigate ship with Dio, the two of them in front of a long table populated with Mothers, some frowning, some smiling. Mother Keara, Mother Anemone, Mother Yana, and Elana—*Mother Elana*, Andy reminded herself—fell into the latter category.

Bela sat on Andy's right, and Camille gripped the chair on Andy's left, looking slightly green, like she had since they set sail from Sri Lanka three days ago, moving like the salt- and flower-scented wind thanks to all the air Sibyls on board. Andy and her group all had on casual clothes—jeans and tanks and sneakers—eschewing the formal robes of their orders absolutely on purpose. Now, somewhere south of Tahiti and west of the Pitcairns, out of French Polynesian territory and deep in uncharted international waters, floating in the calm, quiet sea Andy had dreamed about so many times, the Mothers in their oh-so-formal browns and greens and blues (and one godawful yellow) had finally fought their way to decisions on the matters laid before them.

"It is decreed," Mother Yana said in serious tones, "that Dionysia Allard may train to use her veather making in battle. Ve shall support her in all ways possible, and in due time, offer children born vith such abilities to her for consideration of apprenticeship. Ve vill, in fact and here forward, apprentice all adepts born vith projective powers to those Sibyls with the talent to advise them."

The sunlight exploding through the frigate's rows of

round windows lightened the heavy words, but nothing could take away the monumental nature of that ruling. Andy felt like her fighting group, the quad that had once been considered a collection of hopeless, weak losers and misfits, had finally been validated.

Not that they needed validation to kick ass, take names, and save the world. They had already done that three times, by her count.

Andy sensed the powerful links between herself and her sister Sibyls, the pulse of happiness traveling through all four hearts, and the easy flow of earth, fire, air, and water joined as one for a common purpose. Together again, and strong, maybe stronger than ever.

Look out, New York City. We'll be back soon, and we'll rule.

Elana took over from Mother Yana, announcing, "I formally accept the position of eldest Mother at Motherhouse Atanua, and I will assume primary responsibility for the accelerated and basic training programs. As recent events have made obvious, there is little of greater urgency than preparing our young water adepts to take their places among fighting groups all across the world. The importance of water can never be underestimated, and we have much to learn—and to remember—about its flow and power."

Andy saw the sideways looks Elana got, not because of her accepting the title of eldest water Sibyl Mother despite her demon infection, or because she mentioned accelerated training or feeding young adepts into fighting groups even faster than they had first planned. No, the looks came from her announcement of Motherhouse Atanua.

The name had come to Andy after they sailed away from civilization. Atanua, the Polynesian goddess of the dawn, maker of oceans and mother of humankind. Andy couldn't think of anything more fitting. The fact that

Motherhouse Atanua didn't yet exist—that was what caused all the funny stares.

What they don't know won't hurt them. Not yet, anyway.

Bela gave Andy her own version of the funny stare, as if she sensed Andy might be up to something, but Andy ignored her mortar. If everybody was just coming to that realization despite being on a boat full of Mothers, water babies and water adepts, young Sibyls of all varieties with projective talents, and an odd assortment of Bengal fighters who just needed to be away from the mainstream world, Andy didn't know how to help them.

The Council of Mothers wasn't finished yet, and this next part . . . well, this next part made Andy squirm a little bit.

Mother Anemone took the lead, fixing Andy with her misty green-blue eyes. Her unusually stern stare and deep frown said a lot, and Andy fidgeted with the sunglasses in her lap.

"As for our consideration of your situation, Andrea Myles, you submitted yourself for judgment because of your negligence of your quad and the safety of the child Neala."

Bela shifted in her chair and glared at the table full of Mothers. So did Camille. Dio grumbled under her breath. None of them liked this, but they weren't Mothers. Andy knew she had a greater responsibility, that lack of experience was no excuse, and that she had done the right thing by following the code of justice the Mothers adhered to among themselves. This ruling would do its part to continue setting the flow—*her* flow—to rights again.

Mother Anemone pulled a packet of papers from the folds of her light blue robes and placed them on the center of the long table. "We have collected statements from your peers, your friends, your associates—thorough testimony, if not all of it serious and helpful."

Andy stared at the pile of papers, a new level of disquiet forming in her chest. She hadn't expected this. What did the old hags do, perp-style interviews with everybody she knew?

"This from a Mr. Jake Lowell, police officer and Astaroth demon," Mother Anemone said, a note of affection in her voice. " 'Andy's the best cop I know and a kick-ass Sibyl, too.' "

Andy swallowed, her throat suddenly dry as Dio and Bela put their hands on her knees. She felt the soft touch of Camille's fingers on the back of her neck, and the quiet, powerful rush of blended elemental energy surrounded her, supporting her, holding her upright in the chair as Mother Anemone kept reading and turning pages.

"Cynda Flynn Lowell, mother of the child in question, says, 'No better friend and no better goddess-mother. I'll kick her teeth in if she puts my daughter in danger again, but I know Andy would have died to save Neala.' "

Paper rustled as Mother Anemone flipped to the next paper. " 'Fight with her any day.' " Mother Anemone glanced at Andy. "That was Nick Lowell, Neala's father, though the sentiment was closely echoed by his brother Creed; by Creed's wife, Riana Dumain Lowell; by Jake's wife, Merilee Alexander Lowell; by Sheila Gray's Ranger group; and by any number of Sibyl triads and OCU patrol squads."

Mother Anemone waited as if wishing to see if Andy had anything to add, but Andy couldn't have spoken if she'd wanted to try. So Mother Anemone went on, this time with a disapproving frown. "A Mr. Saul Brent opined, 'She's hot. Nothing more to say.' From Dio Allard in your own quad, 'She's a bitch and I love her,' with 'Ditto' signed by Bela Argos Sharp and Camille Fitzgerald Cole." Mother Anemone moved all the papers aside then, focusing on the very bottom page. "And Mr. Jack Blackmore, a man with a most colorful past and at best a questionable history in his relations with the Dark Crescent Sisterhood, wrote, 'I'm still here.'"

Jack.

Andy's heart ached so suddenly and fiercely she couldn't hold back her tears. Damn it, she missed him so much. Nearly a month since she'd seen his handsome face. Those sweet, loving eyes. Almost there. Almost time. Just not quite yet.

I'm still here . . .

Please let him mean that.

In true fire Sibyl fashion, Mother Keara went next, glorying in her role of spouting off the punishments Andy knew she so richly deserved.

"We sentence you to three months of diligent work on the construction of yer new Motherhouse—though frankly I have my troubles seein' what was off about the first one." She let off a small blast of white smoke, tamped a flame on the corner of the parchment, and kept reading. "We order you to be givin' equally diligent attention to the needs of yer quad and the deeper needs of yer own heart. Nurture yer relationships, help with settlin' new initiates and the flippin' unusual assortment of characters you and Elana have seen fit to welcome into yer midst, assist with Dio's rehabilitation, and spend time with yer old friends and your goddess-children Neala and Ethan when they can visit." She looked up and grinned, her wrinkled face taking on a timeless quality as her green eyes—and her hair—blazed. "Will you be acceptin' our discipline, Andrea Myles?"

Andy drew on the strength and support of her quad to find her voice, and she answered with a firm, loud, "I accept."

Mother Keara nodded, spreading smoke in every direction. "Then I pronounce this Council—"

"Wait, wait. One more thing." Elana held up both hands, and all eyes turned to her. Andy stared, too, because she had no idea what the old imp was up to now, but whatever it was, Andy trusted it would be for the best in the long run—no matter how much discomfort it caused in the short run.

"What the hell?" Dio muttered, and Andy could tell she was gearing up for a good blast of thunder if necessary.

"Down, girl," Andy whispered.

Elana performed one of the best dramatic sighs Andy had ever witnessed, then grabbed the front of her slick canary robes. "I'm putting you in charge of picking something besides this goddess-awful yellow chiffon crap. Can you choose something better, Andy? Something a little more . . . *us*?"

The rest of the Mothers at the Council table gaped.

Camille and Bela snickered, and Dio said, "Well, you can't have blue. Blue's taken."

Andy shrugged that off. "How does purple sound?" she asked Elana. "A silk-and-cotton blend? And we need a good supply of sunglasses, too."

Elana considered this while all the other mothers started trying to object, then she banged a hand on the table and loudly announced, "Works for me. And *now* this meeting of the Council of Mothers is closed. Get up on deck, girl. We've got work to do."

"Work?" Bela got up and hustled out of the conference room right behind Andy, with Dio and Camille close behind her. "What work?"

"Come with me on a boat trip," Dio sniped in an awful imitation of Andy's Southern twang. "It'll be a va-caaation. Real relaxing and all."

Camille didn't say anything because she was running to the starboard gunwale to puke again.

Andy waited for her to finish, patted her back, then pointed to the large, unnamed island barely visible in the morning mists off the boat's bow, a little to port. Twenty square miles of tropical paradise with the exact right sand, superlative trees, and smooth, idyllic energy and flow. Even the waves on the beaches sounded right to Andy. The island had no inhabitants, no declared national allegiance, and no registered presence with any nation, though Mother Anemone would take care of all of that soon enough.

For now, though—

Andy put on her sunglasses and grinned at her quad, and also at Elana and Ona as they joined them at the boat's forwardmost point. "I need everybody's help with a little project."

"What kind of little project?" Bela asked, each word sounding more wary than the last.

"Nothing much." Andy gave Bela her best grin. "Just raising a volcano off the western shore there."

Bela's mouth came open. For a moment she seemed speechless, then managed a sputtering, "Volcano? Raising a—you're out of your freaking mind."

"It's been extinct for centuries." Andy waved her hand like it was really no big deal. "Just some minor earth shifting. You know, a little rock and roll. Elana and I will handle the water displacement and protect the boat, and you, Dio, can you take care of the air displacement and weather pattern shifts? And Camille, you and Ona make sure to set up a good firewall so we don't accidentally wash away New Zealand or something, okay?"

Everybody but Elana and Ona stared at her. Ona cracked her knuckles like she was getting loose for a big sword fight, and Elana did a deep knee bend, followed by some impressive yogic breathing. A few seconds later, she dived into the ocean to warn off all sentient sea creatures that might be affected by their energy-working and landscape contouring.

Camille surrendered, going to join Ona and starting to

discuss which lines of subterranean ore they needed to stabilize.

"It'll be a vaa-caaation," Dio groused again, but she squinted at the sky, and Andy sensed her reading air currents and getting ready to shove some clouds back and forth.

Bela pointed her finger in Andy's face. "Damn your hide. Next time I'm taking a Carnival Cruise, just so you know."

Andy blew her a kiss. Then she squared her stance and got ready to do a little tango with the South Pacific.

44

Sibyls.

Jack gripped the railing on the rickety skiff he and Saul had rented from one of the five hundred or so people living on tiny, remote Rapa Iti—which just happened to include one small group of retired members of the Dark Crescent Sisterhood who used to cover American Samoa, the Cook Islands, and French Polynesia.

Why was it that his relationship with one particular Sibyl seemed to frequently involve him riding through paradise in a boat that should have been retired from service about a century ago—and wondering if he might get drowned for his trouble?

He'd spent a long few weeks weighing whether he should give Andy space and leave her alone or plow after her like Tarzan beating his chest and claiming his Jane. Last time the space thing had been the wrong choice, and Jack couldn't see Andy doing anything with Tarzan save for a quick and merciless disemboweling.

So he'd sent her messages. A lot of them, all saying the same thing. That he was here. That he was waiting. And finally that he'd wait forever if he had to, but he hoped it didn't come to that.

Her summons had arrived yesterday, and it made him laugh.

So show up already. Two words for you: South Pacific. Now I'm the one waiting for you.

Jack hadn't wasted any time getting himself to the nearest fire Sibyl to start his journey. This time he'd get it right, damn it, even if he couldn't find any swinging vines.

Jack liked getting things right.

For Andy, he could even get used to the whole chest-beating thing. She was woman enough to wake all the primal urges lurking deep in his essence. He'd just have to be on the lookout for warning glares if he wanted to avoid the disemboweling. He thought he was up to the task.

Saul drove the skiff, shirtless as usual, his tattoos and scars already turning pink under the relentless South Pacific sunlight. Jack had picked jeans and a sleeveless T-shirt. He had one bag full of the same gear, plus a trunk with his wet suit and scuba gear.

"She really might kill you," Saul shouted over the engine's puttering and snuffling and the not-so-quiet rush of the natural surf.

"This time I've got an invitation," Jack shouted back, not giving a shit what Saul thought.

Saul flipped him off. "I'm betting she'll regret that."

Jack decided to ignore Saul, and he focused instead on the island slowly coming into view.

Whoa.

Duncan and John hadn't been kidding when they told him the place was un-fucking-believable.

Dark blue seas gave way to sky-blue waves rushing to crest on white quartz beaches. The sand twinkled and gleamed under the flawless sunlight, showing off patches of purple and green and light pink blended like highlights. Farther inland, the sand feathered into swaths of lush green and amber grasses and a thick tree cover. Silky green knolls dotted one end of the island, and Jack could make out cottages in various stages of construction. Elana's other family of the heart, the Bengals who needed out of the cities, had selected that end for their quiet little society, finally safe from Rakshasa and suspicious paranormals and humans who didn't understand what they were, or the pain they had been through to reclaim their sanity from unwanted supernatural infections. Jack had heard that a few of the Astaroths and some Cursons had elected to build homes or vacation spots in the same location, giving rise to the spot's new nickname—Demon Beach.

On the other end of the island, more cottages—some crystalline in appearance, some of stone, and a few of high-grade teak—and some larger all-purpose structures had been raised around flat farmlike fields. Air and fire and earth Sibyls with projective talents would visit these little homes to train, and to live permanently if the need arose. Saul pointed at those houses. "Chaos Beach. I heard Andy nicknamed it herself."

Fitting, Jack thought, and finally let himself look at the island's crowning feature. Less than a tenth of a mile off the flat end of the island, rising like a breathtaking phantasm born straight from the breaking waves, stood a huge dormant volcano so old it was bleached white and laced with coral caves already turned into amazing sea-view quarters for the water Sibyls. Though he couldn't see it, Jack knew the volcano's outer slopes hid a gigantic caldera within, a hollow, protected basin that already housed the heart of Motherhouse Atanua, built right into the natural formations of the coral-crusted structure itself. Andy had made sure her water Sibyls would never again fall prey to a tidal surge, natural or otherwise. Even the largest, fiercest wave would break into so much foam against the massive mountain, and her adepts would be nestled safe within those towering walls no matter what the oceans and skies tried to do to them.

His gaze moved upward. Higher. Higher still, to a plateau near the top of the mountain. That's where Andy had built her quarters. John and Duncan told him she had pronounced it the best possible spot because she could see anything coming and be ready to meet it.

"Are you ready to meet me?" he whispered into the rushing wind, his arms already aching to hold her.

Probably his imagination, but Jack thought he could make out small figures on a white coral balcony, staring out across the waves.

One of them had red hair.

"Is that him?" Dio asked, her voice as soft and smooth as the light wind coursing across the lip of the volcano.

"It's him." Andy's breath came short as her fingers curled around the soft, polished coral on the rail of the balcony.

Dio shook her head, watching the boat approach. "Why didn't he just come straight here through the mirrors?"

"It's not his style." Andy wanted to climb over and dive right off the mountain. She wanted to plunge into the clear blue surf below and sweep through the waves until she reached Jack, until she pulled him into the warm depths with her and claimed him forever. She didn't think she had ever missed anyone so badly. She knew she had never wanted anyone more, mind and body and soul.

It took all her strength, but she turned away from the sea view and focused on Camille, who was standing beside Bela in her bedroom. She hadn't moved much furniture into the large room, just a big bed with a good mattress and soft sea-blue sheets, a teak chair and writing table, and a teakwood sofa and chairs with blue cushions for her quad to use when they were in residence. She hadn't been able to bring herself to hang anything on the gorgeous coral walls, or even put blinds on the huge windows that gave her a 360-degree view of the ocean.

Camille came forward and gave Andy a quick, tight hug. "I won't let you down, honey. Give us two hours— three, tops—and we'll be ready."

As she finished her sentence, she stepped toward the center of the floor. The polished coral beneath her feet shimmered, and Camille melted into the earth's ever-flowing channels of energy. Bela and Dio didn't dissolve, but they got out fast, hurrying off to gather Elana and Ona and the adepts.

Andy waited, wondering how she looked in her new light purple robes. Probably a stupid color, but a hell of a lot better than canary yellow. The soft fabric teased her skin, making her feel electric, doubling her excitement as seconds passed, and minutes, and she sensed him coming closer.

When Jack finally opened her door and walked inside toting a small trunk and travel bag, she was treated to a full, delicious view of his tanned muscles and handsome face. All she could do was ache all over. All she could say was, "You're here."

She covered her mouth and just let her heart pound.

Jack dropped his stuff on the floor, closed the door behind him, took off his sunglasses, and gazed at her like he wanted to kiss every inch of her, toes to lips and back again.

"I'm wherever you are," he said, his voice so low it gave her chills. "If you're ready. If that's what you want."

She couldn't stop looking at him. "I want you. You're my present and my future. You're my home, Jack."

He walked toward her. Closer. Close enough to touch, then only a breath away from her. "Want to get married?" he murmured. "I brought a ring just in case you decided not to kill me for all those messages."

Andy gazed into his warm brown eyes, already getting lost in the depths. "How does an hour from now sound? Two? We really should give everybody time to get ready for us."

Jack gave it a little thought. "Two hours. Just about right."

He wrapped her in his powerful arms and kissed her,

long and deep and hot, just like she'd been missing, just like she wanted, and her entire body started to tingle.

Jack bit her lip, her neck, tasting her, touching her all over through the soft fabric of her robes. "I love you, Andy."

She felt whole again. Completed. She wanted him to feel the same way.

He lifted her and carried her straight to the big bed she had picked out, hoping he'd share it with her. Light-headed, she held him tight as he stretched her out on the downy comforter and kissed her again. The few times Andy opened her eyes, she realized she could see hints of their reflections in the polished coral ceiling, in the windows and walls. She could see Jack kissing her with a backdrop of clouds and sky and endless, welcoming ocean waves.

In a hazy sort of trance, she opened herself to excitement, to relief, to satisfaction and crazy need. His emotions flowed through her, matching hers with each thrust of his tongue and stroke of his strong, talented hands.

"Incredible," he said as he opened her robes, as he found her breasts and teased the nipples until she screamed into his mouth and molded her body to his, tugging at his jeans until he slid them off, until he took off his shirt and let her have all of him, skin to skin, kissing her, sliding his hard length against her belly.

She raised her hand and let her fingers trace the scars on his arms and chest. "If I'm incredible, you're amazing."

His next kiss came more gently, so soft it teased deep spots in her soul.

"Can you see us?" he whispered, his bass tone giving her shivers on top of shivers.

She forgot about talking and nodded, watching from a dozen angles as he lowered his mouth to her nipple and nibbled the sensitive tip.

Torture.

And perfect.

Andy pressed both hands against the sides of his head and pushed his face down, down, groaning as he took her breast in his mouth and really drove her insane.

She couldn't get over the silk of his mouth on her skin, the force of his hands moving across all the right spots—and everywhere, everywhere, she could see him massaging her, pressing his fingers into her soft lower curls as he relieved the burning ache in her other breast. She could see herself touching him, running her fingers along his erection, then not even struggling as he pushed away her hand and pressed his thighs between her legs.

"I'm watching us together," she said, her voice nothing but a gasp against the steady, rocking rush of the surf far below on the mountain. "I can see us together forever."

"I love you," Jack told her as he drove into her, taking her completely with one stroke, making love to her all over the room wherever she looked, but the best place to look was right in front of her, directly into the heat and passion of his gaze.

Andy moaned from the hot motion of him thrusting inside her, and too fast, too fast, her orgasm shattered her heart and put it back together again all in the same moment. She let herself scream, let herself stay wide open physically and emotionally, and Jack gave her everything. All his strength. All his energy. All his feelings. He didn't hold anything back, including his roar of pleasure and possession when he came inside her, pulsing and thrusting until Andy knew she couldn't take another second, but wanted hours and hours and hours more. She didn't stop the conception. She welcomed it, adoring the sense of life blooming in her depths, his existence and hers joining in the most complete and permanent way she could imagine. She especially adored the pure, unfettered joy that washed across Jack's features when she pulled his face to hers, kissed him, and said, "It's happening. Our first baby. She's happening right this second."

Jack felt crazy again, but this time, it was crazy-happy. He could definitely get used to crazy-happy.

He'd been on the island less than three hours, but all of his dreams were about to come true. Andy stood a few feet away from him with Dio, her maid of honor. Andy wore a simple white dress, strapless with soft lines that showed off her knockout figure. She had a pearl and shell necklace, bare feet, a bracelet and anklet made out of white star-shaped flowers that seemed to be growing all over the island, and a crown of the same flowers draped over her rich red curls.

Jack had on jeans and a white shirt he had borrowed from Saul. At least the shirt was pressed. At least Saul had combed his hair into a neat ponytail. He stood beside Jack, his tattooed hand resting firmly on Ethan Lowell's shoulder. The little fellow wore such a solemn expression it almost made Jack laugh, but the boy had a death grip on the little black box with Andy's ring— a two-carat natural blue diamond set in white gold, as rare and intricate as she was. Jack had been gratified to see that the stone mirrored the lighter shades of the ocean surrounding the mountain. He'd gotten the matching men's band, just in case, hoping for the best. Andy had been glad for his foresight.

Meant to be, she had told him as she lay naked in his arms, gazing at the rings he had picked out while he rubbed and kissed her belly and whispered to the little girl already growing inside her.

Meant to be.

Jack had never let himself believe in that kind of sap, but he embraced it now. Bring on the sap, damn it. He felt like a man who had stepped into the best dream of his life and he never, ever wanted to wake.

Andy's quad and the adepts and seemingly the entire island had decorated the base of the caldera in tropical flowers, and strands of twinkling lights rose along the slopes, straight into the sunbathed sky. Jack waited with Andy inside a flower-laced entrance to the basin as onlookers formed groups and made a path for them, a path leading to Elana, who as eldest Mother on the island and perhaps the oldest priestess on the planet next to Ona, waited on a carpet of flower petals to join them forever.

"They're here," Dio said to Andy, and Andy immediately turned to Jack.

He was surprised to see the nervousness on her face.

He moved to her and drew her against him, worried as he brushed his lips across hers, tasting honey and mint and woman, and breathing in that sweet vanilla-and-ocean smell he had come to love so much. "Second thoughts, sweetheart?"

"No. But there's something I want you to do for me before all this gets started." She touched his cheek with her fingertips and seemed even more nervous.

"Name it."

Andy managed a smile. "Go find Camille. She has something for you, okay? Something from me."

Okay. That was strange, but if it would make her feel better, he was all over it. Jack turned Andy loose and headed through the archway, passing by Cynda and Nick, who were both busy encouraging a too-excited Neala not to torch all the flower petals she was supposed to scatter in front of Andy when she walked down the aisle.

A minute or so later, Jack spotted Camille standing with Bela, Duncan, and John near the front, a few yards away from Elana. He walked straight up to them, wondering what the hell was going on, and that's when he saw the two women standing with them.

The younger one of the pair was dark-headed and nervous-looking. The older woman had gray hair, neatly trimmed against her lined but pretty face. Both women had great big brown eyes.

Eyes he knew.

Eyes he stared at each morning in the mirror.

Oh, God.

Jack stopped.

His mother and sister broke into sobs and smiles and threw themselves into his arms before he even had a chance to grasp what was happening.

"Sibyls have amazing archives," Camille was saying. "I didn't take any chances tracking them down or do anything to tip their identity to the human world, I promise. I can bring them to the island safely anytime you guys want to see each other. Nobody here will ever reveal their identity."

Jack barely heard her. He kissed the top of his mother's head, then Ginger's, holding them tight so they couldn't vanish. His chest ached as one of the deepest, darkest holes in his heart stitched itself shut and finally, finally, finally started to heal.

His mother pulled back and cupped his face in her hands. "Thank you for our life," she said. "For our safety. For all your sacrifices. I can't wait to meet this special woman of yours. I can't wait to get to know her—and you."

"I'm still me," Jack said, and he realized that for the first time in his adult life, he really was himself, fully and completely, all of his secrets thrown aside or shared—or just not necessary anymore. He felt as clear as the ocean outside the mountain.

Ginger grinned at him, and Jack felt years peeling off his life, shedding off his soul. For a few seconds, he was seventeen again, plotting to ruffle her hair to tick her off and make her laugh. "So," she said, her grown-up voice startling him back to the here and now. "You gonna marry this chick, or what?"

"Oh, yeah," he said, messing up his sister's hair and knowing it was a sacred privilege he'd always honor. "You wait right here and watch."

And they did watch, his mother and his sister and all the friends he had in the world, as Jack walked back to the basin entry and kissed Andy, and kissed her again. Then he made his way back down the aisle with Saul and waited with Elana, less than patient, for Dio to make her walk. Ethan followed, holding the black box in his small, shaking hands. Neala came next, laughing and smoking and scattering burning flower petals all over the ground as the crowd hummed and sang something light and tropical and just right for the moment.

When Andy started toward Jack, her smile told him everything.

I want you.

I love you.

My life and your life, joined from this point forward, and even death won't end us.

"I'm yours," he told her a few moments later as he slid the blue diamond onto her finger. "And you're mine."

"Yes," she whispered as he kissed her and Elana said the words to seal what Jack already knew, what he already felt at a level so deep nothing could ever shake it.

"I'll be here," he told Andy, then lifted her off her feet and turned to face the cheering crowd. "I'll be right here beside you, now and forever."

(acknowledgments)

Of all the characters I have ever written, Andy Myles has gotten the most reaction. From emails and letters about her to emails and letters *to* her, Andy has garnered quite a bit of attention. She really struck a chord with female readers, perhaps because she's smart, strong, fiery, and honest—soft and wounded, but also strong as good Southern steel. Writing her story brought me both joy and sorrow. I'm glad she's gotten her tale, but sorry I won't get to look forward to it any longer. For all the readers who care for Andy, this is for you. I hope you get lost in her world and never want to leave.

Thanks to my family for doing without me while I followed Andy's path. Thanks to my friend Judy for long walks that helped me think. Thanks to my friend Chris for being funny and fixing stuff so I never lost my mind. Thanks to my readers where I work, for bugging me about when the story would be written.

To my editor, Kate Collins, I'm glad Andy and Jack surprised you, and as always, you helped me to make the story stronger. Kelli, you're still keeping me in line and on target. Beth, I owe you and your entire staff much gratitude for all your patience related to my map-reading impairment. I'm so glad you guys have eagle eyes . . . and a good sense of direction.

And Nancy—how much chocolate do I owe you now? I have to be getting toward a truckload.